big
NATE

Other *Big Nate* Books

Big Nate: In a Class by Himself

Big Nate Strikes Again

big NATE

FROM THE TOP

by LINCOLN PEIRCE

Andrews McMeel
Publishing, LLC

Kansas City • Sydney • London

Big Nate is distributed internationally by United Feature Syndicate.

Big Nate copyright © 2010 by United Feature Syndicate. All rights reserved. Printed in the United States of America. No part of this book may be used or reproduced in any manner whatsoever without written permission except in the case of reprints in the context of reviews.

Andrews McMeel Publishing, LLC
an Andrews McMeel Universal company
1130 Walnut Street, Kansas City, Missouri 64106

www.andrewsmcmeel.com

11 12 13 14 RR2 10 9 8 7 6 5 4

ISBN: 978-1-4494-0232-7

Library of Congress Control Number: 2010930552

These strips appeared in newspapers from
August 28, 2006, through April 1, 2007.

Big Nate can be viewed on the Internet at
www.comics.com/big_nate

**To JDP,
the original Big Nate**

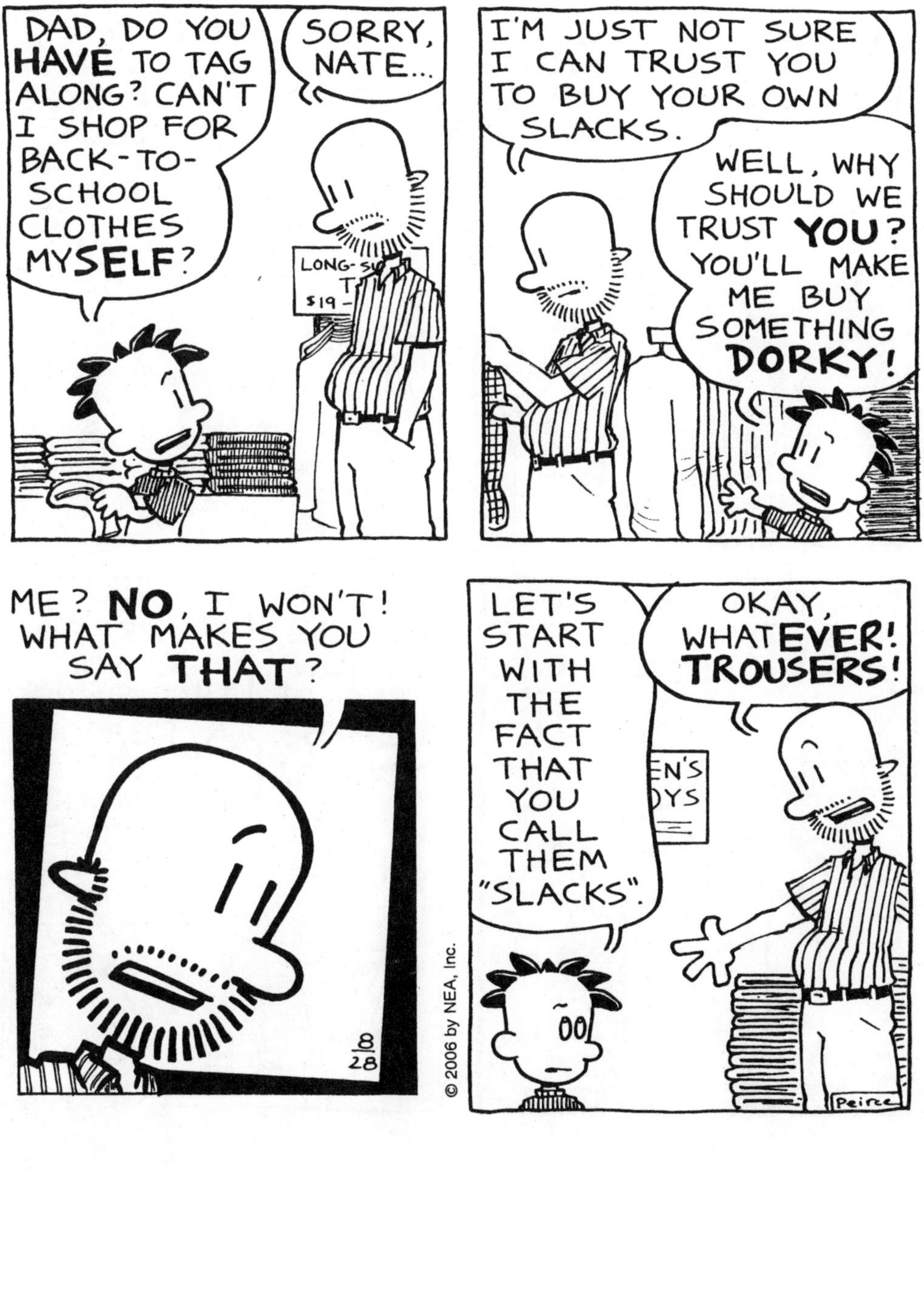
DAD, DO YOU **HAVE** TO TAG ALONG? CAN'T I SHOP FOR BACK-TO-SCHOOL CLOTHES MY**SELF**?
SORRY, NATE...
LONG-SL T $19 -
I'M JUST NOT SURE I CAN TRUST YOU TO BUY YOUR OWN SLACKS.
WELL, WHY SHOULD WE TRUST **YOU**? YOU'LL MAKE ME BUY SOMETHING **DORKY**!
ME? **NO**, I WON'T! WHAT MAKES YOU SAY **THAT**?
8/28
LET'S START WITH THE FACT THAT YOU CALL THEM "SLACKS".
OKAY, WHAT**EVER**! **TROUSERS**!
EN'S
YS
Peirce

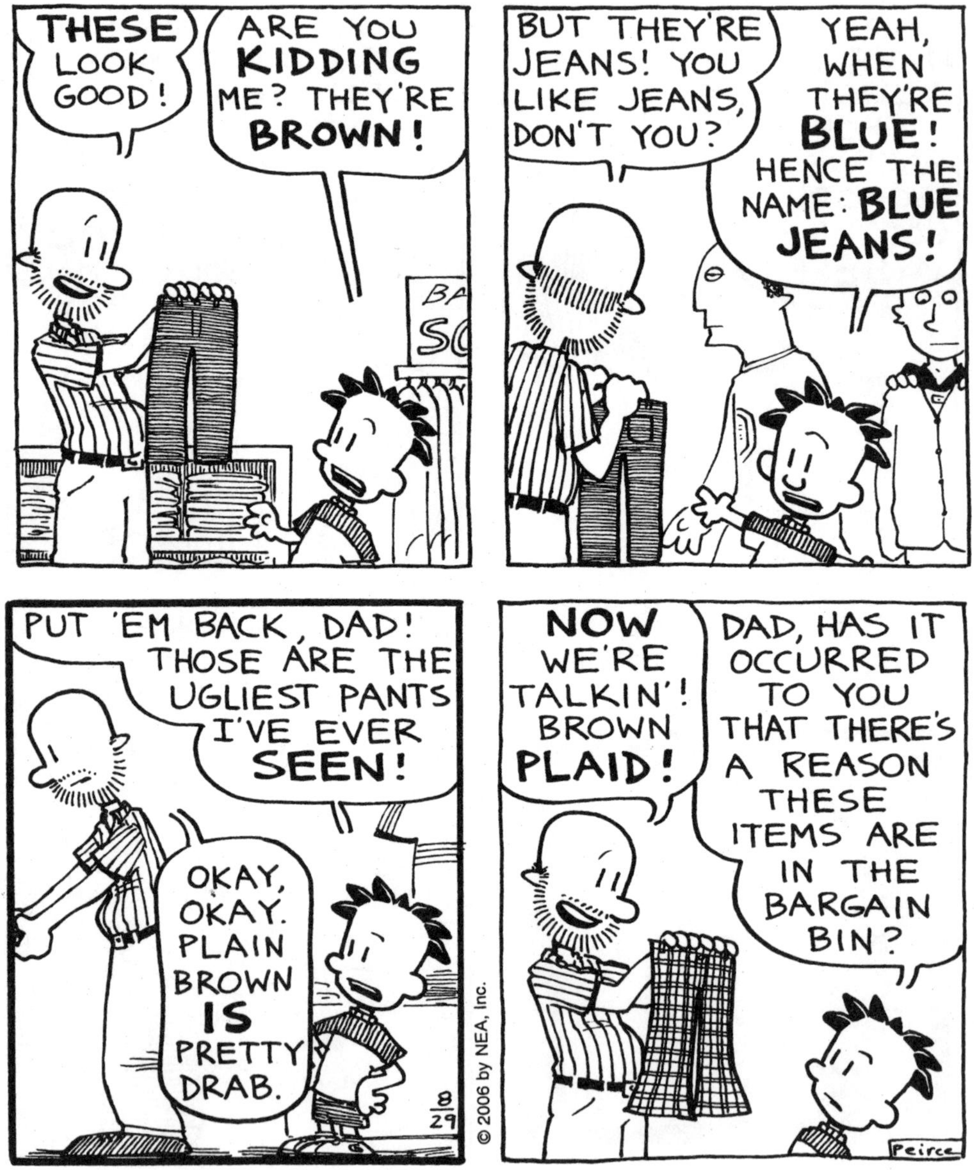
THESE LOOK GOOD!
ARE YOU KIDDING ME? THEY'RE BROWN!
BUT THEY'RE JEANS! YOU LIKE JEANS, DON'T YOU?
YEAH, WHEN THEY'RE BLUE! HENCE THE NAME: BLUE JEANS!
PUT 'EM BACK, DAD! THOSE ARE THE UGLIEST PANTS I'VE EVER SEEN!
OKAY, OKAY. PLAIN BROWN IS PRETTY DRAB.
8/29
© 2006 by NEA, Inc.
NOW WE'RE TALKIN'! BROWN PLAID!
DAD, HAS IT OCCURRED TO YOU THAT THERE'S A REASON THESE ITEMS ARE IN THE BARGAIN BIN?
Peirce

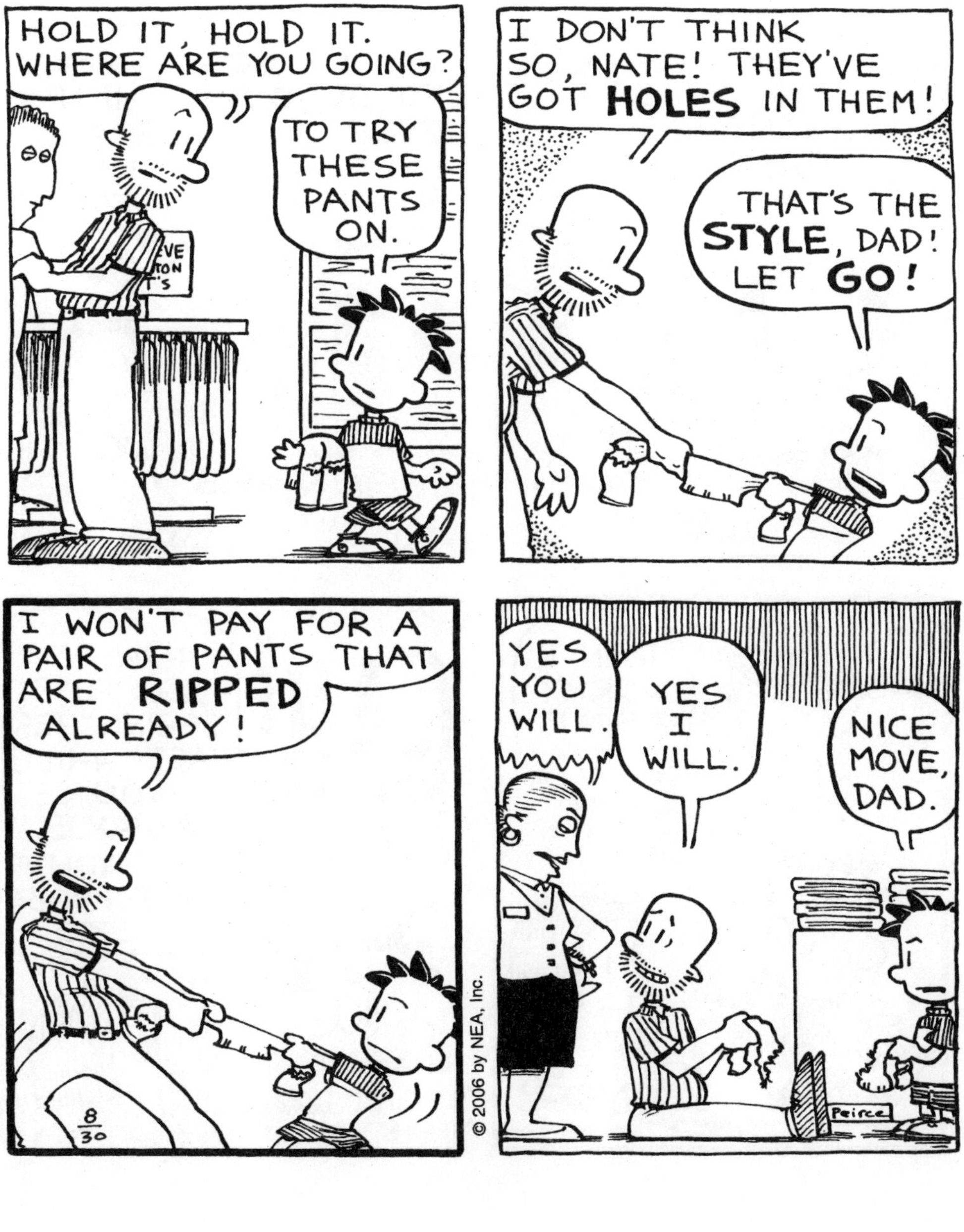
HOLD IT, HOLD IT. WHERE ARE YOU GOING?
TO TRY THESE PANTS ON.
I DON'T THINK SO, NATE! THEY'VE GOT HOLES IN THEM!
THAT'S THE STYLE, DAD! LET GO!
I WON'T PAY FOR A PAIR OF PANTS THAT ARE RIPPED ALREADY!
8/30
© 2006 by NEA, Inc.
YES YOU WILL.
YES I WILL.
NICE MOVE, DAD.
Peirce

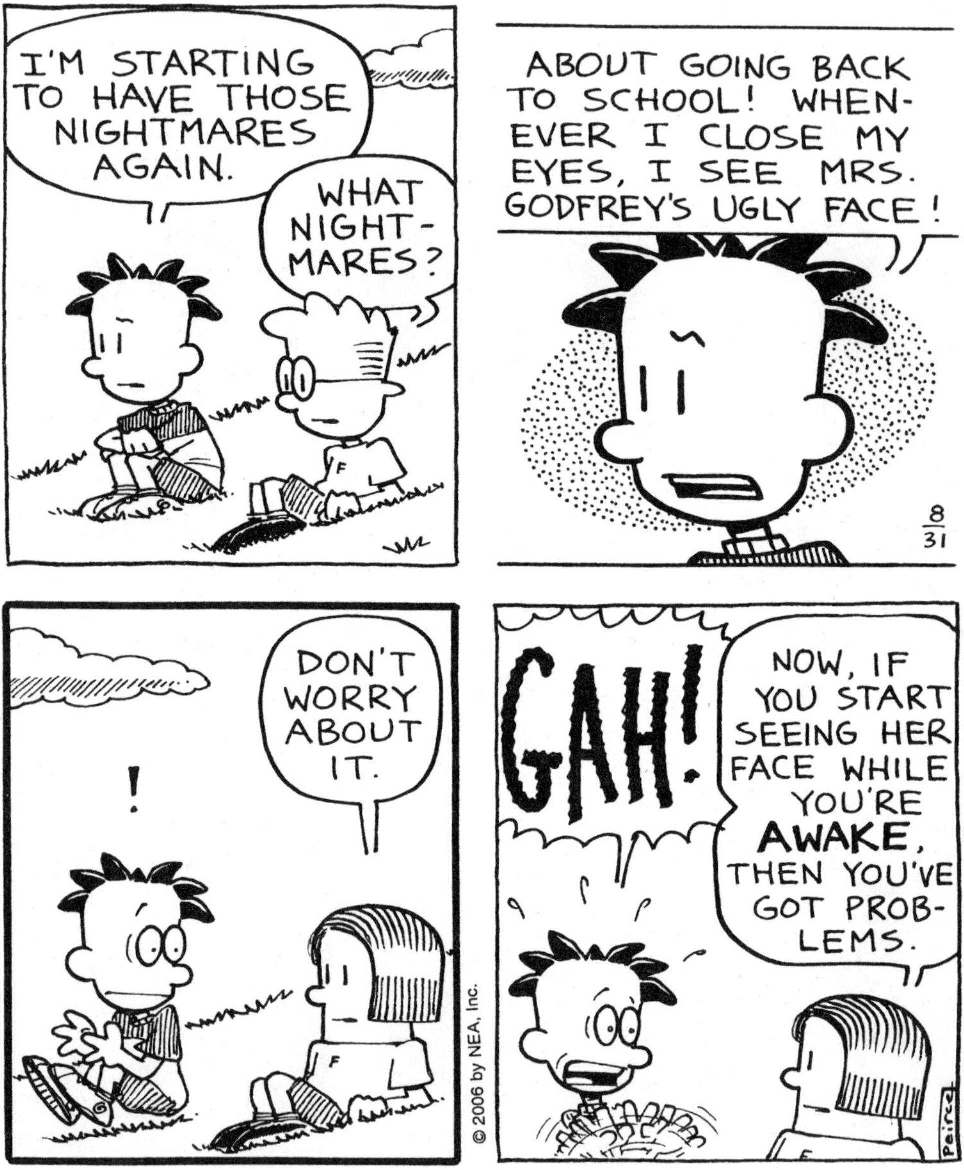
I'M STARTING TO HAVE THOSE NIGHTMARES AGAIN.
WHAT NIGHT-MARES?
ABOUT GOING BACK TO SCHOOL! WHEN-EVER I CLOSE MY EYES, I SEE MRS. GODFREY'S UGLY FACE!
8/31
!
DON'T WORRY ABOUT IT.
© 2006 by NEA, Inc.
GAH!
NOW, IF YOU START SEEING HER FACE WHILE YOU'RE AWAKE, THEN YOU'VE GOT PROB-LEMS.
Peirce

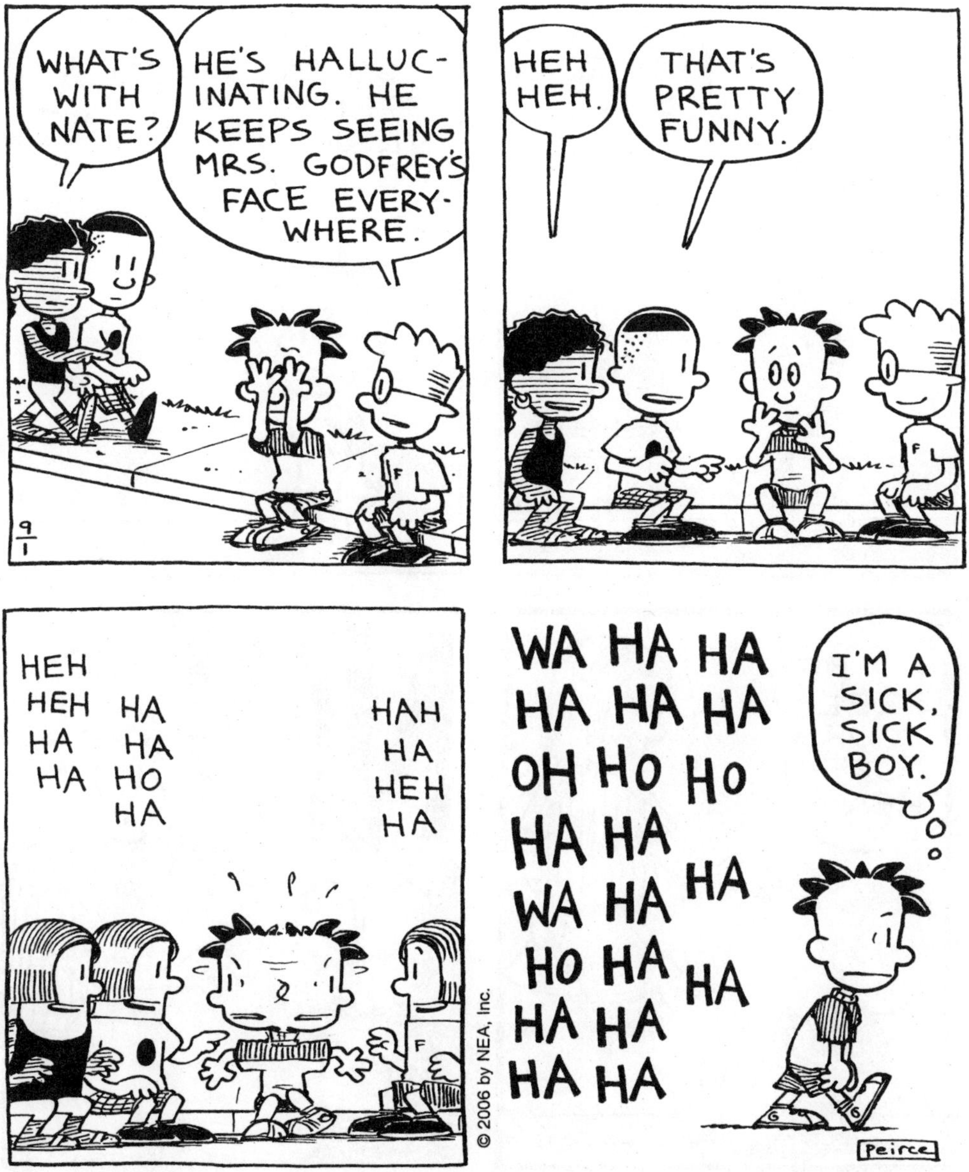
WHAT'S WITH NATE?
HE'S HALLUCINATING. HE KEEPS SEEING MRS. GODFREY'S FACE EVERYWHERE.
9/1
HEH HEH.
THAT'S PRETTY FUNNY.
HEH HEH HA HA
HA HA HO HA
HAH HA HEH HA
© 2006 by NEA, Inc.
WA HA HA HA HA HA OH HO HO HA HA WA HA HA HO HA HA HA HA HA HA
I'M A SICK, SICK BOY.
Peirce

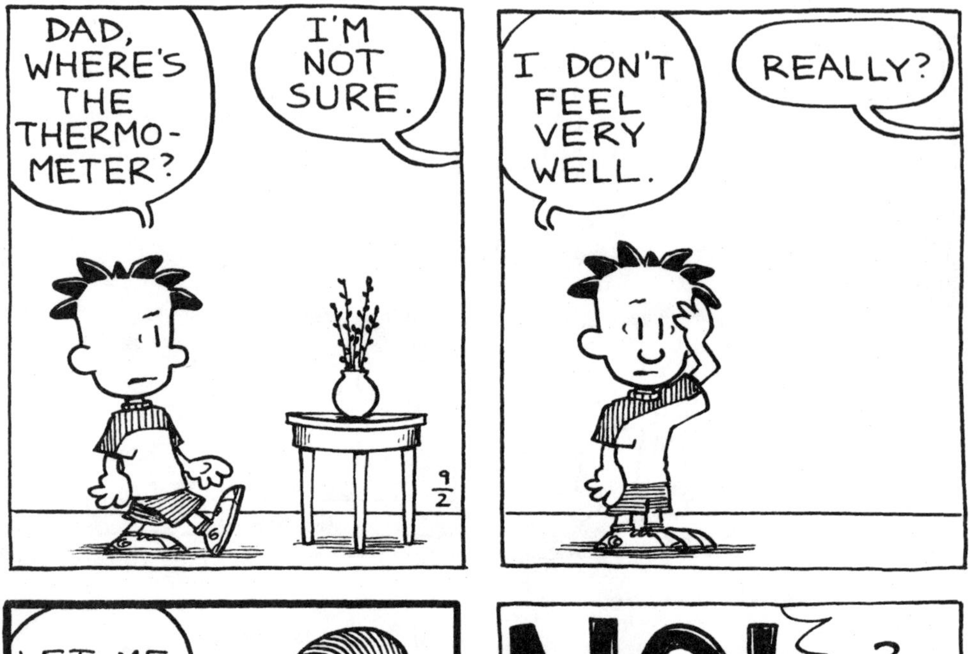
DAD, WHERE'S THE THERMO- METER?
I'M NOT SURE.
I DON'T FEEL VERY WELL.
REALLY?
LET ME FEEL YOUR FORE- HEAD.
NO!
?

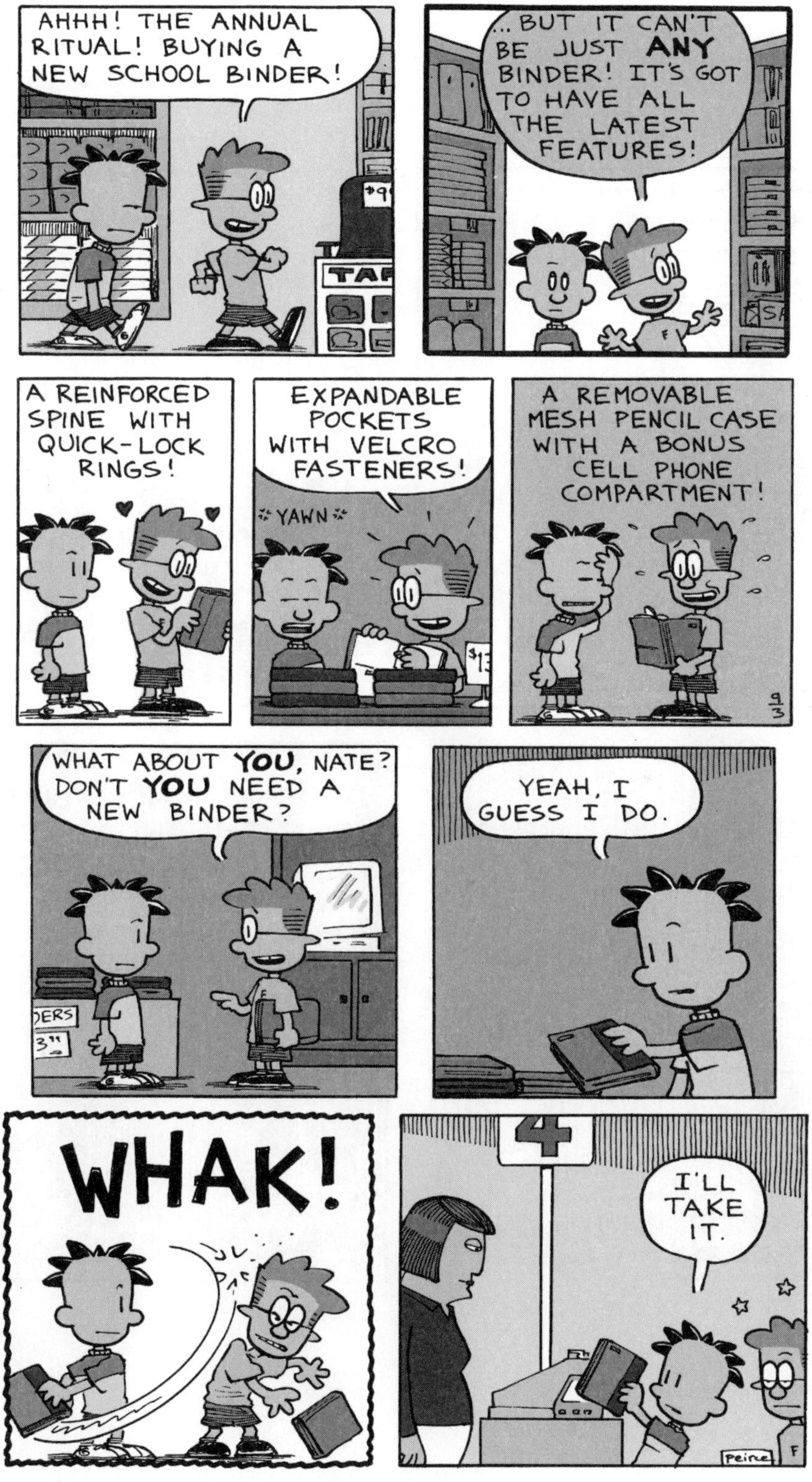
AHHH! THE ANNUAL RITUAL! BUYING A NEW SCHOOL BINDER!
... BUT IT CAN'T BE JUST **ANY** BINDER! IT'S GOT TO HAVE ALL THE LATEST FEATURES!
A REINFORCED SPINE WITH QUICK-LOCK RINGS!
EXPANDABLE POCKETS WITH VELCRO FASTENERS!
YAWN
A REMOVABLE MESH PENCIL CASE WITH A BONUS CELL PHONE COMPARTMENT!
WHAT ABOUT **YOU**, NATE? DON'T **YOU** NEED A NEW BINDER?
YEAH, I GUESS I DO.
WHAK!
4
I'LL TAKE IT.
Peirce

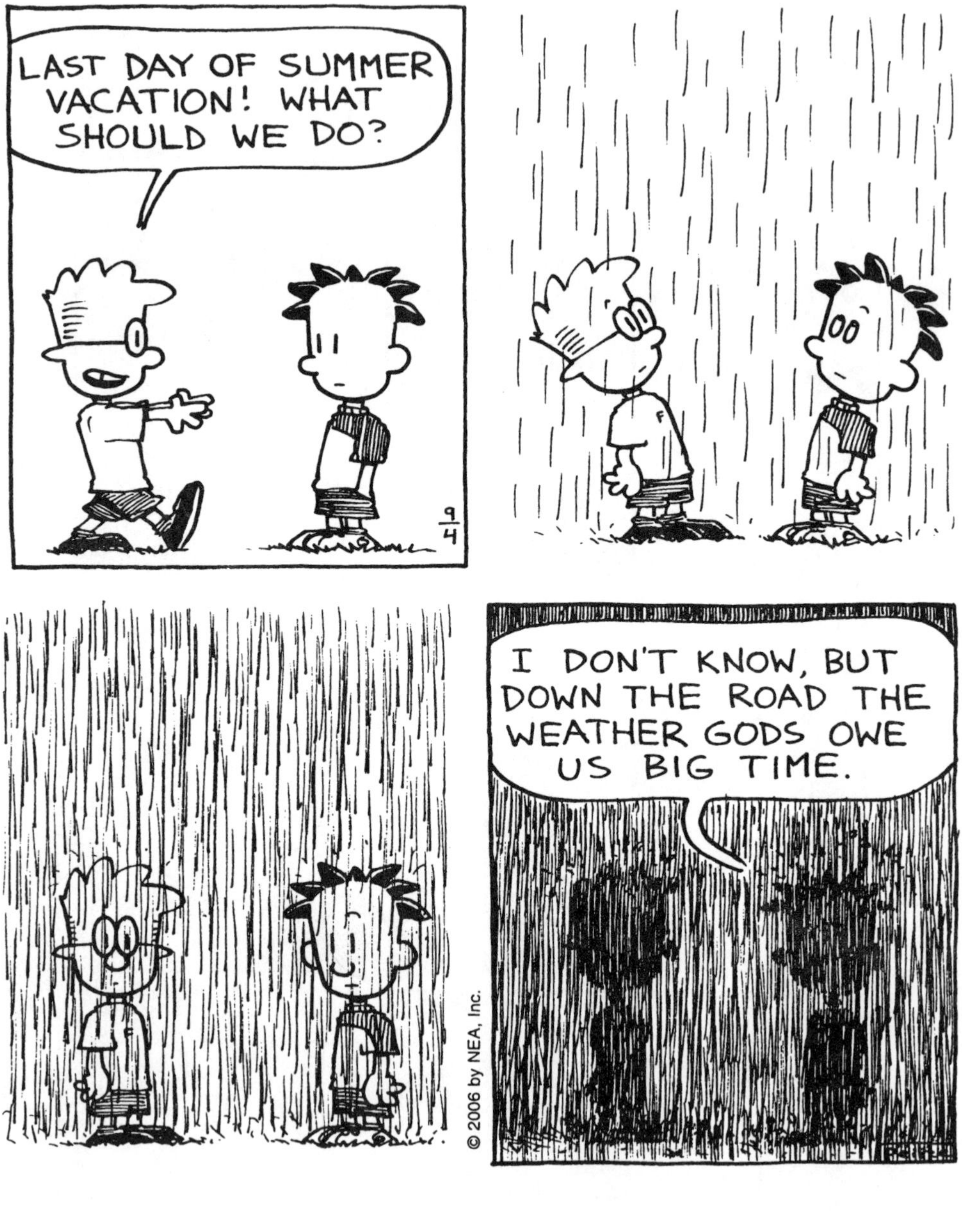
LAST DAY OF SUMMER VACATION! WHAT SHOULD WE DO?
9/4
I DON'T KNOW, BUT DOWN THE ROAD THE WEATHER GODS OWE US BIG TIME.

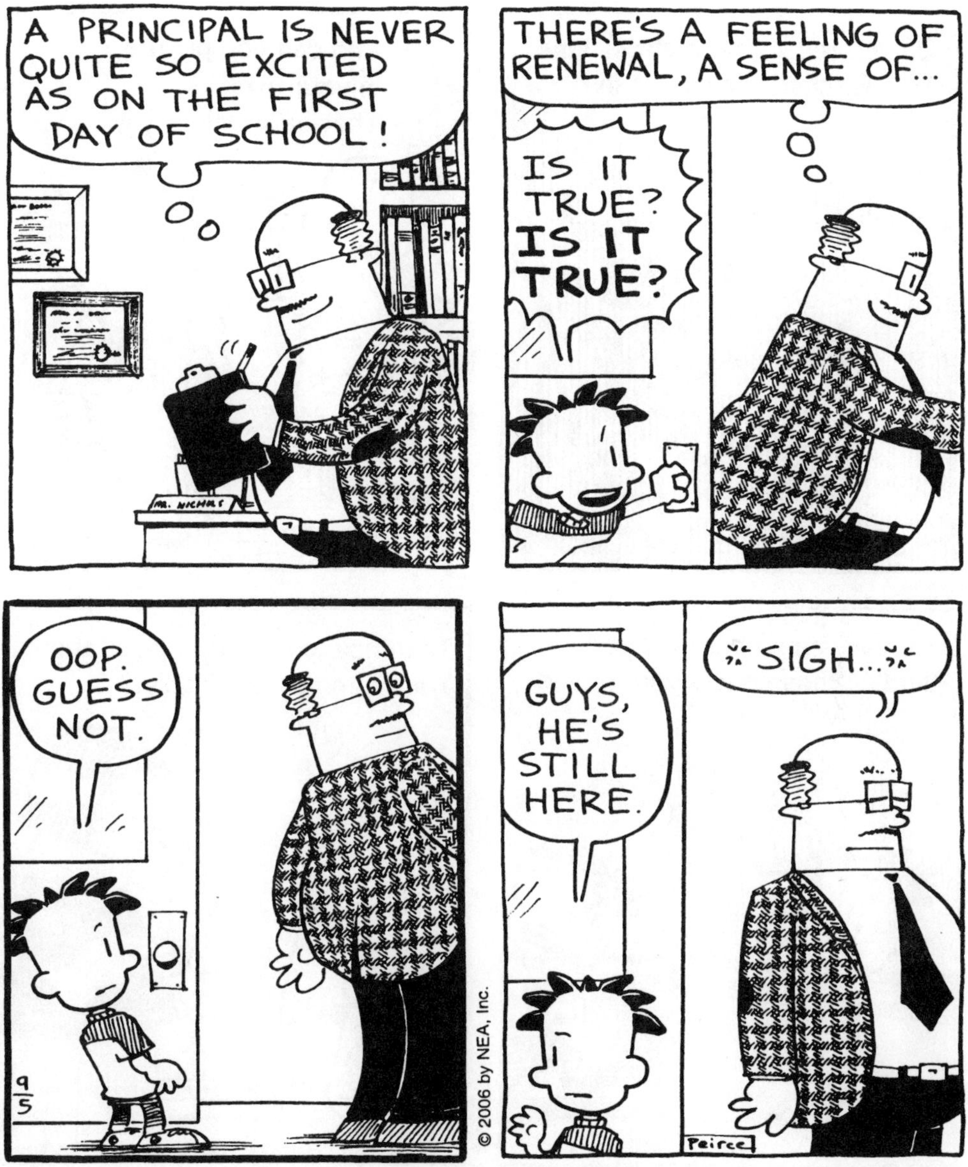
A PRINCIPAL IS NEVER QUITE SO EXCITED AS ON THE FIRST DAY OF SCHOOL!
MR. NICHOLS
THERE'S A FEELING OF RENEWAL, A SENSE OF...
IS IT TRUE? **IS IT TRUE?**
OOP. GUESS NOT.
9/5
© 2006 by NEA, Inc.
GUYS, HE'S STILL HERE.
SIGH...
Peirce

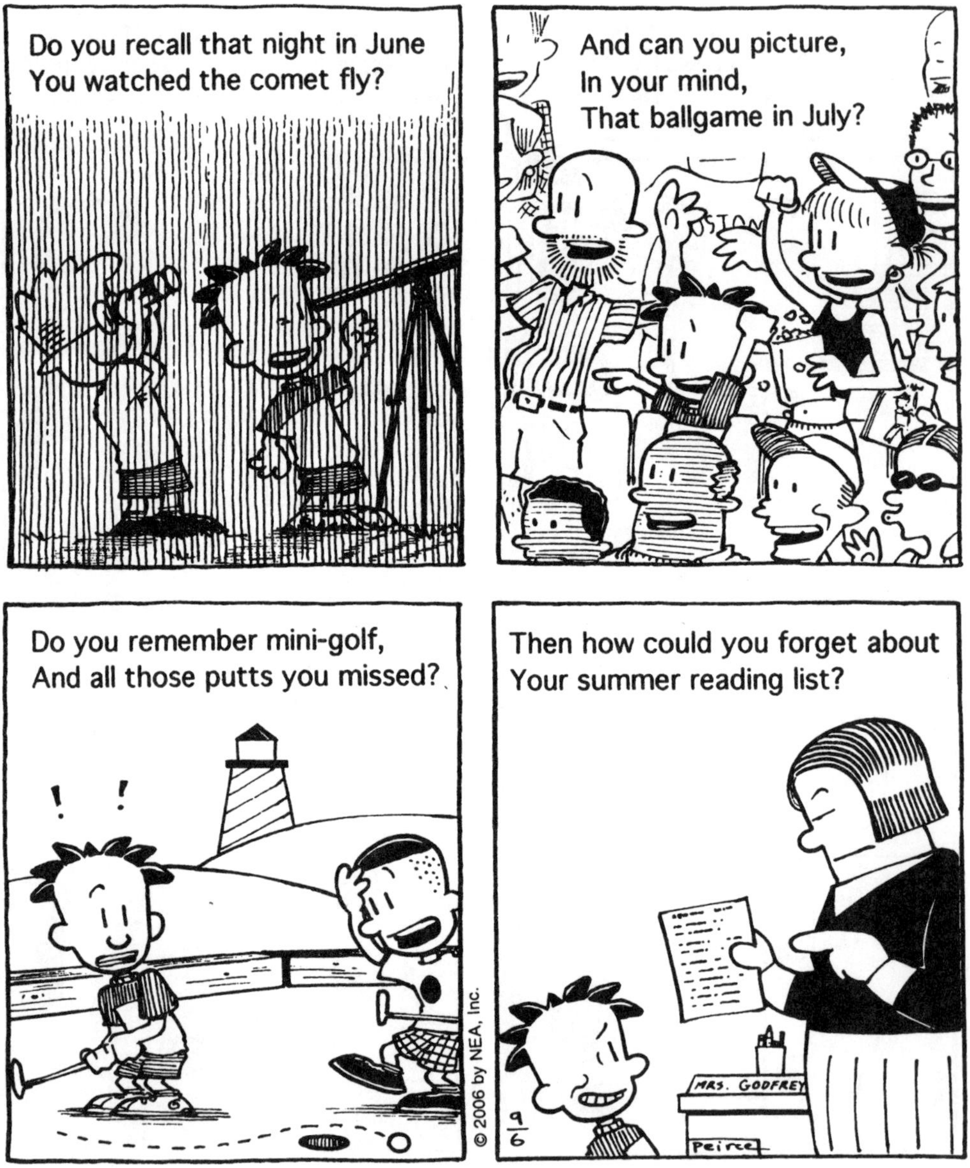
Do you recall that night in June
You watched the comet fly?
And can you picture,
In your mind,
That ballgame in July?
Do you remember mini-golf,
And all those putts you missed?
© 2006 by NEA, Inc.
Then how could you forget about
Your summer reading list?
MRS. GODFREY
Peirce

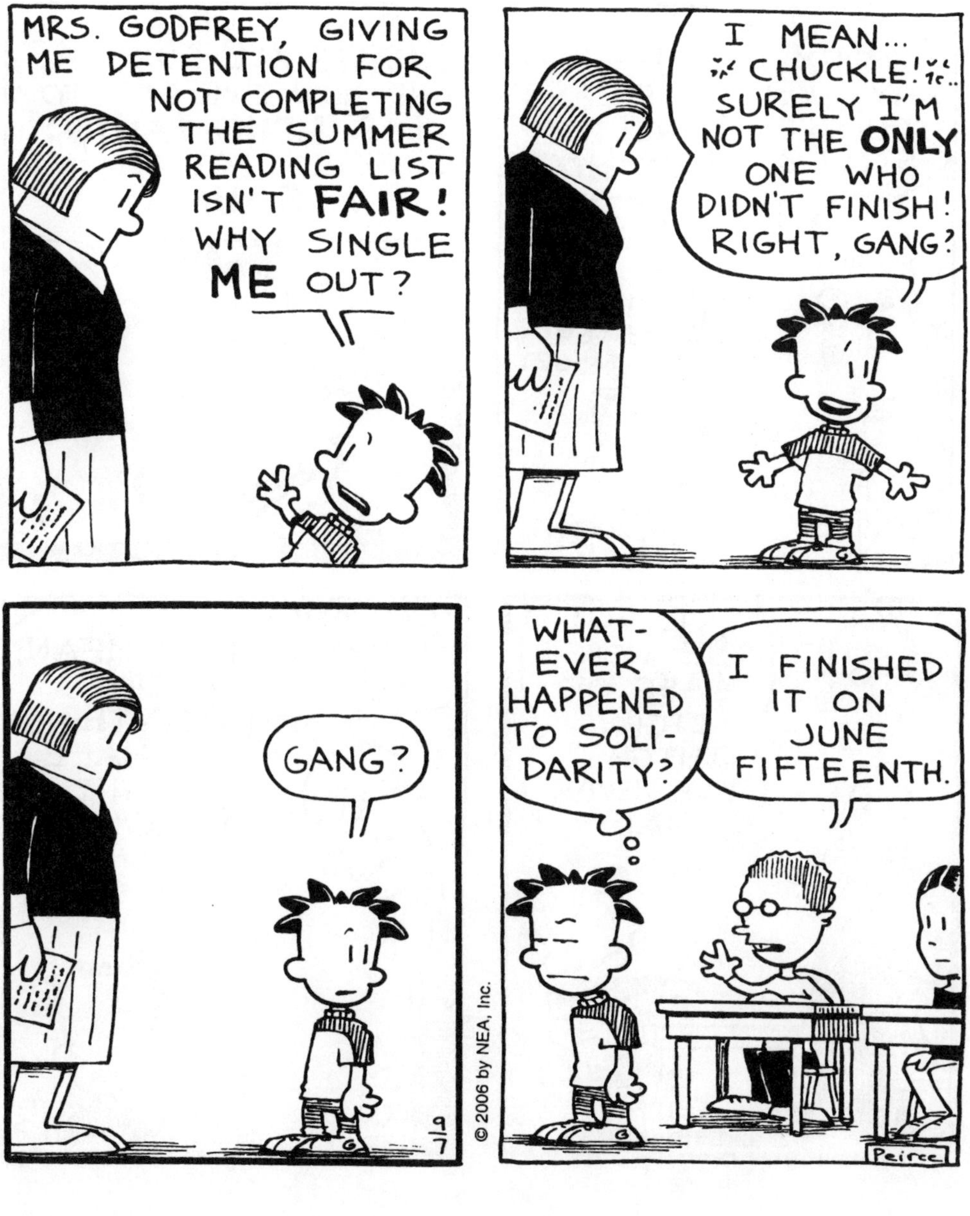
MRS. GODFREY, GIVING ME DETENTION FOR NOT COMPLETING THE SUMMER READING LIST ISN'T FAIR! WHY SINGLE ME OUT?
I MEAN... *CHUCKLE!* SURELY I'M NOT THE ONLY ONE WHO DIDN'T FINISH! RIGHT, GANG?
GANG?
WHAT-EVER HAPPENED TO SOLI-DARITY?
I FINISHED IT ON JUNE FIFTEENTH.
9/7
© 2006 by NEA, Inc.
Peirce

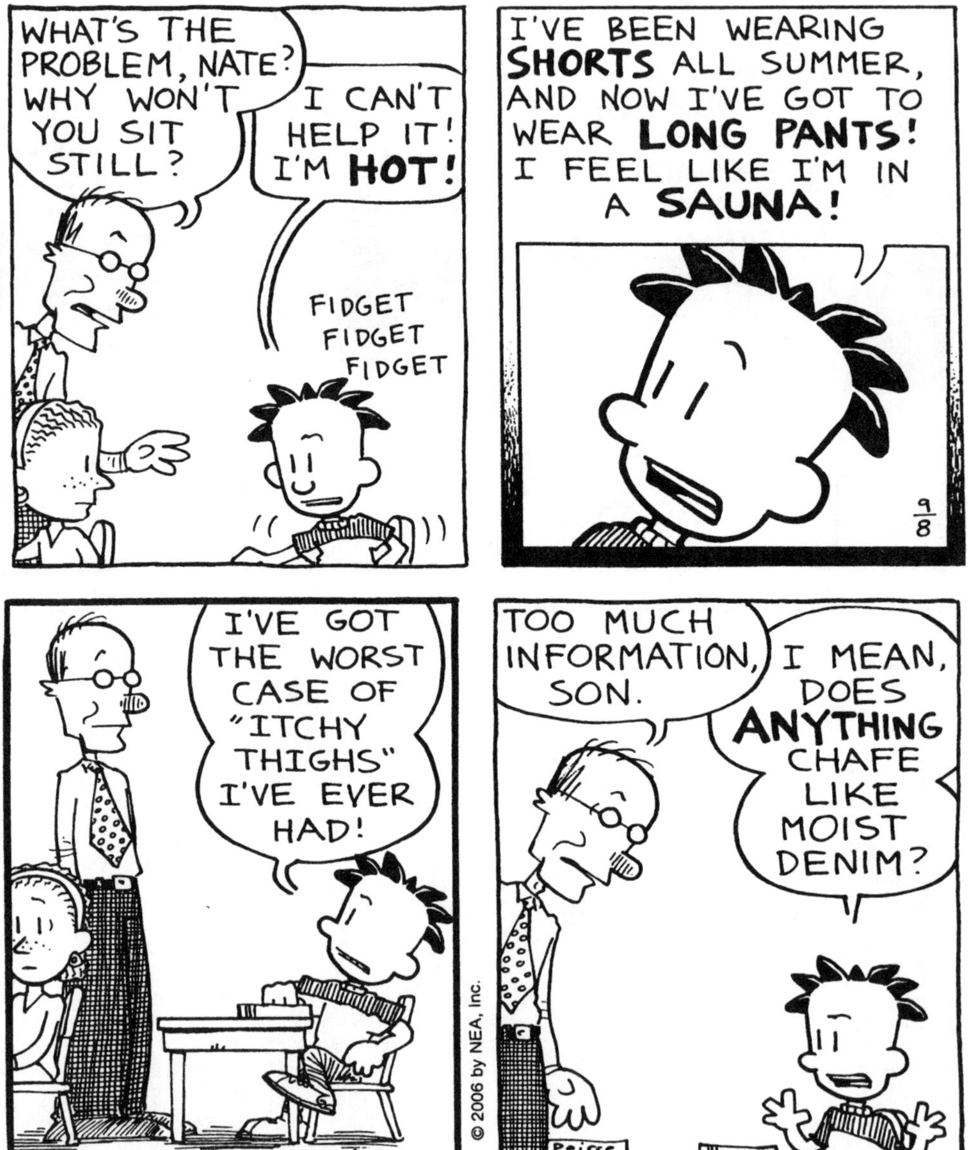
WHAT'S THE PROBLEM, NATE? WHY WON'T YOU SIT STILL?
I CAN'T HELP IT! I'M **HOT**!
FIDGET FIDGET FIDGET
I'VE BEEN WEARING **SHORTS** ALL SUMMER, AND NOW I'VE GOT TO WEAR **LONG PANTS**! I FEEL LIKE I'M IN A **SAUNA**!
9/8
I'VE GOT THE WORST CASE OF "ITCHY THIGHS" I'VE EVER HAD!
© 2006 by NEA, Inc.
TOO MUCH INFORMATION, SON.
I MEAN, DOES **ANYTHING** CHAFE LIKE MOIST DENIM?
Peirce

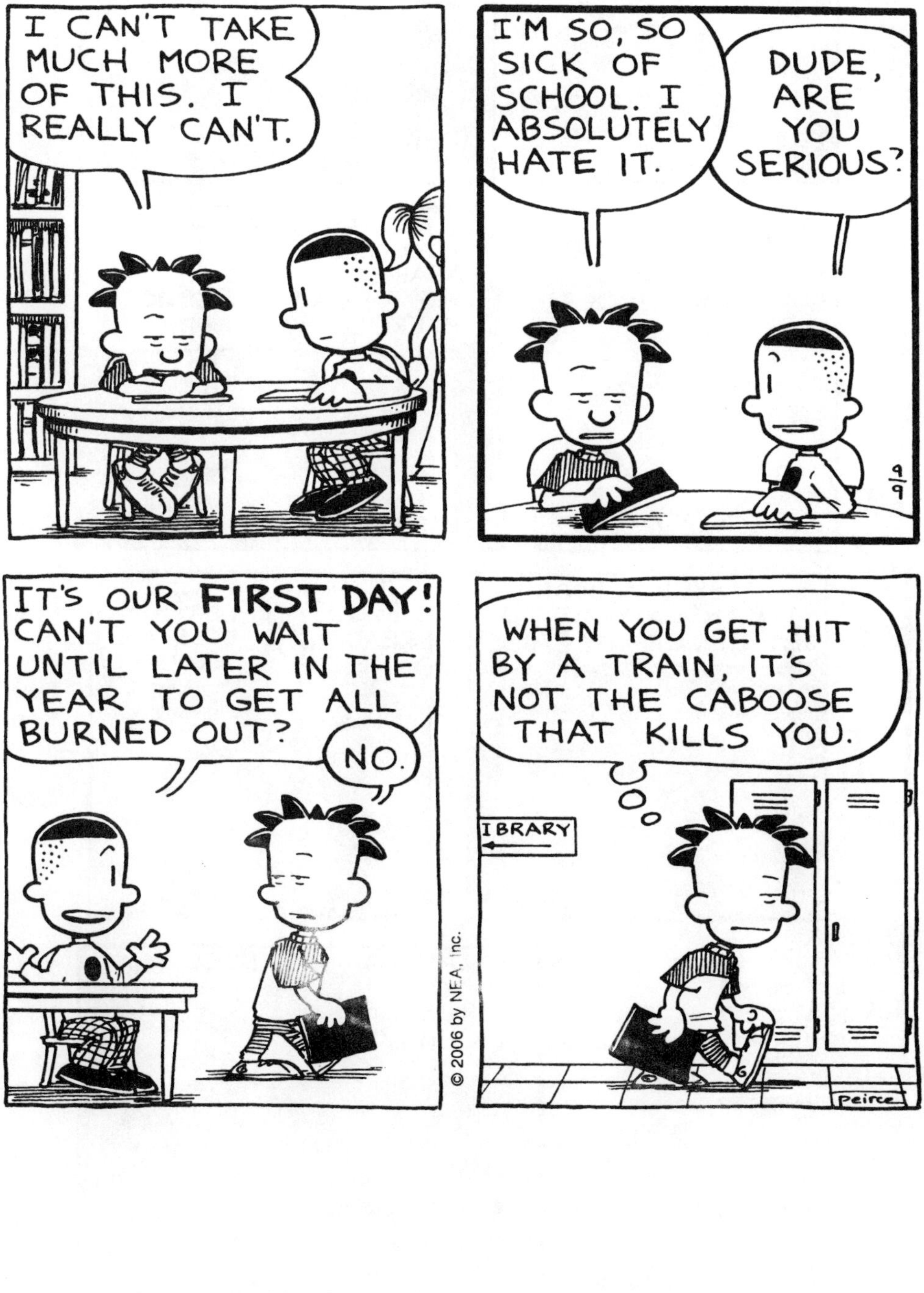
I CAN'T TAKE MUCH MORE OF THIS. I REALLY CAN'T.
I'M SO, SO SICK OF SCHOOL. I ABSOLUTELY HATE IT.
DUDE, ARE YOU SERIOUS?
9/9
IT'S OUR **FIRST DAY**! CAN'T YOU WAIT UNTIL LATER IN THE YEAR TO GET ALL BURNED OUT?
NO.
© 2006 by NEA, Inc.
WHEN YOU GET HIT BY A TRAIN, IT'S NOT THE CABOOSE THAT KILLS YOU.
IBRARY
peirce

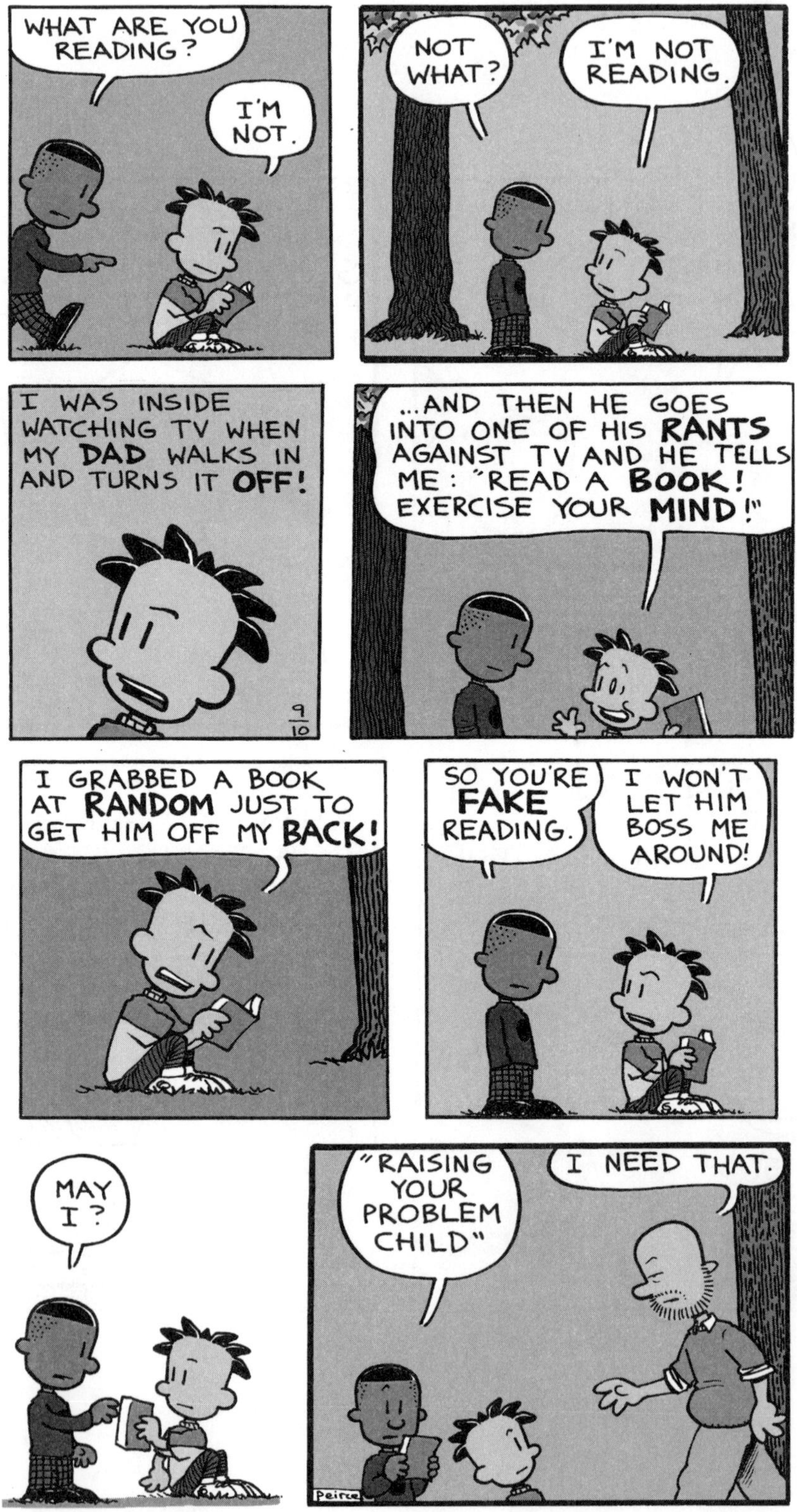
WHAT ARE YOU READING?
I'M NOT.
NOT WHAT?
I'M NOT READING.
I WAS INSIDE WATCHING TV WHEN MY DAD WALKS IN AND TURNS IT OFF!
9/10
...AND THEN HE GOES INTO ONE OF HIS RANTS AGAINST TV AND HE TELLS ME: "READ A BOOK! EXERCISE YOUR MIND!"
I GRABBED A BOOK AT RANDOM JUST TO GET HIM OFF MY BACK!
SO YOU'RE FAKE READING.
I WON'T LET HIM BOSS ME AROUND!
MAY I?
"RAISING YOUR PROBLEM CHILD"
I NEED THAT.
Peirce

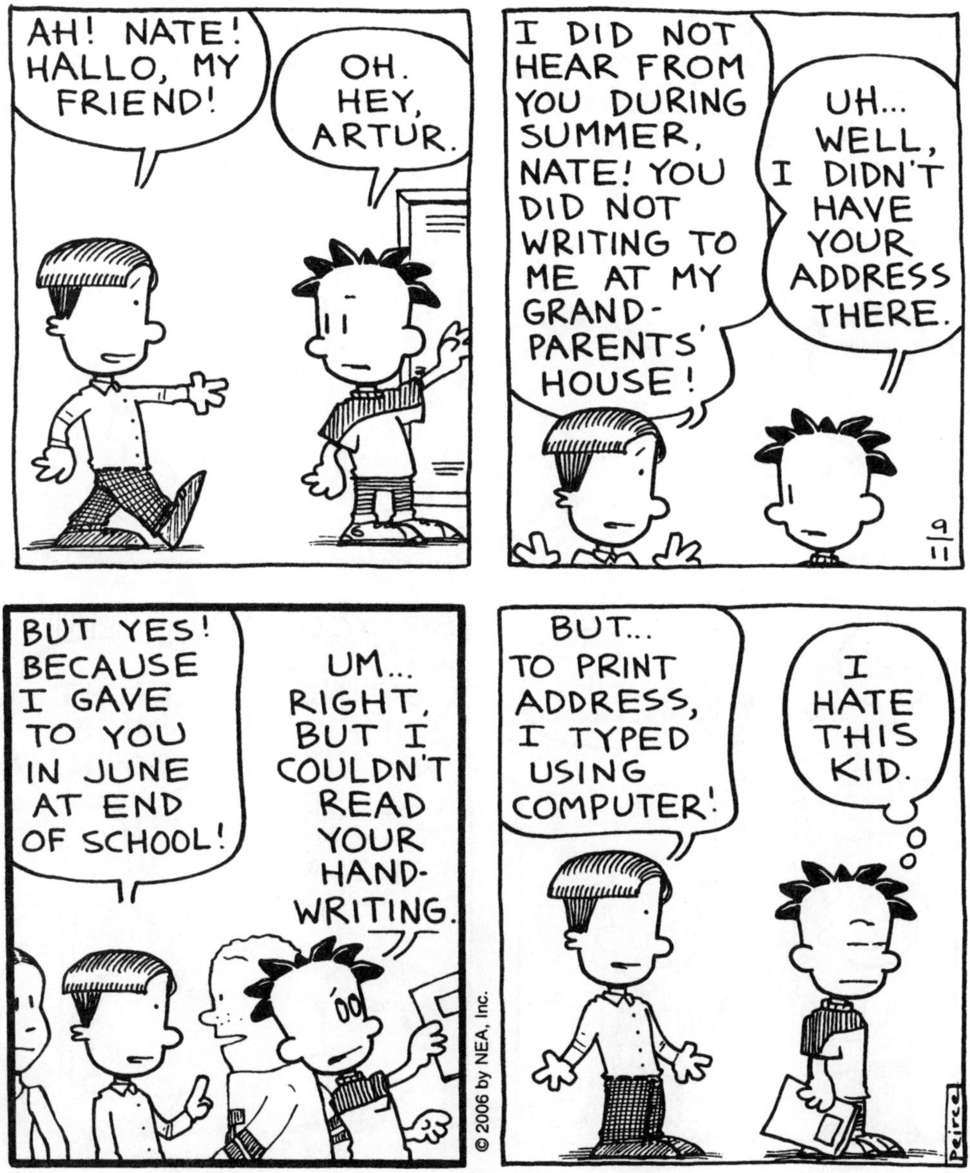
AH! NATE! HALLO, MY FRIEND!
OH. HEY, ARTUR.
I DID NOT HEAR FROM YOU DURING SUMMER, NATE! YOU DID NOT WRITING TO ME AT MY GRAND-PARENTS' HOUSE!
UH... WELL, I DIDN'T HAVE YOUR ADDRESS THERE.
9/11
BUT YES! BECAUSE I GAVE TO YOU IN JUNE AT END OF SCHOOL!
UM... RIGHT, BUT I COULDN'T READ YOUR HAND-WRITING.
© 2006 by NEA, Inc.
BUT... TO PRINT ADDRESS, I TYPED USING COMPUTER!
I HATE THIS KID.
Peirce

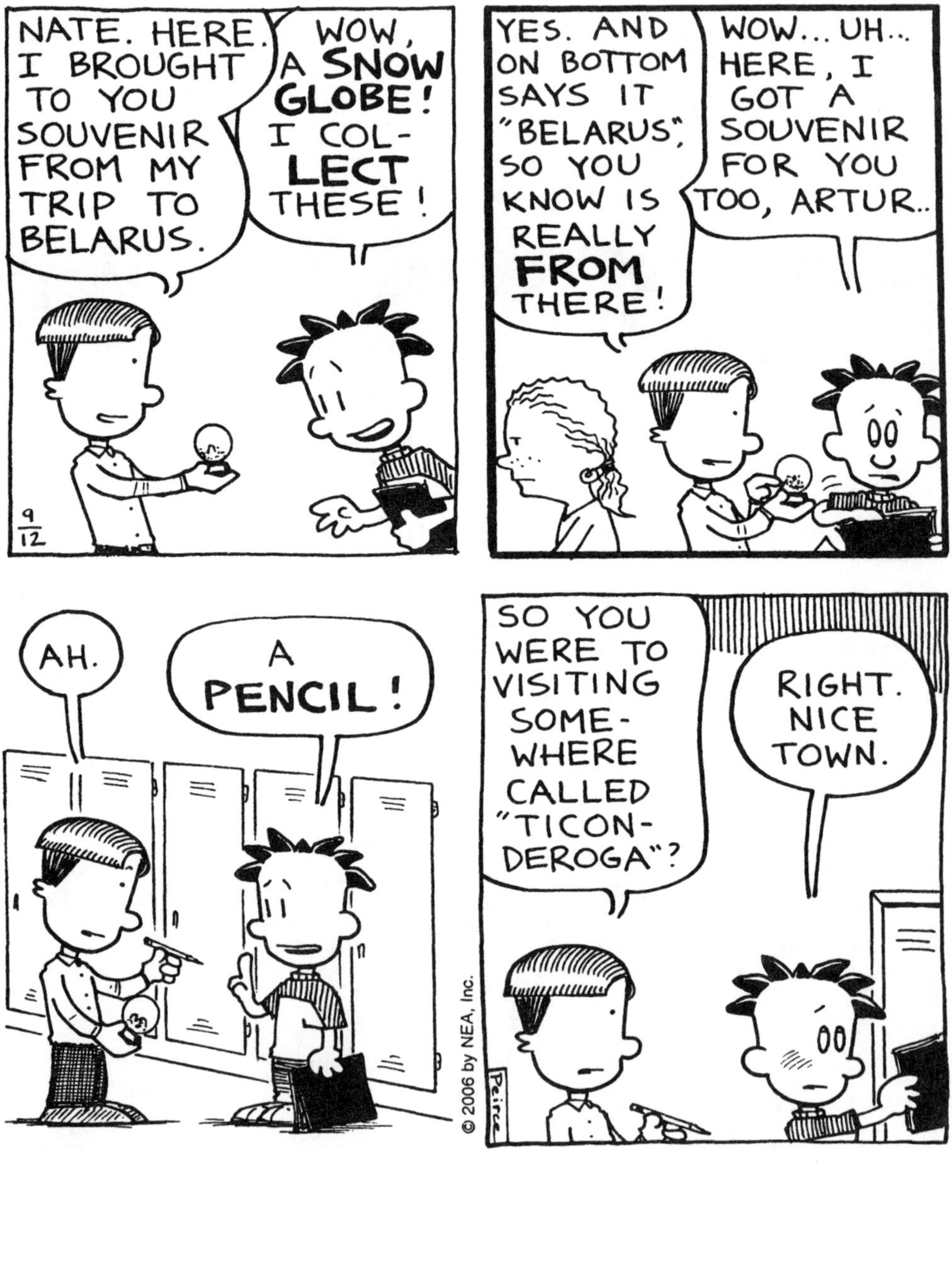
NATE. HERE. I BROUGHT TO YOU SOUVENIR FROM MY TRIP TO BELARUS.
WOW, A **SNOW GLOBE**! I COL-**LECT** THESE!
9/12
YES. AND ON BOTTOM SAYS IT "BELARUS", SO YOU KNOW IS REALLY **FROM** THERE!
WOW... UH... HERE, I GOT A SOUVENIR FOR YOU TOO, ARTUR..
AH.
A **PENCIL**!
SO YOU WERE TO VISITING SOME-WHERE CALLED "TICON-DEROGA"?
RIGHT. NICE TOWN.
Peirce

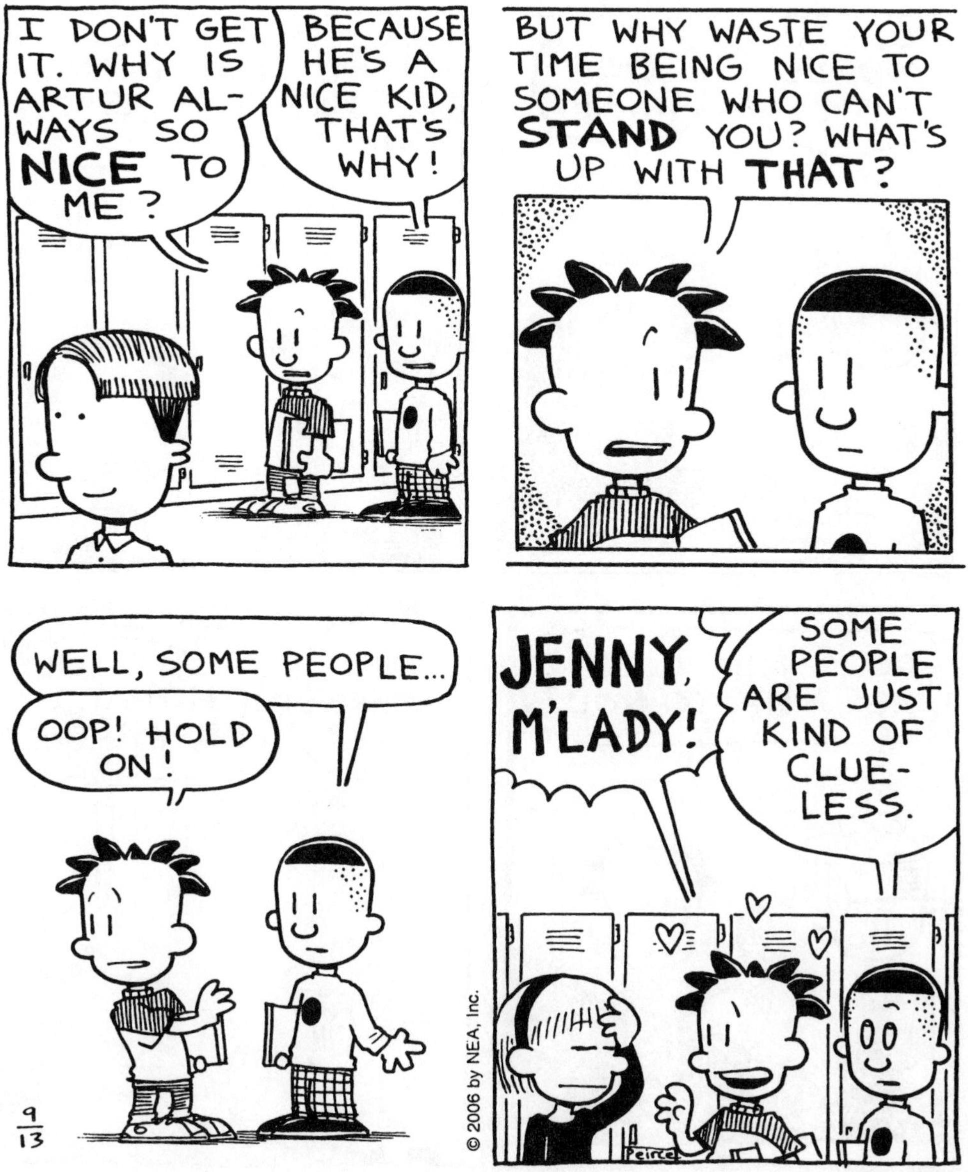
I DON'T GET IT. WHY IS ARTUR ALWAYS SO NICE TO ME?
BECAUSE HE'S A NICE KID, THAT'S WHY!
BUT WHY WASTE YOUR TIME BEING NICE TO SOMEONE WHO CAN'T STAND YOU? WHAT'S UP WITH THAT?
WELL, SOME PEOPLE...
OOP! HOLD ON!
JENNY, M'LADY!
SOME PEOPLE ARE JUST KIND OF CLUELESS.
9/13
© 2006 by NEA, Inc.
Peirce

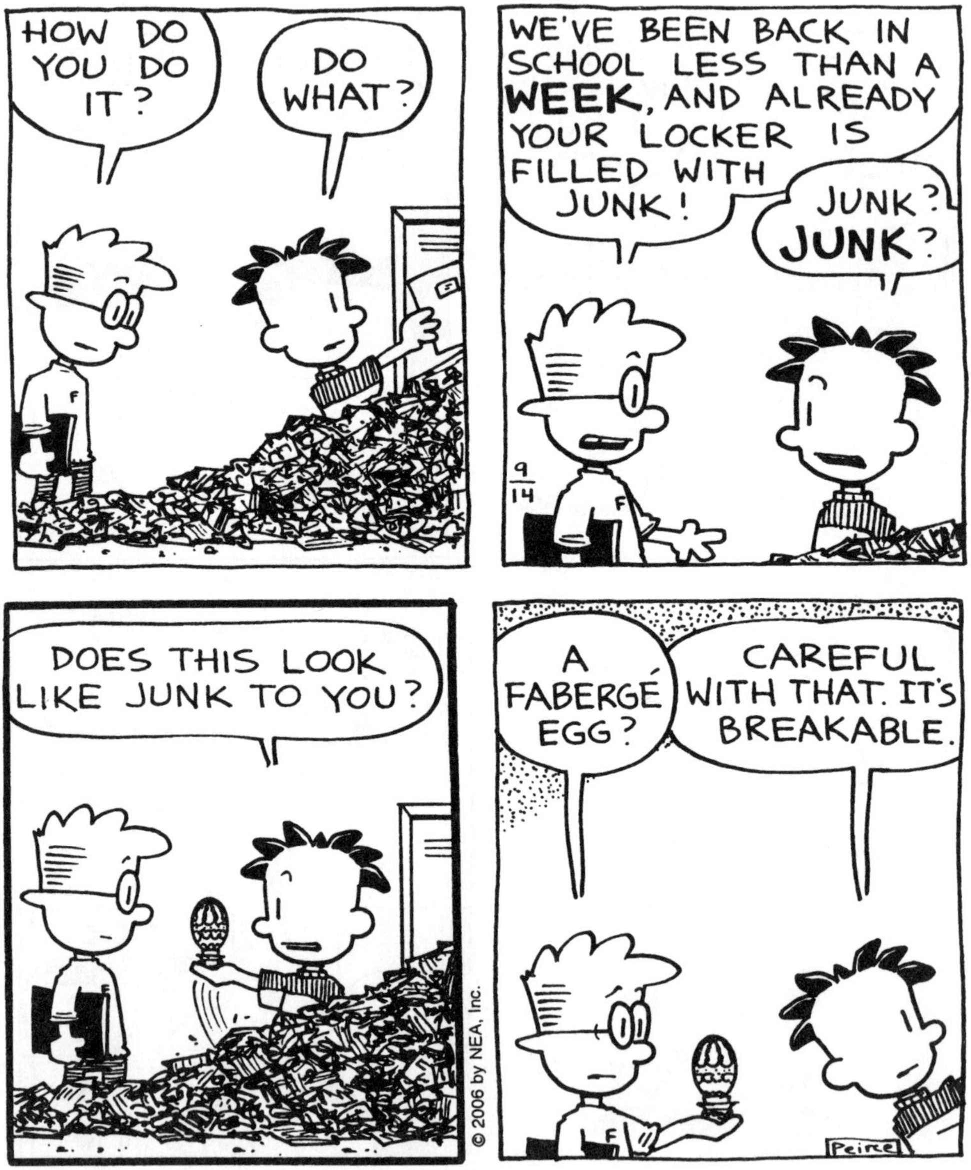
HOW DO YOU DO IT?
DO WHAT?
WE'VE BEEN BACK IN SCHOOL LESS THAN A **WEEK**, AND ALREADY YOUR LOCKER IS FILLED WITH JUNK!
JUNK? **JUNK**?
9/14
DOES THIS LOOK LIKE JUNK TO YOU?
A FABERGÉ EGG?
CAREFUL WITH THAT. IT'S BREAKABLE.
Peirce

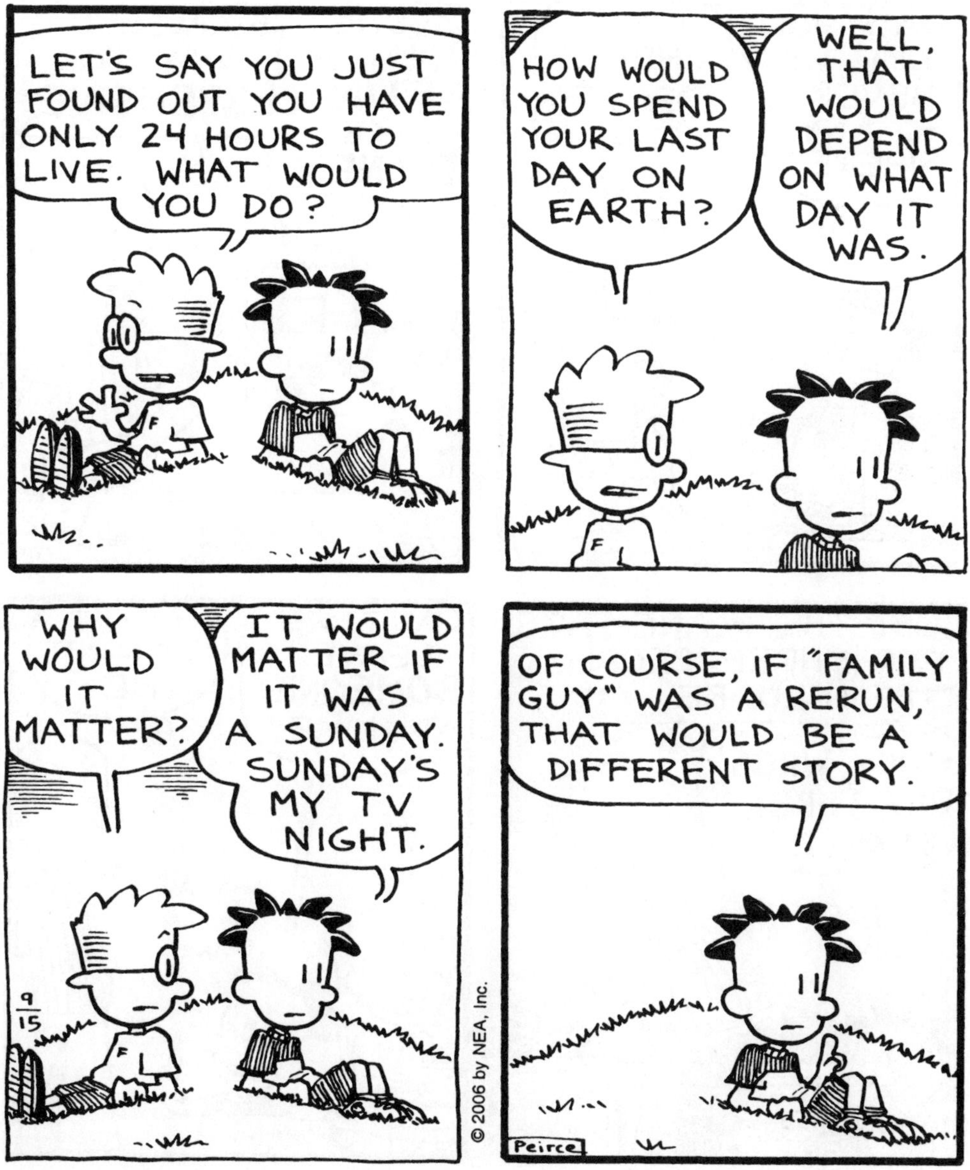
LET'S SAY YOU JUST FOUND OUT YOU HAVE ONLY 24 HOURS TO LIVE. WHAT WOULD YOU DO?
HOW WOULD YOU SPEND YOUR LAST DAY ON EARTH?
WELL, THAT WOULD DEPEND ON WHAT DAY IT WAS.
WHY WOULD IT MATTER?
IT WOULD MATTER IF IT WAS A SUNDAY. SUNDAY'S MY TV NIGHT.
9/15
© 2006 by NEA, Inc.
OF COURSE, IF "FAMILY GUY" WAS A RERUN, THAT WOULD BE A DIFFERENT STORY.
Peirce

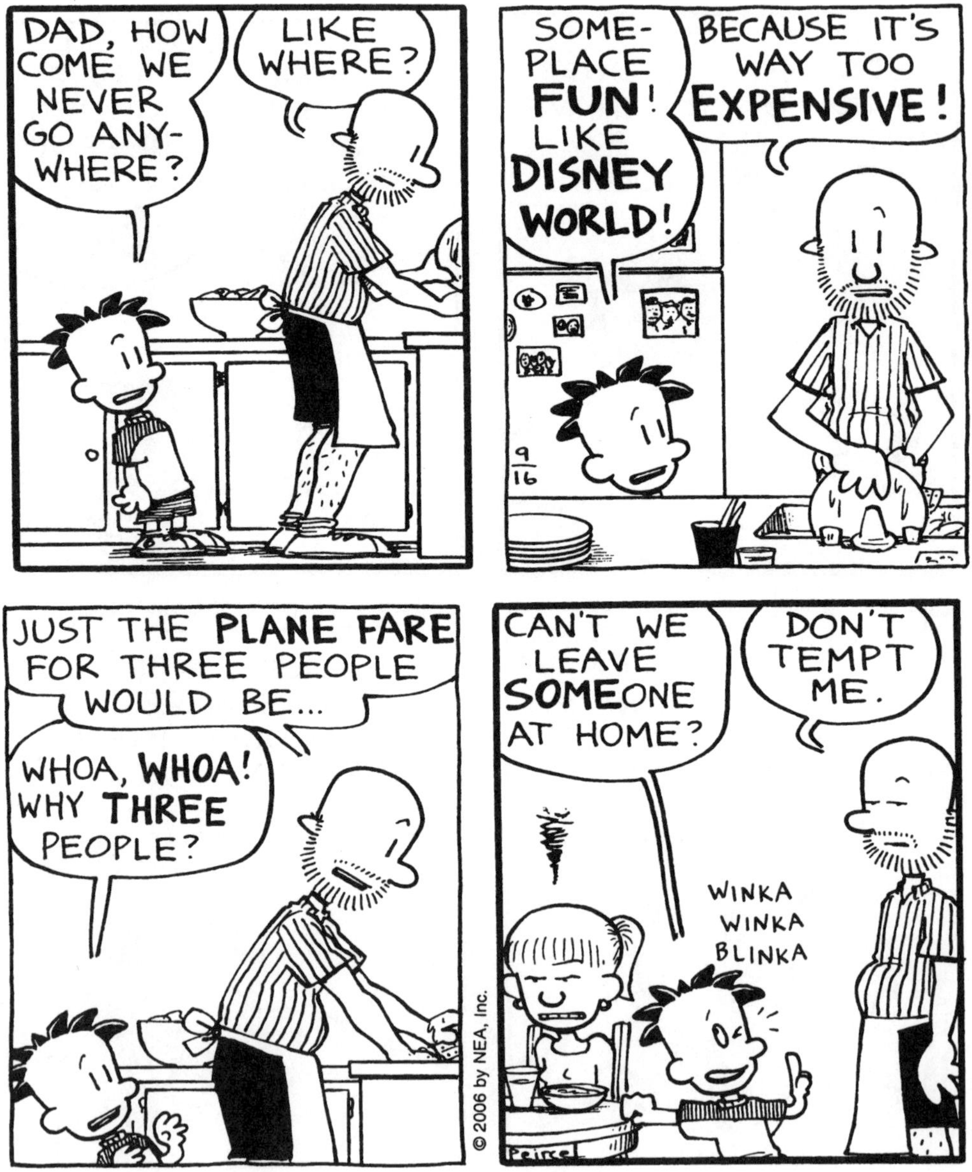
DAD, HOW COME WE NEVER GO ANYWHERE?
LIKE WHERE?
SOMEPLACE FUN! LIKE DISNEY WORLD!
BECAUSE IT'S WAY TOO EXPENSIVE!
9/16
JUST THE PLANE FARE FOR THREE PEOPLE WOULD BE...
WHOA, WHOA! WHY THREE PEOPLE?
CAN'T WE LEAVE SOMEONE AT HOME?
DON'T TEMPT ME.
WINKA WINKA BLINKA
Peirce

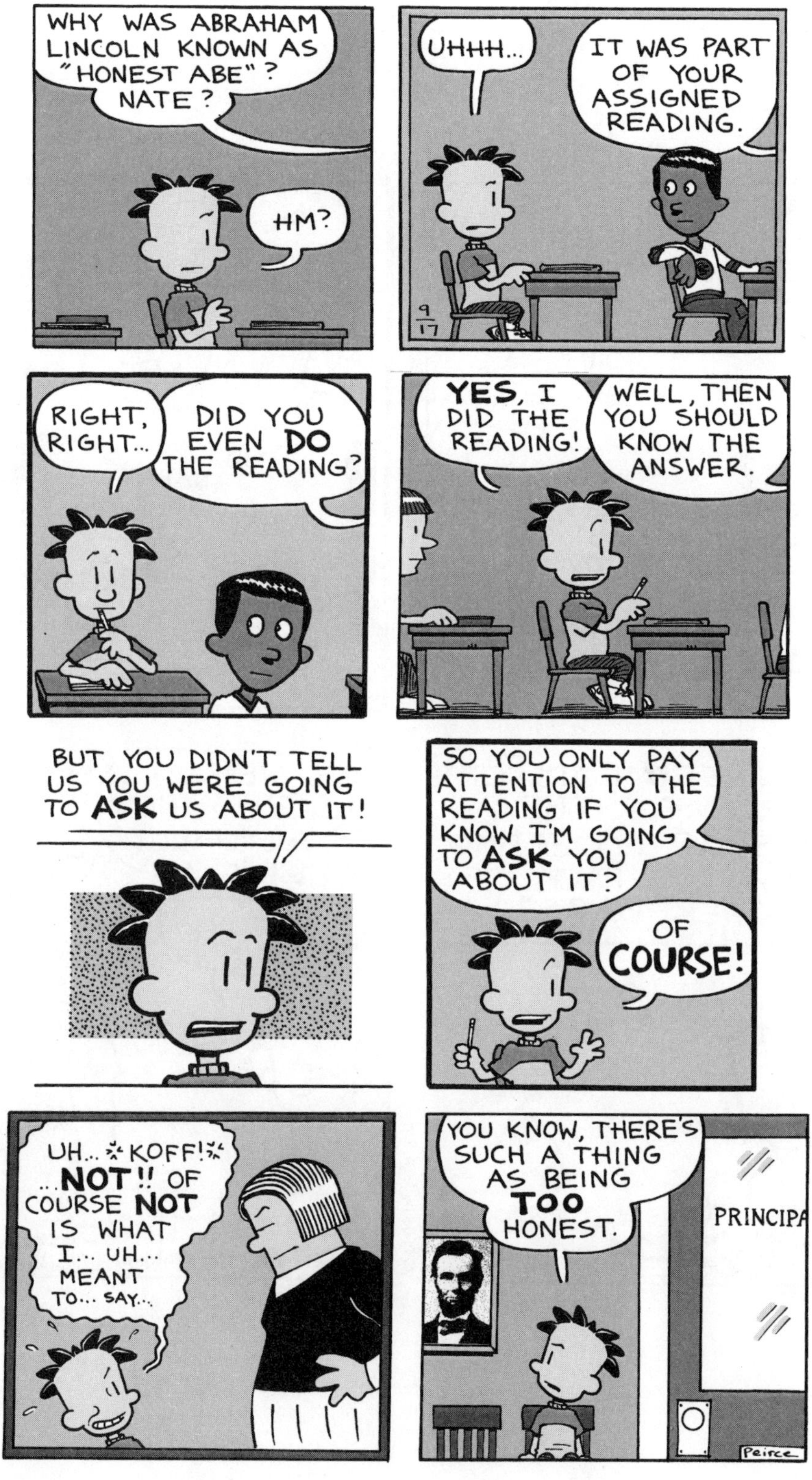
WHY WAS ABRAHAM LINCOLN KNOWN AS "HONEST ABE"? NATE?
HM?
UHHH...
IT WAS PART OF YOUR ASSIGNED READING.
9/17
RIGHT, RIGHT...
DID YOU EVEN DO THE READING?
YES, I DID THE READING!
WELL, THEN YOU SHOULD KNOW THE ANSWER.
BUT YOU DIDN'T TELL US YOU WERE GOING TO ASK US ABOUT IT!
SO YOU ONLY PAY ATTENTION TO THE READING IF YOU KNOW I'M GOING TO ASK YOU ABOUT IT?
OF COURSE!
UH... KOFF! ...NOT!! OF COURSE NOT IS WHAT I... UH... MEANT TO... SAY...
YOU KNOW, THERE'S SUCH A THING AS BEING TOO HONEST.
PRINCIPA
Peirce

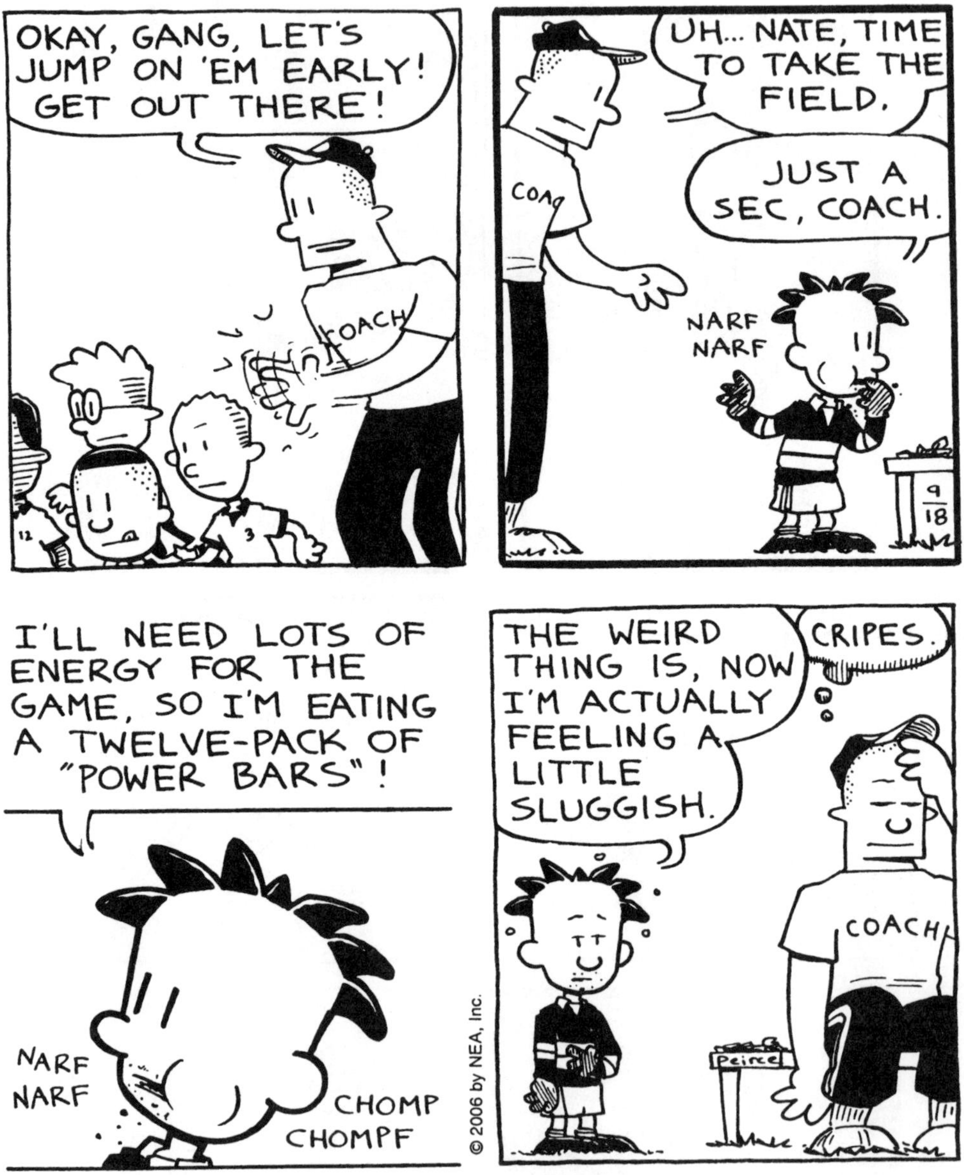
OKAY, GANG, LET'S JUMP ON 'EM EARLY! GET OUT THERE!
COACH
12
3
UH... NATE, TIME TO TAKE THE FIELD.
JUST A SEC, COACH.
COACH
NARF NARF
9/18
I'LL NEED LOTS OF ENERGY FOR THE GAME, SO I'M EATING A TWELVE-PACK OF "POWER BARS"!
NARF NARF
CHOMP CHOMPF
THE WEIRD THING IS, NOW I'M ACTUALLY FEELING A LITTLE SLUGGISH.
CRIPES.
COACH
Peirce

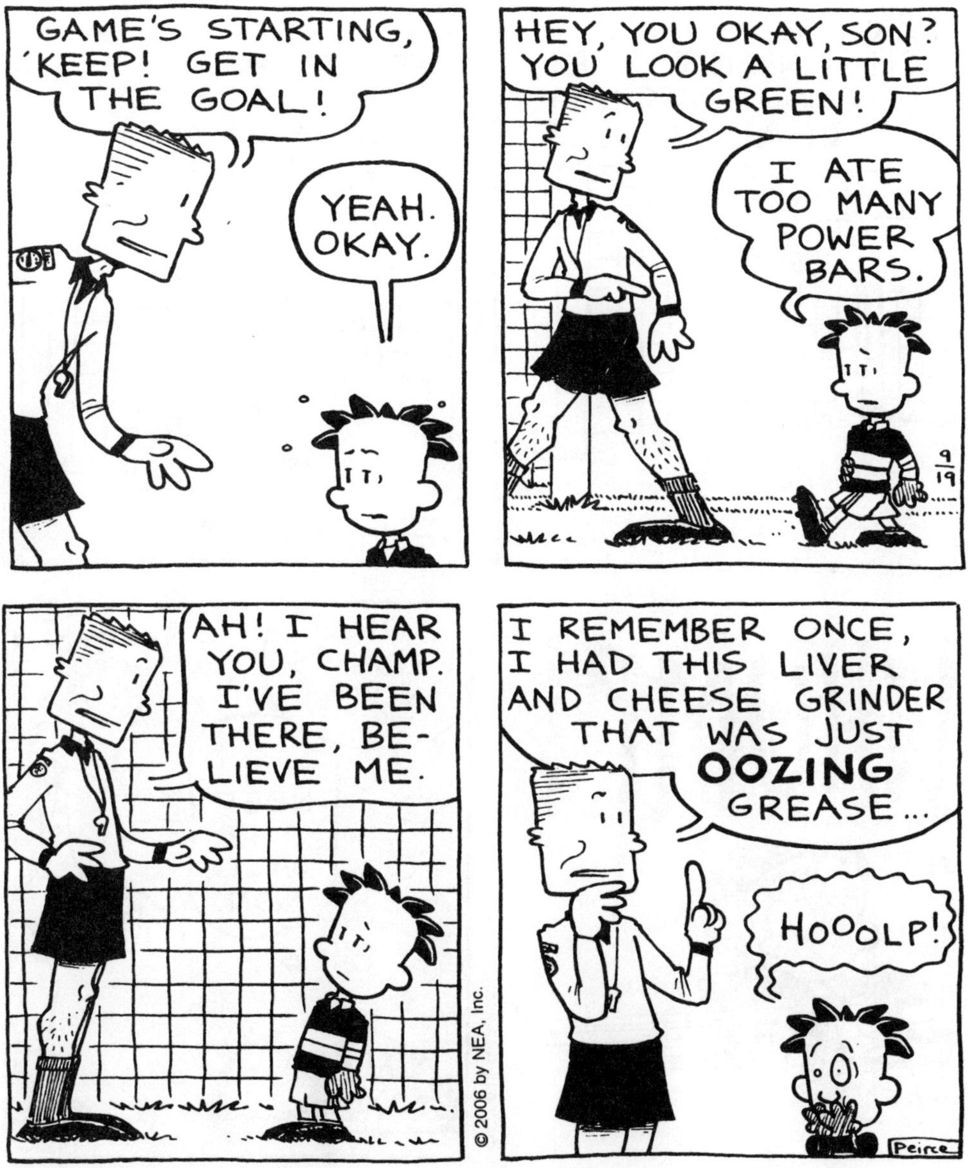
GAME'S STARTING, 'KEEP! GET IN THE GOAL!
YEAH. OKAY.
HEY, YOU OKAY, SON? YOU LOOK A LITTLE GREEN!
I ATE TOO MANY POWER BARS.
9/19
AH! I HEAR YOU, CHAMP. I'VE BEEN THERE, BELIEVE ME.
© 2006 by NEA, Inc.
I REMEMBER ONCE, I HAD THIS LIVER AND CHEESE GRINDER THAT WAS JUST **OOZING** GREASE...
HOOOLP!
Peirce

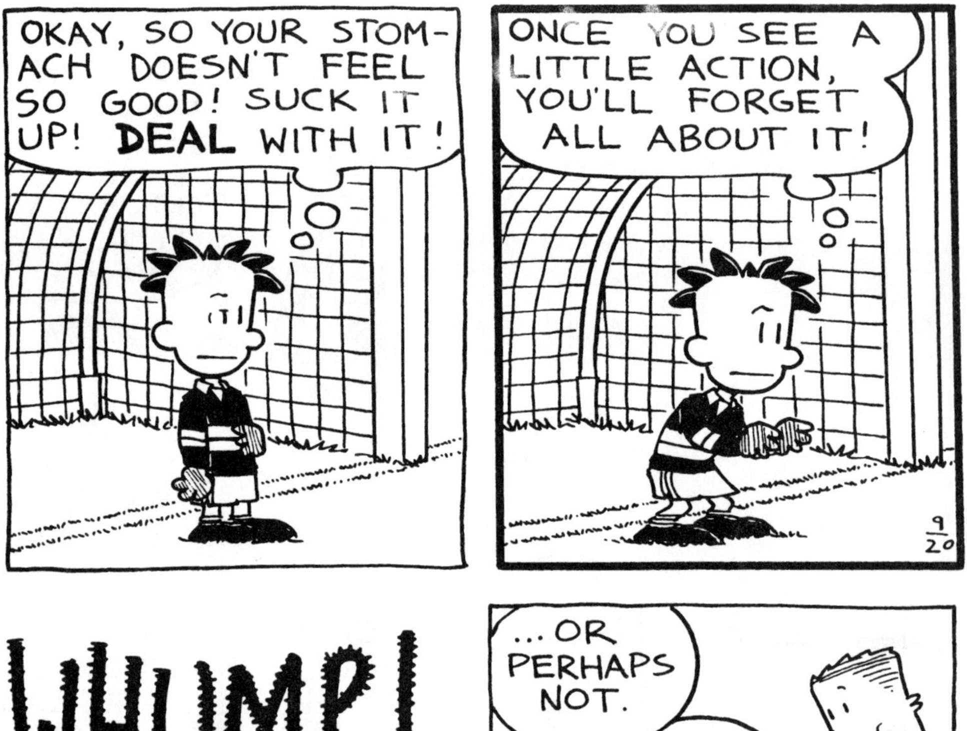
OKAY, SO YOUR STOMACH DOESN'T FEEL SO GOOD! SUCK IT UP! **DEAL** WITH IT!
ONCE YOU SEE A LITTLE ACTION, YOU'LL FORGET ALL ABOUT IT!
9/20
WHUMP!
...OR PERHAPS NOT.
WE'LL NEED THE BALL, SON.
Peirce

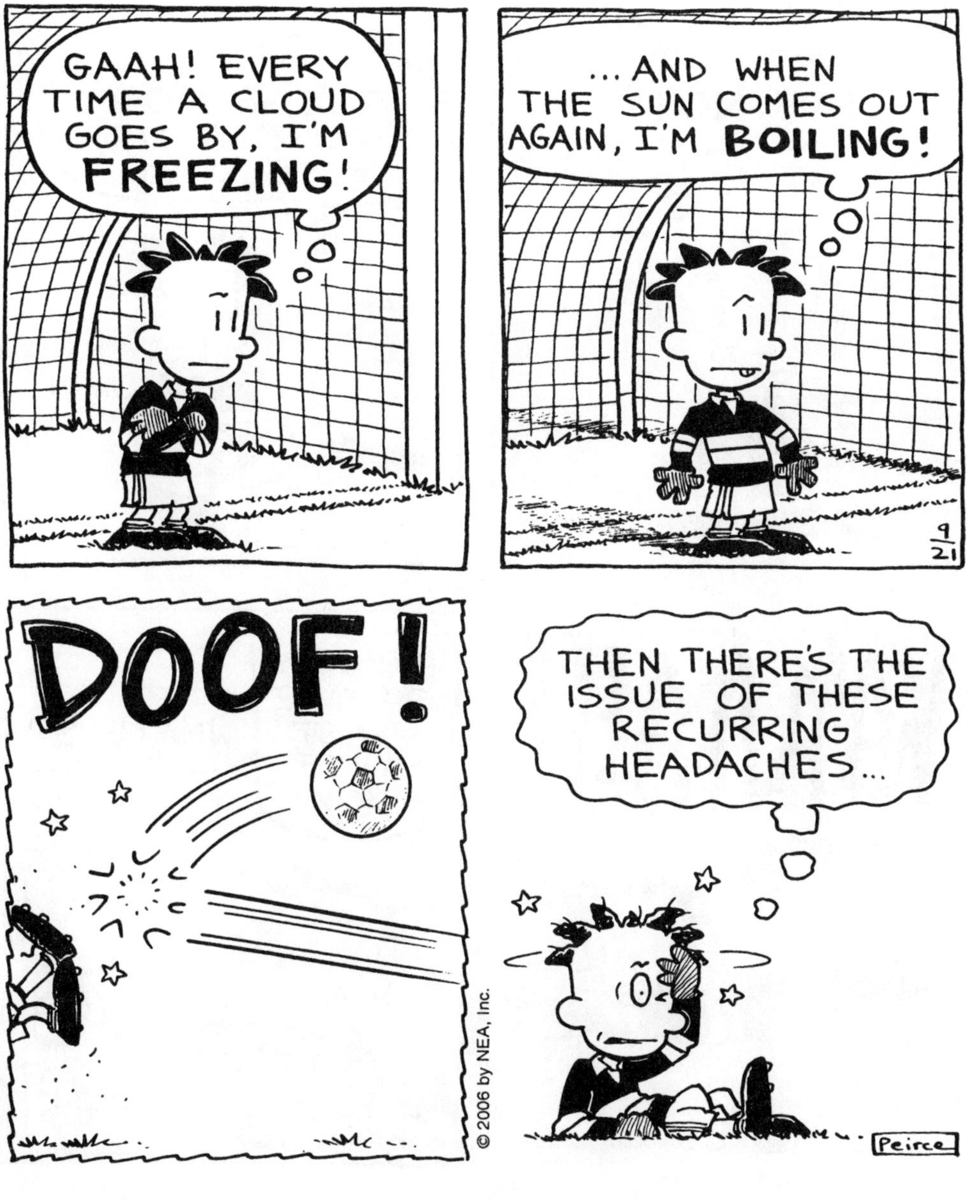
GAAH! EVERY TIME A CLOUD GOES BY, I'M **FREEZING**!
...AND WHEN THE SUN COMES OUT AGAIN, I'M **BOILING**!
9/21
DOOF!
THEN THERE'S THE ISSUE OF THESE RECURRING HEADACHES...
Peirce

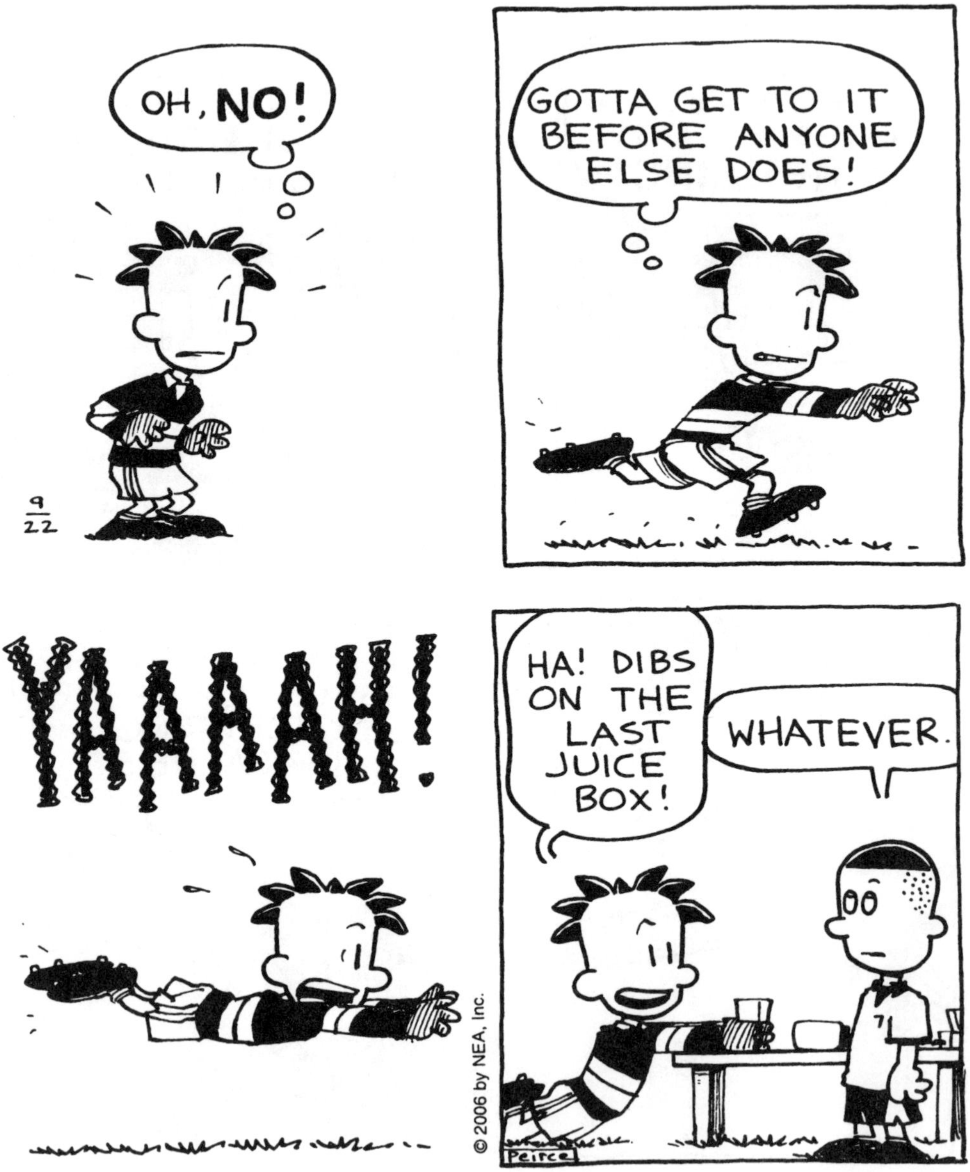
OH, NO!
9/22
GOTTA GET TO IT BEFORE ANYONE ELSE DOES!
YAAAAH!
HA! DIBS ON THE LAST JUICE BOX!
WHATEVER.
Peirce

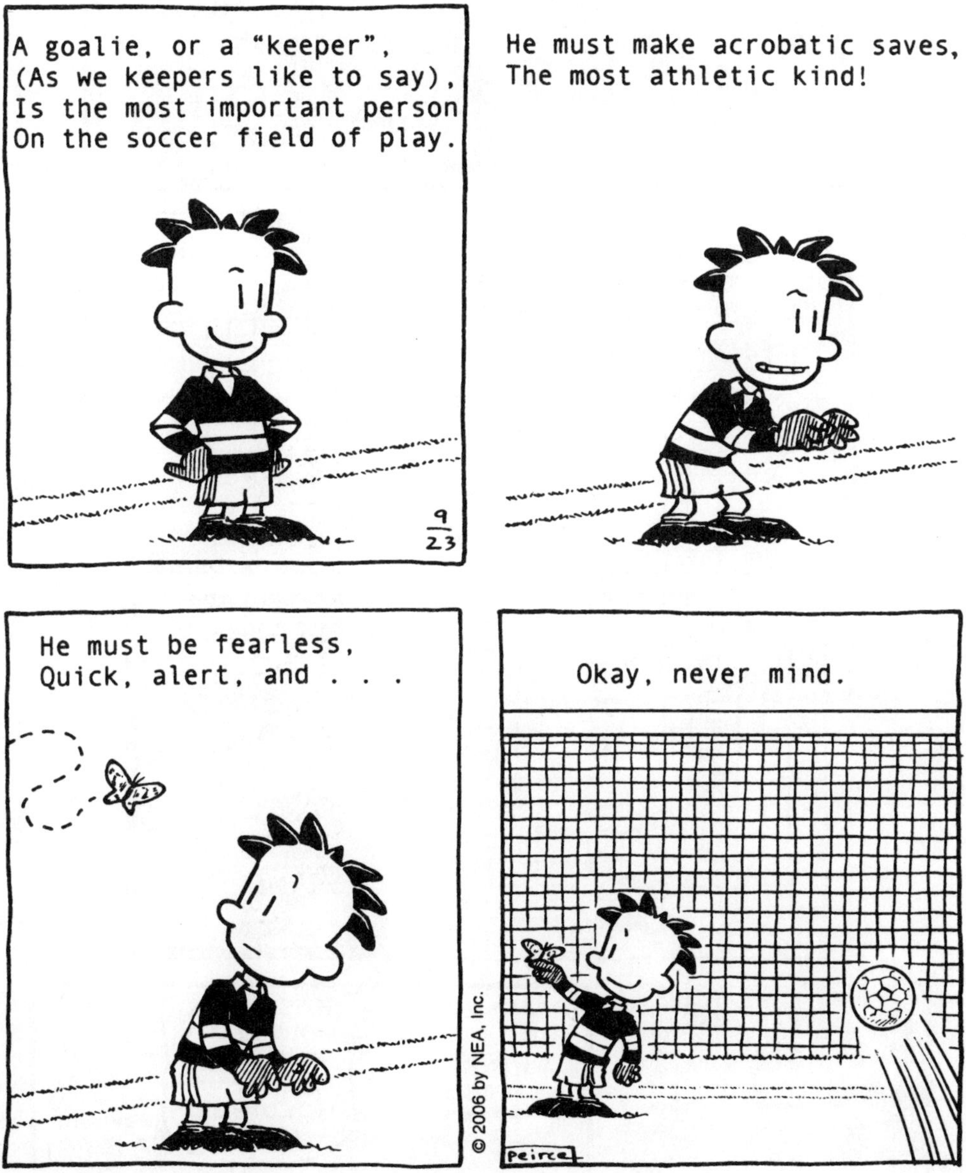
A goalie, or a "keeper",
(As we keepers like to say),
Is the most important person
On the soccer field of play.
9/23
He must make acrobatic saves,
The most athletic kind!
He must be fearless,
Quick, alert, and . . .
Okay, never mind.
© 2006 by NEA, Inc.
Peirce

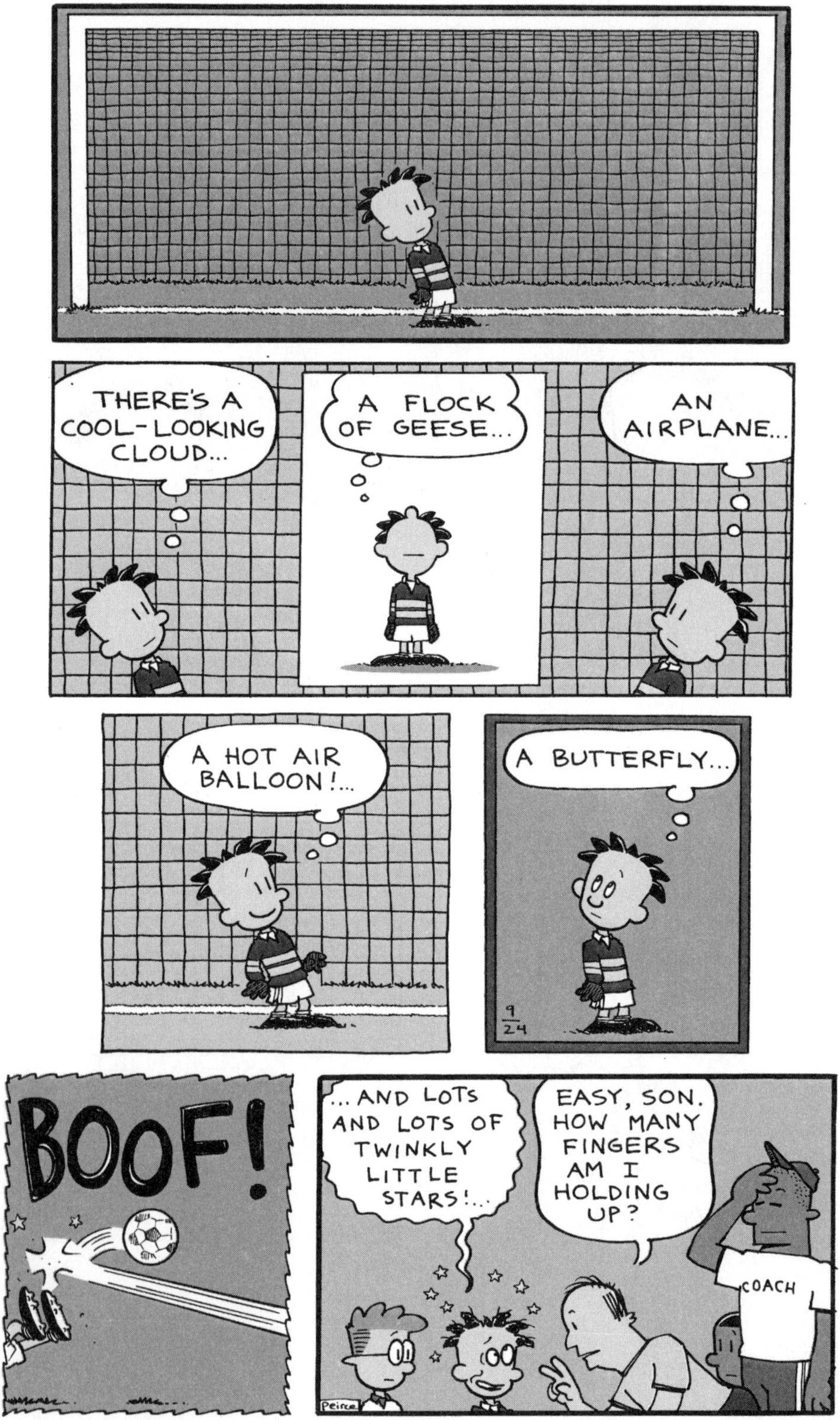
THERE'S A COOL-LOOKING CLOUD...
A FLOCK OF GEESE...
AN AIRPLANE...
A HOT AIR BALLOON!...
A BUTTERFLY...
9
24
BOOF!
...AND LOTS AND LOTS OF TWINKLY LITTLE STARS!...
EASY, SON. HOW MANY FINGERS AM I HOLDING UP?
COACH
Peirce

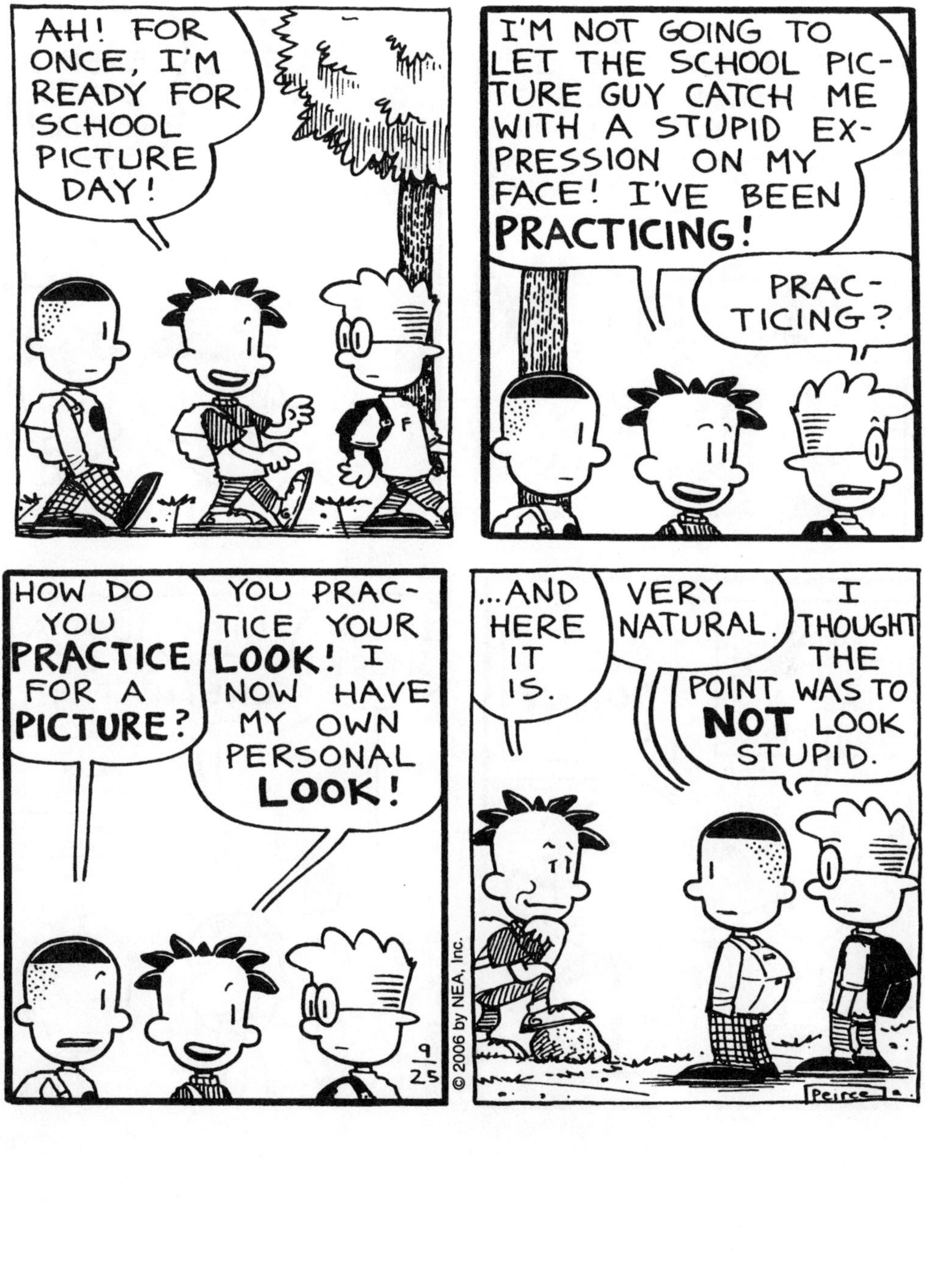
AH! FOR ONCE, I'M READY FOR SCHOOL PICTURE DAY!
I'M NOT GOING TO LET THE SCHOOL PICTURE GUY CATCH ME WITH A STUPID EXPRESSION ON MY FACE! I'VE BEEN PRACTICING!
PRACTICING?
HOW DO YOU PRACTICE FOR A PICTURE?
YOU PRACTICE YOUR LOOK! I NOW HAVE MY OWN PERSONAL LOOK!
9/25
© 2006 by NEA, Inc.
...AND HERE IT IS.
VERY NATURAL.
I THOUGHT THE POINT WAS TO NOT LOOK STUPID.
Peirce

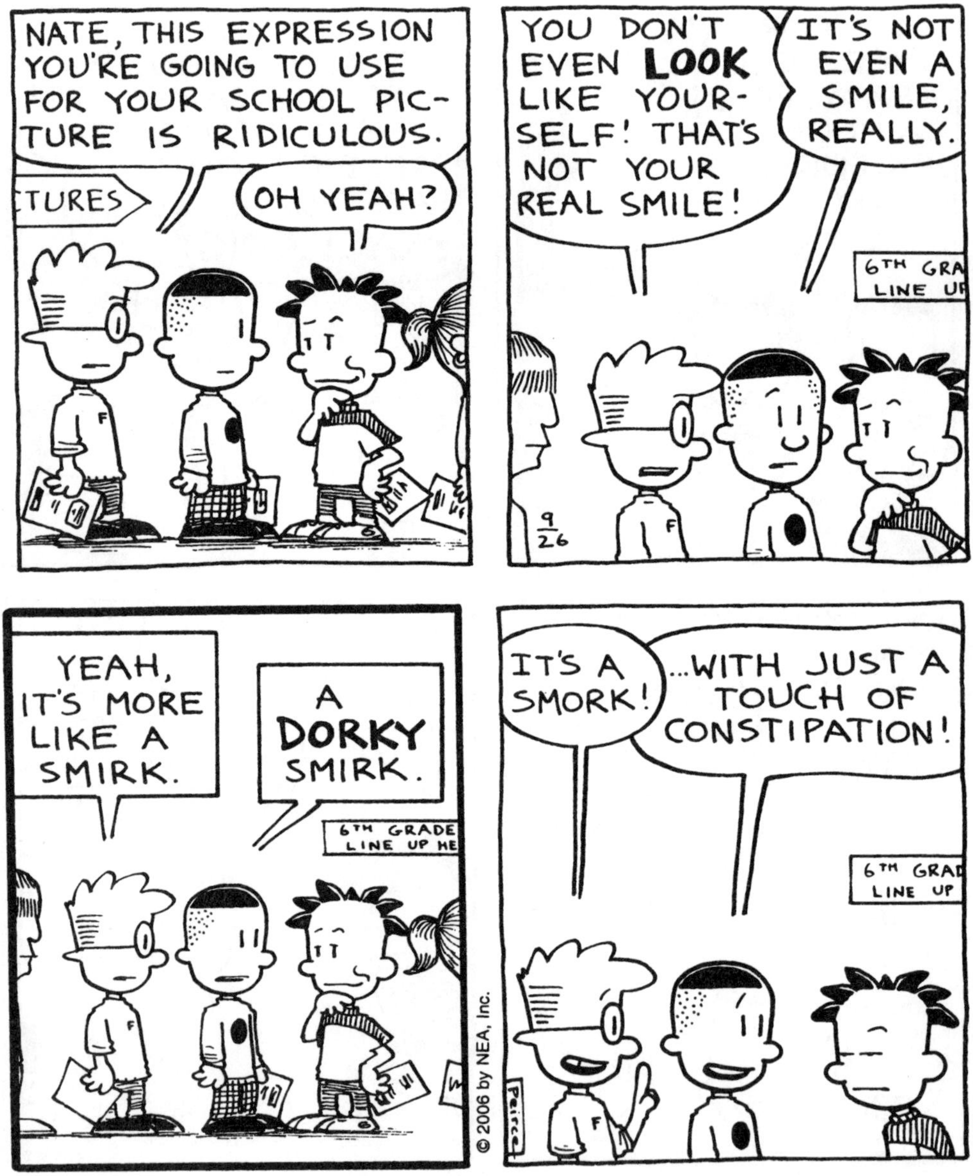
NATE, THIS EXPRESSION YOU'RE GOING TO USE FOR YOUR SCHOOL PICTURE IS RIDICULOUS.
TURES
OH YEAH?
YOU DON'T EVEN LOOK LIKE YOURSELF! THAT'S NOT YOUR REAL SMILE!
IT'S NOT EVEN A SMILE, REALLY.
6TH GRA
LINE UP
9/26
YEAH, IT'S MORE LIKE A SMIRK.
A DORKY SMIRK.
6TH GRADE
LINE UP HE
IT'S A SMORK!
...WITH JUST A TOUCH OF CONSTIPATION!
6TH GRAD
LINE UP
Peirce
© 2006 by NEA, Inc.

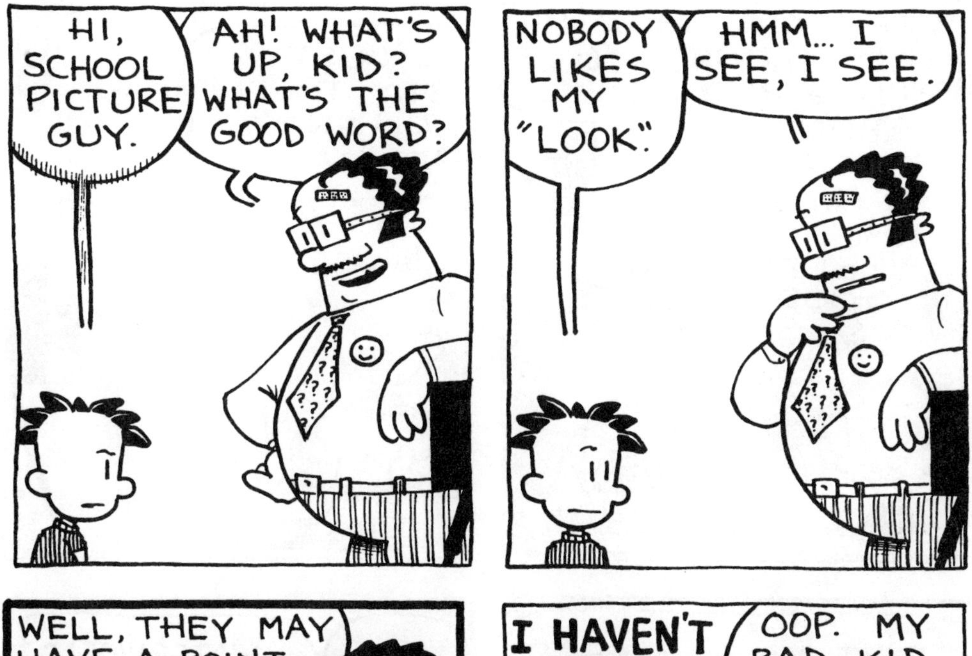
HI, SCHOOL PICTURE GUY.
AH! WHAT'S UP, KID? WHAT'S THE GOOD WORD?
NOBODY LIKES MY "LOOK."
HMM... I SEE, I SEE.
WELL, THEY MAY HAVE A POINT, AMIGO. THE HAIR-STYLE IS A BIT EXTREME.
I HAVEN'T EVEN SHOWN YOU THE "LOOK" YET!!
OOP. MY BAD, KID. CARRY ON.
9/27
Peirce

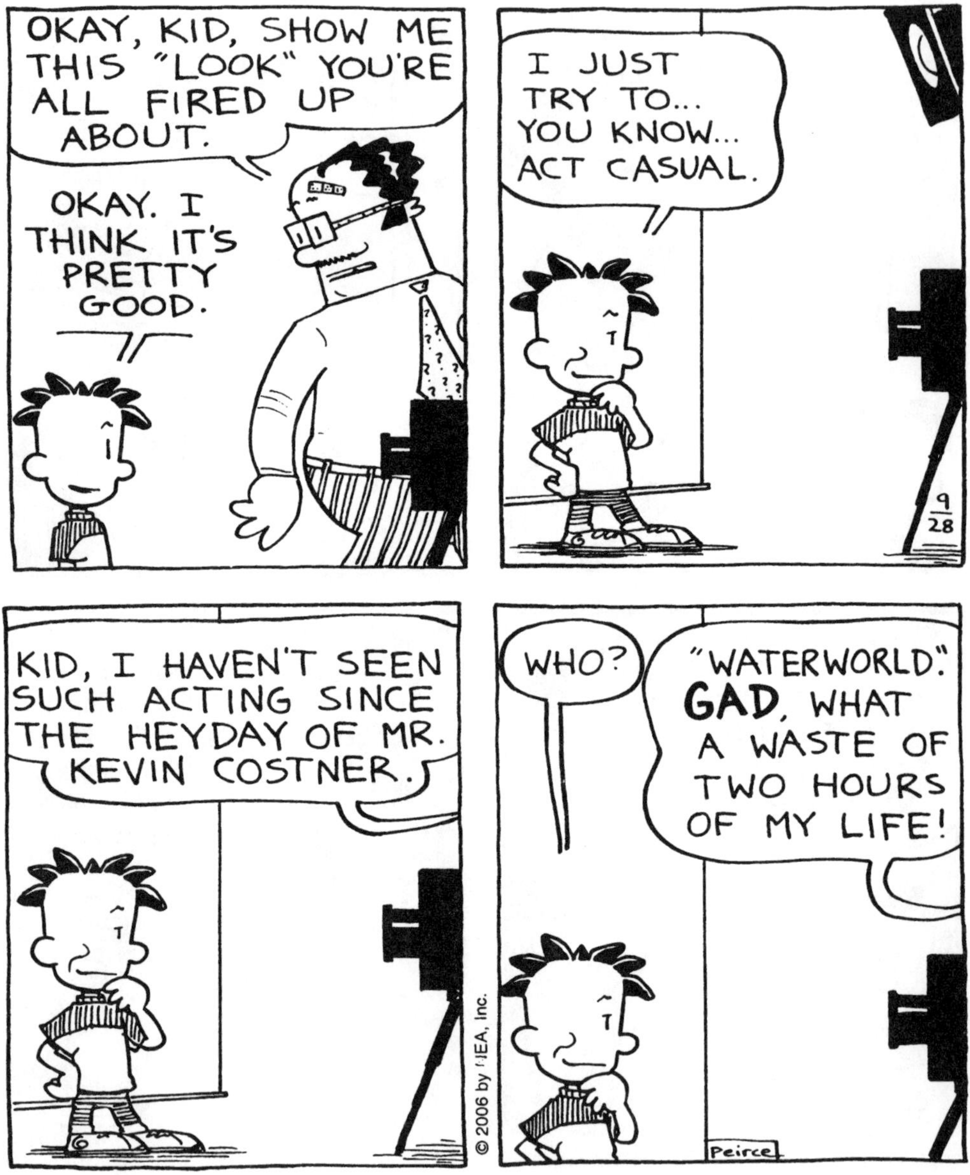
OKAY, KID, SHOW ME THIS "LOOK" YOU'RE ALL FIRED UP ABOUT.
OKAY. I THINK IT'S PRETTY GOOD.
I JUST TRY TO... YOU KNOW... ACT CASUAL.
9/28
KID, I HAVEN'T SEEN SUCH ACTING SINCE THE HEYDAY OF MR. KEVIN COSTNER.
WHO?
"WATERWORLD." GAD, WHAT A WASTE OF TWO HOURS OF MY LIFE!
Peirce

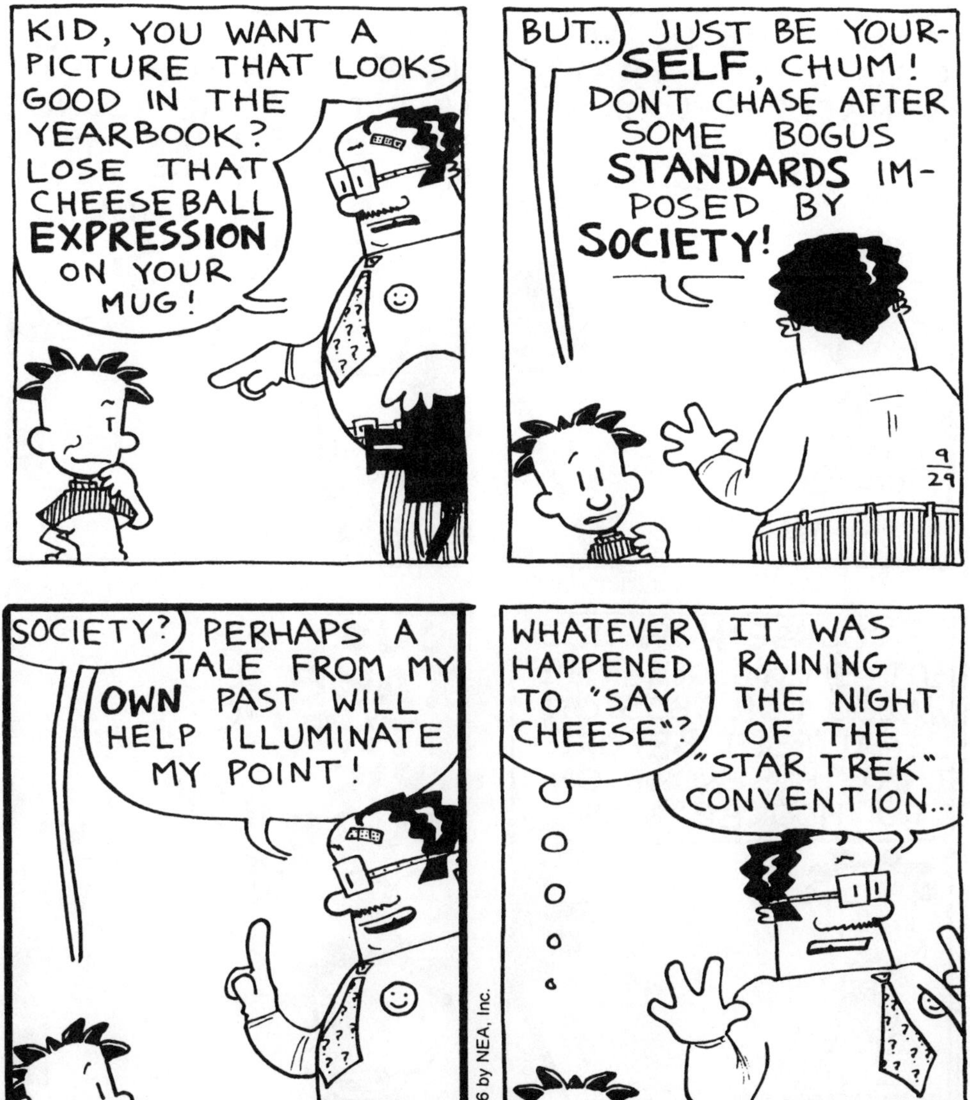
KID, YOU WANT A PICTURE THAT LOOKS GOOD IN THE YEARBOOK? LOSE THAT CHEESEBALL **EXPRESSION** ON YOUR MUG!
BUT...
JUST BE YOUR-**SELF**, CHUM! DON'T CHASE AFTER SOME BOGUS **STANDARDS** IM-POSED BY **SOCIETY**!
9/29
SOCIETY?
PERHAPS A TALE FROM MY **OWN** PAST WILL HELP ILLUMINATE MY POINT!
WHATEVER HAPPENED TO "SAY CHEESE"?
IT WAS RAINING THE NIGHT OF THE "STAR TREK" CONVENTION...
Peirce

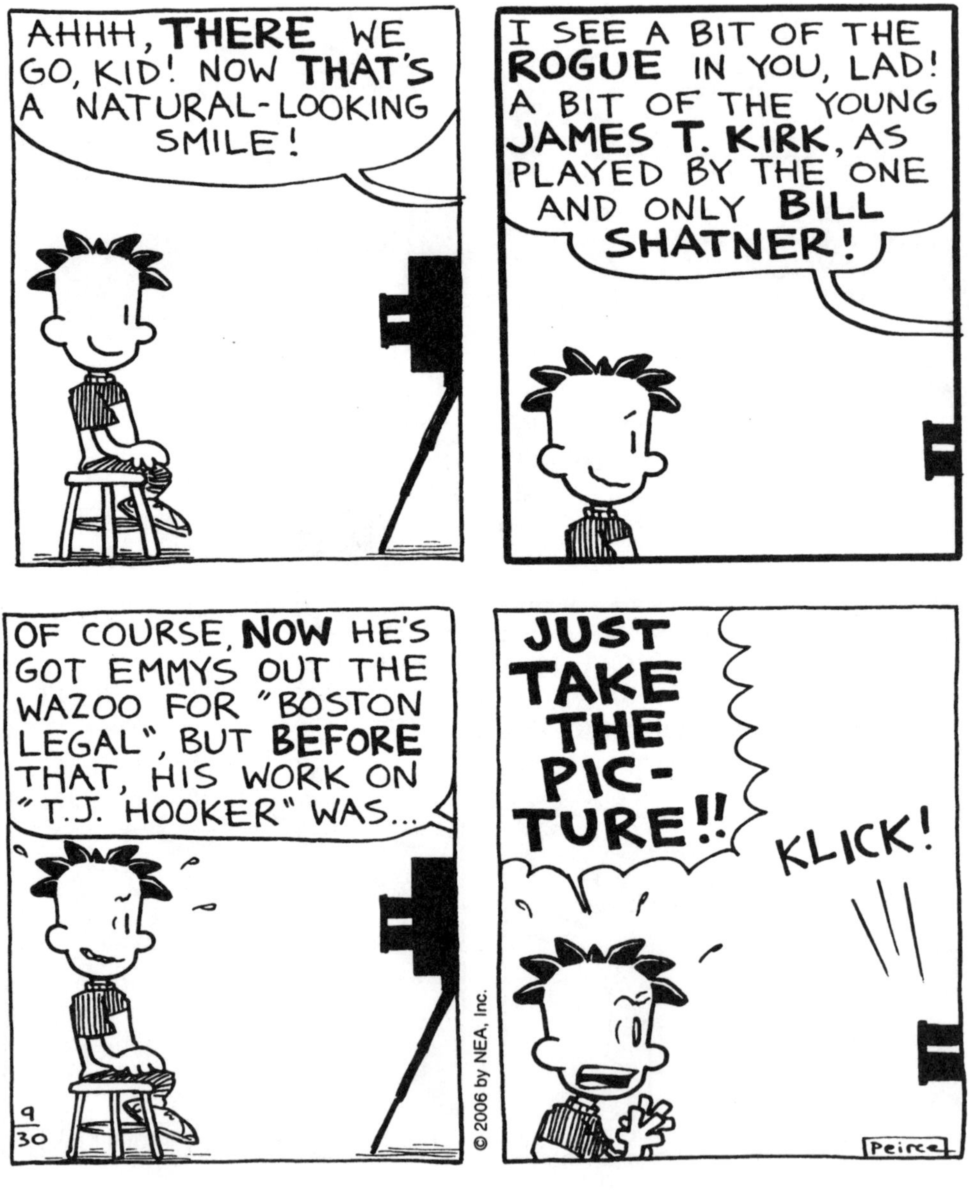
AHHH, THERE WE GO, KID! NOW THAT'S A NATURAL-LOOKING SMILE!
I SEE A BIT OF THE ROGUE IN YOU, LAD! A BIT OF THE YOUNG JAMES T. KIRK, AS PLAYED BY THE ONE AND ONLY BILL SHATNER!
OF COURSE, NOW HE'S GOT EMMYS OUT THE WAZOO FOR "BOSTON LEGAL", BUT BEFORE THAT, HIS WORK ON "T.J. HOOKER" WAS...
9/30
JUST TAKE THE PIC-TURE!!
KLICK!
Peirce

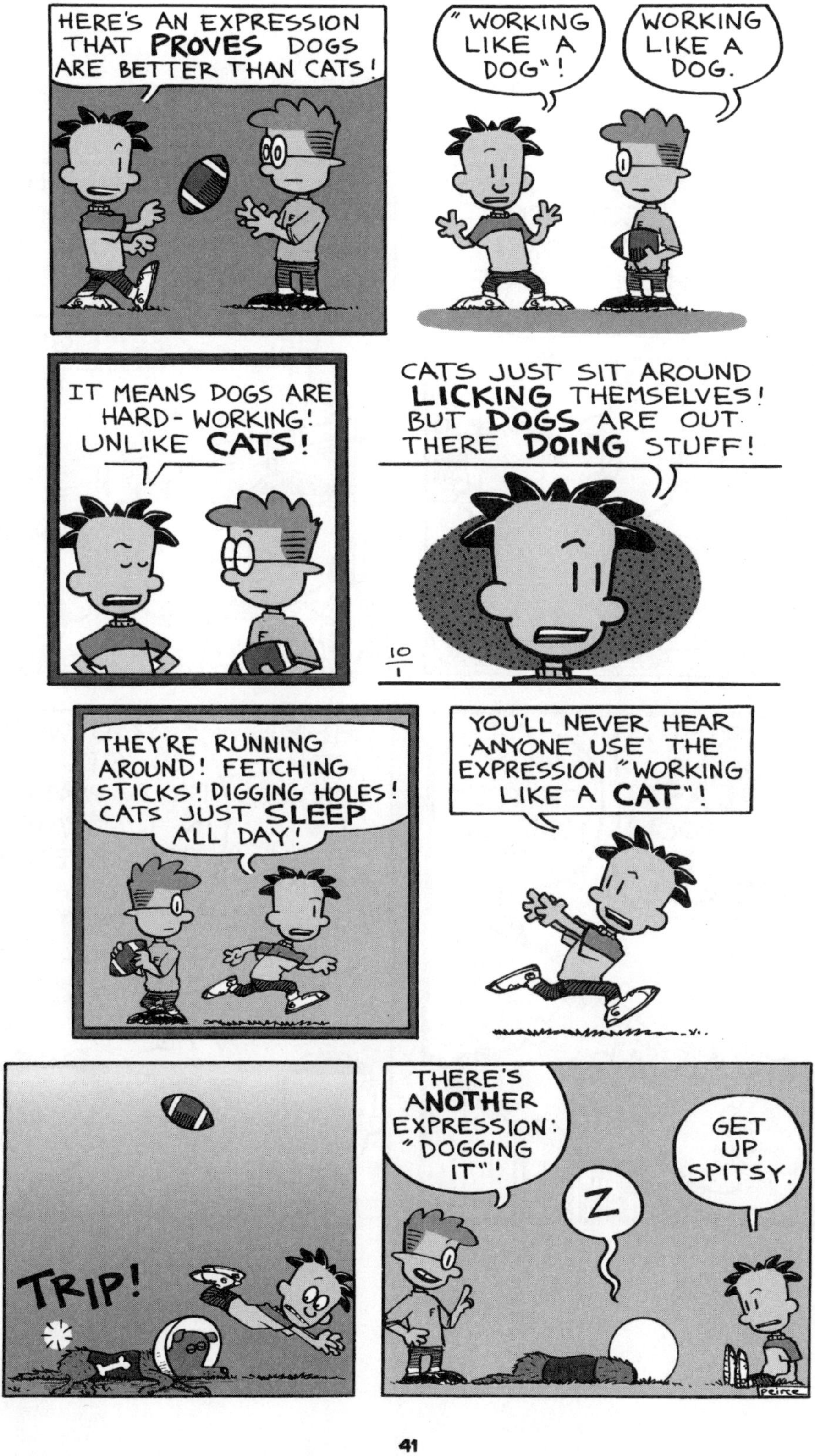
HERE'S AN EXPRESSION THAT PROVES DOGS ARE BETTER THAN CATS!
"WORKING LIKE A DOG"!
WORKING LIKE A DOG.
IT MEANS DOGS ARE HARD-WORKING! UNLIKE CATS!
CATS JUST SIT AROUND LICKING THEMSELVES! BUT DOGS ARE OUT THERE DOING STUFF!
10/1
THEY'RE RUNNING AROUND! FETCHING STICKS! DIGGING HOLES! CATS JUST SLEEP ALL DAY!
YOU'LL NEVER HEAR ANYONE USE THE EXPRESSION "WORKING LIKE A CAT"!
TRIP!
THERE'S ANOTHER EXPRESSION: "DOGGING IT"!
Z
GET UP, SPITSY.
peirce

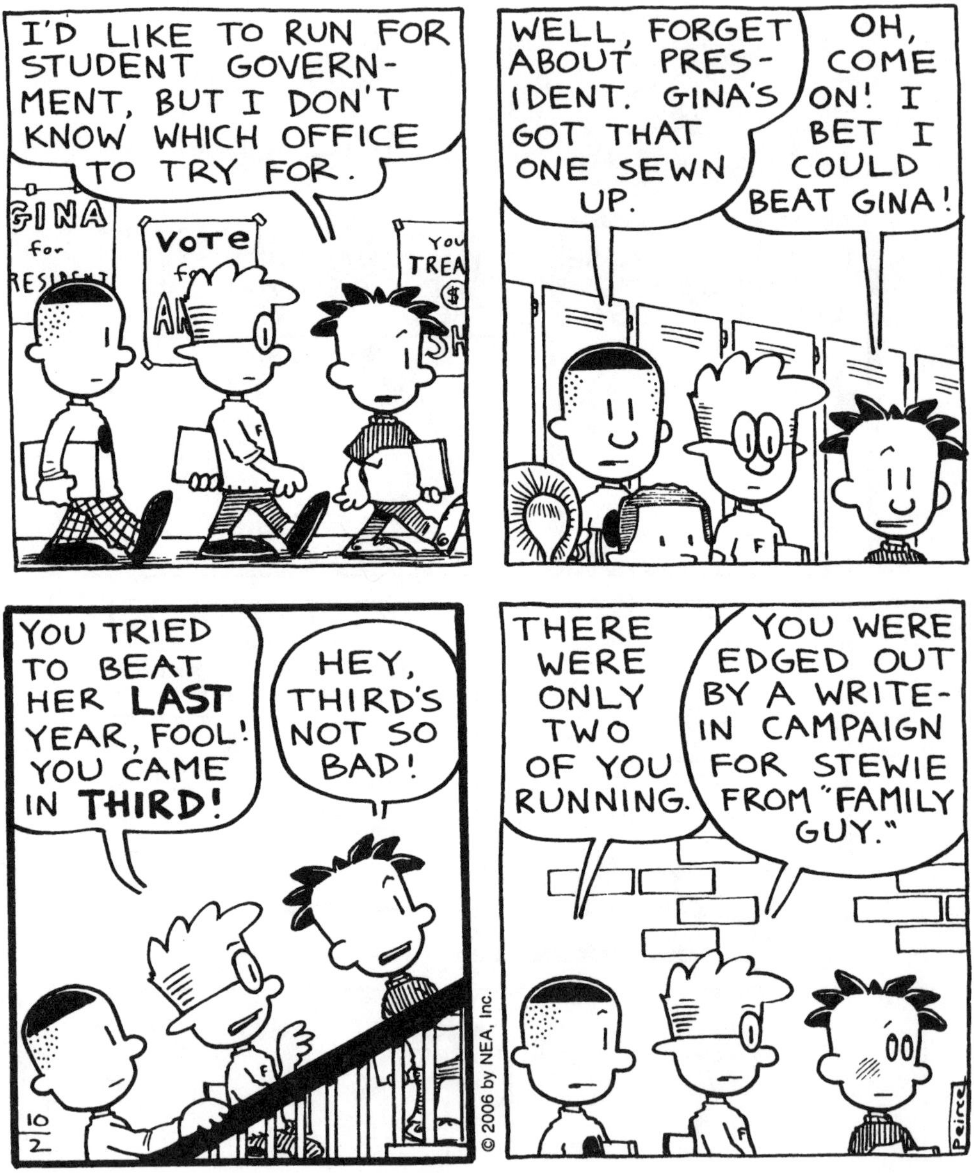
I'D LIKE TO RUN FOR STUDENT GOVERNMENT, BUT I DON'T KNOW WHICH OFFICE TO TRY FOR.
GINA for PRESIDENT
VOTE
WELL, FORGET ABOUT PRESIDENT. GINA'S GOT THAT ONE SEWN UP.
OH, COME ON! I BET I COULD BEAT GINA!
YOU TRIED TO BEAT HER **LAST** YEAR, FOOL! YOU CAME IN **THIRD**!
HEY, THIRD'S NOT SO BAD!
10/2
© 2006 by NEA, Inc.
THERE WERE ONLY TWO OF YOU RUNNING.
YOU WERE EDGED OUT BY A WRITE-IN CAMPAIGN FOR STEWIE FROM "FAMILY GUY."
Peirce

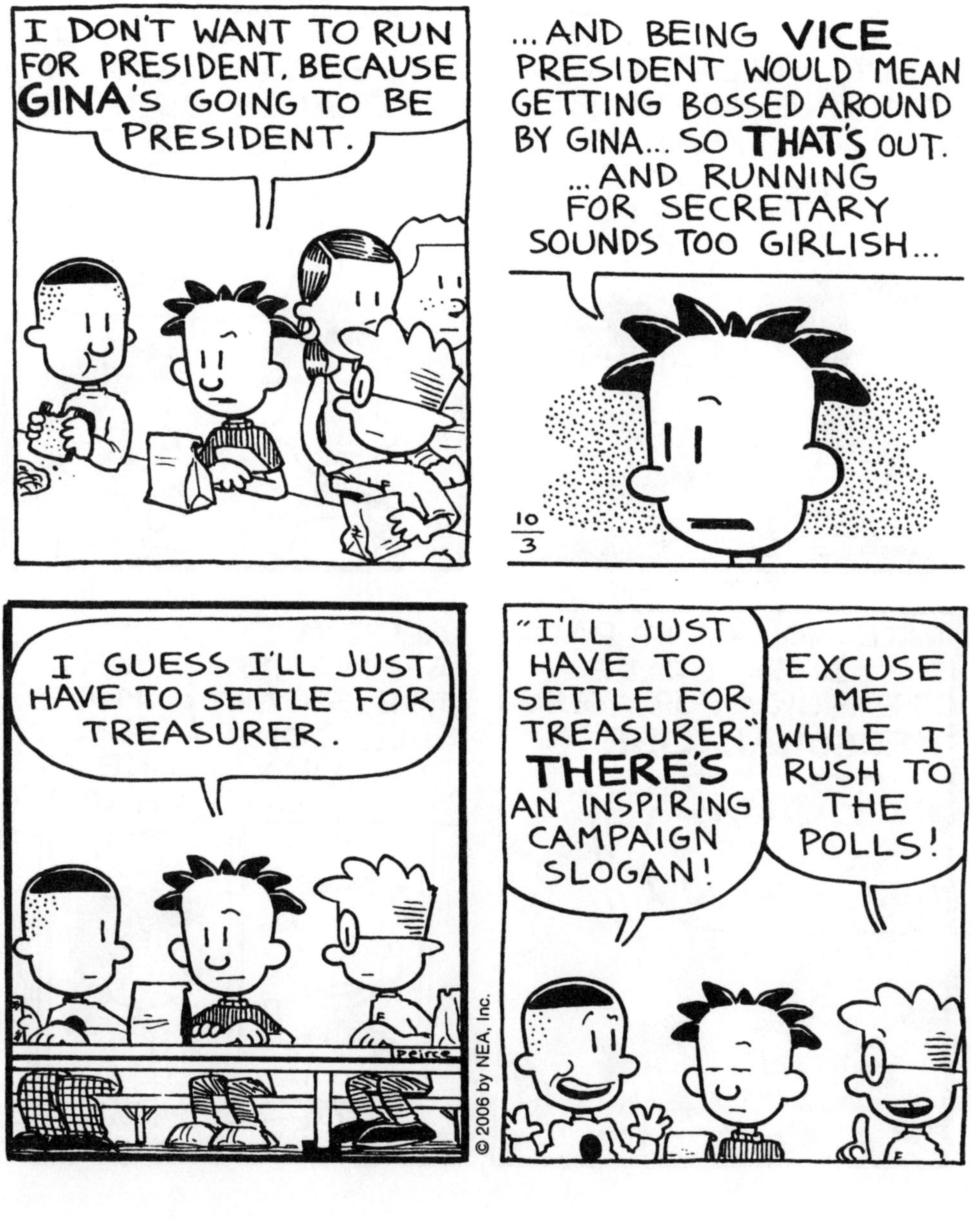
I DON'T WANT TO RUN FOR PRESIDENT, BECAUSE GINA'S GOING TO BE PRESIDENT.
...AND BEING VICE PRESIDENT WOULD MEAN GETTING BOSSED AROUND BY GINA... SO THAT'S OUT.
...AND RUNNING FOR SECRETARY SOUNDS TOO GIRLISH...
10/3
I GUESS I'LL JUST HAVE TO SETTLE FOR TREASURER.
PEIRCE
"I'LL JUST HAVE TO SETTLE FOR TREASURER." THERE'S AN INSPIRING CAMPAIGN SLOGAN!
EXCUSE ME WHILE I RUSH TO THE POLLS!

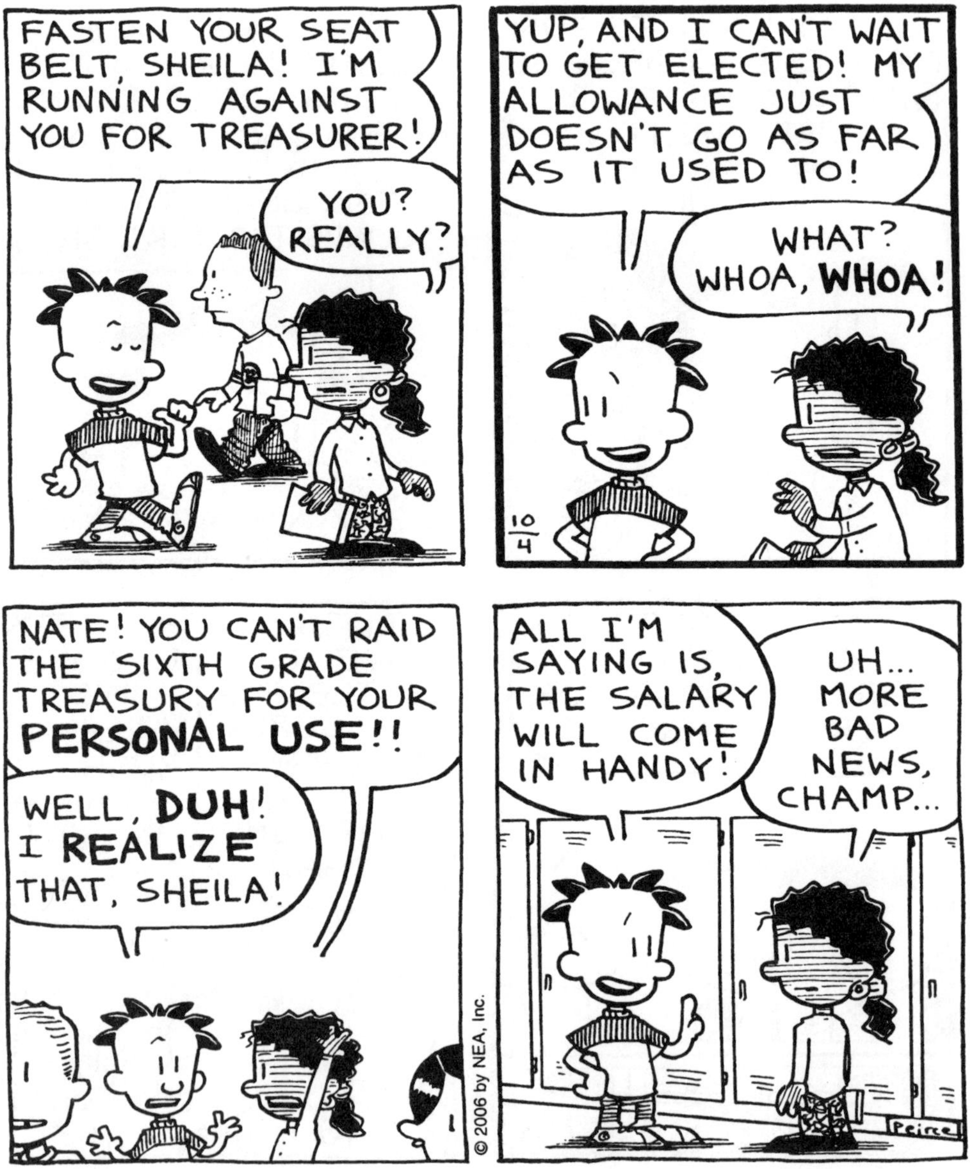
FASTEN YOUR SEAT BELT, SHEILA! I'M RUNNING AGAINST YOU FOR TREASURER!
YOU? REALLY?
YUP, AND I CAN'T WAIT TO GET ELECTED! MY ALLOWANCE JUST DOESN'T GO AS FAR AS IT USED TO!
WHAT? WHOA, **WHOA**!
10/4
NATE! YOU CAN'T RAID THE SIXTH GRADE TREASURY FOR YOUR **PERSONAL USE**!!
WELL, **DUH**! I **REALIZE** THAT, SHEILA!
© 2006 by NEA, Inc.
ALL I'M SAYING IS, THE SALARY WILL COME IN HANDY!
UH... MORE BAD NEWS, CHAMP...
Peirce

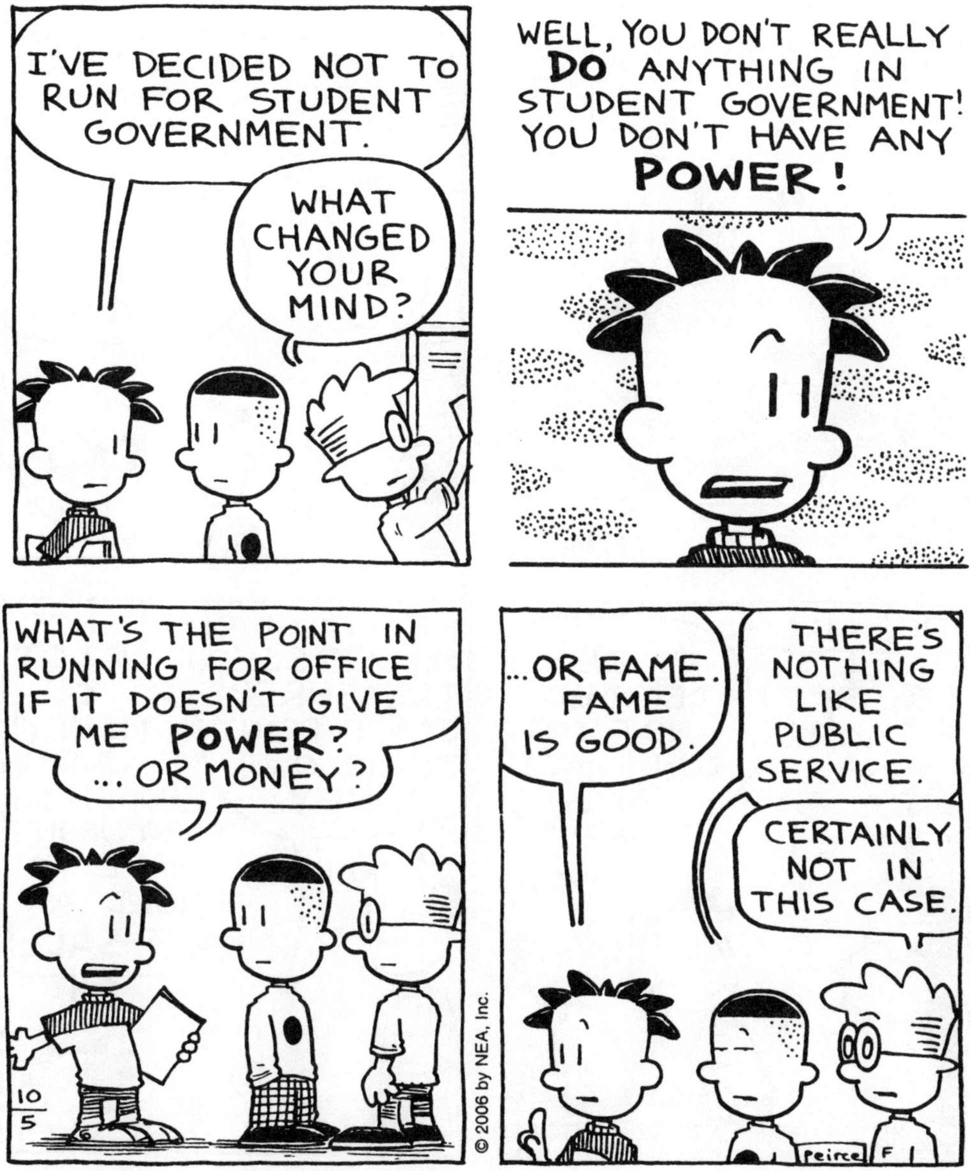
I'VE DECIDED NOT TO RUN FOR STUDENT GOVERNMENT.
WHAT CHANGED YOUR MIND?
WELL, YOU DON'T REALLY **DO** ANYTHING IN STUDENT GOVERNMENT! YOU DON'T HAVE ANY **POWER**!
WHAT'S THE POINT IN RUNNING FOR OFFICE IF IT DOESN'T GIVE ME **POWER**? ... OR MONEY?
...OR FAME. FAME IS GOOD.
THERE'S NOTHING LIKE PUBLIC SERVICE.
CERTAINLY NOT IN THIS CASE.
10/5
© 2006 by NEA, Inc.
Peirce

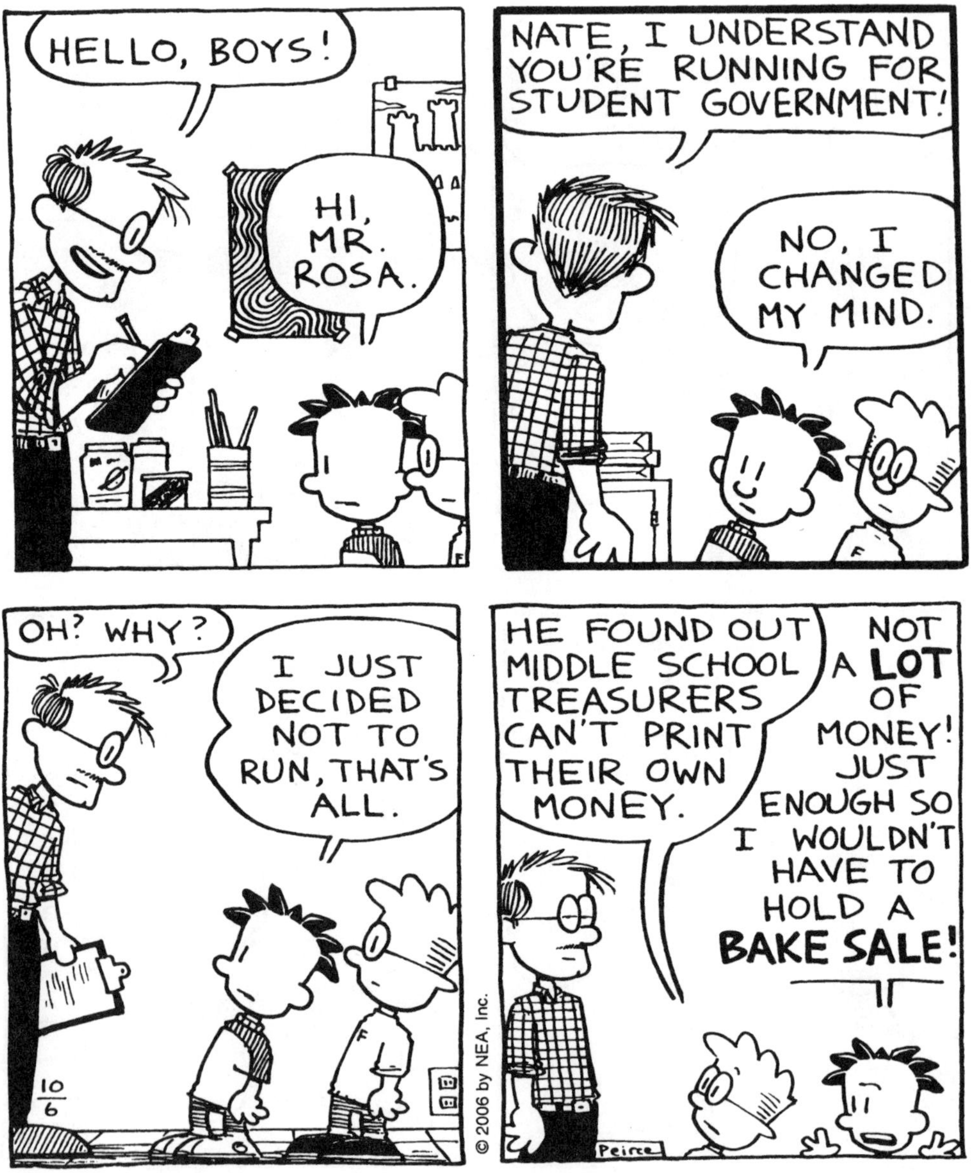
HELLO, BOYS!
HI, MR. ROSA.
NATE, I UNDERSTAND YOU'RE RUNNING FOR STUDENT GOVERNMENT!
NO, I CHANGED MY MIND.
OH? WHY?
I JUST DECIDED NOT TO RUN, THAT'S ALL.
10/6
HE FOUND OUT MIDDLE SCHOOL TREASURERS CAN'T PRINT THEIR OWN MONEY.
NOT A **LOT** OF MONEY! JUST ENOUGH SO I WOULDN'T HAVE TO HOLD A **BAKE SALE**!
Peirce

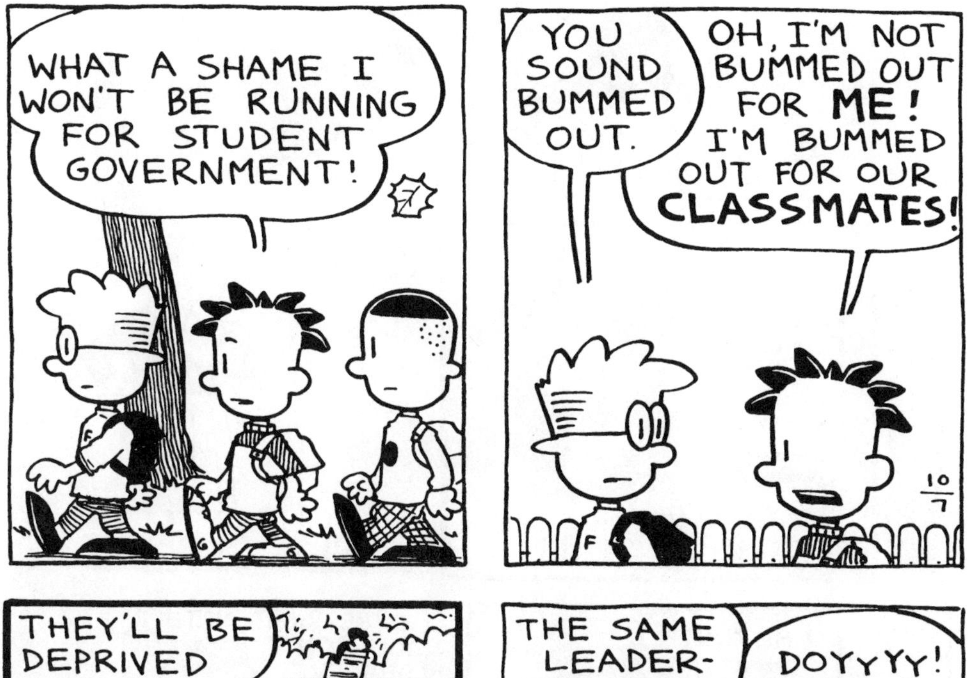
WHAT A SHAME I WON'T BE RUNNING FOR STUDENT GOVERNMENT!
YOU SOUND BUMMED OUT.
OH, I'M NOT BUMMED OUT FOR ME! I'M BUMMED OUT FOR OUR CLASSMATES!
10/7
THEY'LL BE DEPRIVED OF MY LEADERSHIP!
LEADER-SHIP?
© 2006 by NEA, Inc.
THE SAME LEADERSHIP YOU DISPLAYED DURING OUR CAMPING TRIP LAST SUMMER?
DOYYYY! "FOLLOW ME, GUYS! THE TENT'S THIS WAY!"
Peirce

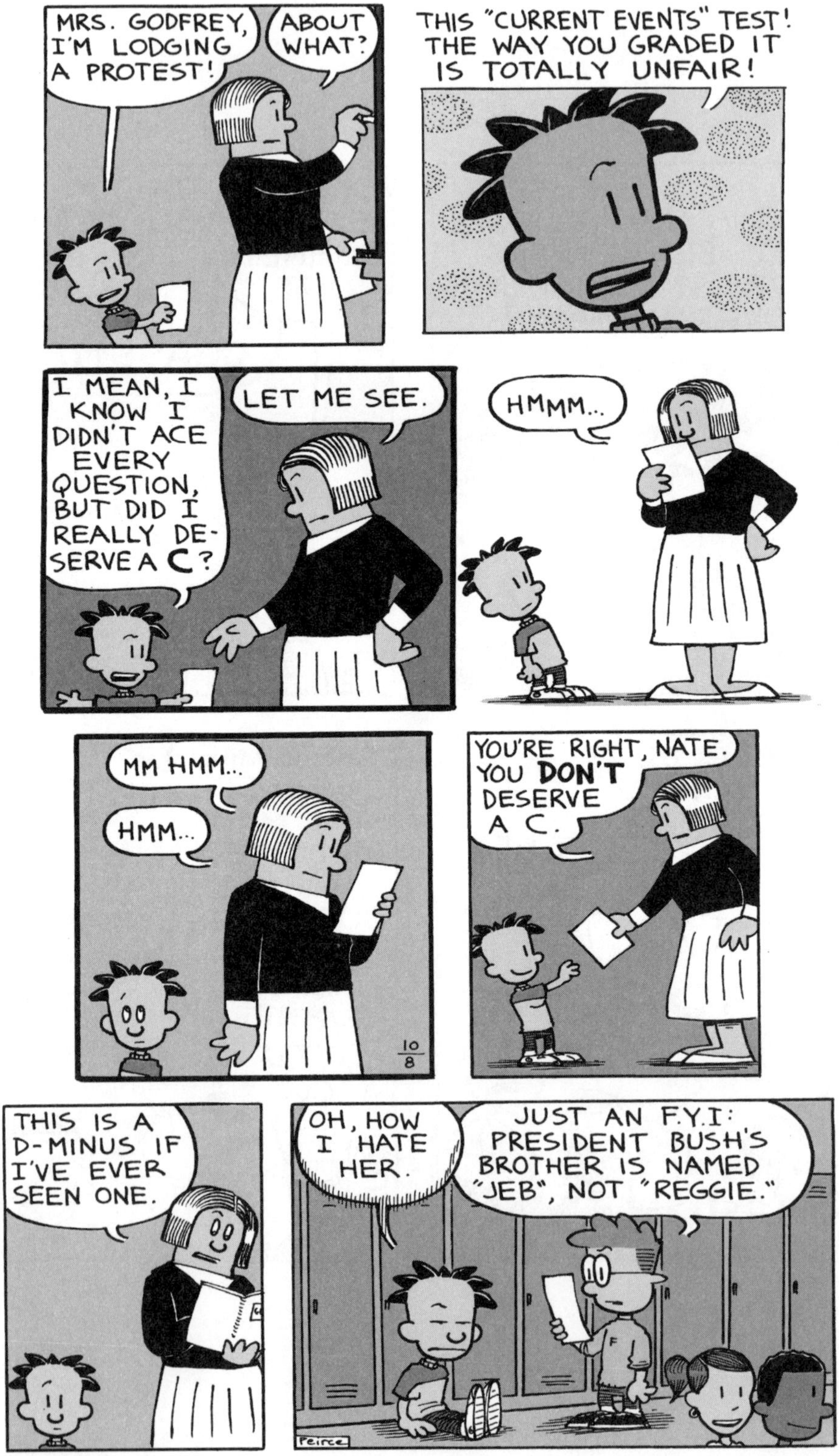
MRS. GODFREY, I'M LODGING A PROTEST!
ABOUT WHAT?
THIS "CURRENT EVENTS" TEST! THE WAY YOU GRADED IT IS TOTALLY UNFAIR!
I MEAN, I KNOW I DIDN'T ACE EVERY QUESTION, BUT DID I REALLY DESERVE A **C**?
LET ME SEE.
HMMM...
MM HMM...
HMM...
YOU'RE RIGHT, NATE. YOU **DON'T** DESERVE A C.
THIS IS A D-MINUS IF I'VE EVER SEEN ONE.
OH, HOW I HATE HER.
JUST AN F.Y.I: PRESIDENT BUSH'S BROTHER IS NAMED "JEB", NOT "REGGIE."
Peirce

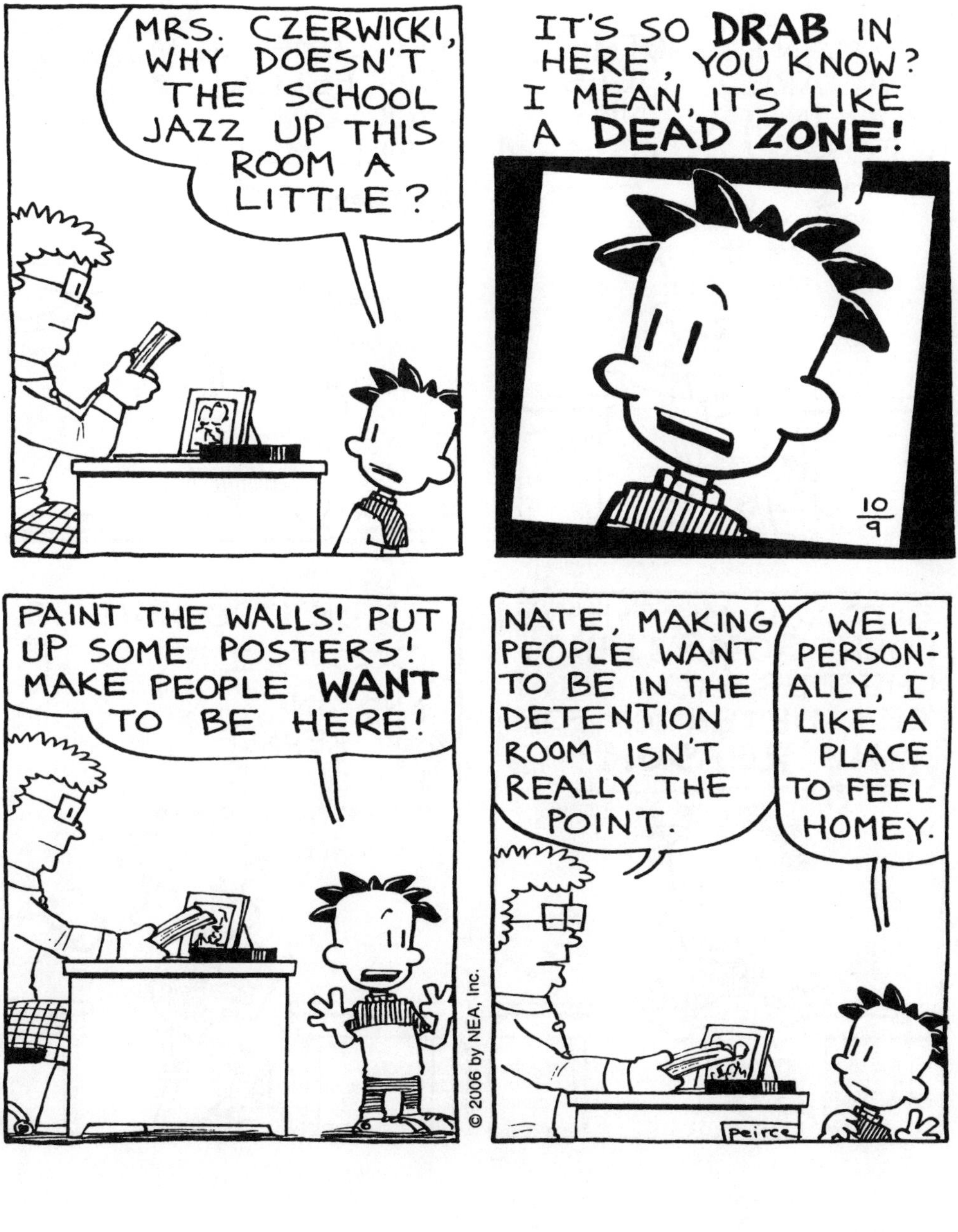
MRS. CZERWICKI, WHY DOESN'T THE SCHOOL JAZZ UP THIS ROOM A LITTLE?
IT'S SO DRAB IN HERE, YOU KNOW? I MEAN, IT'S LIKE A DEAD ZONE!
10/9
PAINT THE WALLS! PUT UP SOME POSTERS! MAKE PEOPLE WANT TO BE HERE!
© 2006 by NEA, Inc.
NATE, MAKING PEOPLE WANT TO BE IN THE DETENTION ROOM ISN'T REALLY THE POINT.
WELL, PERSONALLY, I LIKE A PLACE TO FEEL HOMEY.
peirce

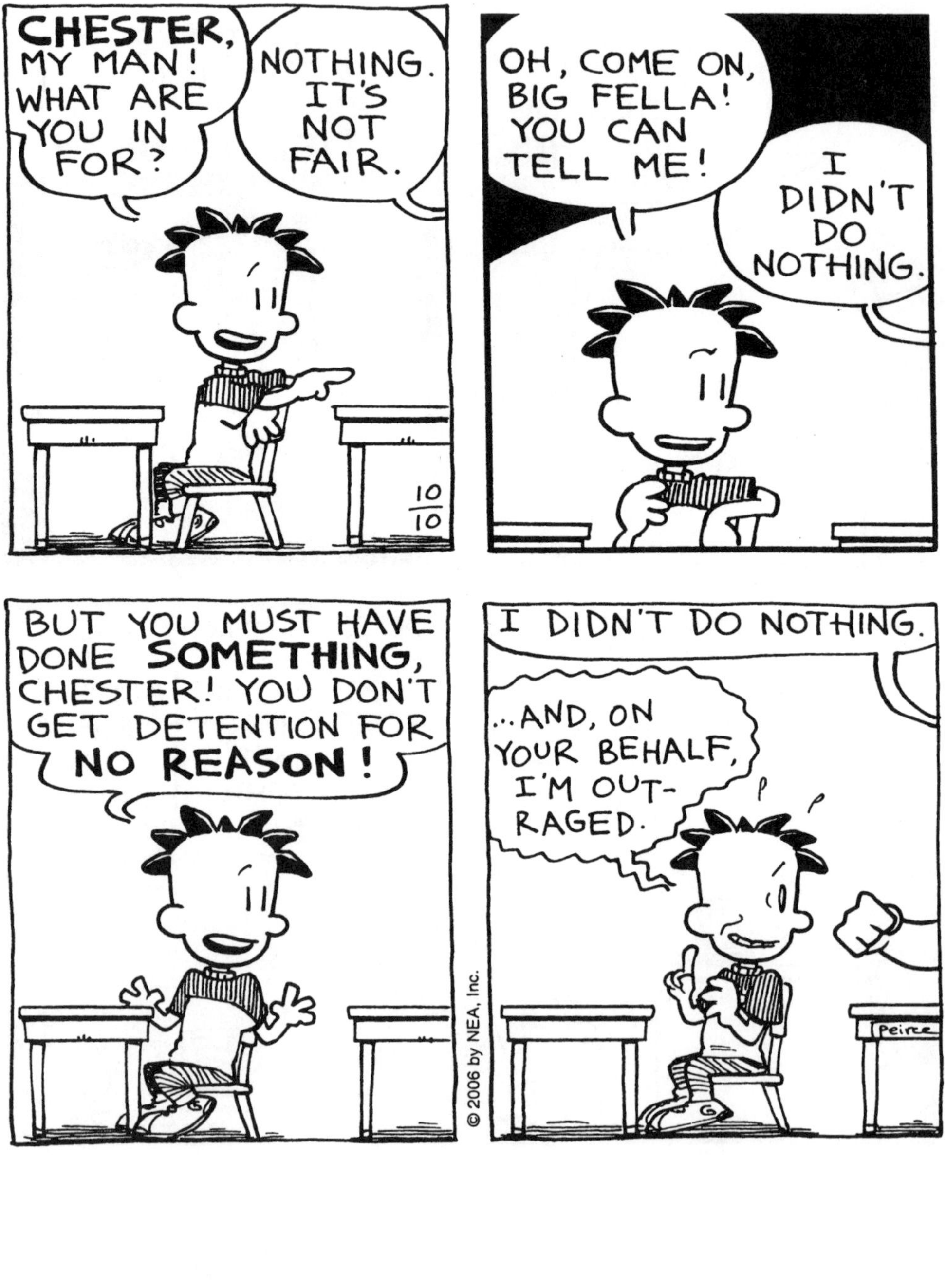
CHESTER, MY MAN! WHAT ARE YOU IN FOR?
NOTHING. IT'S NOT FAIR.
10/10
OH, COME ON, BIG FELLA! YOU CAN TELL ME!
I DIDN'T DO NOTHING.
BUT YOU MUST HAVE DONE SOMETHING, CHESTER! YOU DON'T GET DETENTION FOR NO REASON!
I DIDN'T DO NOTHING.
...AND, ON YOUR BEHALF, I'M OUT-RAGED.
Peirce
© 2006 by NEA, Inc.

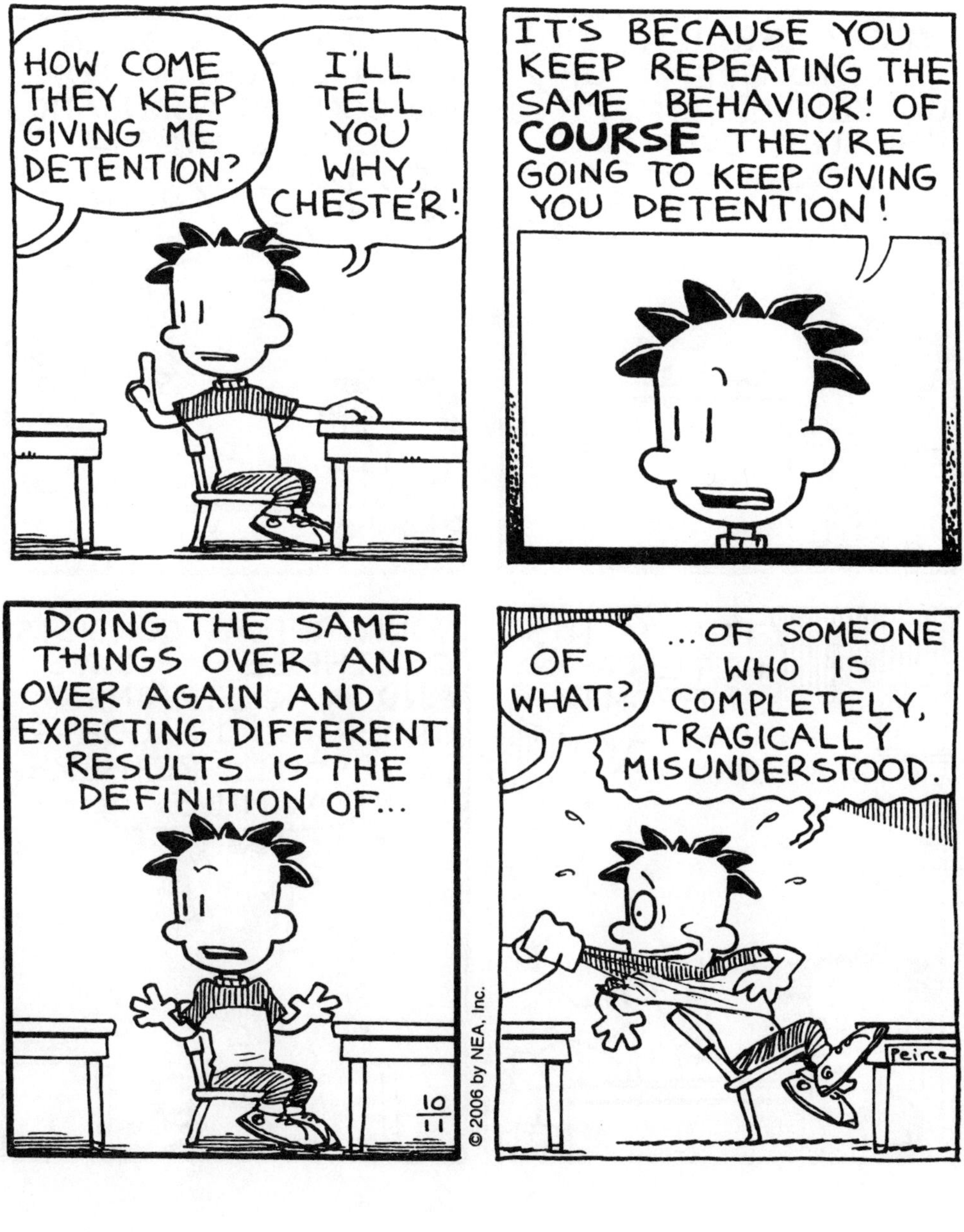
HOW COME THEY KEEP GIVING ME DETENTION?
I'LL TELL YOU WHY, CHESTER!
IT'S BECAUSE YOU KEEP REPEATING THE SAME BEHAVIOR! OF **COURSE** THEY'RE GOING TO KEEP GIVING YOU DETENTION!
DOING THE SAME THINGS OVER AND OVER AGAIN AND EXPECTING DIFFERENT RESULTS IS THE DEFINITION OF...
OF WHAT?
...OF SOMEONE WHO IS COMPLETELY, TRAGICALLY MISUNDERSTOOD.
10/11
© 2006 by NEA, Inc.
Peirce

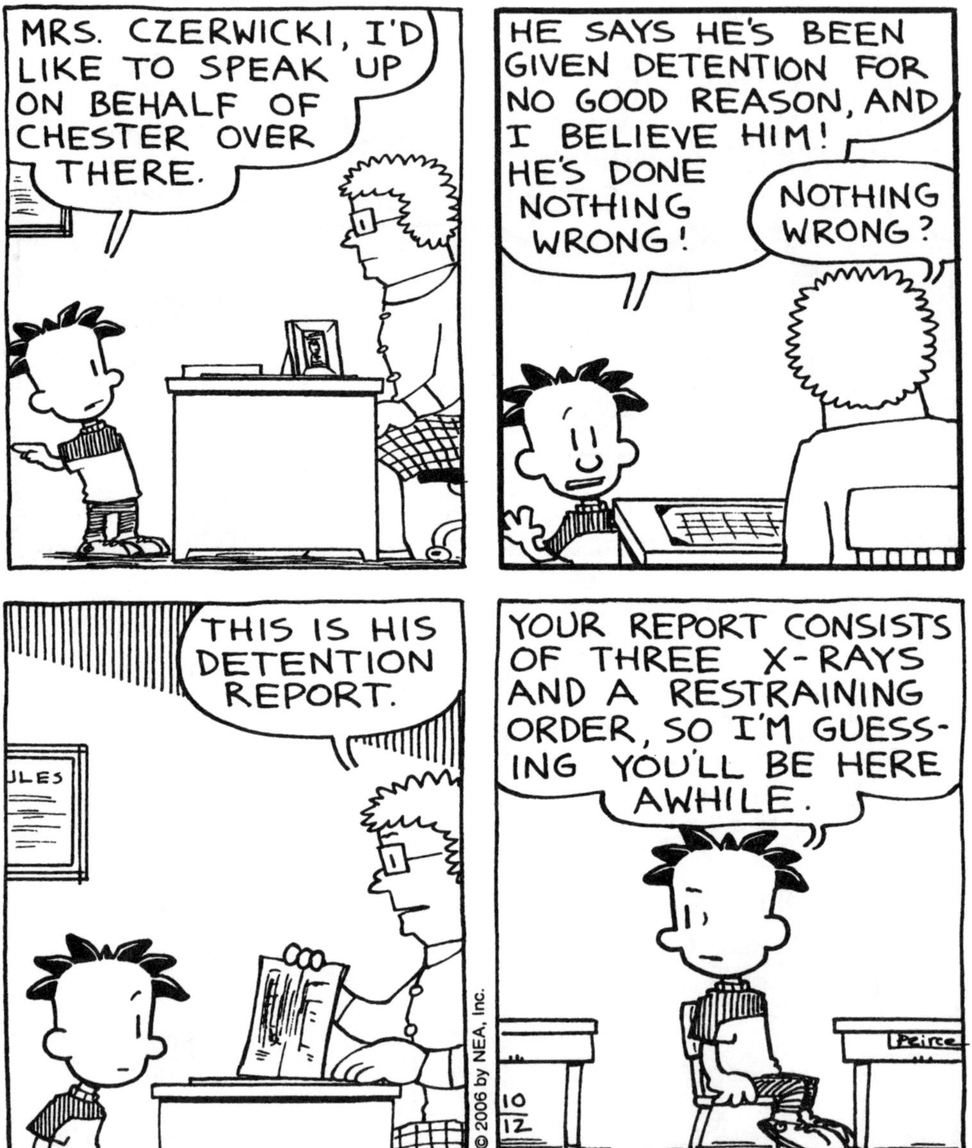
MRS. CZERWICKI, I'D LIKE TO SPEAK UP ON BEHALF OF CHESTER OVER THERE.
HE SAYS HE'S BEEN GIVEN DETENTION FOR NO GOOD REASON, AND I BELIEVE HIM! HE'S DONE NOTHING WRONG!
NOTHING WRONG?
THIS IS HIS DETENTION REPORT.
ULES
YOUR REPORT CONSISTS OF THREE X-RAYS AND A RESTRAINING ORDER, SO I'M GUESSING YOU'LL BE HERE AWHILE.
Peirce
10
12

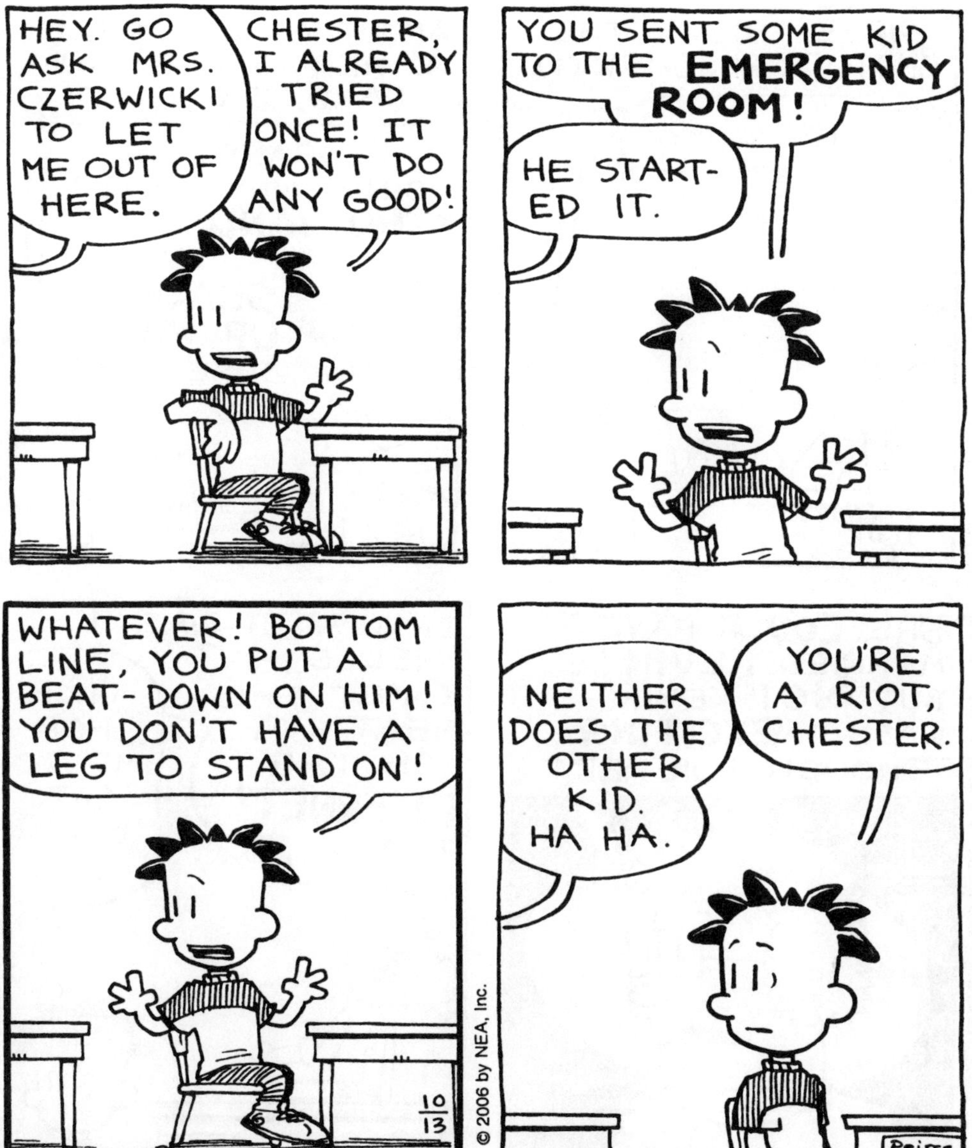
HEY. GO ASK MRS. CZERWICKI TO LET ME OUT OF HERE.
CHESTER, I ALREADY TRIED ONCE! IT WON'T DO ANY GOOD!
YOU SENT SOME KID TO THE EMERGENCY ROOM!
HE STARTED IT.
WHATEVER! BOTTOM LINE, YOU PUT A BEAT-DOWN ON HIM! YOU DON'T HAVE A LEG TO STAND ON!
10/13
© 2006 by NEA, Inc.
NEITHER DOES THE OTHER KID. HA HA.
YOU'RE A RIOT, CHESTER.
Peirce

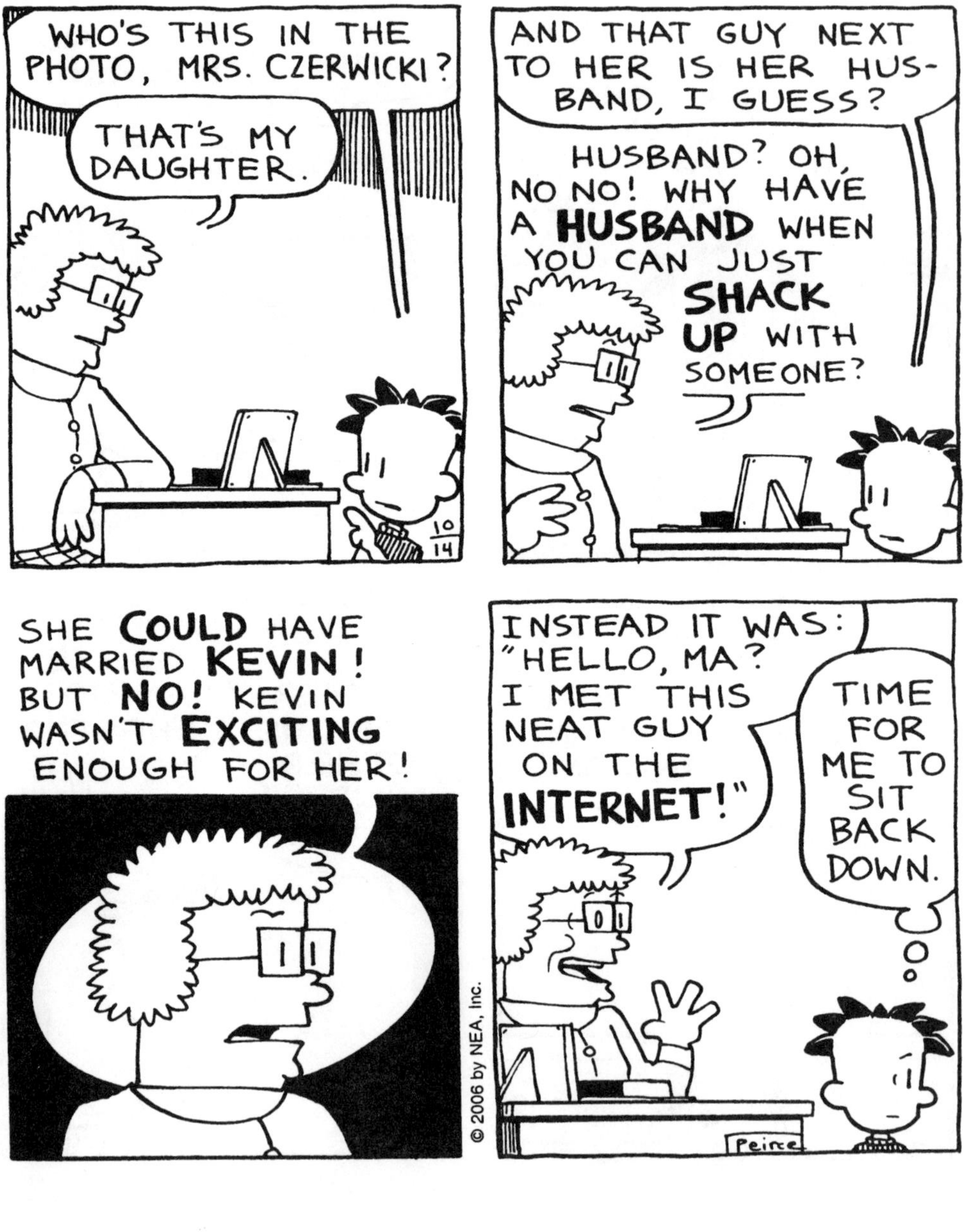
WHO'S THIS IN THE PHOTO, MRS. CZERWICKI?
THAT'S MY DAUGHTER.
10/14
AND THAT GUY NEXT TO HER IS HER HUSBAND, I GUESS?
HUSBAND? OH, NO NO! WHY HAVE A HUSBAND WHEN YOU CAN JUST SHACK UP WITH SOMEONE?
SHE COULD HAVE MARRIED KEVIN! BUT NO! KEVIN WASN'T EXCITING ENOUGH FOR HER!
© 2006 by NEA, Inc.
INSTEAD IT WAS: "HELLO, MA? I MET THIS NEAT GUY ON THE INTERNET!"
TIME FOR ME TO SIT BACK DOWN.
Peirce

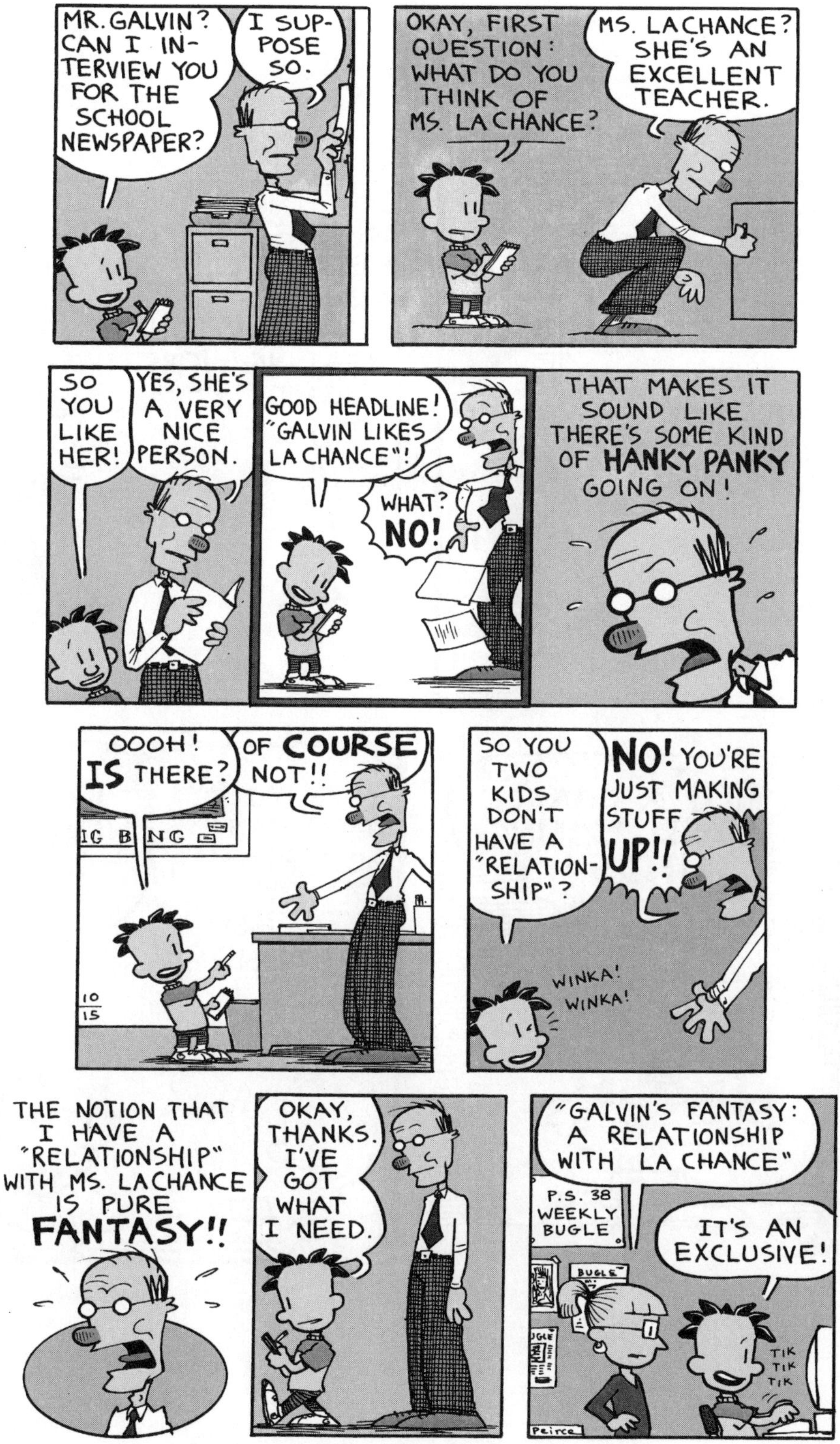
MR. GALVIN? CAN I INTERVIEW YOU FOR THE SCHOOL NEWSPAPER?
I SUPPOSE SO.
OKAY, FIRST QUESTION: WHAT DO YOU THINK OF MS. LACHANCE?
MS. LACHANCE? SHE'S AN EXCELLENT TEACHER.
SO YOU LIKE HER!
YES, SHE'S A VERY NICE PERSON.
GOOD HEADLINE! "GALVIN LIKES LACHANCE"!
WHAT? NO!
THAT MAKES IT SOUND LIKE THERE'S SOME KIND OF **HANKY PANKY** GOING ON!
OOOH! **IS** THERE?
OF **COURSE** NOT!!
10
15
SO YOU TWO KIDS DON'T HAVE A "RELATIONSHIP"?
NO! YOU'RE JUST MAKING STUFF **UP!!**
WINKA! WINKA!
THE NOTION THAT I HAVE A "RELATIONSHIP" WITH MS. LACHANCE IS PURE **FANTASY!!**
OKAY, THANKS. I'VE GOT WHAT I NEED.
"GALVIN'S FANTASY: A RELATIONSHIP WITH LA CHANCE"
P.S. 38 WEEKLY BUGLE
IT'S AN EXCLUSIVE!
TIK TIK TIK
Peirce

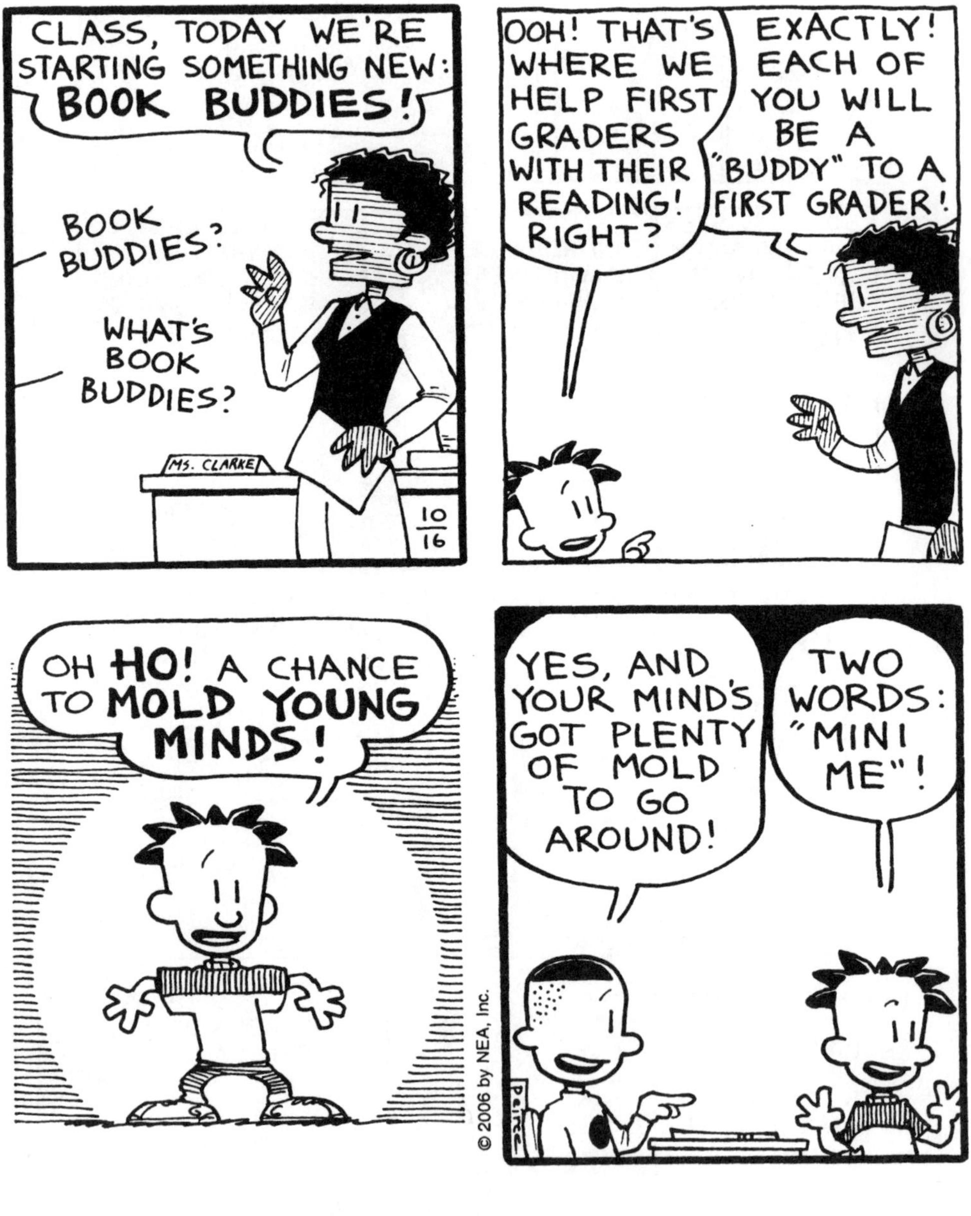
CLASS, TODAY WE'RE STARTING SOMETHING NEW: **BOOK BUDDIES!**
BOOK BUDDIES?
WHAT'S BOOK BUDDIES?
MS. CLARKE
10/16
OOH! THAT'S WHERE WE HELP FIRST GRADERS WITH THEIR READING! RIGHT?
EXACTLY! EACH OF YOU WILL BE A "BUDDY" TO A FIRST GRADER!
OH **HO!** A CHANCE TO **MOLD YOUNG MINDS!**
YES, AND YOUR MIND'S GOT PLENTY OF MOLD TO GO AROUND!
TWO WORDS: "MINI ME"!
PEIRCE

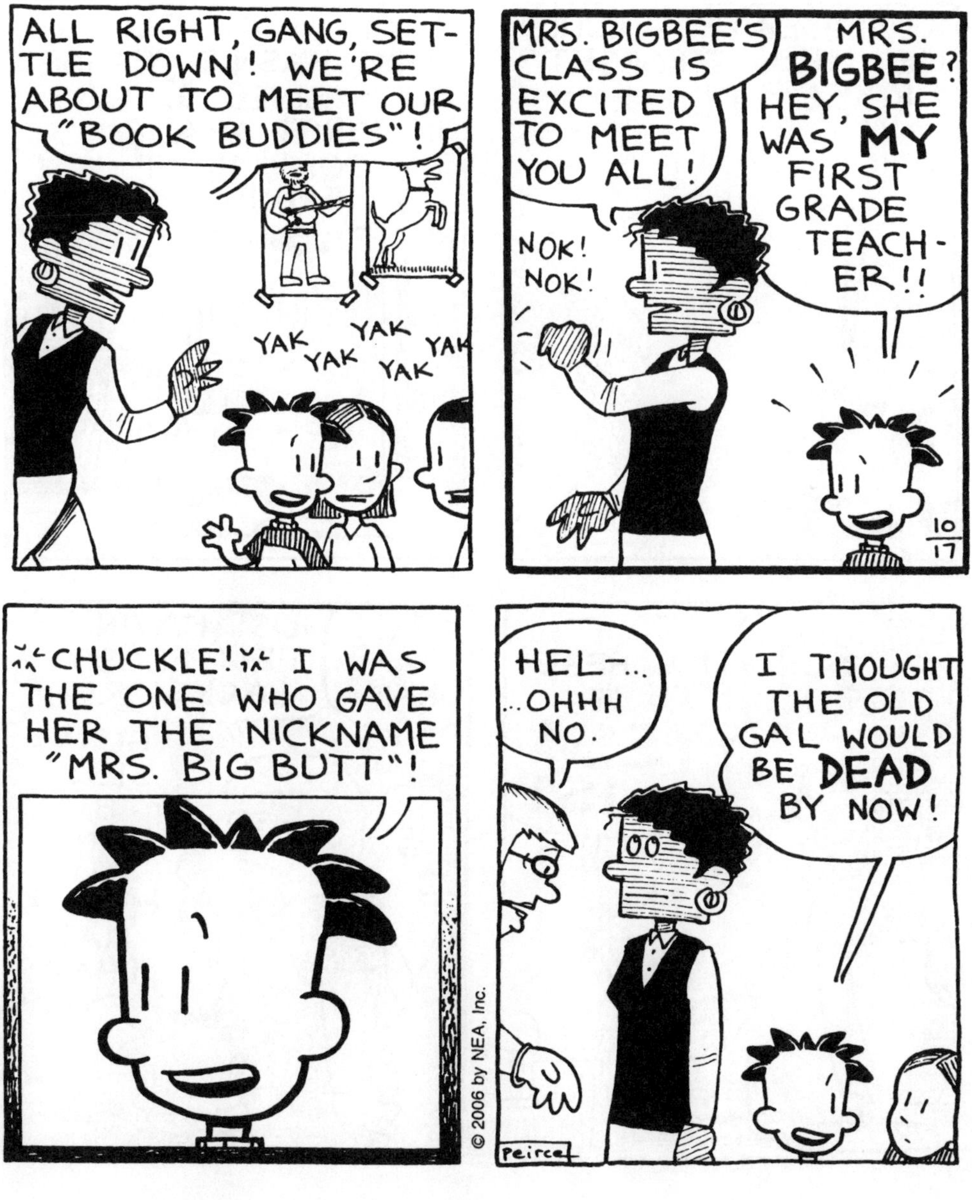
ALL RIGHT, GANG, SETTLE DOWN! WE'RE ABOUT TO MEET OUR "BOOK BUDDIES"!
YAK YAK YAK YAK YAK
MRS. BIGBEE'S CLASS IS EXCITED TO MEET YOU ALL!
NOK! NOK!
MRS. BIGBEE? HEY, SHE WAS MY FIRST GRADE TEACHER!!
10/17
CHUCKLE! I WAS THE ONE WHO GAVE HER THE NICKNAME "MRS. BIG BUTT"!
HEL-... ...OHHH NO.
I THOUGHT THE OLD GAL WOULD BE DEAD BY NOW!
Peirce

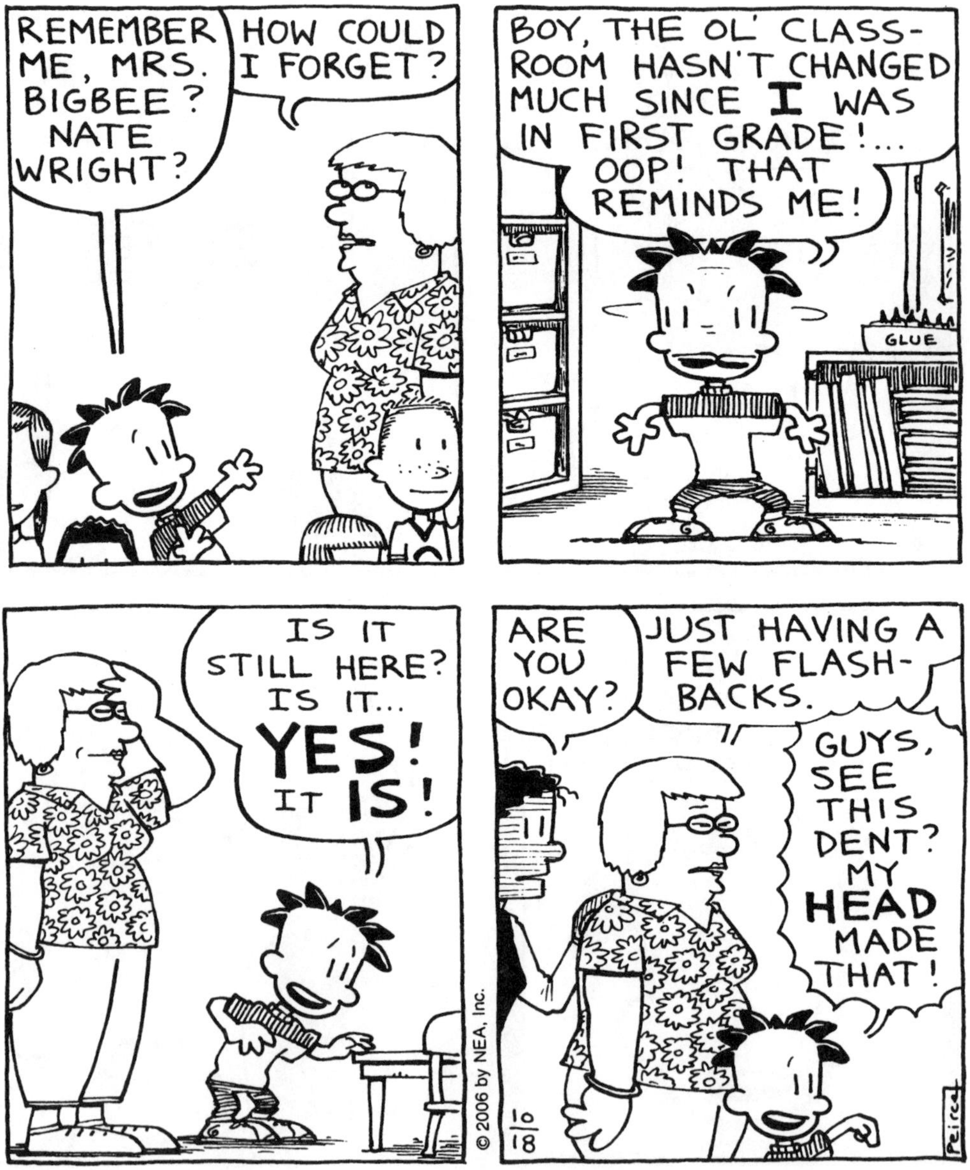
REMEMBER ME, MRS. BIGBEE? NATE WRIGHT?
HOW COULD I FORGET?
BOY, THE OL' CLASS-ROOM HASN'T CHANGED MUCH SINCE I WAS IN FIRST GRADE!...
OOP! THAT REMINDS ME!
GLUE
IS IT STILL HERE? IS IT... YES! IT IS!
ARE YOU OKAY?
JUST HAVING A FEW FLASH-BACKS.
GUYS, SEE THIS DENT? MY HEAD MADE THAT!
© 2006 by NEA, Inc.
10/18
Peirce

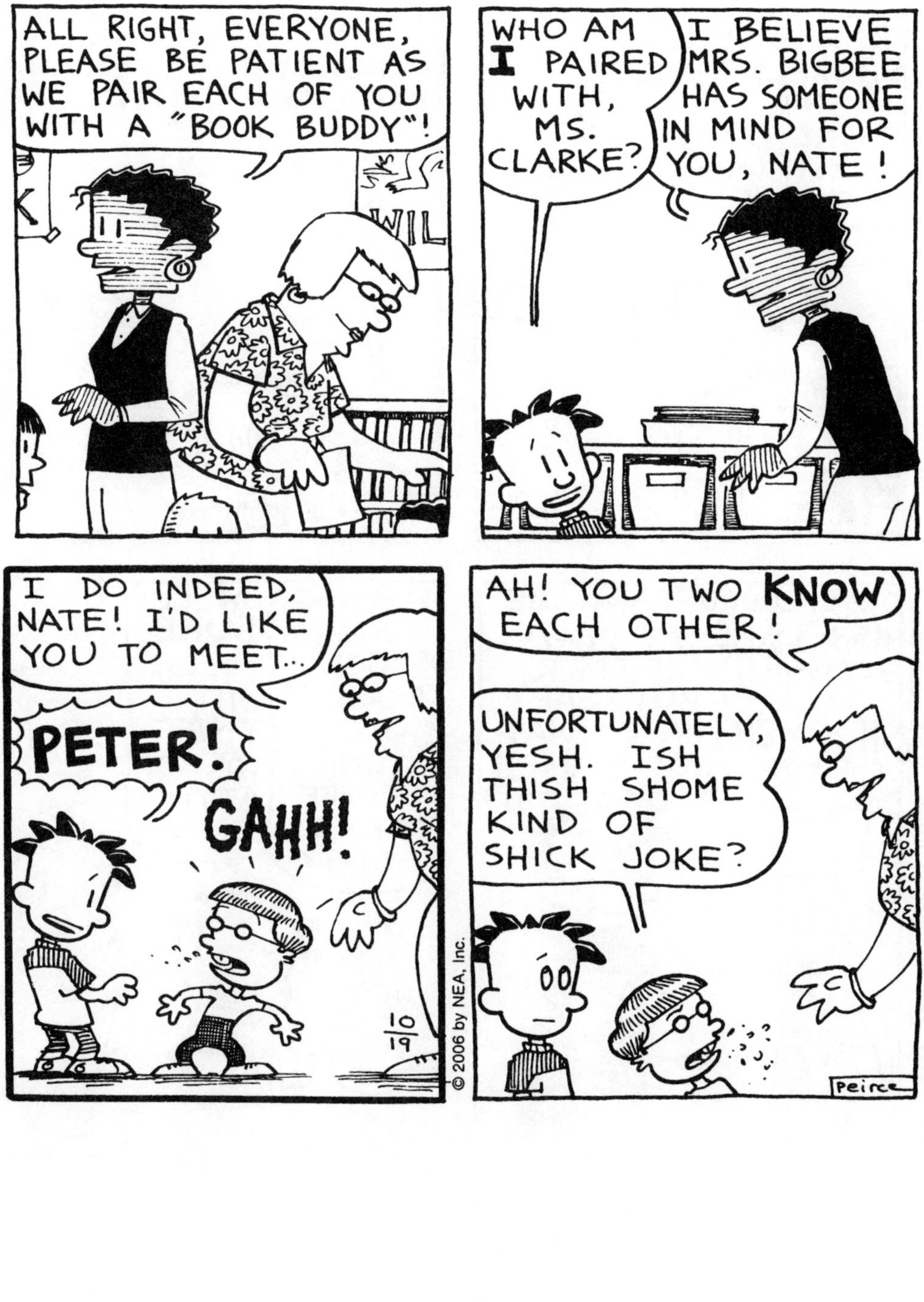
ALL RIGHT, EVERYONE, PLEASE BE PATIENT AS WE PAIR EACH OF YOU WITH A "BOOK BUDDY"!
WHO AM **I** PAIRED WITH, MS. CLARKE?
I BELIEVE MRS. BIGBEE HAS SOMEONE IN MIND FOR YOU, NATE!
I DO INDEED, NATE! I'D LIKE YOU TO MEET...
PETER!
GAHH!
© 2006 by NEA, Inc.
10/19
AH! YOU TWO **KNOW** EACH OTHER!
UNFORTUNATELY, YESH. ISH THISH SHOME KIND OF SHICK JOKE?
Peirce

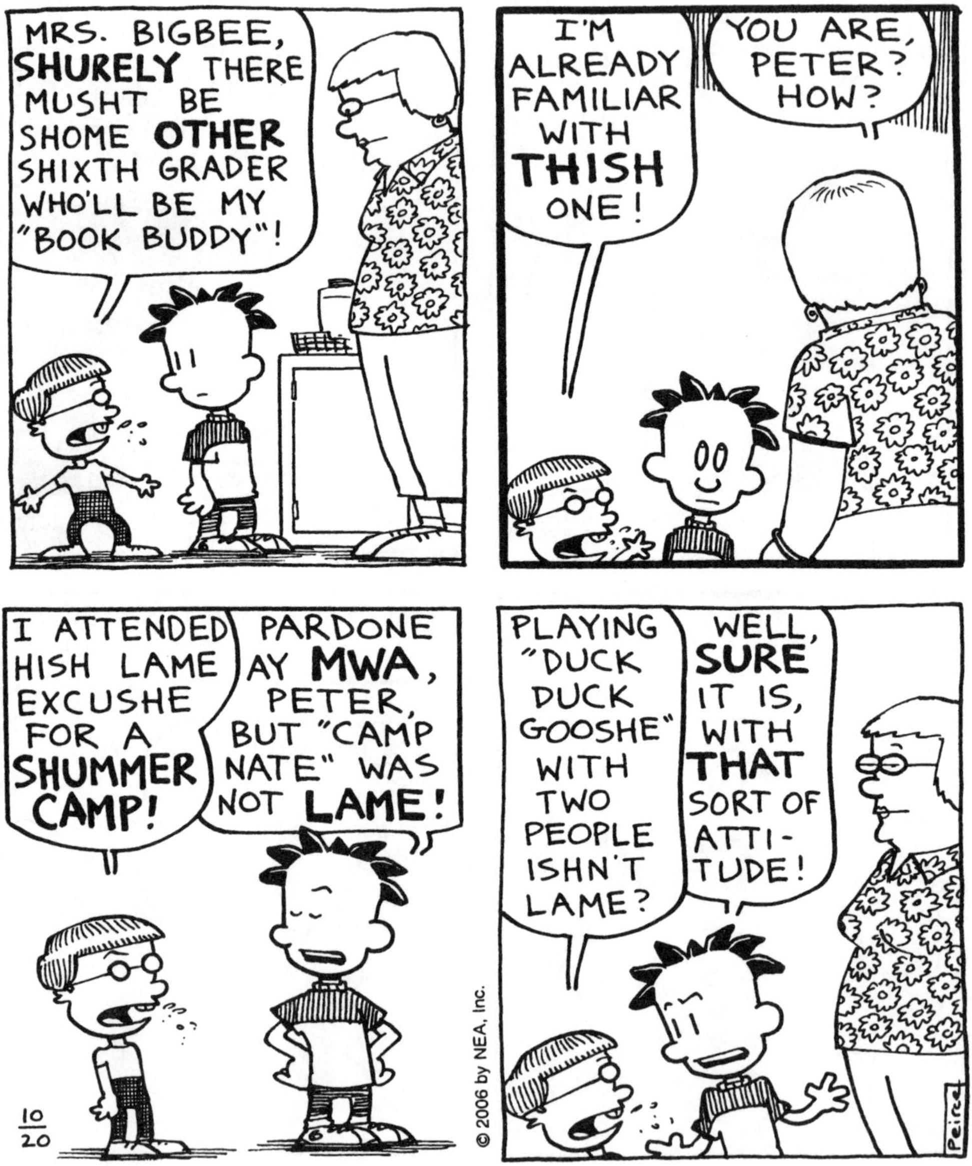
MRS. BIGBEE, SHURELY THERE MUSHT BE SHOME OTHER SHIXTH GRADER WHO'LL BE MY "BOOK BUDDY"!
I'M ALREADY FAMILIAR WITH THISH ONE!
YOU ARE, PETER? HOW?
I ATTENDED HISH LAME EXCUSHE FOR A SHUMMER CAMP!
PARDONE AY MWA, PETER, BUT "CAMP NATE" WAS NOT LAME!
PLAYING "DUCK DUCK GOOSHE" WITH TWO PEOPLE ISHN'T LAME?
WELL, SURE IT IS, WITH THAT SORT OF ATTITUDE!
10/20
Peirce

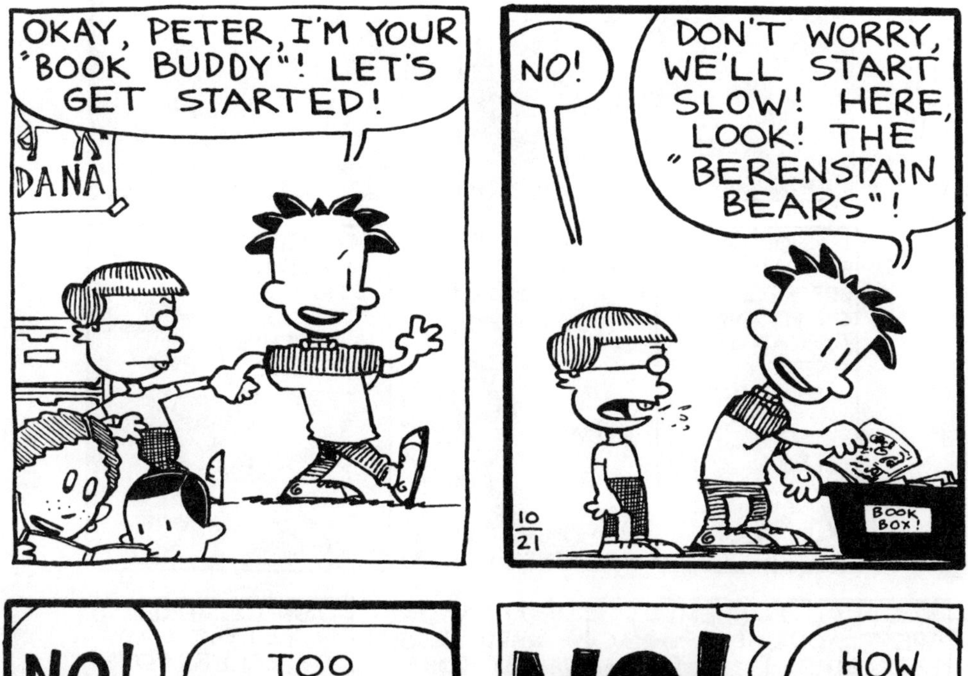
OKAY, PETER, I'M YOUR "BOOK BUDDY"! LET'S GET STARTED!
DANA
NO!
DON'T WORRY, WE'LL START SLOW! HERE, LOOK! THE "BERENSTAIN BEARS"!
10/21
BOOK BOX!
NO!
TOO ADVANCED?
BOOK BOX!
© 2006 by NEA, Inc.
NO!
HOW 'BOUT "PAT THE BUNNY"?
Peirce

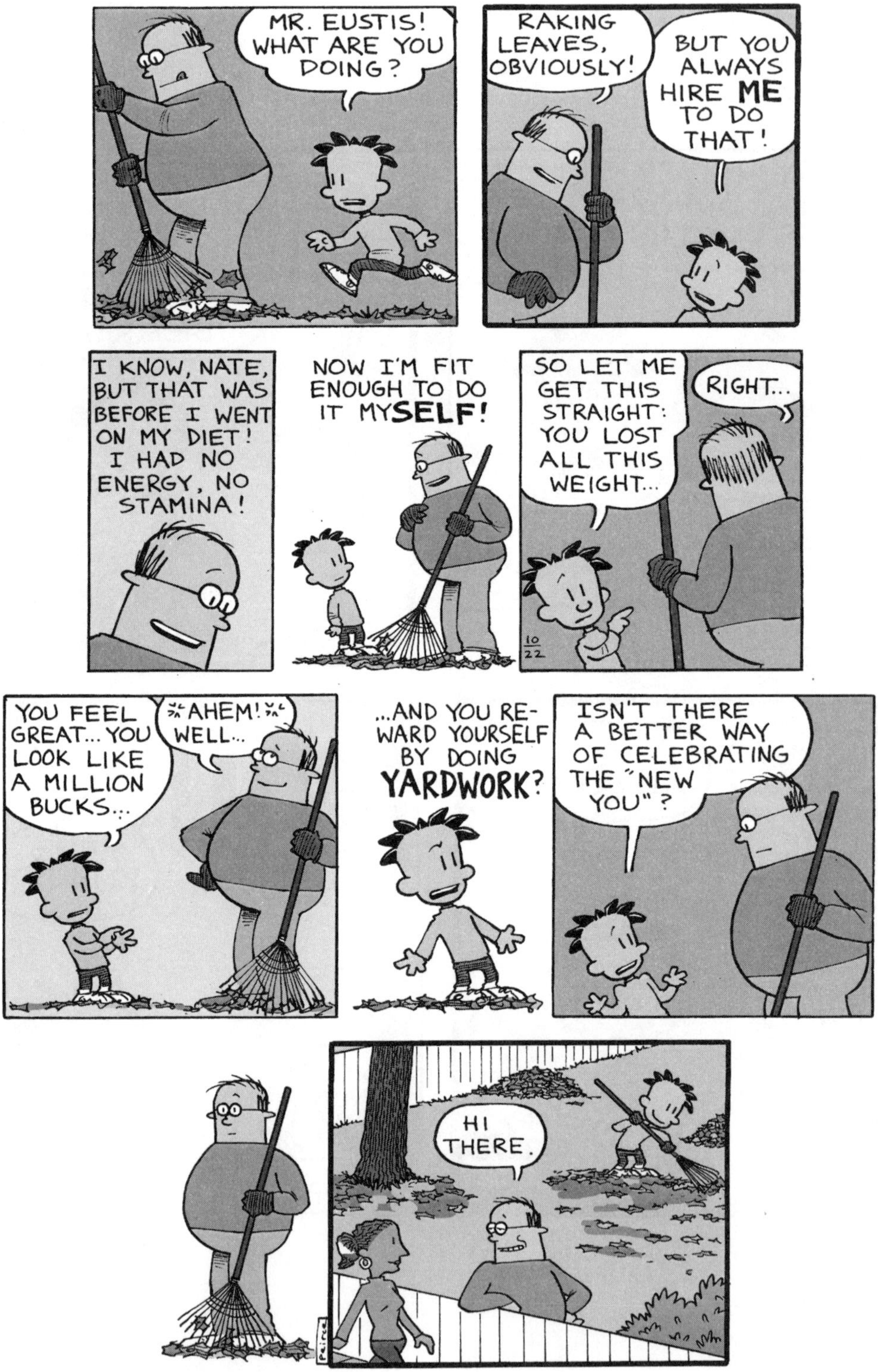
MR. EUSTIS! WHAT ARE YOU DOING?
RAKING LEAVES, OBVIOUSLY!
BUT YOU ALWAYS HIRE ME TO DO THAT!
I KNOW, NATE, BUT THAT WAS BEFORE I WENT ON MY DIET! I HAD NO ENERGY, NO STAMINA!
NOW I'M FIT ENOUGH TO DO IT MYSELF!
SO LET ME GET THIS STRAIGHT: YOU LOST ALL THIS WEIGHT...
RIGHT...
10 22
YOU FEEL GREAT... YOU LOOK LIKE A MILLION BUCKS...
AHEM! WELL...
...AND YOU REWARD YOURSELF BY DOING YARDWORK?
ISN'T THERE A BETTER WAY OF CELEBRATING THE "NEW YOU"?
HI THERE.
Peirce

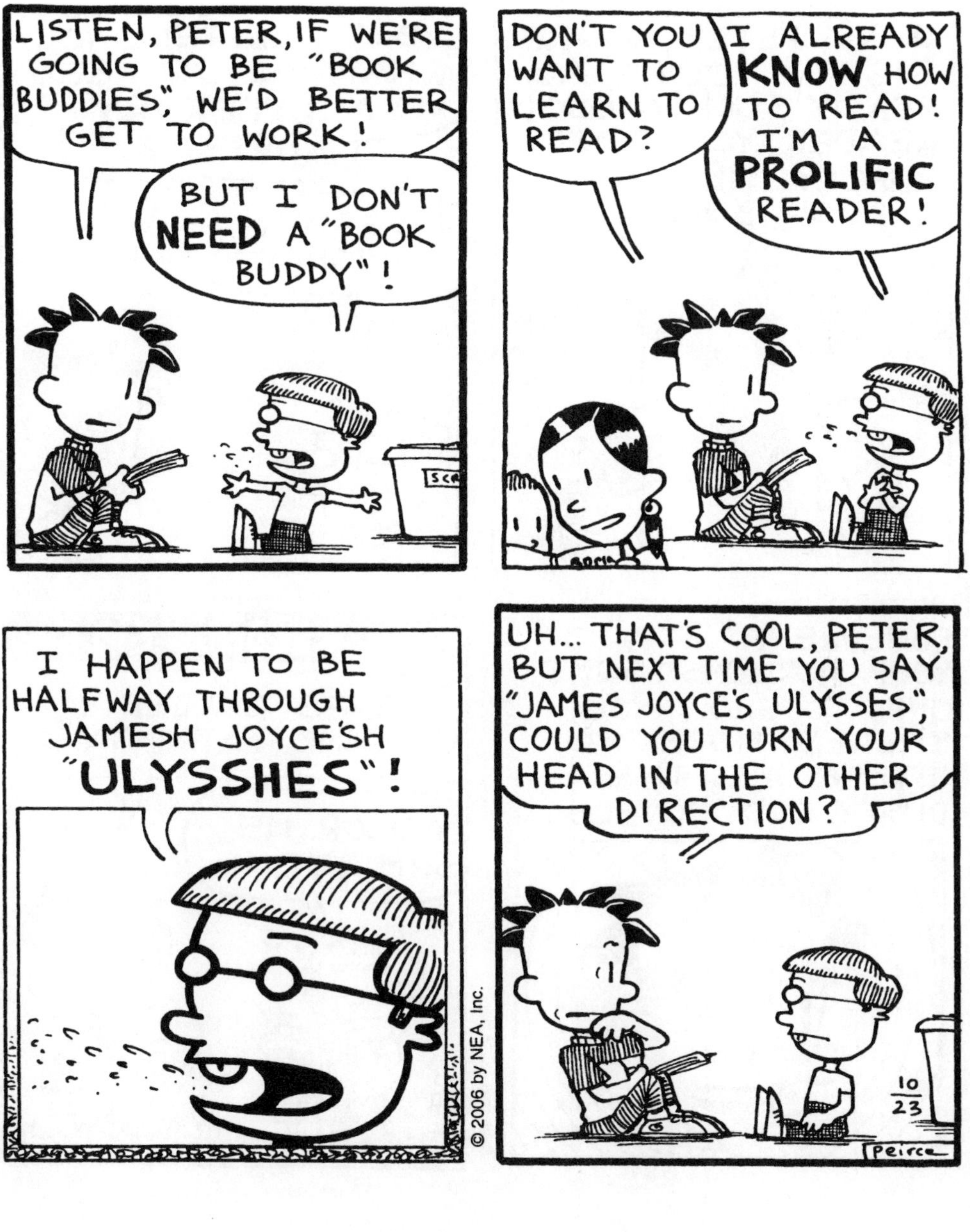
LISTEN, PETER, IF WE'RE GOING TO BE "BOOK BUDDIES," WE'D BETTER GET TO WORK!
BUT I DON'T NEED A "BOOK BUDDY"!
DON'T YOU WANT TO LEARN TO READ?
I ALREADY KNOW HOW TO READ! I'M A PROLIFIC READER!
I HAPPEN TO BE HALFWAY THROUGH JAMESH JOYCE'SH "ULYSSHES"!
© 2006 by NEA, Inc.
UH... THAT'S COOL, PETER, BUT NEXT TIME YOU SAY "JAMES JOYCE'S ULYSSES," COULD YOU TURN YOUR HEAD IN THE OTHER DIRECTION?
10/23
Peirce

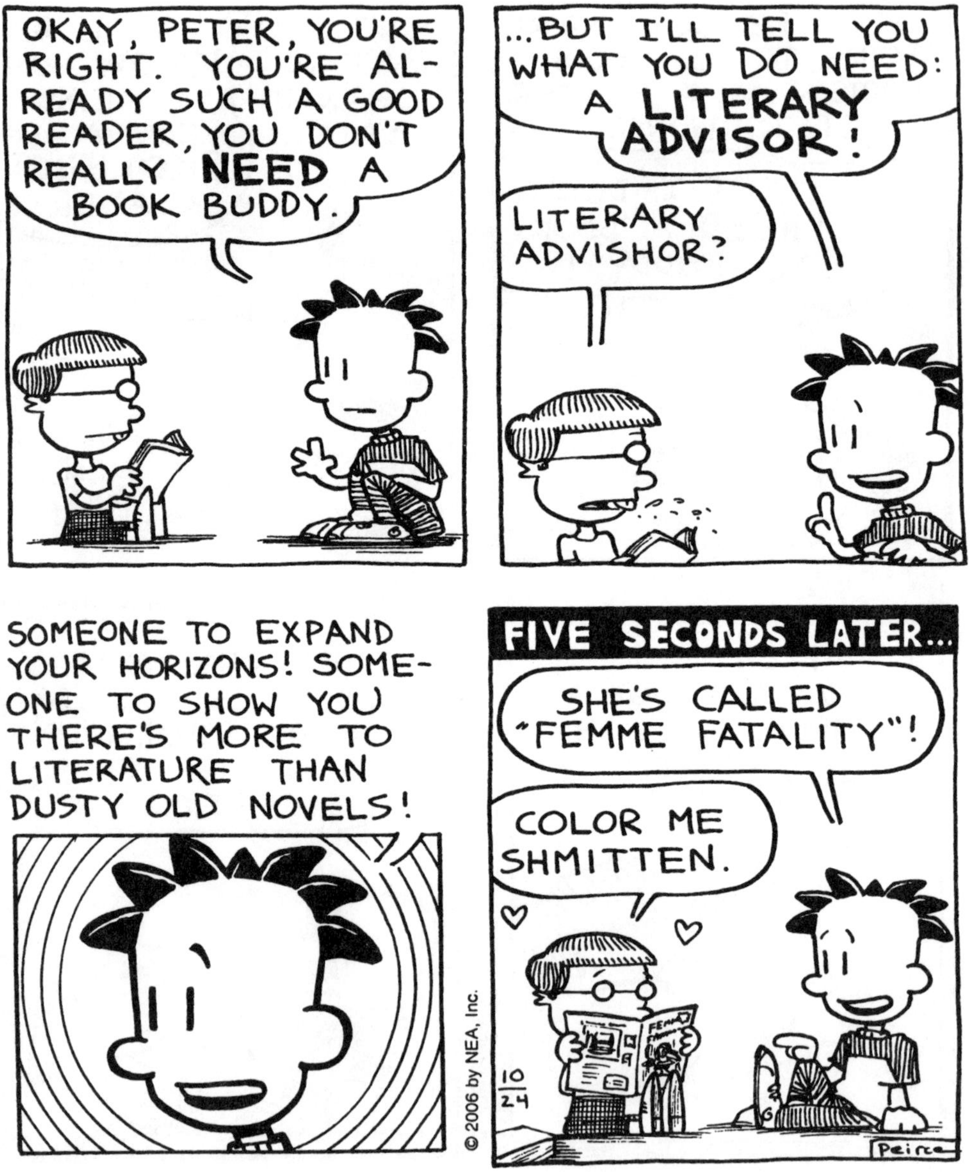
OKAY, PETER, YOU'RE RIGHT. YOU'RE ALREADY SUCH A GOOD READER, YOU DON'T REALLY **NEED** A BOOK BUDDY.
...BUT I'LL TELL YOU WHAT YOU DO NEED: A **LITERARY ADVISOR**!
LITERARY ADVISHOR?
SOMEONE TO EXPAND YOUR HORIZONS! SOMEONE TO SHOW YOU THERE'S MORE TO LITERATURE THAN DUSTY OLD NOVELS!
FIVE SECONDS LATER...
SHE'S CALLED "FEMME FATALITY"!
COLOR ME SHMITTEN.
10/24
Peirce

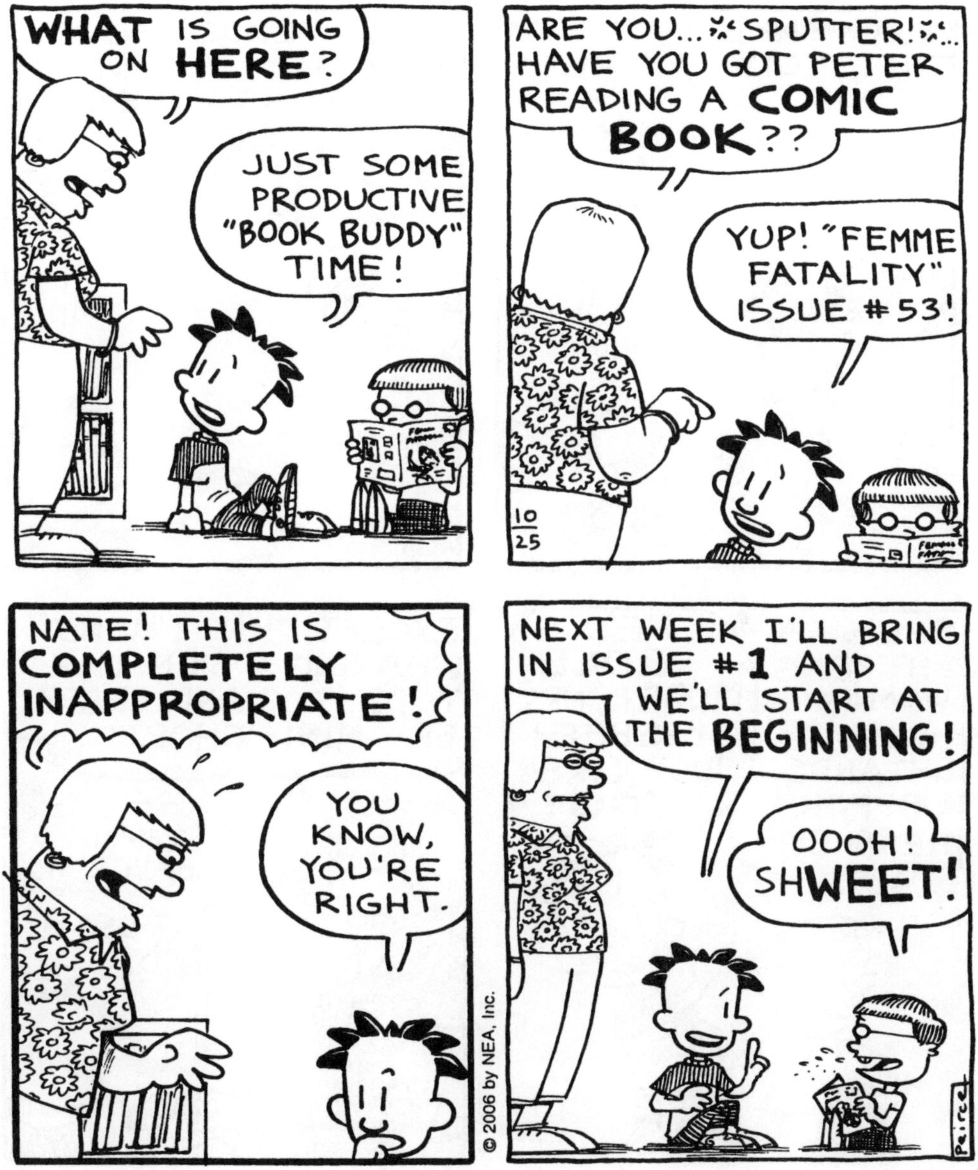
WHAT IS GOING ON HERE?
JUST SOME PRODUCTIVE "BOOK BUDDY" TIME!
ARE YOU... SPUTTER!... HAVE YOU GOT PETER READING A COMIC BOOK??
YUP! "FEMME FATALITY" ISSUE #53!
10 25
NATE! THIS IS COMPLETELY INAPPROPRIATE!
YOU KNOW, YOU'RE RIGHT.
© 2006 by NEA, Inc.
NEXT WEEK I'LL BRING IN ISSUE #1 AND WE'LL START AT THE BEGINNING!
OOOH! SHWEET!
Peirce

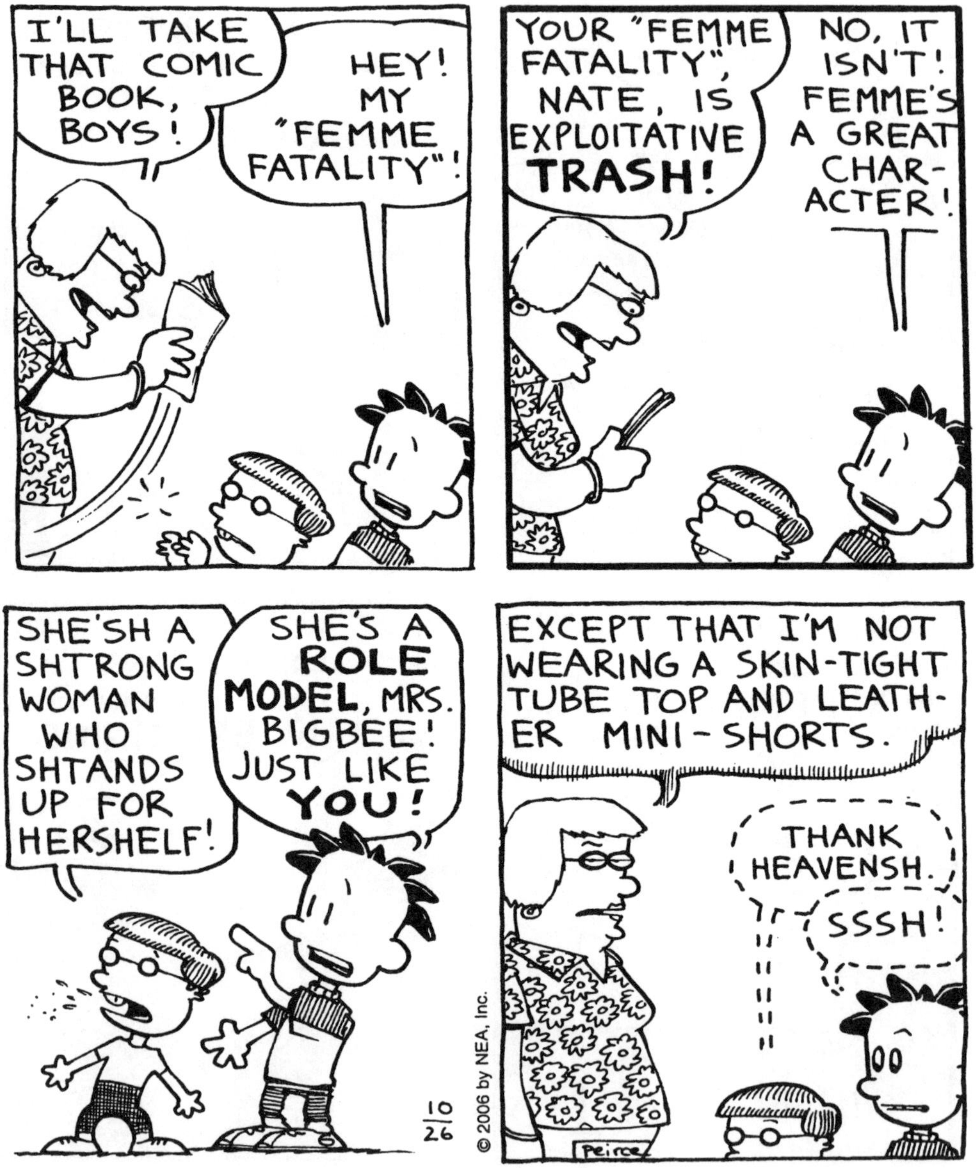
I'LL TAKE THAT COMIC BOOK, BOYS!
HEY! MY "FEMME FATALITY"!
YOUR "FEMME FATALITY", NATE, IS EXPLOITATIVE **TRASH!**
NO, IT ISN'T! FEMME'S A GREAT CHARACTER!
SHE'SH A SHTRONG WOMAN WHO SHTANDS UP FOR HERSHELF!
SHE'S A **ROLE MODEL**, MRS. BIGBEE! JUST LIKE **YOU!**
EXCEPT THAT I'M NOT WEARING A SKIN-TIGHT TUBE TOP AND LEATHER MINI-SHORTS.
THANK HEAVENSH.
SSSH!
10/26
© 2006 by NEA, Inc.
Peirce

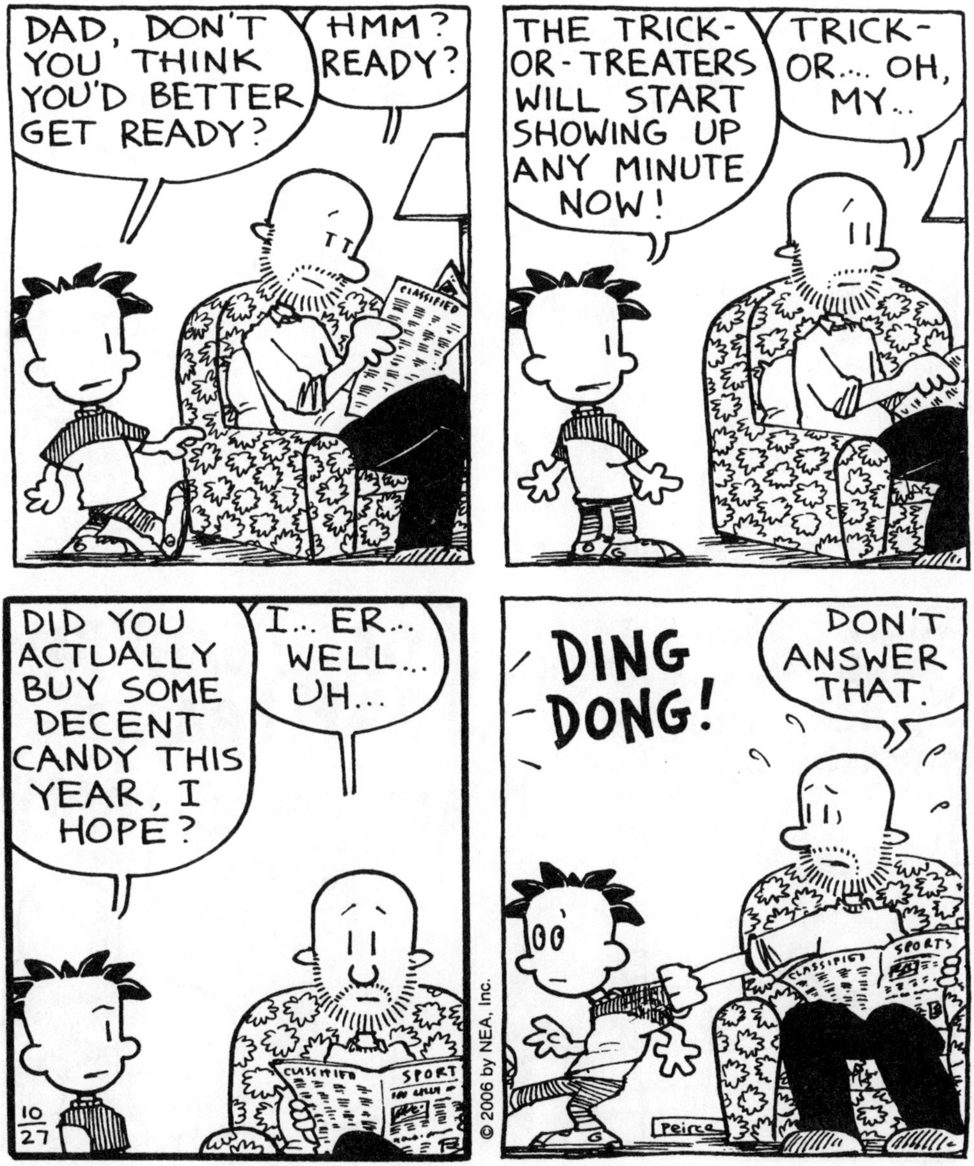
DAD, DON'T YOU THINK YOU'D BETTER GET READY?
HMM? READY?
THE TRICK-OR-TREATERS WILL START SHOWING UP ANY MINUTE NOW!
TRICK-OR.... OH, MY...
DID YOU ACTUALLY BUY SOME DECENT CANDY THIS YEAR, I HOPE?
I... ER... WELL... UH...
10/27
© 2006 by NEA, Inc.
DING DONG!
DON'T ANSWER THAT.
Peirce

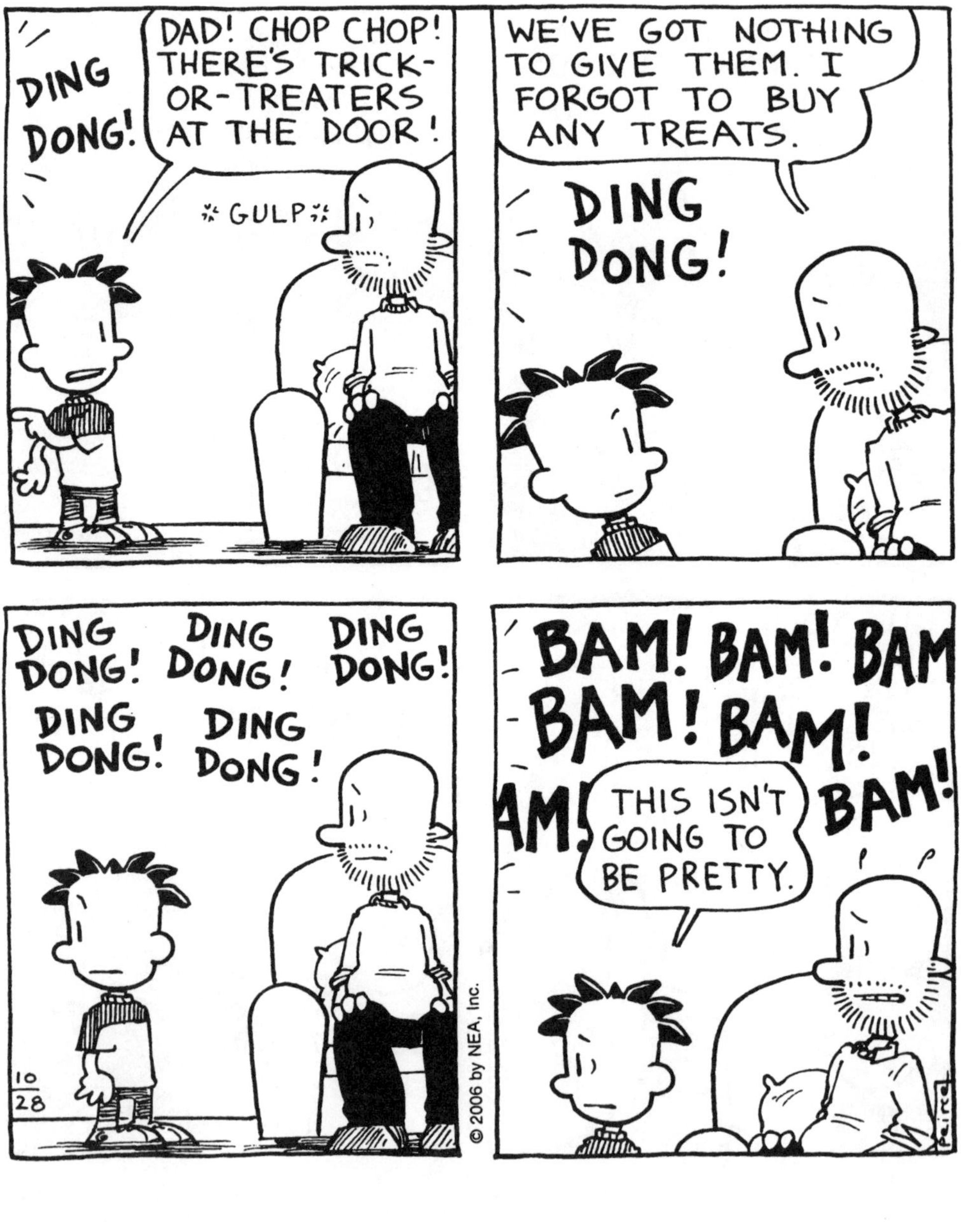
DING DONG!
DAD! CHOP CHOP! THERE'S TRICK-OR-TREATERS AT THE DOOR!
GULP
WE'VE GOT NOTHING TO GIVE THEM. I FORGOT TO BUY ANY TREATS.
DING DONG!
DING DONG! DING DONG! DING DONG!
DING DONG! DING DONG!
10/28
© 2006 by NEA, Inc.
BAM! BAM! BAM
BAM! BAM!
AM! BAM!
THIS ISN'T GOING TO BE PRETTY.
PEIRCE

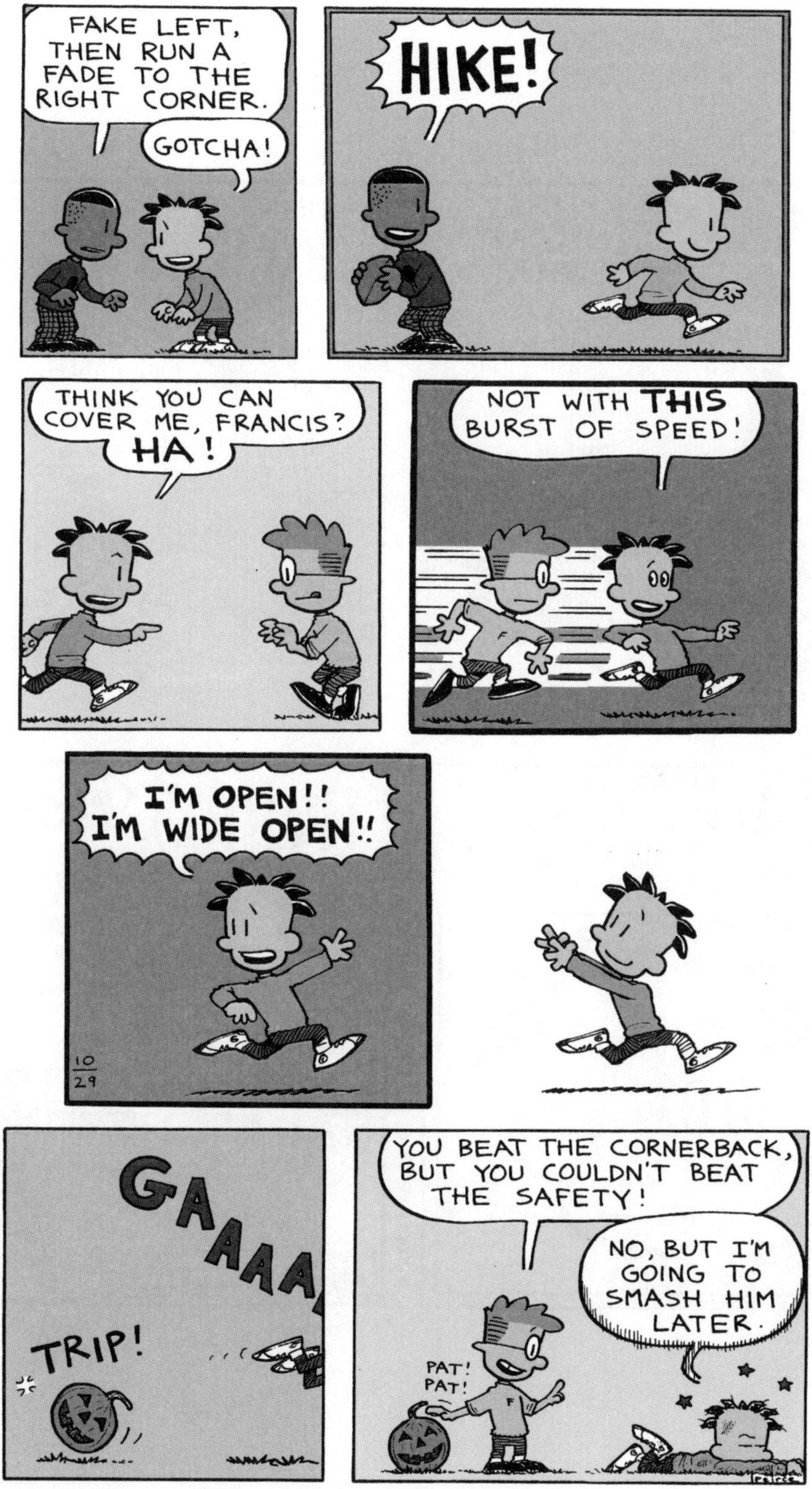
FAKE LEFT, THEN RUN A FADE TO THE RIGHT CORNER.
GOTCHA!
HIKE!
THINK YOU CAN COVER ME, FRANCIS? HA!
NOT WITH THIS BURST OF SPEED!
I'M OPEN!! I'M WIDE OPEN!!
10
29
GAAAA
TRIP!
YOU BEAT THE CORNERBACK, BUT YOU COULDN'T BEAT THE SAFETY!
NO, BUT I'M GOING TO SMASH HIM LATER.
PAT! PAT!

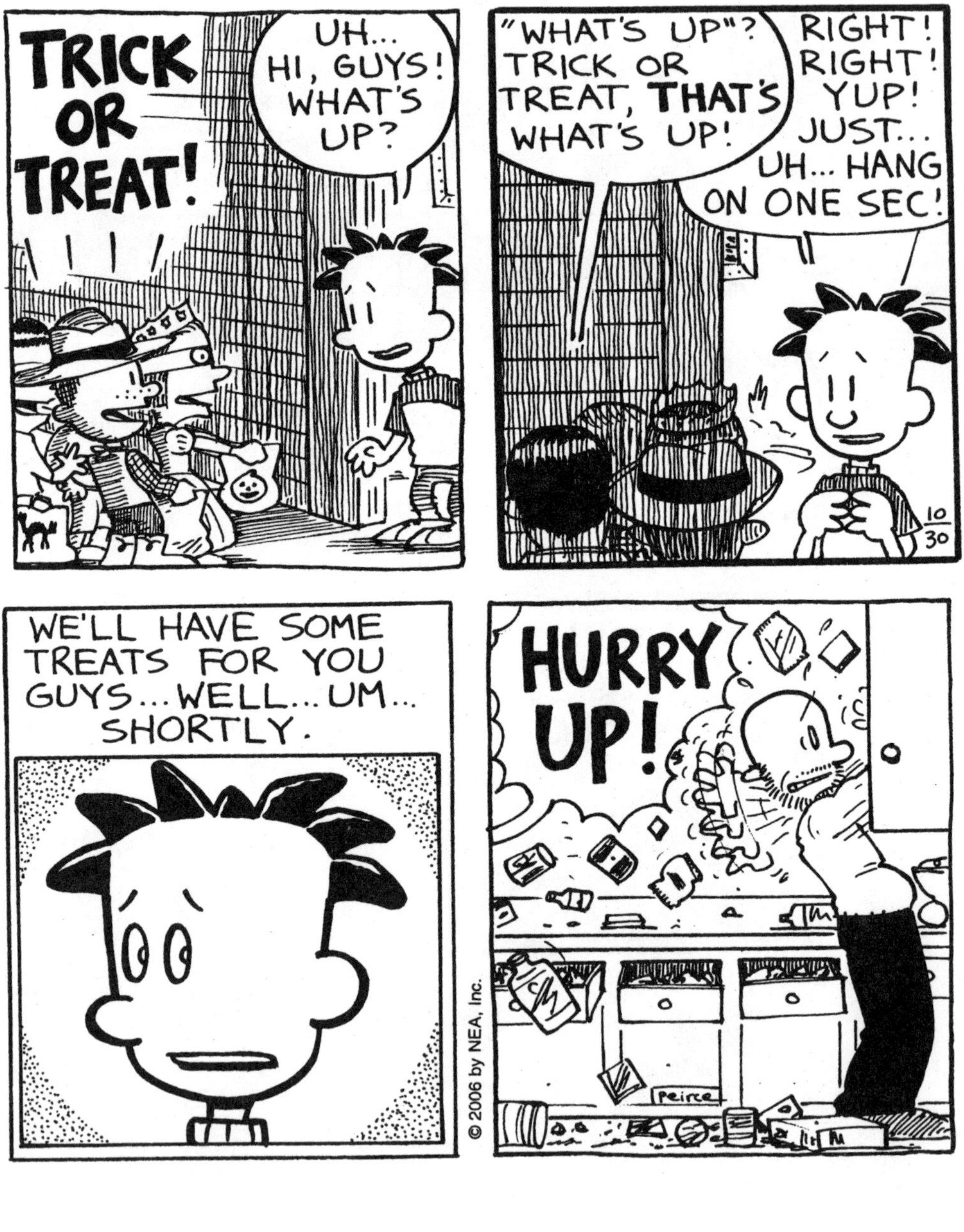
TRICK OR TREAT!
UH... HI, GUYS! WHAT'S UP?
"WHAT'S UP"? TRICK OR TREAT, THAT'S WHAT'S UP!
RIGHT! RIGHT! YUP! JUST... UH... HANG ON ONE SEC!
10 30
WE'LL HAVE SOME TREATS FOR YOU GUYS... WELL... UM... SHORTLY.
© 2006 by NEA, Inc.
HURRY UP!
Peirce

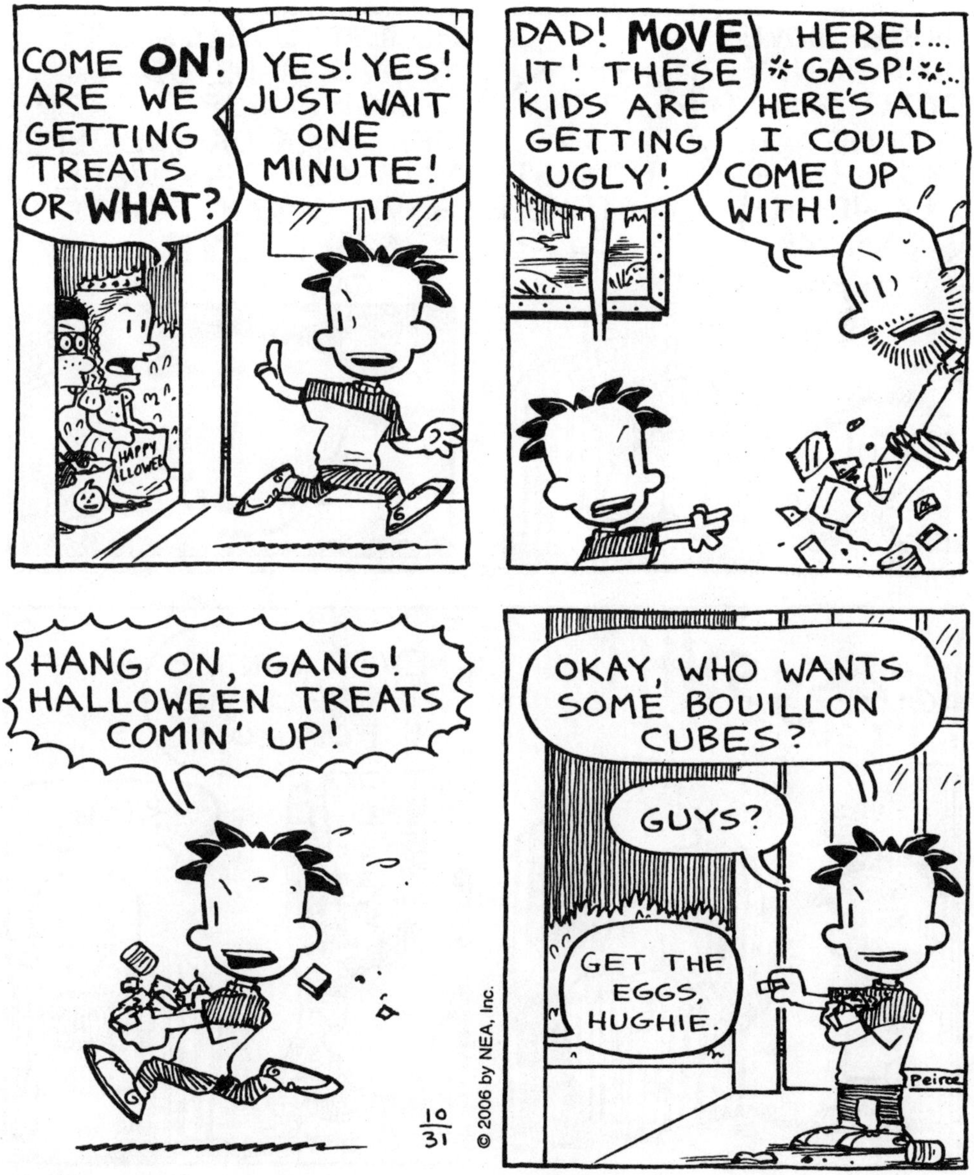
COME ON! ARE WE GETTING TREATS OR WHAT?
YES! YES! JUST WAIT ONE MINUTE!
HAPPY HALLOWEEN
DAD! MOVE IT! THESE KIDS ARE GETTING UGLY!
HERE!... *GASP!*.. HERE'S ALL I COULD COME UP WITH!
HANG ON, GANG! HALLOWEEN TREATS COMIN' UP!
10/31
OKAY, WHO WANTS SOME BOUILLON CUBES?
GUYS?
GET THE EGGS, HUGHIE.
Peirce

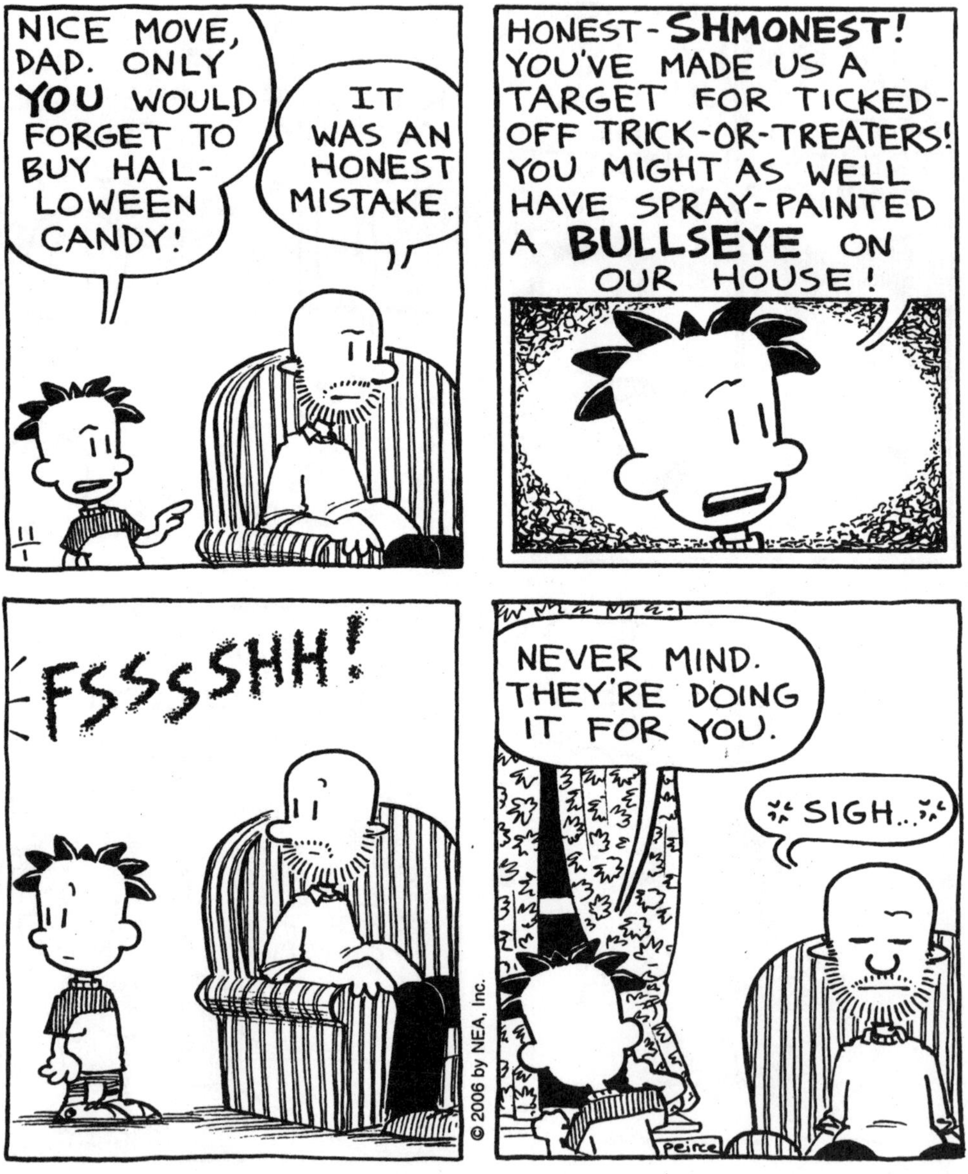
NICE MOVE, DAD. ONLY YOU WOULD FORGET TO BUY HAL-LOWEEN CANDY!
IT WAS AN HONEST MISTAKE.
HONEST-SHMONEST! YOU'VE MADE US A TARGET FOR TICKED-OFF TRICK-OR-TREATERS! YOU MIGHT AS WELL HAVE SPRAY-PAINTED A BULLSEYE ON OUR HOUSE!
FSSSSHH!
NEVER MIND. THEY'RE DOING IT FOR YOU.
SIGH...
peirce

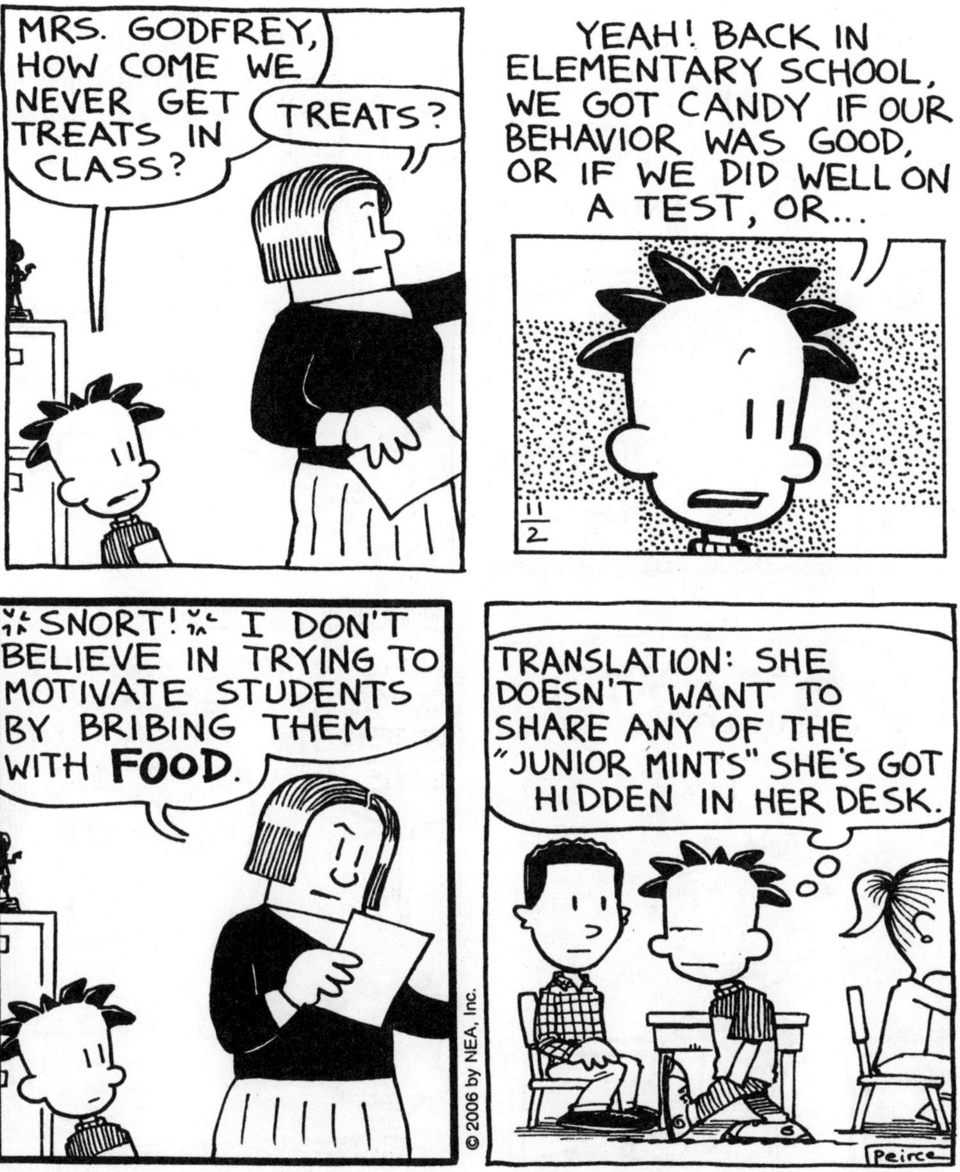
MRS. GODFREY, HOW COME WE NEVER GET TREATS IN CLASS?
TREATS?
YEAH! BACK IN ELEMENTARY SCHOOL, WE GOT CANDY IF OUR BEHAVIOR WAS GOOD, OR IF WE DID WELL ON A TEST, OR...
11/2
SNORT! I DON'T BELIEVE IN TRYING TO MOTIVATE STUDENTS BY BRIBING THEM WITH **FOOD**.
© 2006 by NEA, Inc.
TRANSLATION: SHE DOESN'T WANT TO SHARE ANY OF THE "JUNIOR MINTS" SHE'S GOT HIDDEN IN HER DESK.
Peirce

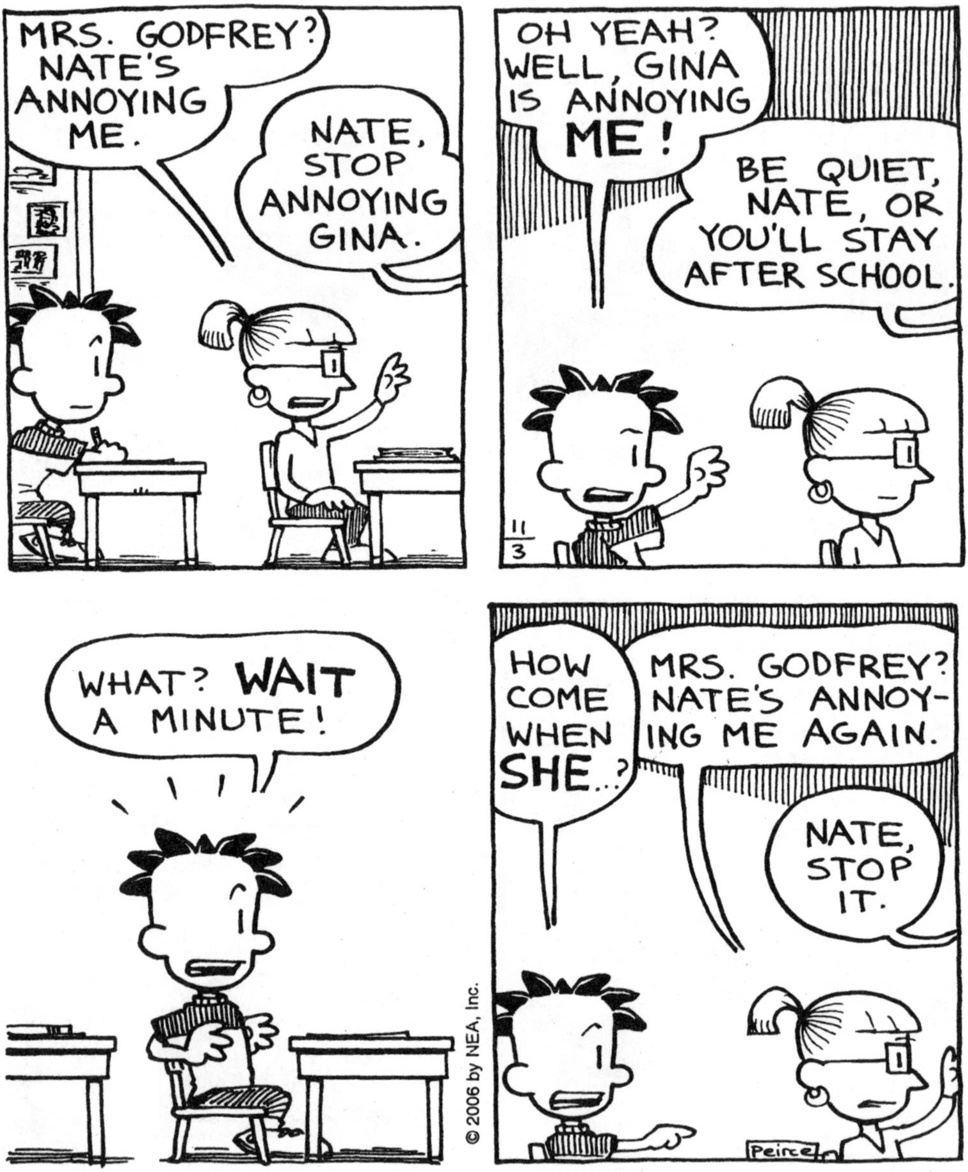
MRS. GODFREY? NATE'S ANNOYING ME.
NATE, STOP ANNOYING GINA.
OH YEAH? WELL, GINA IS ANNOYING **ME**!
BE QUIET, NATE, OR YOU'LL STAY AFTER SCHOOL.
11/3
WHAT? **WAIT** A MINUTE!
© 2006 by NEA, Inc.
MRS. GODFREY? NATE'S ANNOYING ME AGAIN.
HOW COME WHEN **SHE**...?
NATE, STOP IT.
Peirce

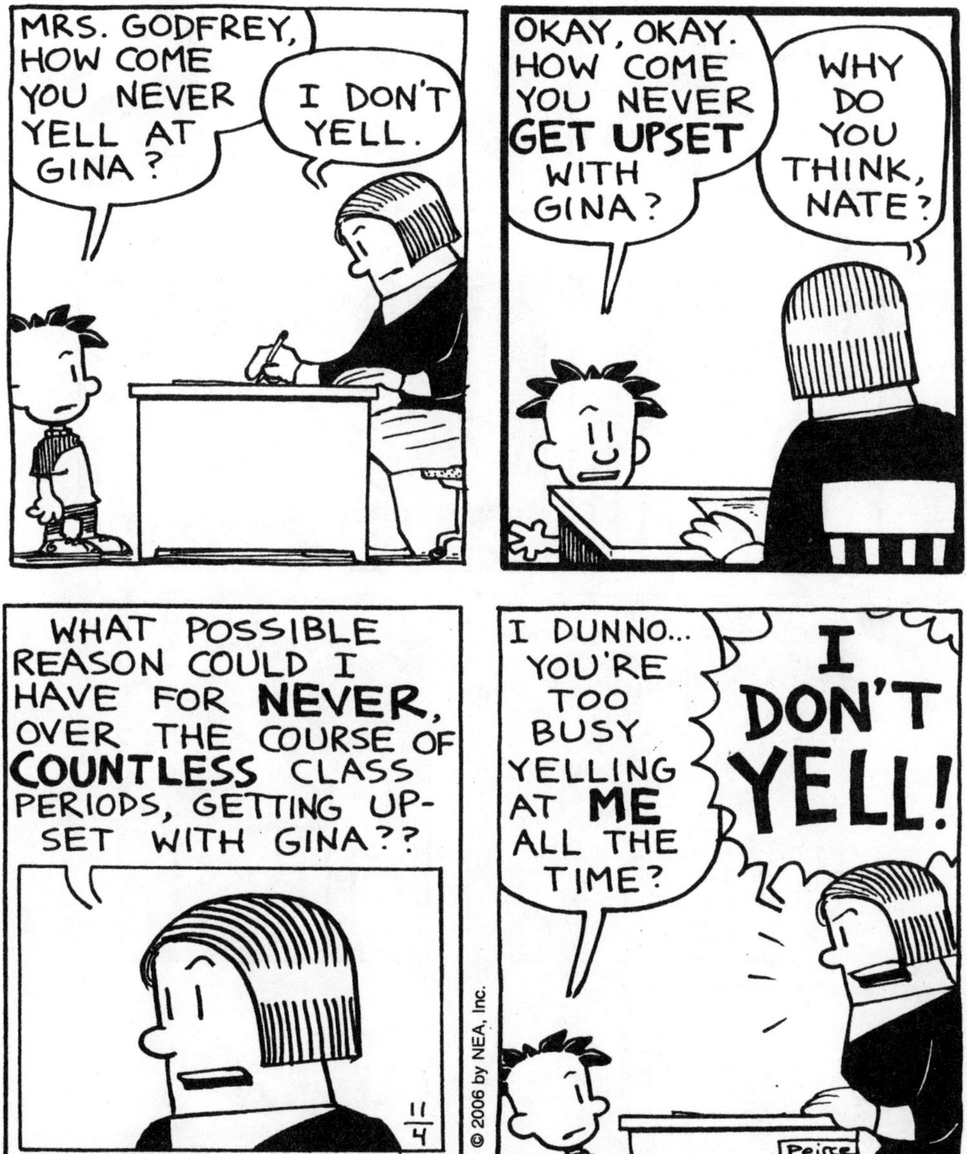
MRS. GODFREY, HOW COME YOU NEVER YELL AT GINA?
I DON'T YELL.
OKAY, OKAY. HOW COME YOU NEVER GET UPSET WITH GINA?
WHY DO YOU THINK, NATE?
WHAT POSSIBLE REASON COULD I HAVE FOR NEVER, OVER THE COURSE OF COUNTLESS CLASS PERIODS, GETTING UP-SET WITH GINA??
11/4
I DUNNO... YOU'RE TOO BUSY YELLING AT ME ALL THE TIME?
I DON'T YELL!
Peirce

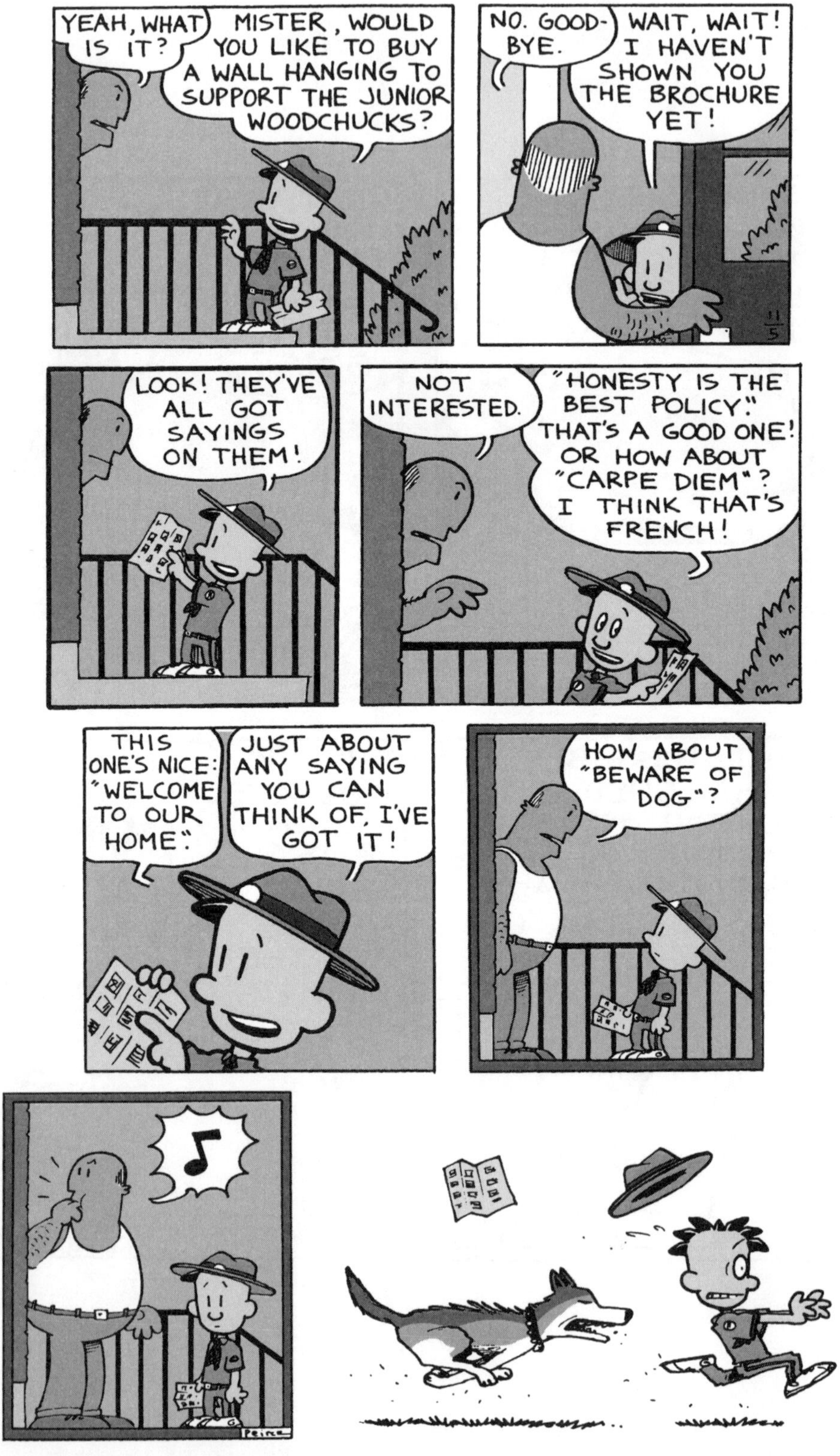
YEAH, WHAT IS IT?
MISTER, WOULD YOU LIKE TO BUY A WALL HANGING TO SUPPORT THE JUNIOR WOODCHUCKS?
NO. GOOD-BYE.
WAIT, WAIT! I HAVEN'T SHOWN YOU THE BROCHURE YET!
LOOK! THEY'VE ALL GOT SAYINGS ON THEM!
NOT INTERESTED.
"HONESTY IS THE BEST POLICY." THAT'S A GOOD ONE! OR HOW ABOUT "CARPE DIEM"? I THINK THAT'S FRENCH!
THIS ONE'S NICE: "WELCOME TO OUR HOME."
JUST ABOUT ANY SAYING YOU CAN THINK OF, I'VE GOT IT!
HOW ABOUT "BEWARE OF DOG"?
PEIRCE

ACCORDING TO THIS ARTICLE, WOMEN ARE ATTRACTED TO "BAD BOYS"!
COSMO
THERE'S SOMETHING ABOUT A REBEL THAT THE LADIES FIND IRRESISTIBLE! HMMM!...
COSMO
11/6
GENTS, I DO BELIEVE I'M GETTING ANOTHER BRILLIANT IDEA!
© 2006 by NEA, Inc.
"ANOTHER"?
YUP! THE HITS JUST KEEP ON COMIN'!
F
PEIRCE

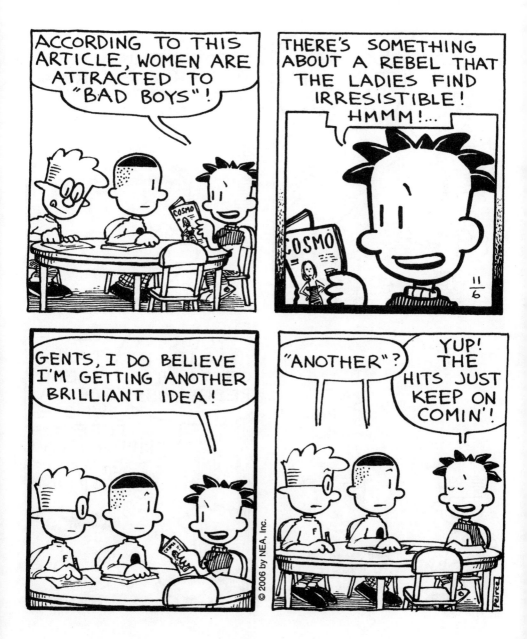

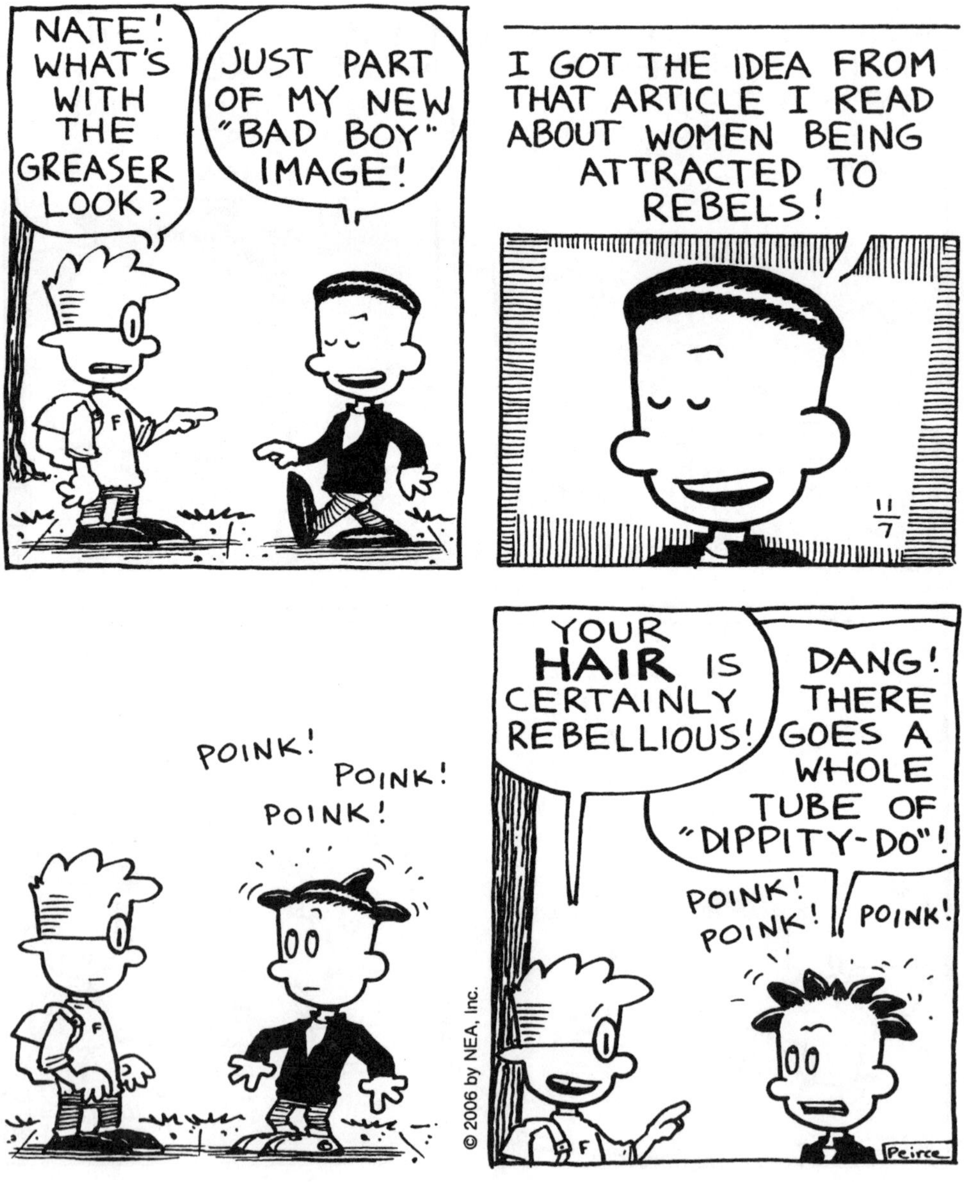
NATE! WHAT'S WITH THE GREASER LOOK?
JUST PART OF MY NEW "BAD BOY" IMAGE!
I GOT THE IDEA FROM THAT ARTICLE I READ ABOUT WOMEN BEING ATTRACTED TO REBELS!
11/7
POINK!
POINK!
POINK!
© 2006 by NEA, Inc.
YOUR HAIR IS CERTAINLY REBELLIOUS!
DANG! THERE GOES A WHOLE TUBE OF "DIPPITY-DO"!
POINK!
POINK!
POINK!
Peirce

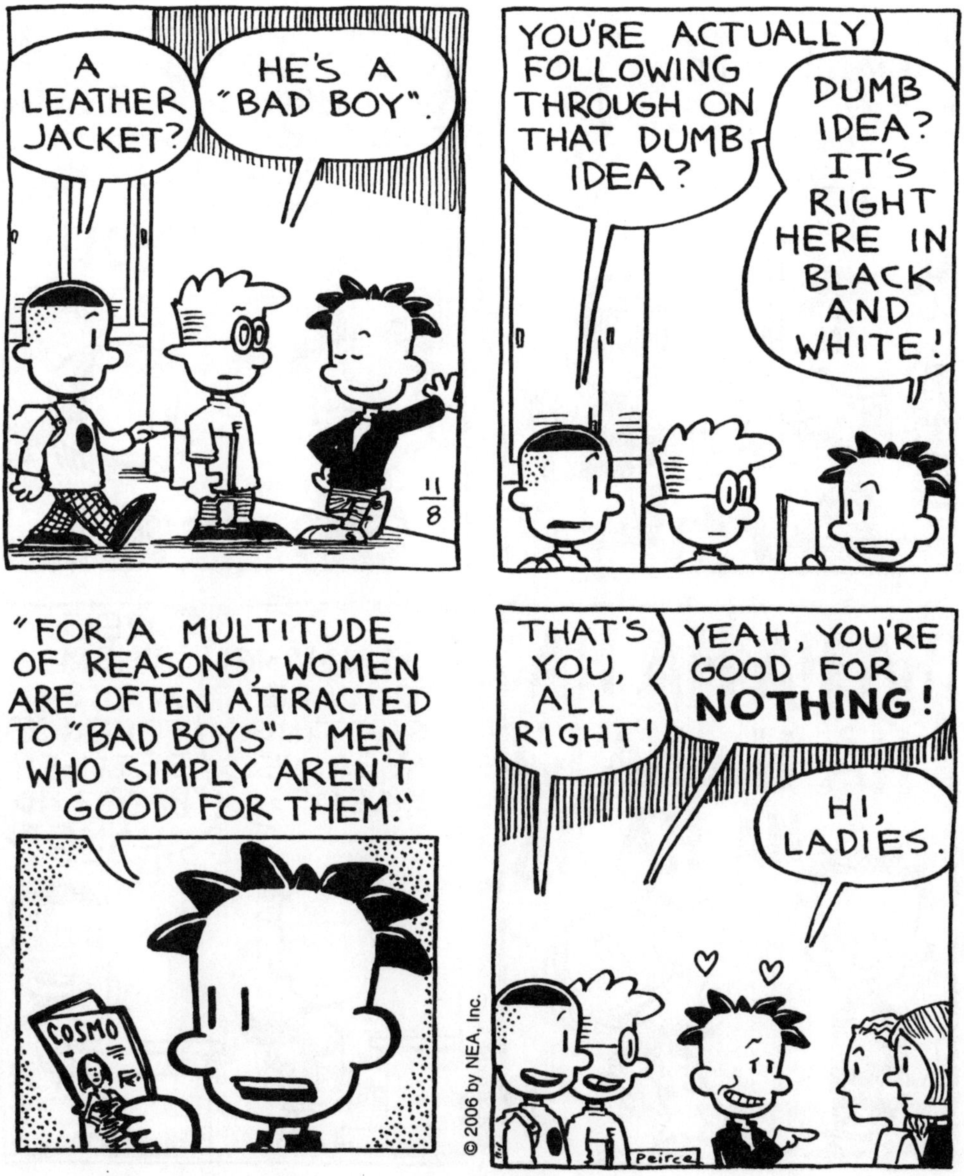
A LEATHER JACKET?
HE'S A "BAD BOY".
11/8
YOU'RE ACTUALLY FOLLOWING THROUGH ON THAT DUMB IDEA?
DUMB IDEA? IT'S RIGHT HERE IN BLACK AND WHITE!
"FOR A MULTITUDE OF REASONS, WOMEN ARE OFTEN ATTRACTED TO "BAD BOYS"– MEN WHO SIMPLY AREN'T GOOD FOR THEM."
COSMO
THAT'S YOU, ALL RIGHT!
YEAH, YOU'RE GOOD FOR **NOTHING**!
HI, LADIES.
© 2006 by NEA, Inc.
Peirce

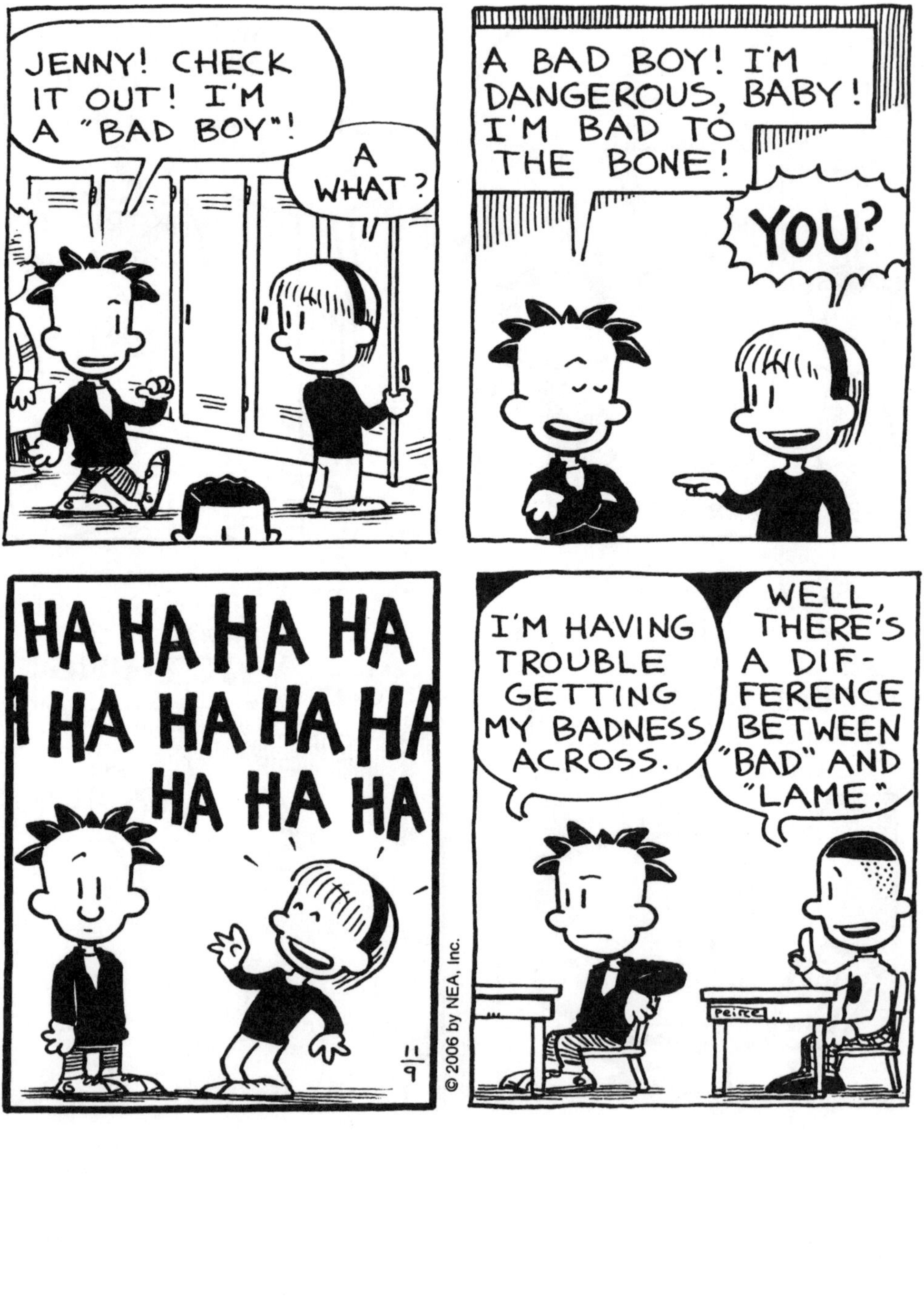
JENNY! CHECK IT OUT! I'M A "BAD BOY"!
A WHAT?
A BAD BOY! I'M DANGEROUS, BABY! I'M BAD TO THE BONE!
YOU?
HA HA HA HA HA HA HA HA HA HA HA HA HA HA
I'M HAVING TROUBLE GETTING MY BADNESS ACROSS.
WELL, THERE'S A DIF-FERENCE BETWEEN "BAD" AND "LAME."
PEIRCE
11/9

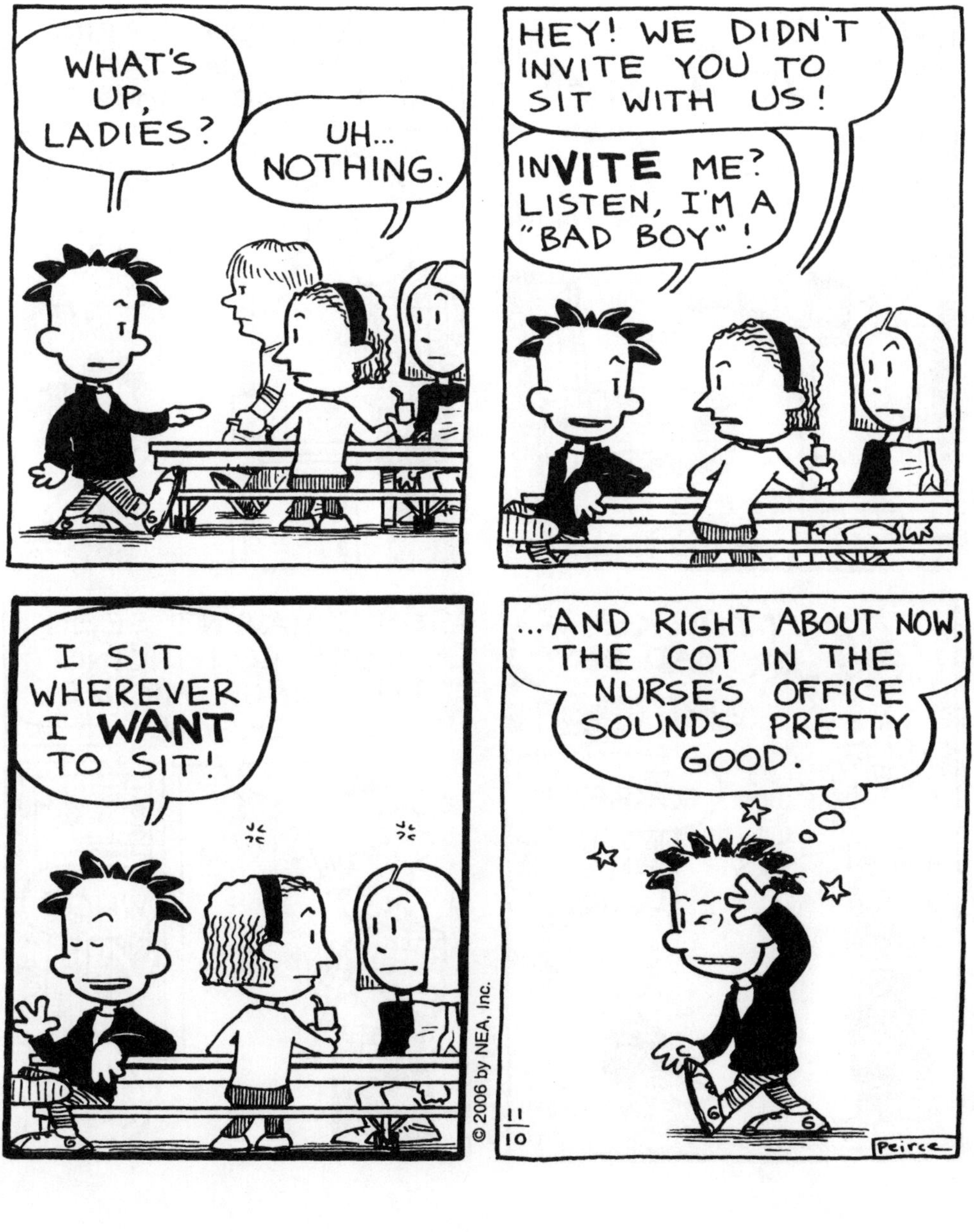
WHAT'S UP, LADIES?
UH... NOTHING.
HEY! WE DIDN'T INVITE YOU TO SIT WITH US!
INVITE ME? LISTEN, I'M A "BAD BOY"!
I SIT WHEREVER I WANT TO SIT!
© 2006 by NEA, Inc.
11/10
...AND RIGHT ABOUT NOW, THE COT IN THE NURSE'S OFFICE SOUNDS PRETTY GOOD.
Peirce

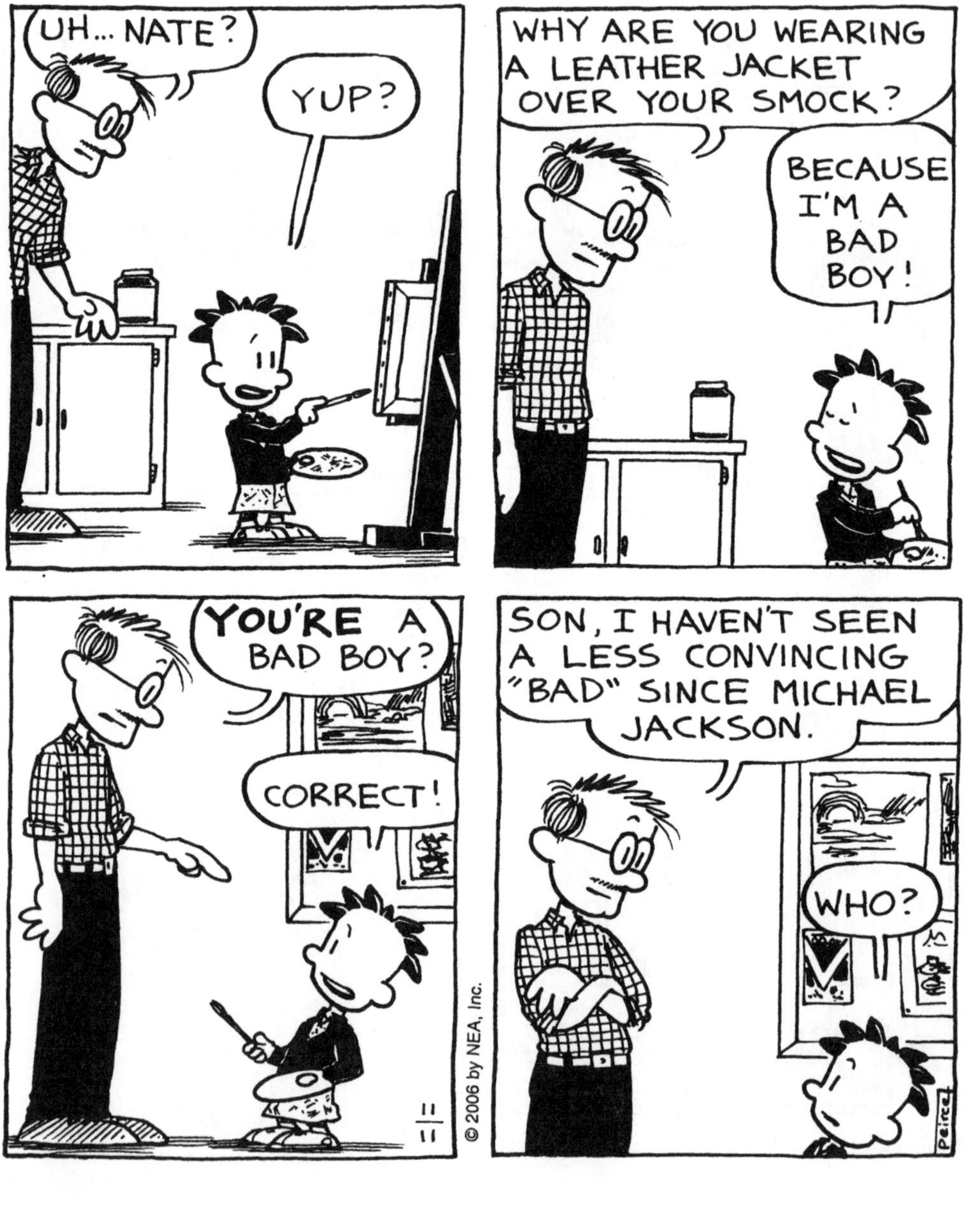
UH... NATE?
YUP?
WHY ARE YOU WEARING A LEATHER JACKET OVER YOUR SMOCK?
BECAUSE I'M A BAD BOY!
YOU'RE A BAD BOY?
CORRECT!
SON, I HAVEN'T SEEN A LESS CONVINCING "BAD" SINCE MICHAEL JACKSON.
WHO?
11/11
PEIRCE

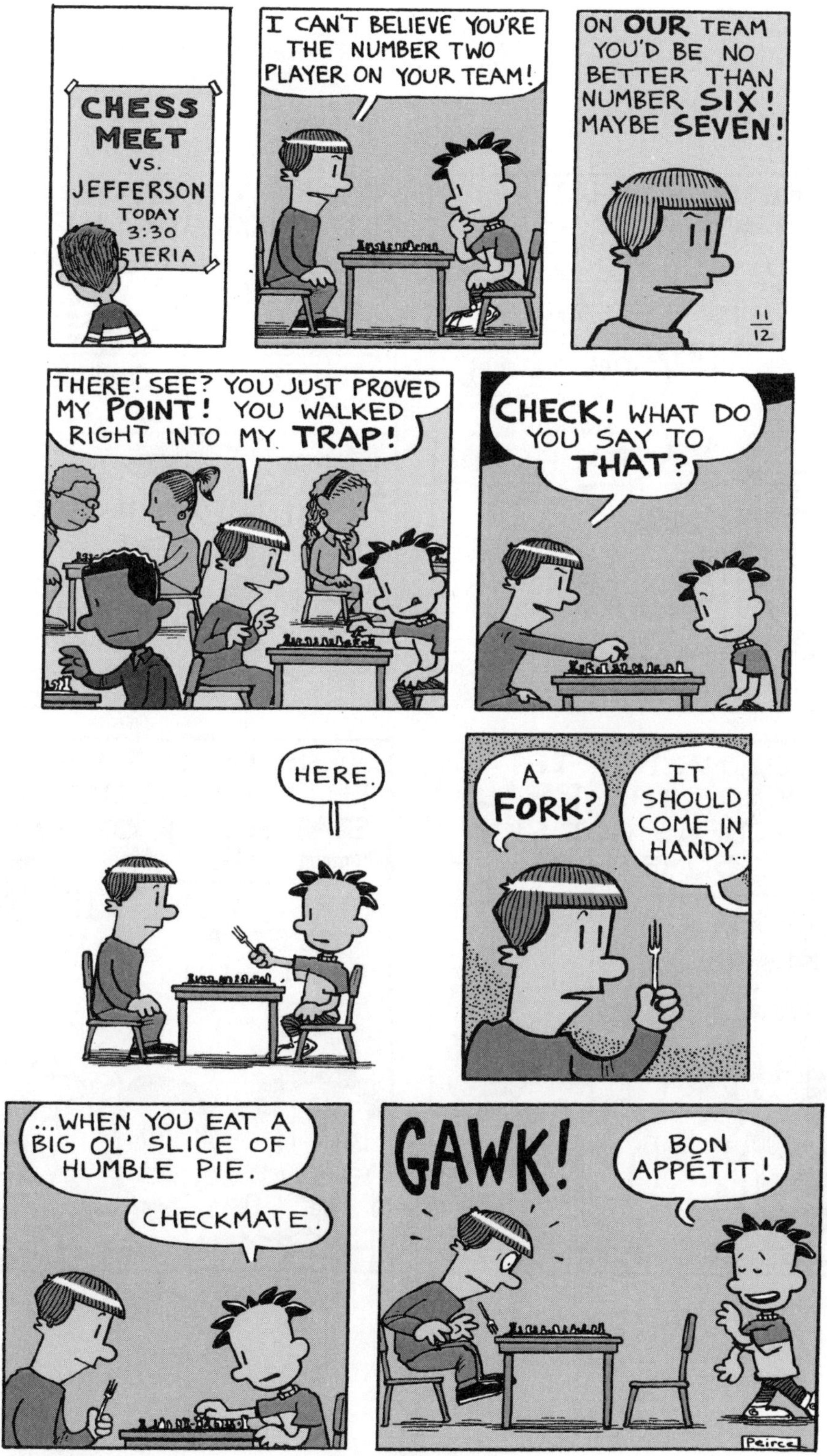
CHESS MEET
VS.
JEFFERSON
TODAY
3:30
ETERIA
I CAN'T BELIEVE YOU'RE THE NUMBER TWO PLAYER ON YOUR TEAM!
ON OUR TEAM YOU'D BE NO BETTER THAN NUMBER SIX! MAYBE SEVEN!
11/12
THERE! SEE? YOU JUST PROVED MY POINT! YOU WALKED RIGHT INTO MY TRAP!
CHECK! WHAT DO YOU SAY TO THAT?
HERE.
A FORK?
IT SHOULD COME IN HANDY...
...WHEN YOU EAT A BIG OL' SLICE OF HUMBLE PIE.
CHECKMATE.
GAWK!
BON APPÉTIT!
Peirce

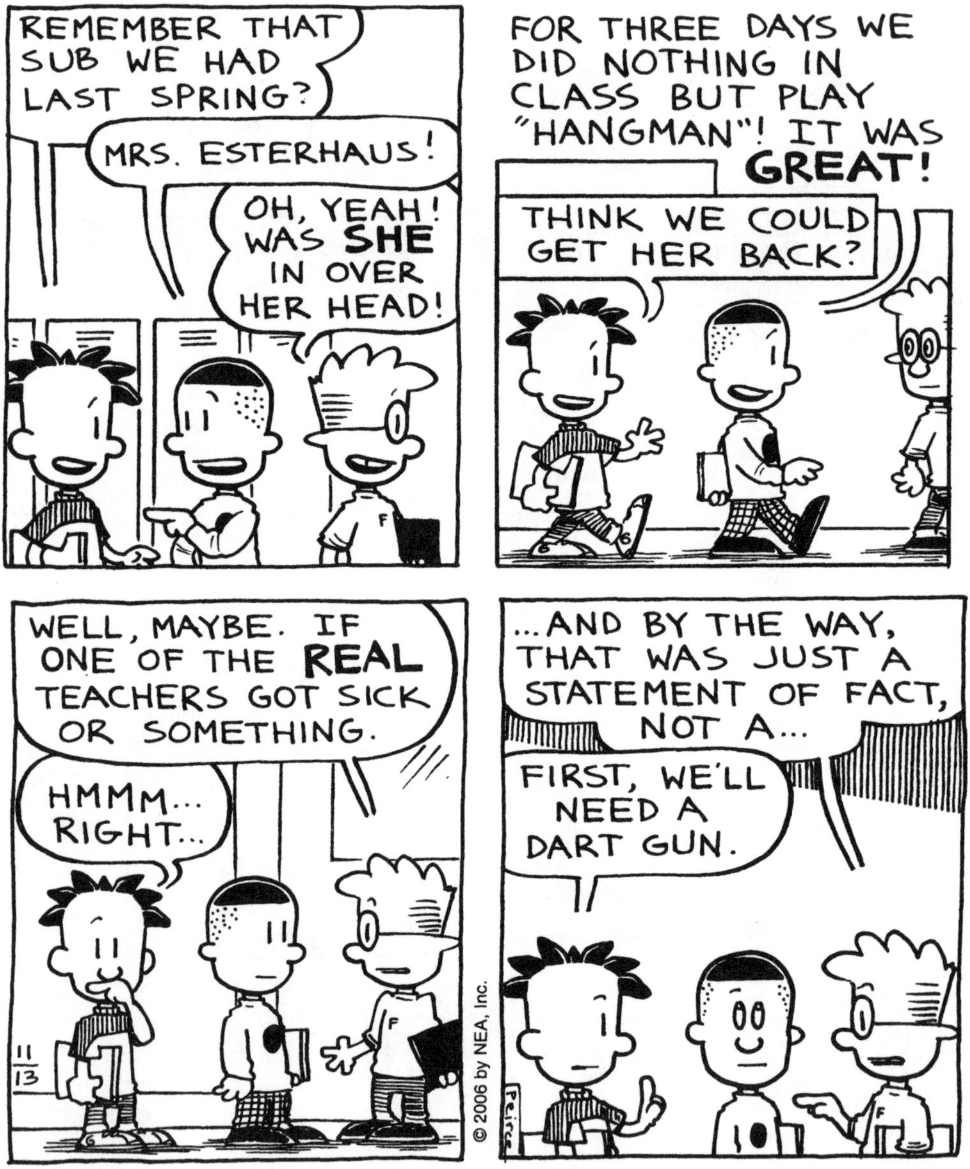
REMEMBER THAT SUB WE HAD LAST SPRING?
MRS. ESTERHAUS!
OH, YEAH! WAS SHE IN OVER HER HEAD!
FOR THREE DAYS WE DID NOTHING IN CLASS BUT PLAY "HANGMAN"! IT WAS GREAT!
THINK WE COULD GET HER BACK?
WELL, MAYBE. IF ONE OF THE REAL TEACHERS GOT SICK OR SOMETHING.
HMMM... RIGHT...
...AND BY THE WAY, THAT WAS JUST A STATEMENT OF FACT, NOT A...
FIRST, WE'LL NEED A DART GUN.
11/13
Peirce

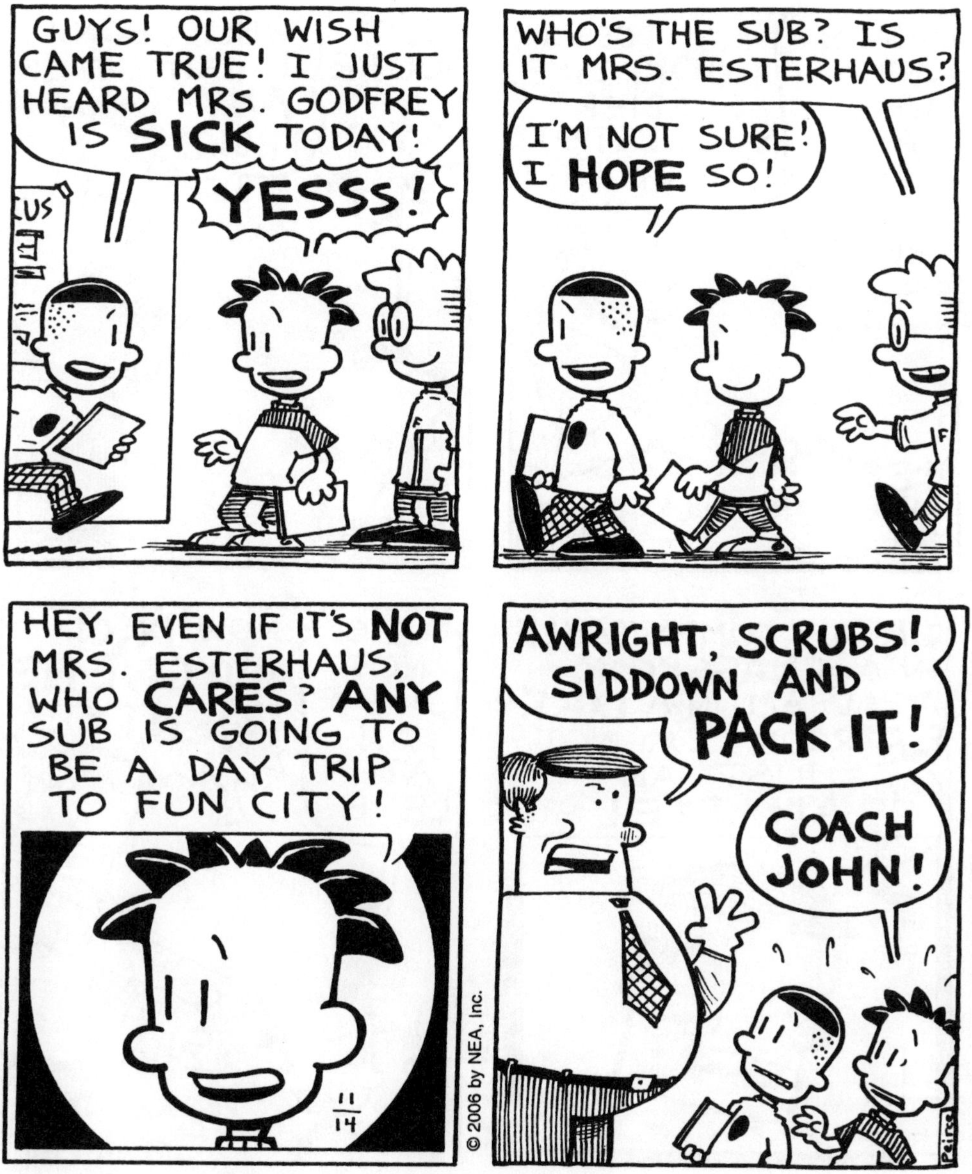
GUYS! OUR WISH CAME TRUE! I JUST HEARD MRS. GODFREY IS SICK TODAY!
YESSS!
WHO'S THE SUB? IS IT MRS. ESTERHAUS?
I'M NOT SURE! I HOPE SO!
HEY, EVEN IF IT'S NOT MRS. ESTERHAUS, WHO CARES? ANY SUB IS GOING TO BE A DAY TRIP TO FUN CITY!
AWRIGHT, SCRUBS! SIDDOWN AND PACK IT!
COACH JOHN!
11/14
Peirce

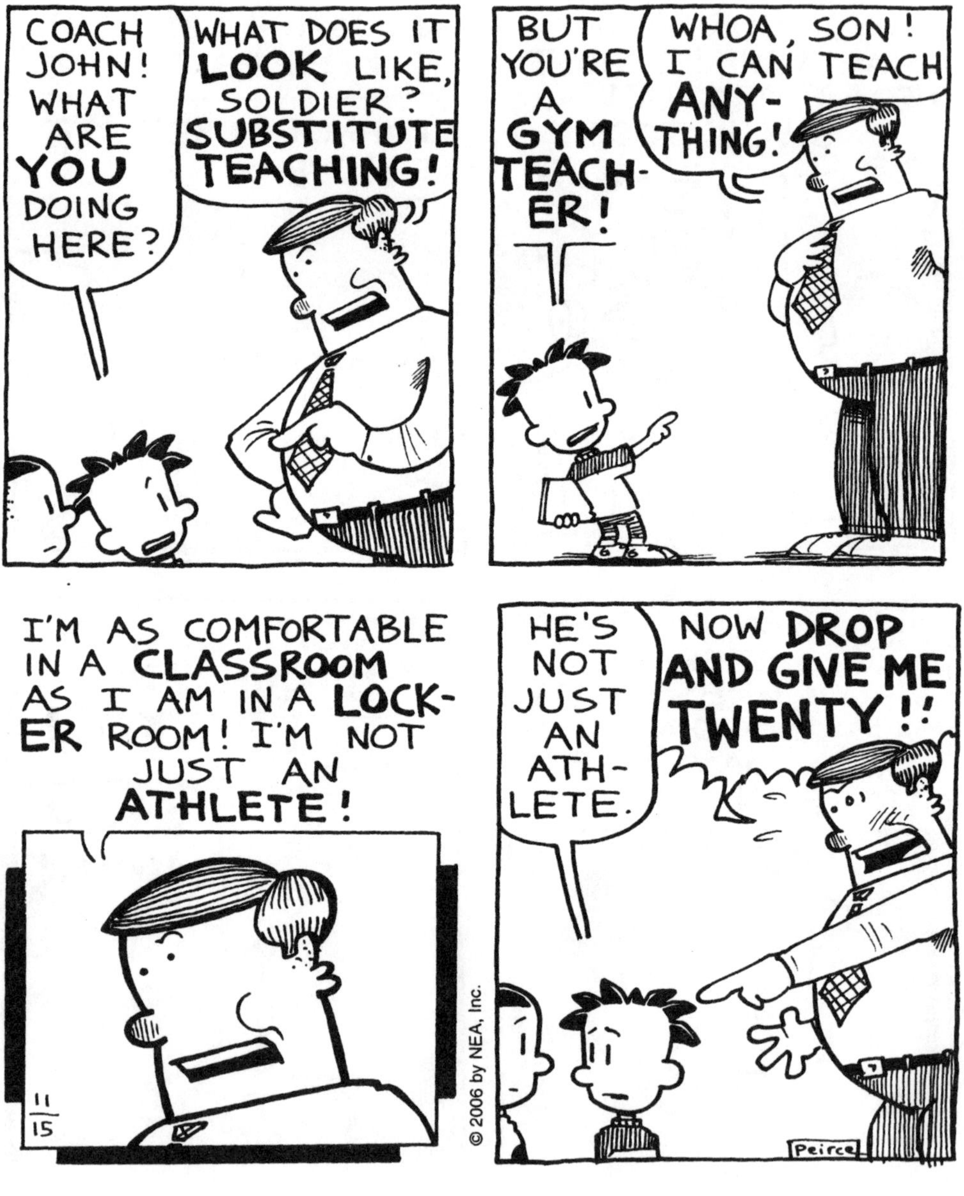
COACH JOHN! WHAT ARE YOU DOING HERE?
WHAT DOES IT LOOK LIKE, SOLDIER? SUBSTITUTE TEACHING!
BUT YOU'RE A GYM TEACHER!
WHOA, SON! I CAN TEACH ANYTHING!
I'M AS COMFORTABLE IN A CLASSROOM AS I AM IN A LOCKER ROOM! I'M NOT JUST AN ATHLETE!
11/15
HE'S NOT JUST AN ATHLETE.
NOW DROP AND GIVE ME TWENTY!!
Peirce

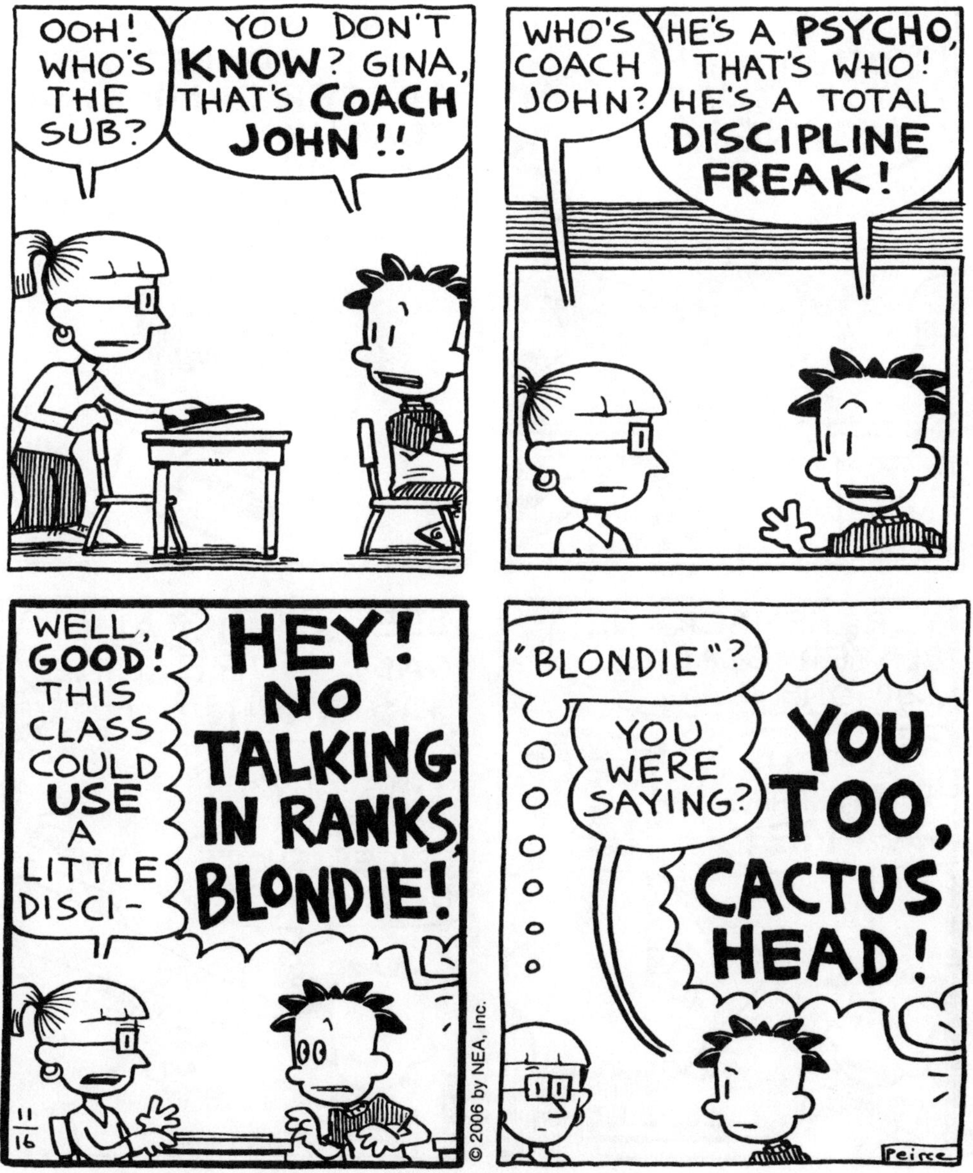
OOH! WHO'S THE SUB?
YOU DON'T KNOW? GINA, THAT'S COACH JOHN!!
WHO'S COACH JOHN?
HE'S A PSYCHO, THAT'S WHO! HE'S A TOTAL DISCIPLINE FREAK!
WELL, GOOD! THIS CLASS COULD USE A LITTLE DISCI-
HEY! NO TALKING IN RANKS, BLONDIE!
11/16
© 2006 by NEA, Inc.
"BLONDIE"?
YOU WERE SAYING?
YOU TOO, CACTUS HEAD!
Peirce

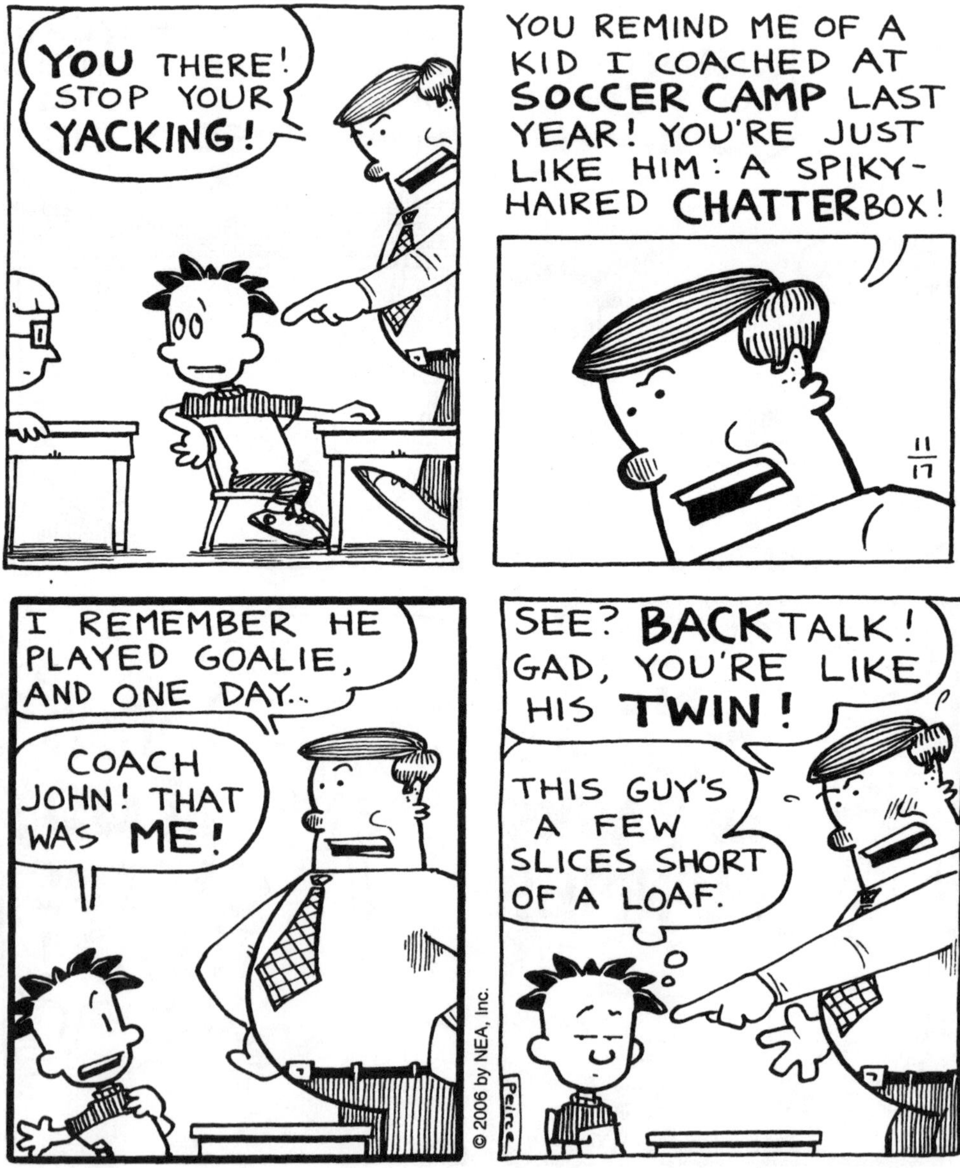
YOU THERE! STOP YOUR YACKING!
YOU REMIND ME OF A KID I COACHED AT SOCCER CAMP LAST YEAR! YOU'RE JUST LIKE HIM: A SPIKY-HAIRED CHATTERBOX!
11/17
I REMEMBER HE PLAYED GOALIE, AND ONE DAY...
COACH JOHN! THAT WAS ME!
SEE? BACKTALK! GAD, YOU'RE LIKE HIS TWIN!
THIS GUY'S A FEW SLICES SHORT OF A LOAF.
Peirce
© 2006 by NEA, Inc.

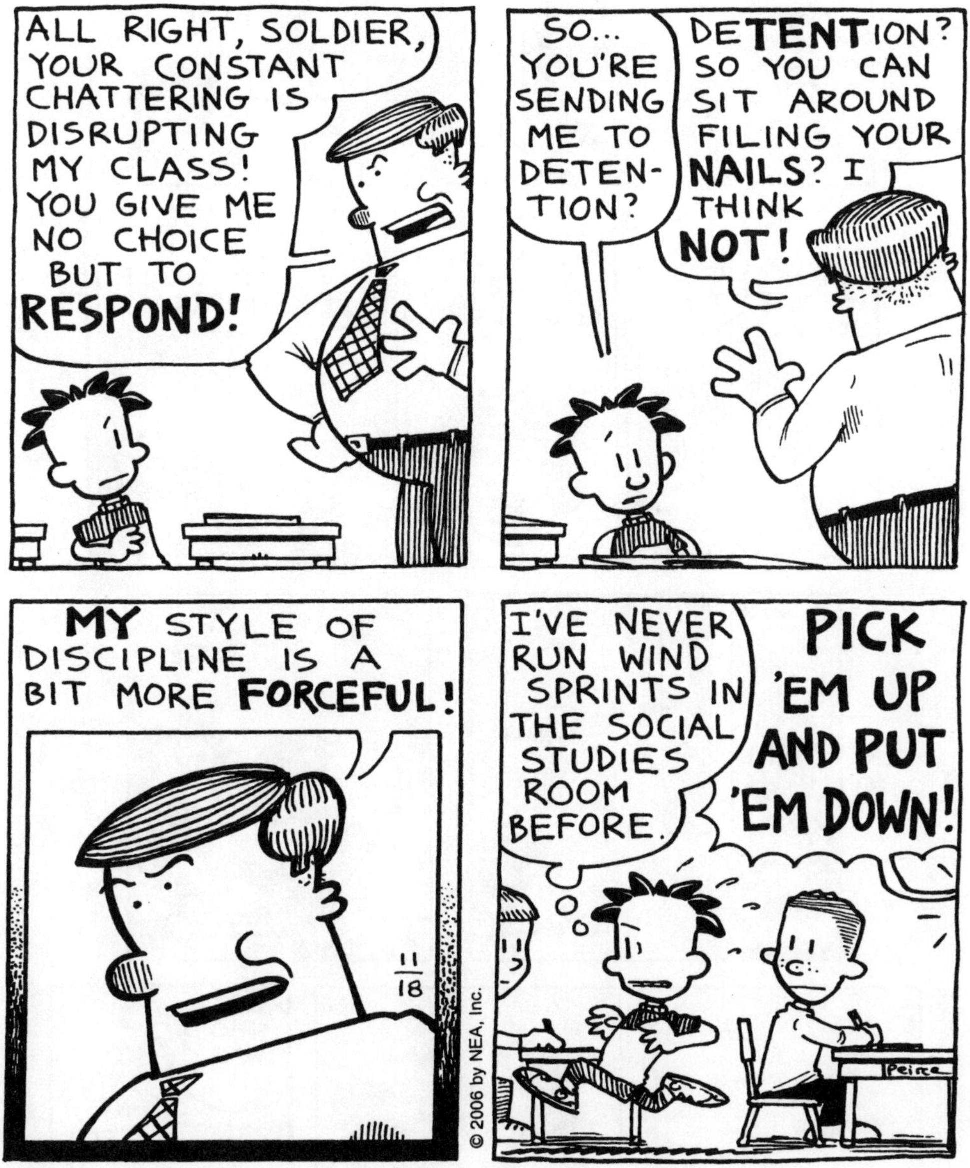
ALL RIGHT, SOLDIER, YOUR CONSTANT CHATTERING IS DISRUPTING MY CLASS! YOU GIVE ME NO CHOICE BUT TO RESPOND!
SO... YOU'RE SENDING ME TO DETEN-TION?
DETENTION? SO YOU CAN SIT AROUND FILING YOUR NAILS? I THINK NOT!
MY STYLE OF DISCIPLINE IS A BIT MORE FORCEFUL!
11/18
© 2006 by NEA, Inc.
I'VE NEVER RUN WIND SPRINTS IN THE SOCIAL STUDIES ROOM BEFORE.
PICK 'EM UP AND PUT 'EM DOWN!
Peirce

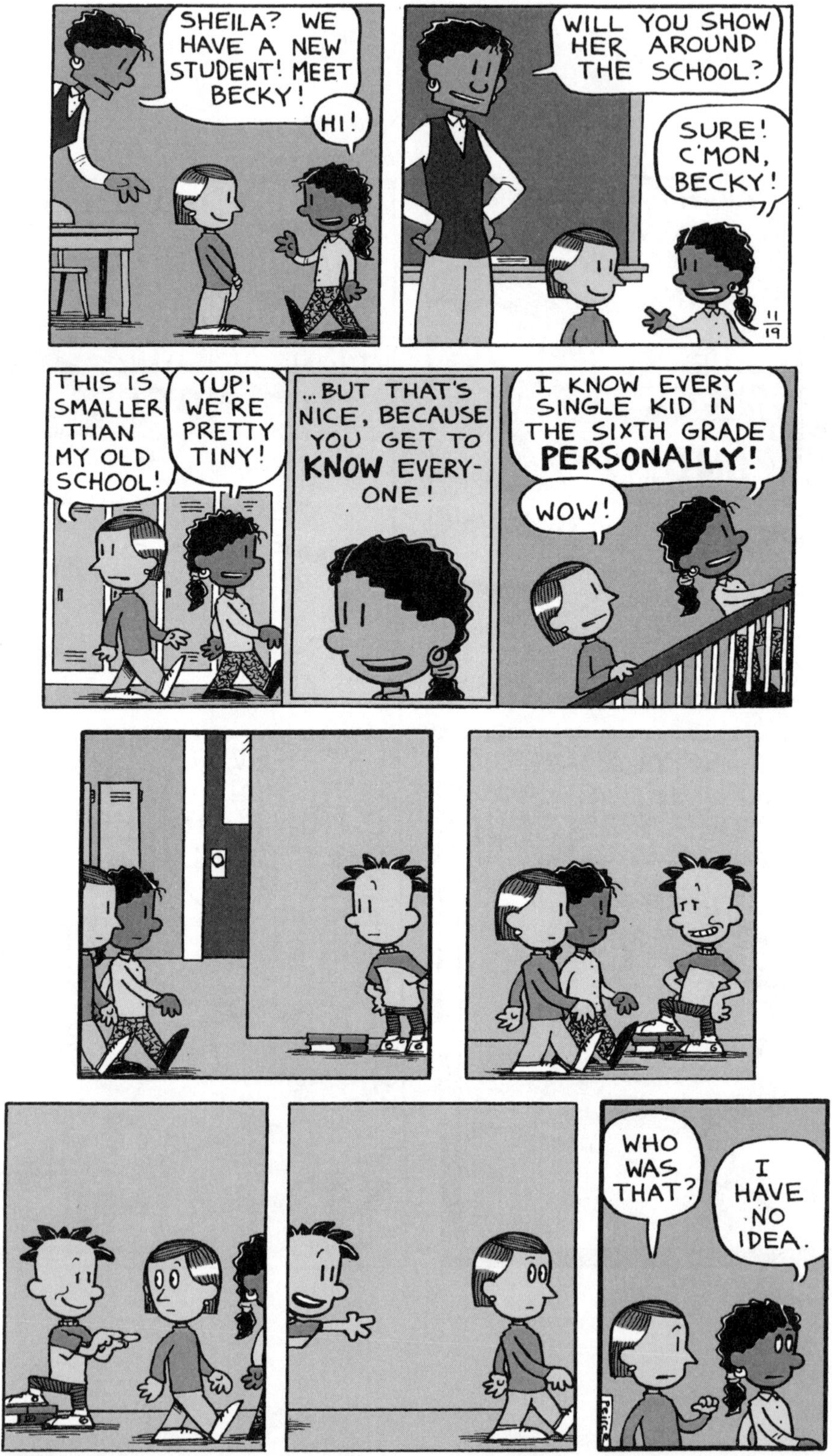
SHEILA? WE HAVE A NEW STUDENT! MEET BECKY!
HI!
WILL YOU SHOW HER AROUND THE SCHOOL?
SURE! C'MON, BECKY!
THIS IS SMALLER THAN MY OLD SCHOOL!
YUP! WE'RE PRETTY TINY!
...BUT THAT'S NICE, BECAUSE YOU GET TO **KNOW** EVERY-ONE!
I KNOW EVERY SINGLE KID IN THE SIXTH GRADE **PERSONALLY**!
WOW!
WHO WAS THAT?
I HAVE NO IDEA.

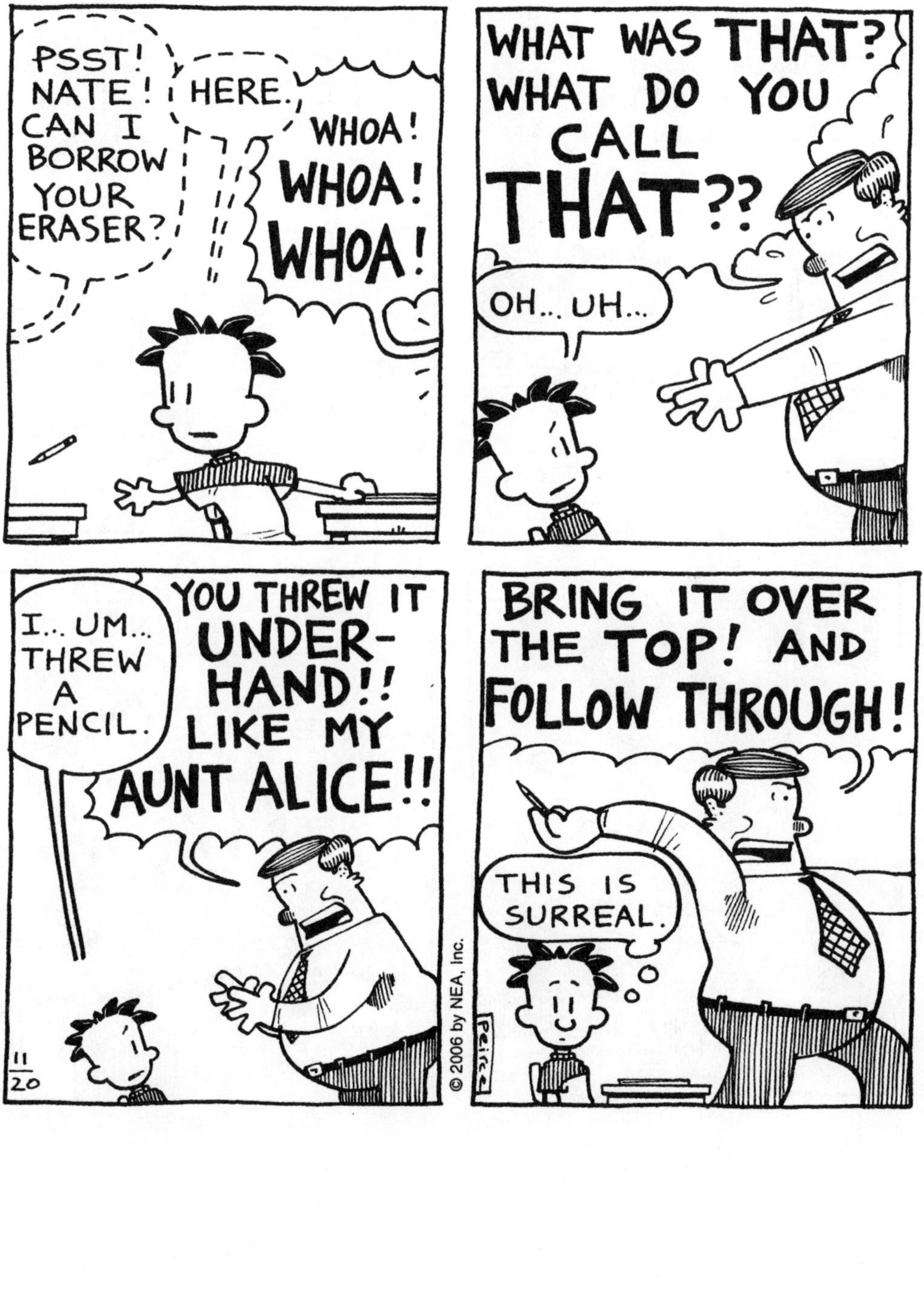
PSST! NATE! CAN I BORROW YOUR ERASER?
HERE.
WHOA! WHOA! WHOA!
WHAT WAS THAT? WHAT DO YOU CALL THAT??
OH... UH...
I... UM... THREW A PENCIL.
YOU THREW IT UNDER-HAND!! LIKE MY AUNT ALICE!!
11/20
© 2006 by NEA, Inc.
Peirce
BRING IT OVER THE TOP! AND FOLLOW THROUGH!
THIS IS SURREAL.

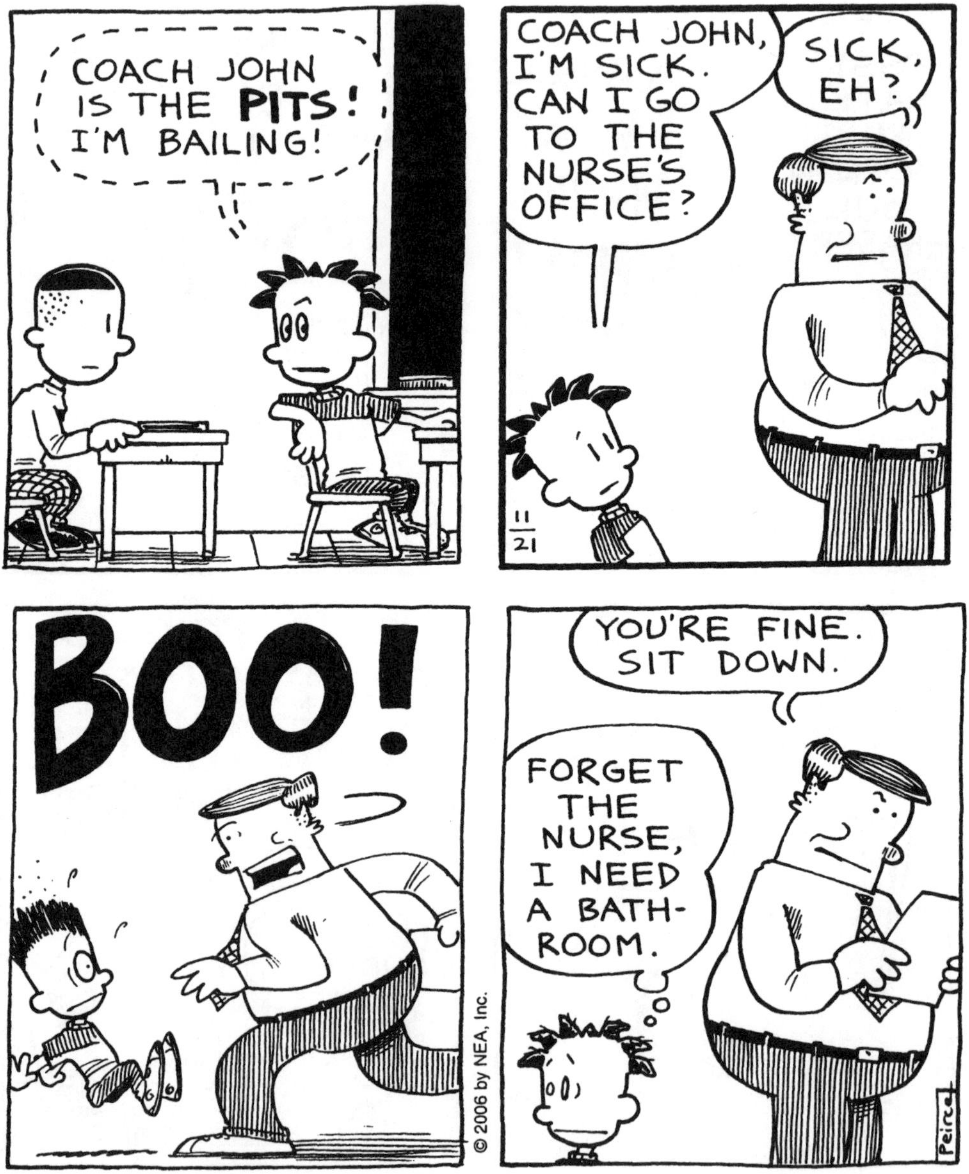
COACH JOHN IS THE **PITS**! I'M BAILING!
COACH JOHN, I'M SICK. CAN I GO TO THE NURSE'S OFFICE?
SICK, EH?
11/21
BOO!
YOU'RE FINE. SIT DOWN.
FORGET THE NURSE, I NEED A BATH-ROOM.
Peirce
© 2006 by NEA, Inc.

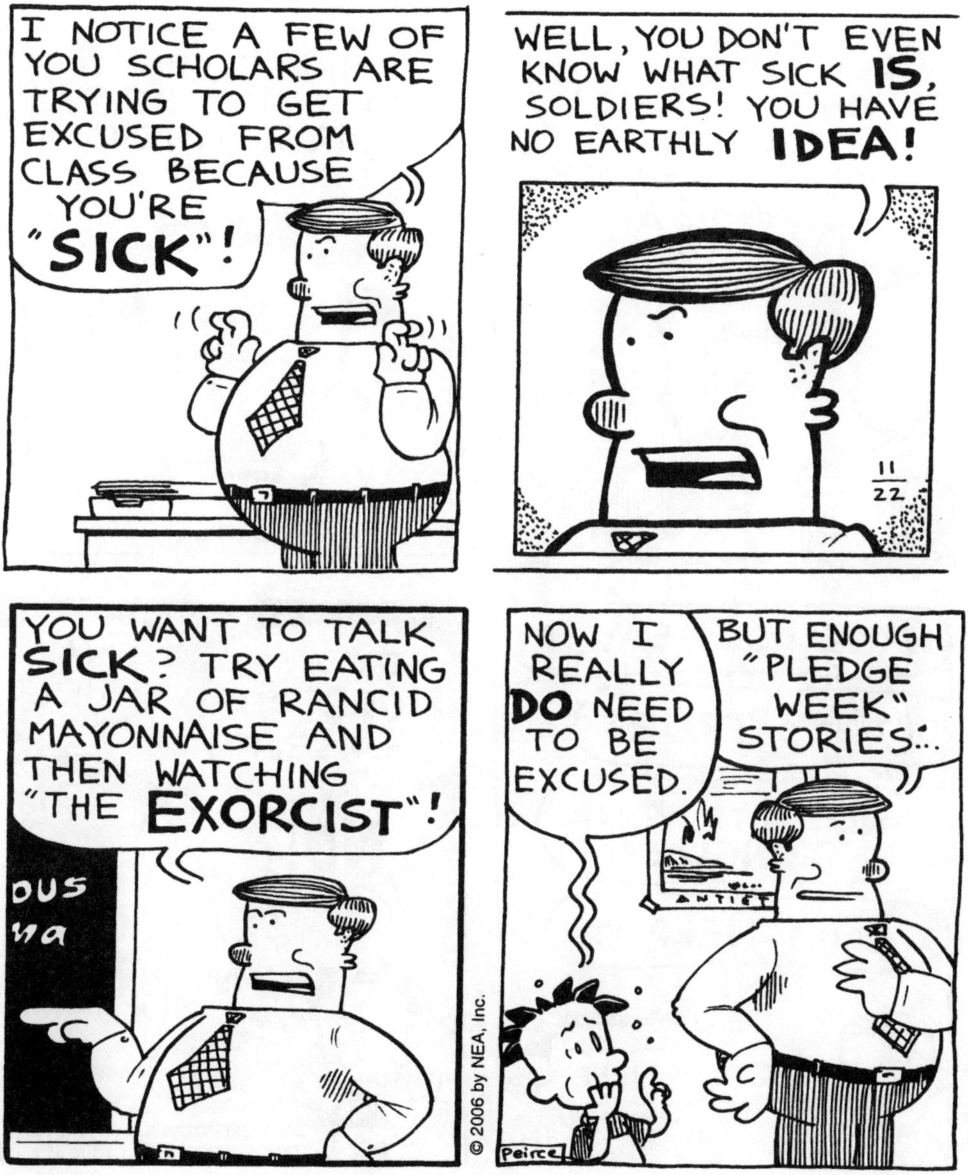
I NOTICE A FEW OF YOU SCHOLARS ARE TRYING TO GET EXCUSED FROM CLASS BECAUSE YOU'RE "SICK"!
WELL, YOU DON'T EVEN KNOW WHAT SICK IS, SOLDIERS! YOU HAVE NO EARTHLY IDEA!
11/22
YOU WANT TO TALK SICK? TRY EATING A JAR OF RANCID MAYONNAISE AND THEN WATCHING "THE EXORCIST"!
NOW I REALLY DO NEED TO BE EXCUSED.
BUT ENOUGH "PLEDGE WEEK" STORIES...
Peirce

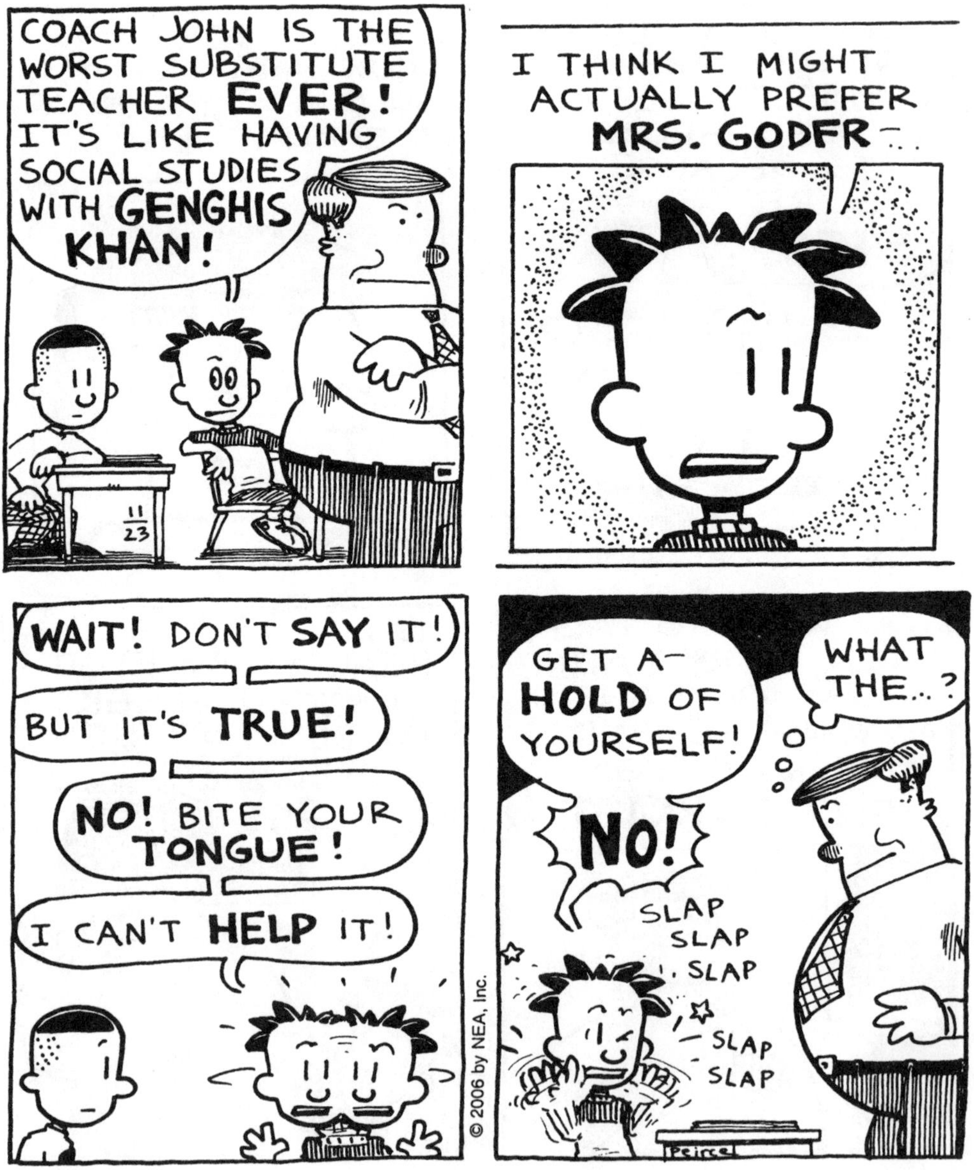

COACH JOHN IS THE WORST SUBSTITUTE TEACHER EVER! IT'S LIKE HAVING SOCIAL STUDIES WITH GENGHIS KHAN!
11/23
I THINK I MIGHT ACTUALLY PREFER MRS. GODFR–...
WAIT! DON'T SAY IT!
BUT IT'S TRUE!
NO! BITE YOUR TONGUE!
I CAN'T HELP IT!
© 2006 by NEA, Inc.
GET A- HOLD OF YOURSELF!
WHAT THE..?
NO!
SLAP
SLAP
SLAP
SLAP
SLAP
Peirce

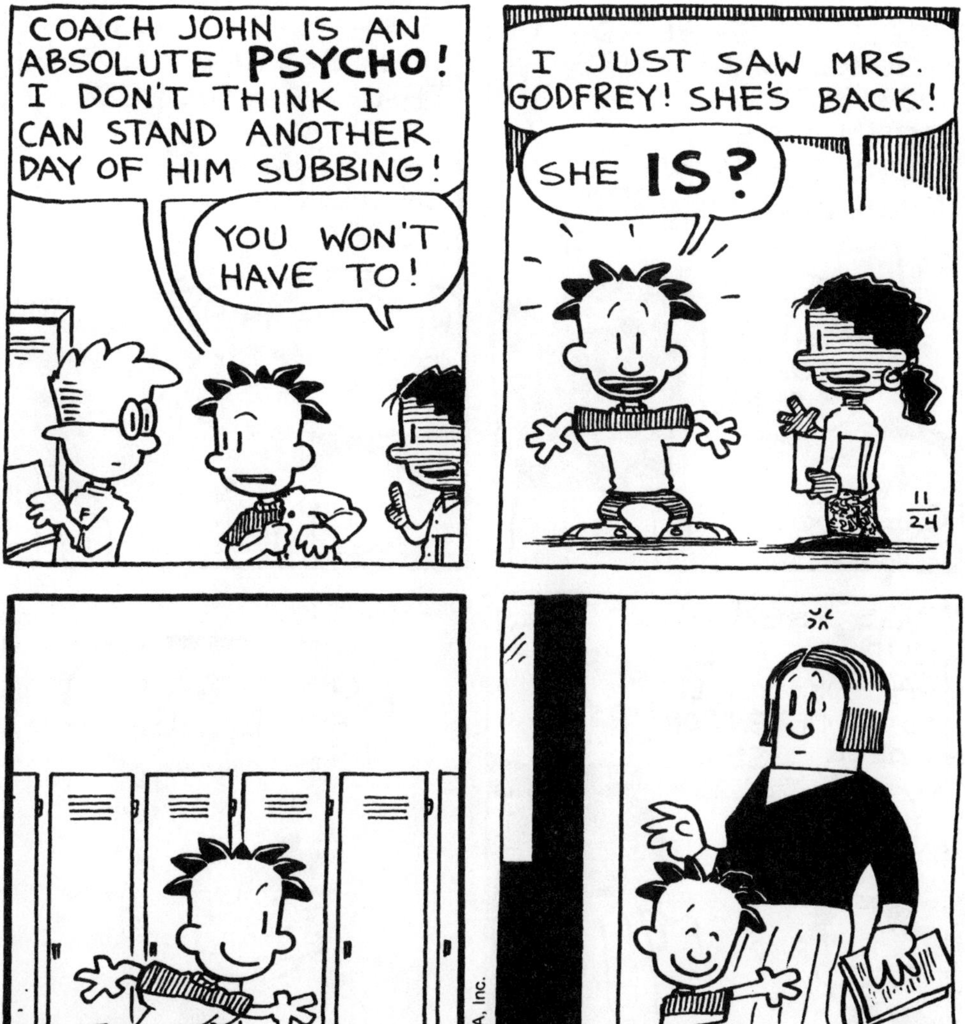
COACH JOHN IS AN ABSOLUTE PSYCHO! I DON'T THINK I CAN STAND ANOTHER DAY OF HIM SUBBING!
YOU WON'T HAVE TO!
I JUST SAW MRS. GODFREY! SHE'S BACK!
SHE IS?
11
24
© 2006 by NEA, Inc.
peirce

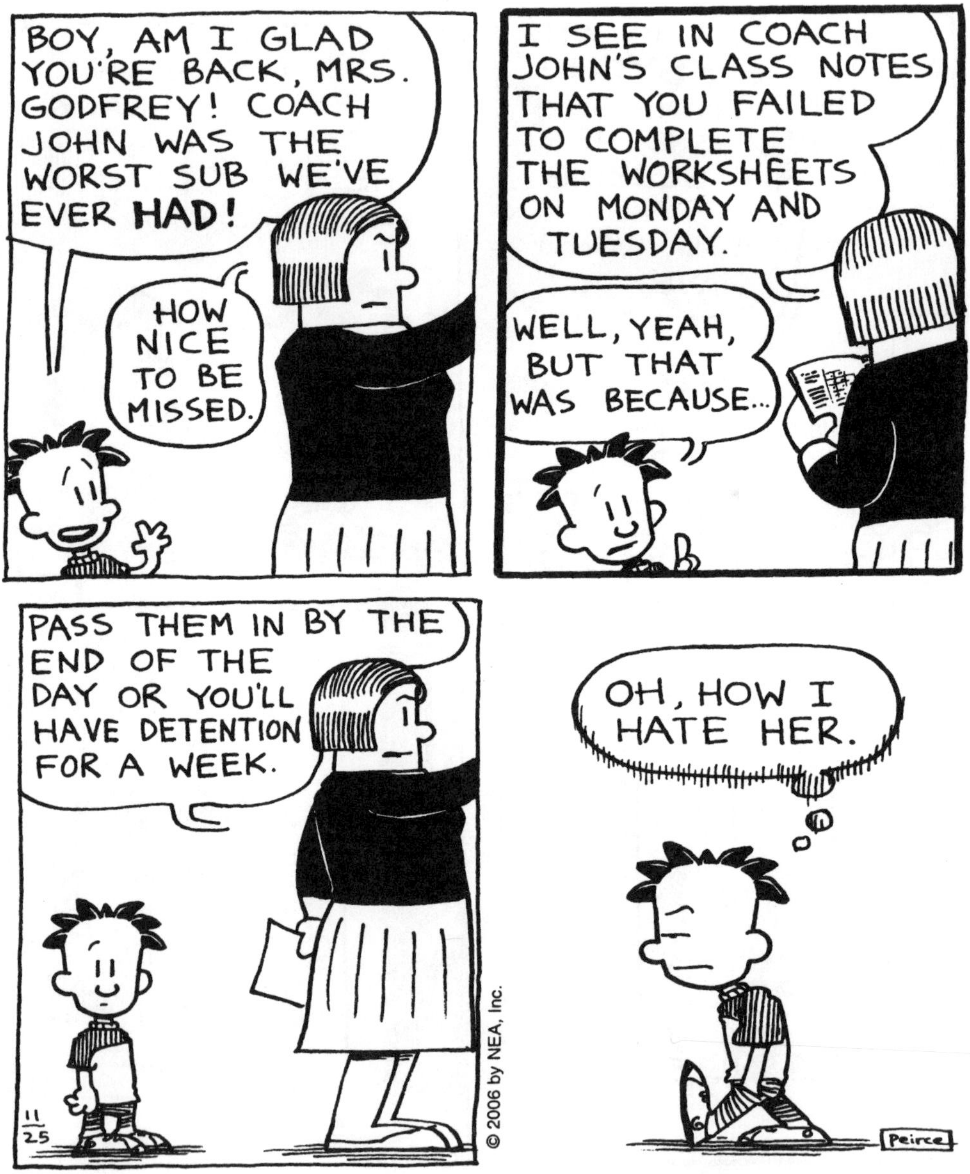
BOY, AM I GLAD YOU'RE BACK, MRS. GODFREY! COACH JOHN WAS THE WORST SUB WE'VE EVER **HAD**!
HOW NICE TO BE MISSED.
I SEE IN COACH JOHN'S CLASS NOTES THAT YOU FAILED TO COMPLETE THE WORKSHEETS ON MONDAY AND TUESDAY.
WELL, YEAH, BUT THAT WAS BECAUSE...
PASS THEM IN BY THE END OF THE DAY OR YOU'LL HAVE DETENTION FOR A WEEK.
OH, HOW I HATE HER.
11/25
© 2006 by NEA, Inc.
Peirce

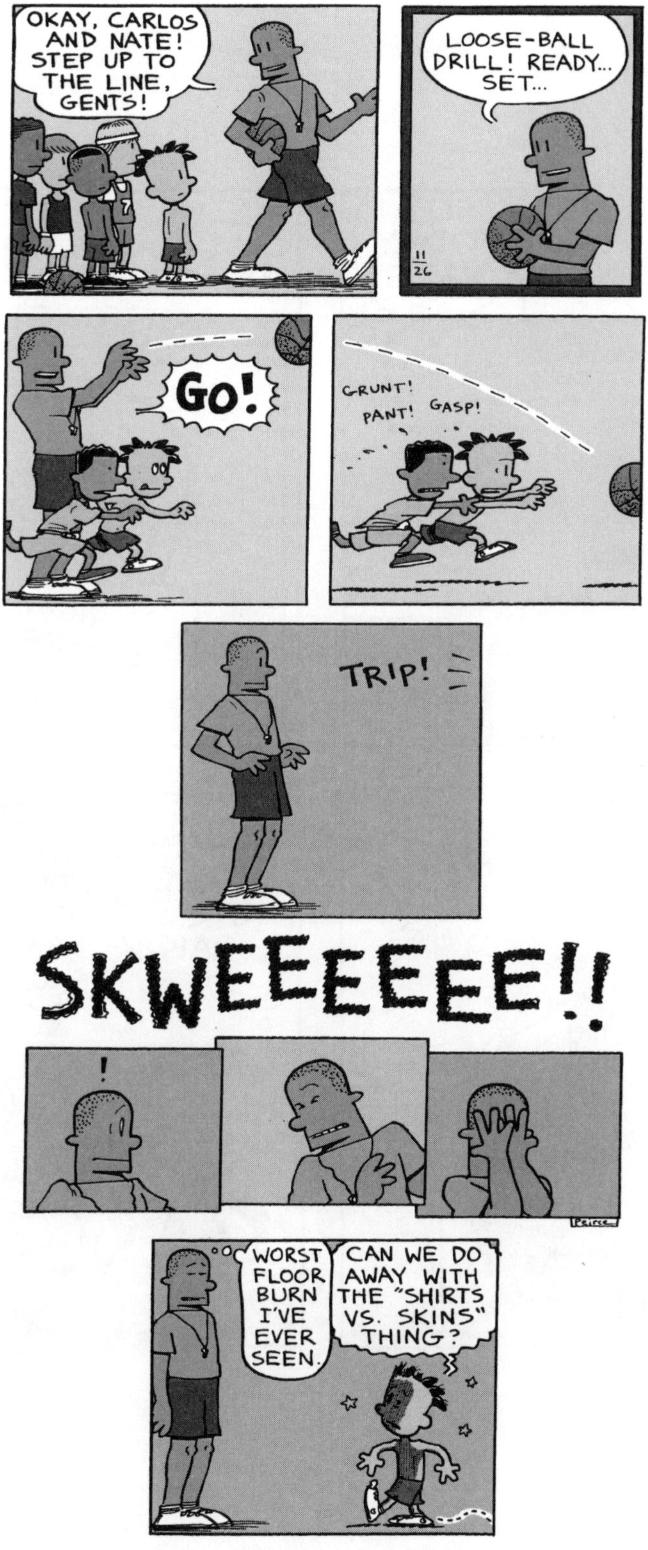
OKAY, CARLOS AND NATE! STEP UP TO THE LINE, GENTS!
LOOSE-BALL DRILL! READY... SET...
GO!
GRUNT!
PANT!
GASP!
TRIP!
SKWEEEEEEE!!
!
WORST FLOOR BURN I'VE EVER SEEN.
CAN WE DO AWAY WITH THE "SHIRTS VS. SKINS" THING?

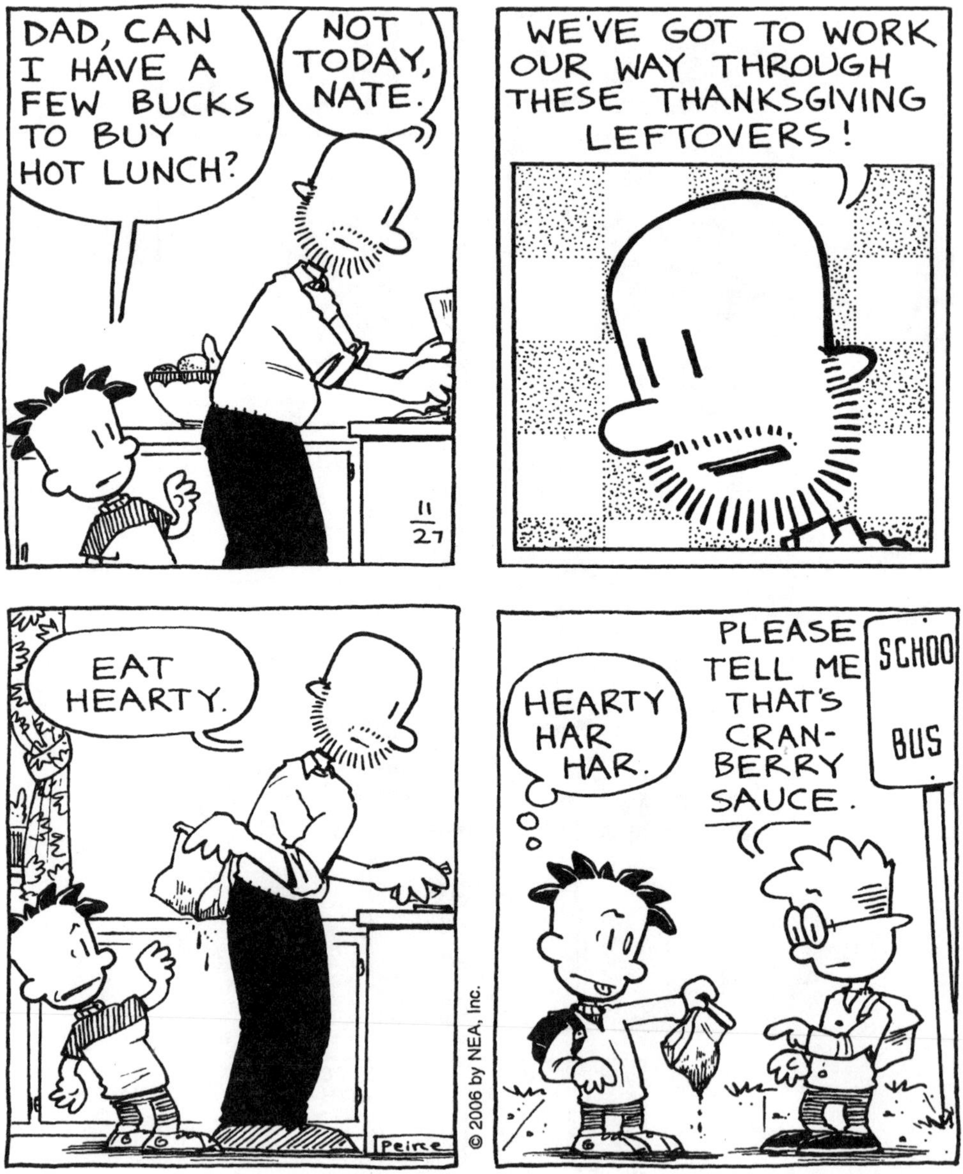
DAD, CAN I HAVE A FEW BUCKS TO BUY HOT LUNCH?
NOT TODAY, NATE.
11/27
WE'VE GOT TO WORK OUR WAY THROUGH THESE THANKSGIVING LEFTOVERS!
EAT HEARTY.
Peirce
© 2006 by NEA, Inc.
HEARTY HAR HAR.
PLEASE TELL ME THAT'S CRAN-BERRY SAUCE.
SCHOO
BUS

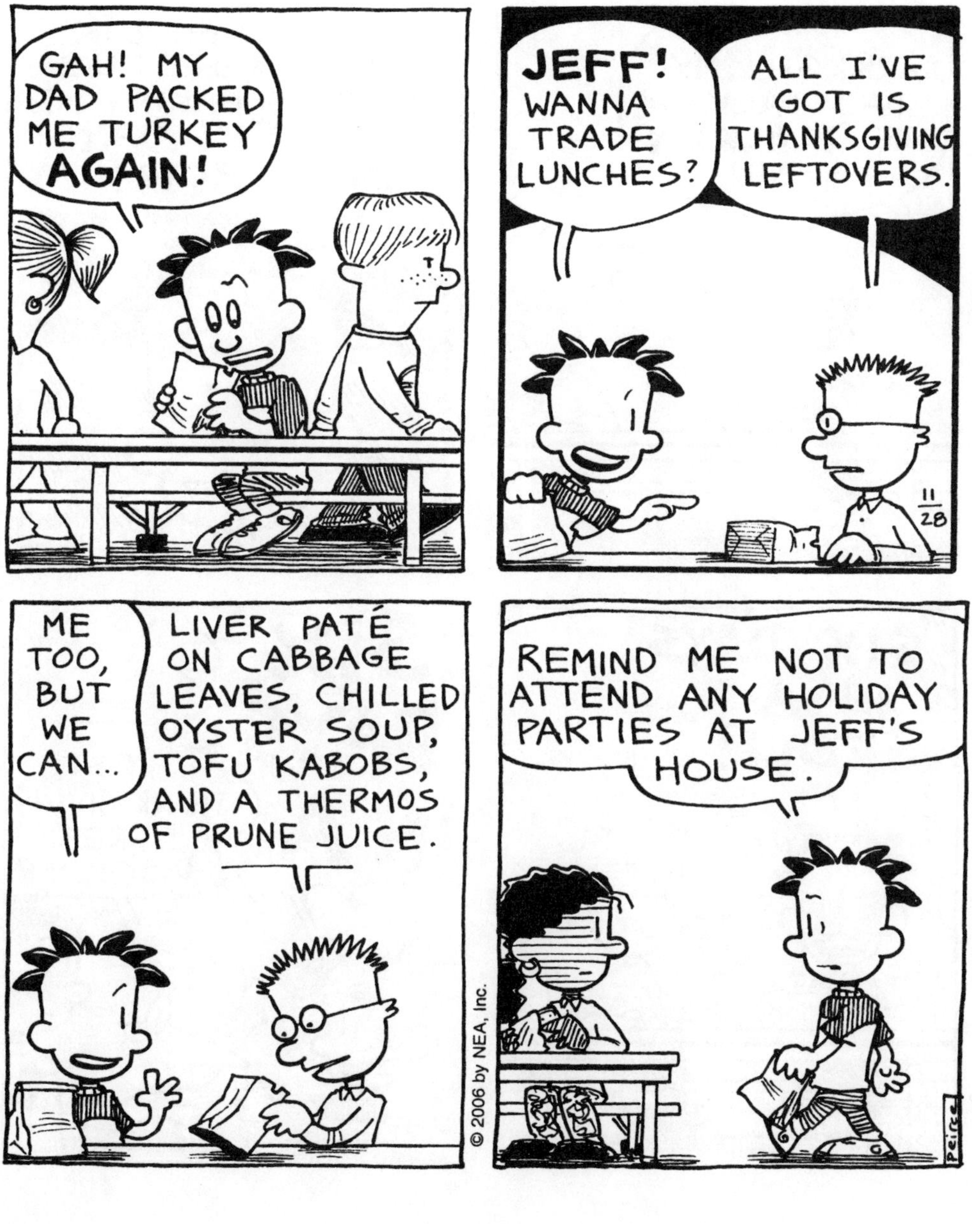
GAH! MY DAD PACKED ME TURKEY **AGAIN**!
JEFF! WANNA TRADE LUNCHES?
ALL I'VE GOT IS THANKSGIVING LEFTOVERS.
11/28
ME TOO, BUT WE CAN...
LIVER PATÉ ON CABBAGE LEAVES, CHILLED OYSTER SOUP, TOFU KABOBS, AND A THERMOS OF PRUNE JUICE.
© 2006 by NEA, Inc.
REMIND ME NOT TO ATTEND ANY HOLIDAY PARTIES AT JEFF'S HOUSE.
PEIRCE

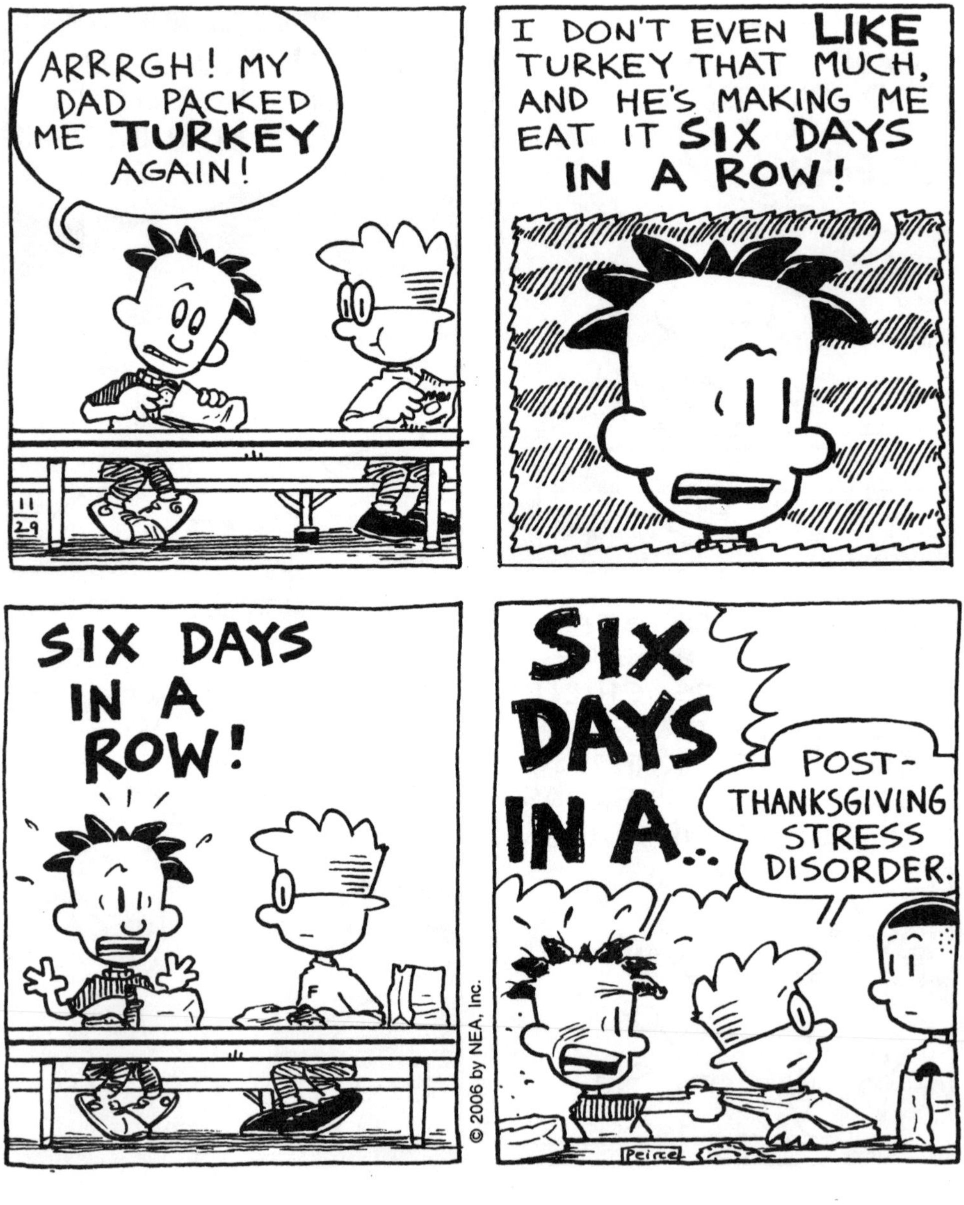
ARRRGH! MY DAD PACKED ME TURKEY AGAIN!
11 29
I DON'T EVEN LIKE TURKEY THAT MUCH, AND HE'S MAKING ME EAT IT SIX DAYS IN A ROW!
SIX DAYS IN A ROW!
© 2006 by NEA, Inc.
SIX DAYS IN A...
POST-THANKSGIVING STRESS DISORDER.
Peirce

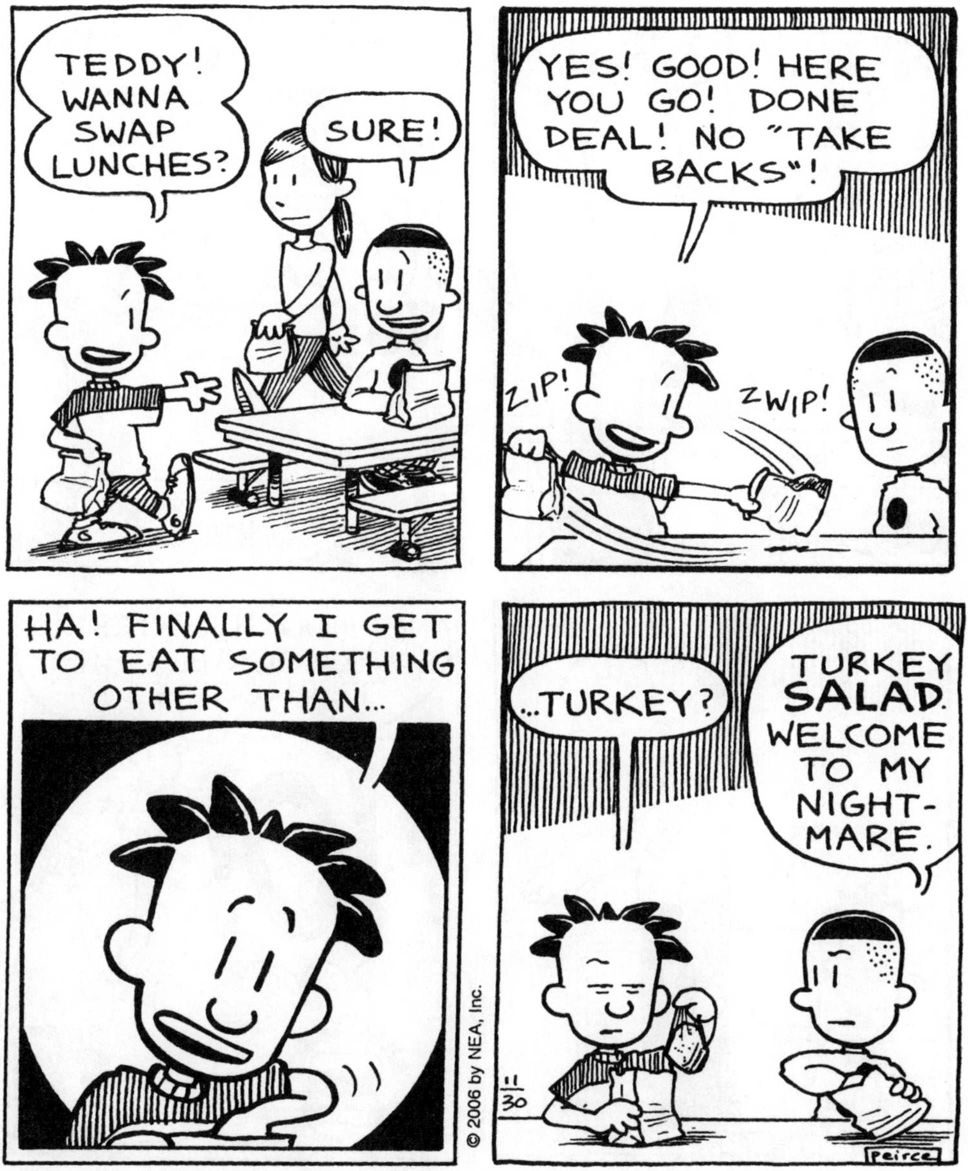
TEDDY! WANNA SWAP LUNCHES?
SURE!
YES! GOOD! HERE YOU GO! DONE DEAL! NO "TAKE BACKS"!
ZIP!
ZWIP!
HA! FINALLY I GET TO EAT SOMETHING OTHER THAN...
...TURKEY?
TURKEY SALAD. WELCOME TO MY NIGHT-MARE.
11 30
© 2006 by NEA, Inc.
peirce

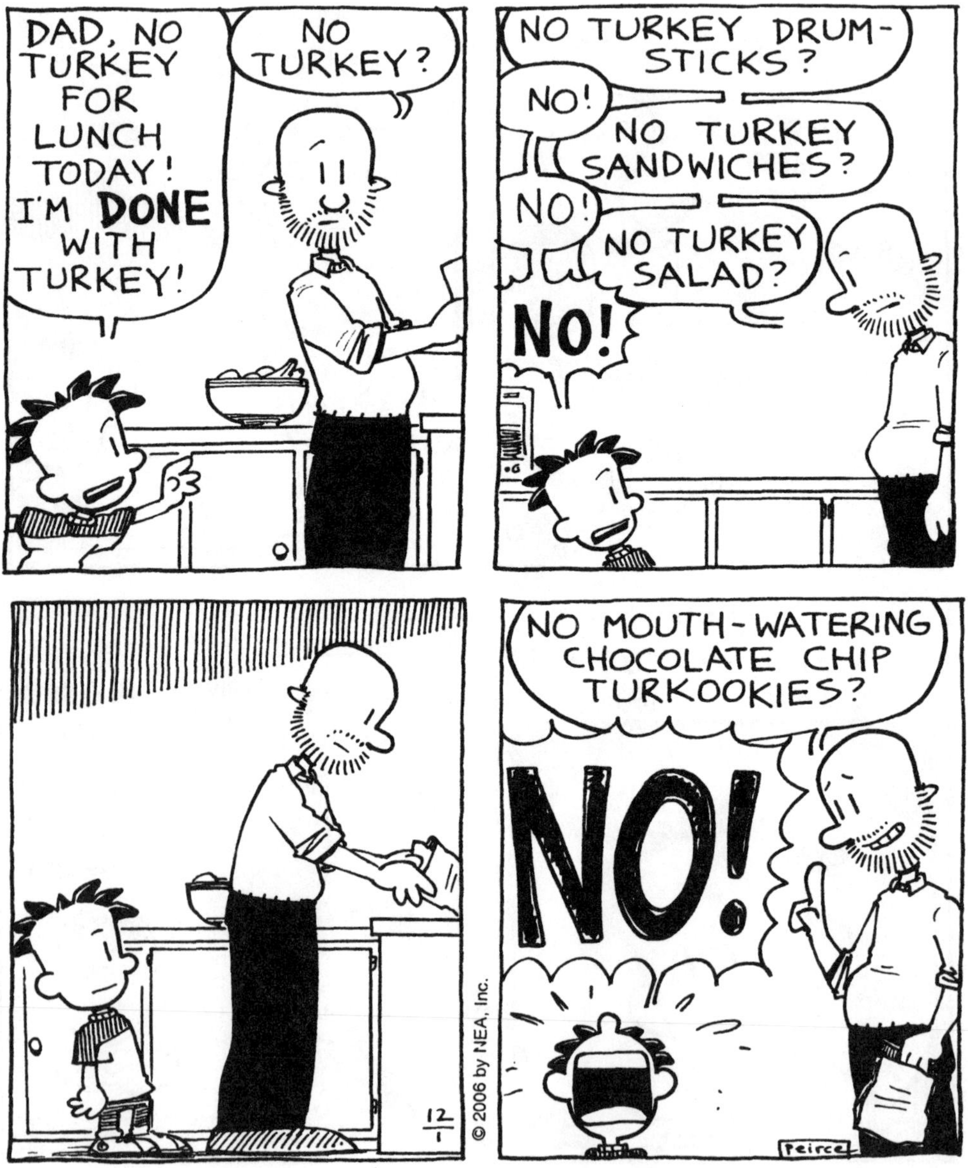
DAD, NO TURKEY FOR LUNCH TODAY! I'M DONE WITH TURKEY!
NO TURKEY?
NO TURKEY DRUM-STICKS?
NO!
NO TURKEY SANDWICHES?
NO!
NO TURKEY SALAD?
NO!
12/1
© 2006 by NEA, Inc.
NO MOUTH-WATERING CHOCOLATE CHIP TURKOOKIES?
NO!
Peirce

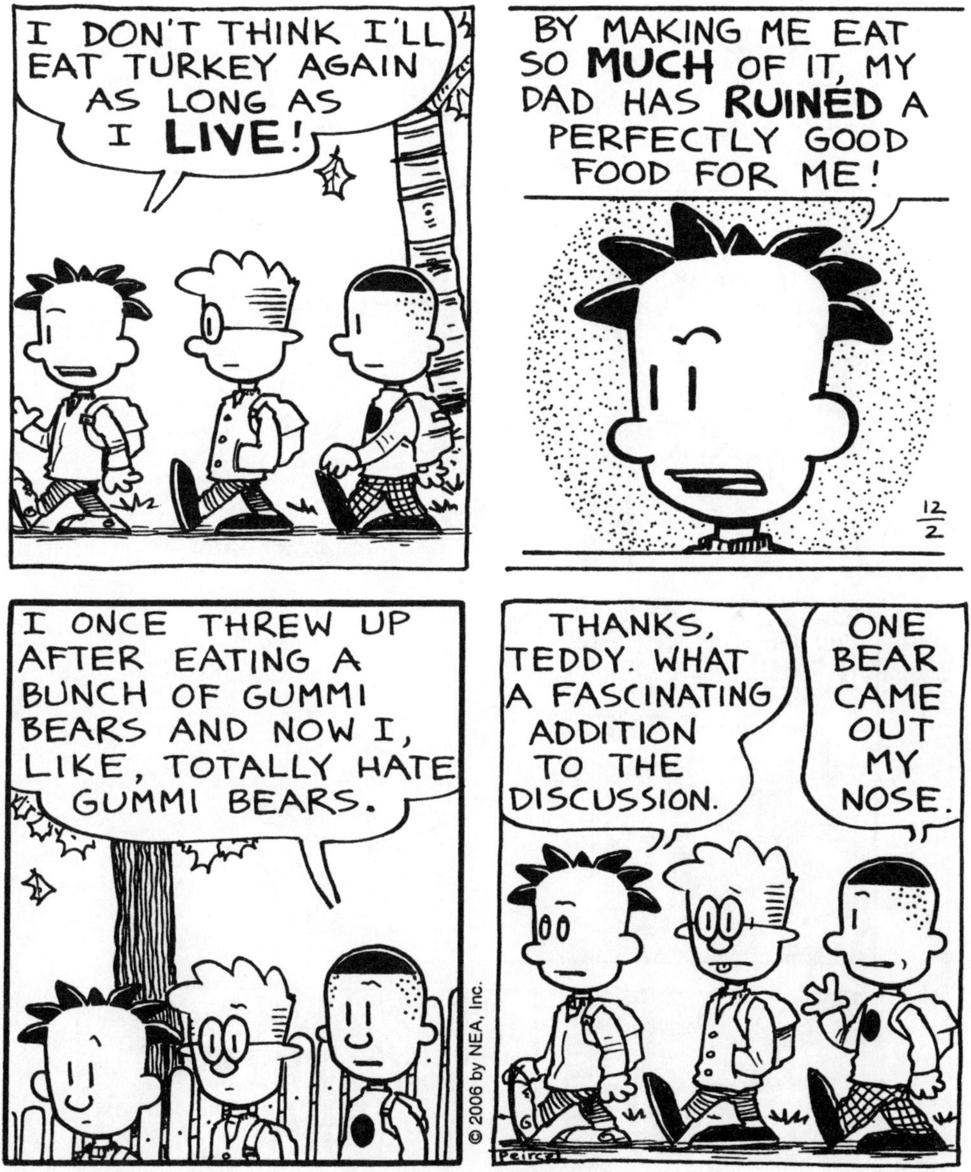
I DON'T THINK I'LL EAT TURKEY AGAIN AS LONG AS I **LIVE**!
BY MAKING ME EAT SO **MUCH** OF IT, MY DAD HAS **RUINED** A PERFECTLY GOOD FOOD FOR ME!
12/2
I ONCE THREW UP AFTER EATING A BUNCH OF GUMMI BEARS AND NOW I, LIKE, TOTALLY HATE GUMMI BEARS.
© 2006 by NEA, Inc.
THANKS, TEDDY. WHAT A FASCINATING ADDITION TO THE DISCUSSION.
ONE BEAR CAME OUT MY NOSE.
Peircz

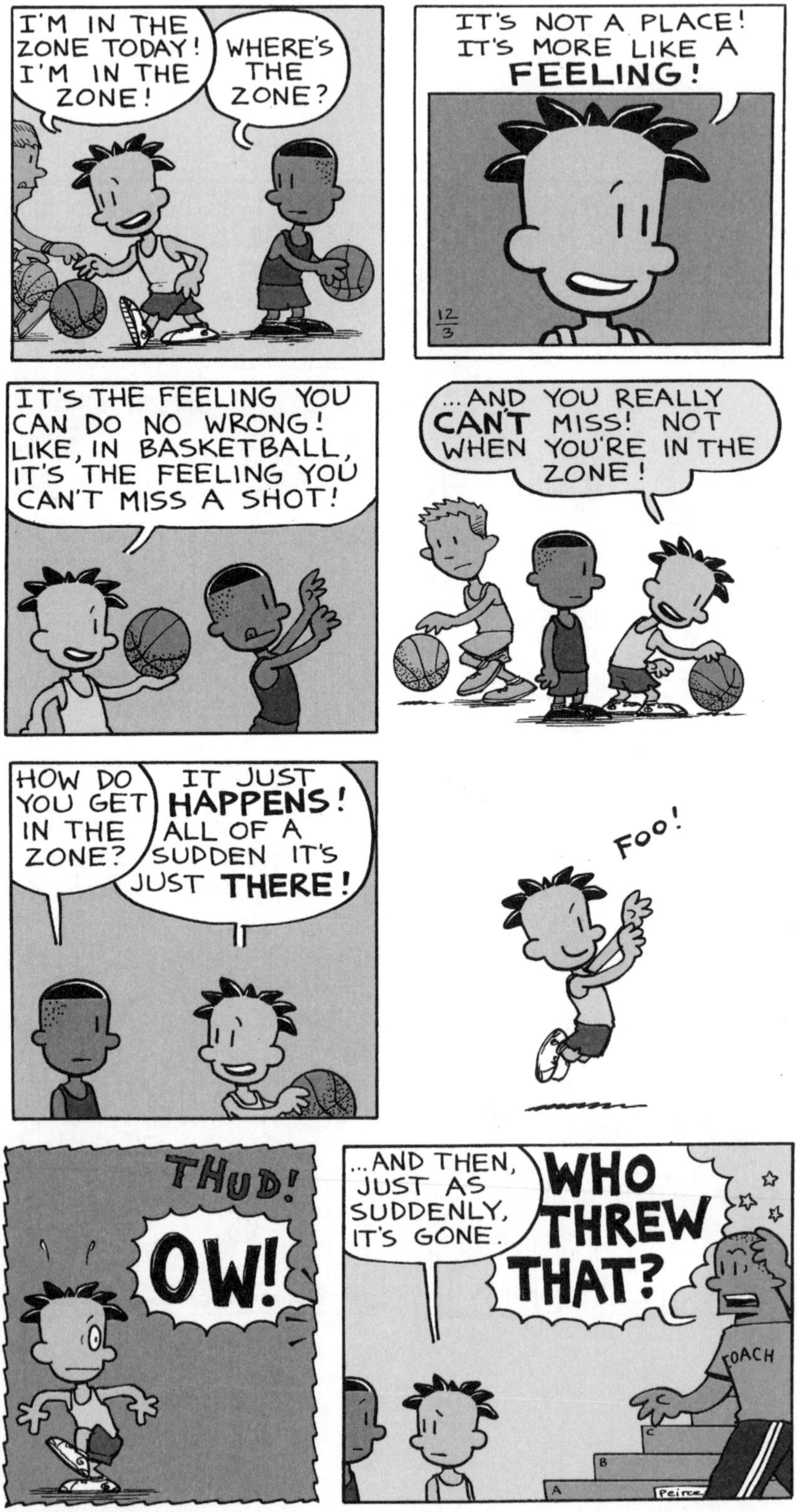
I'M IN THE ZONE TODAY! I'M IN THE ZONE!
WHERE'S THE ZONE?
IT'S NOT A PLACE! IT'S MORE LIKE A FEELING!
12/3
IT'S THE FEELING YOU CAN DO NO WRONG! LIKE, IN BASKETBALL, IT'S THE FEELING YOU CAN'T MISS A SHOT!
...AND YOU REALLY CAN'T MISS! NOT WHEN YOU'RE IN THE ZONE!
HOW DO YOU GET IN THE ZONE?
IT JUST HAPPENS! ALL OF A SUDDEN IT'S JUST THERE!
FOO!
THUD!
OW!
...AND THEN, JUST AS SUDDENLY, IT'S GONE.
WHO THREW THAT?
COACH
Peirce

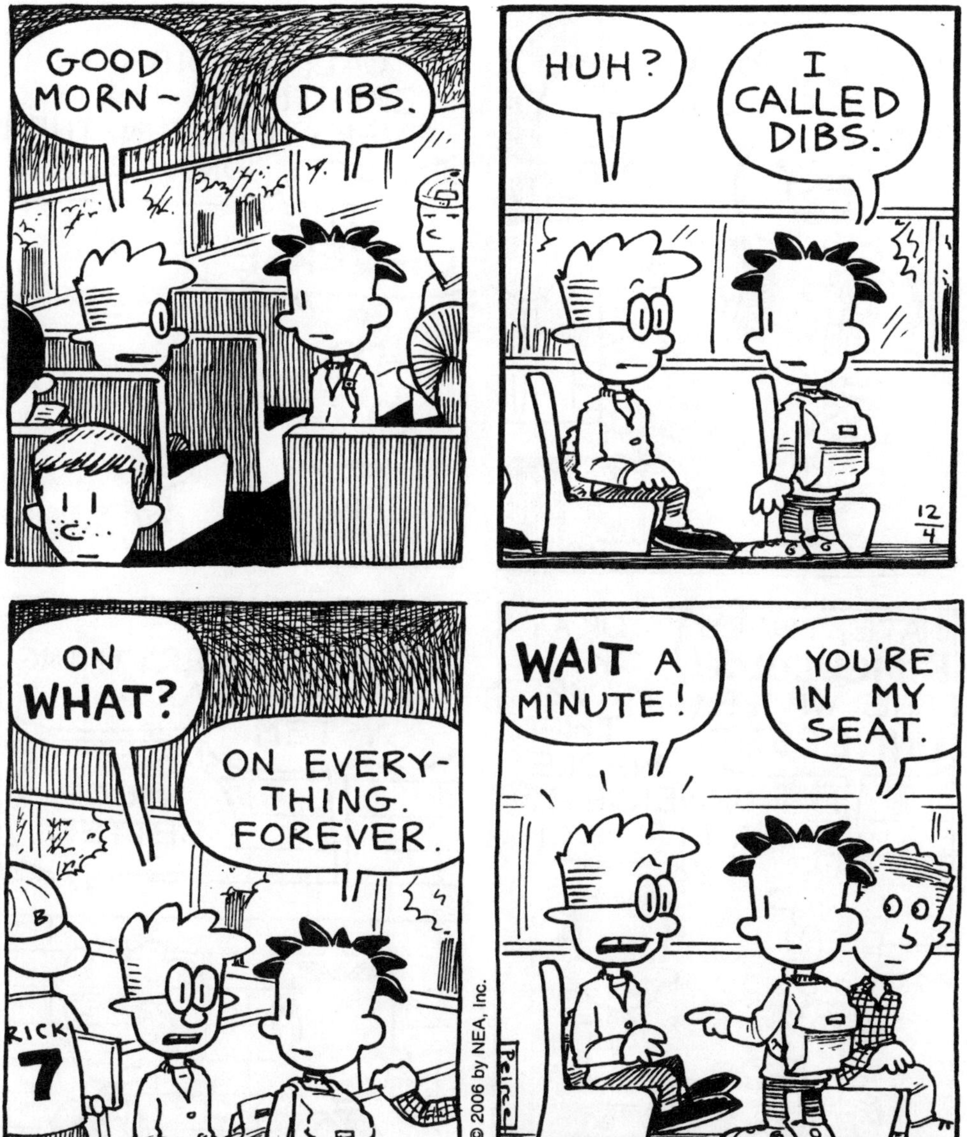
GOOD MORN~
DIBS.
HUH?
I CALLED DIBS.
12/4
ON WHAT?
ON EVERY-THING. FOREVER.
RICK
7
B
© 2006 by NEA, Inc.
Peirce
WAIT A MINUTE!
YOU'RE IN MY SEAT.

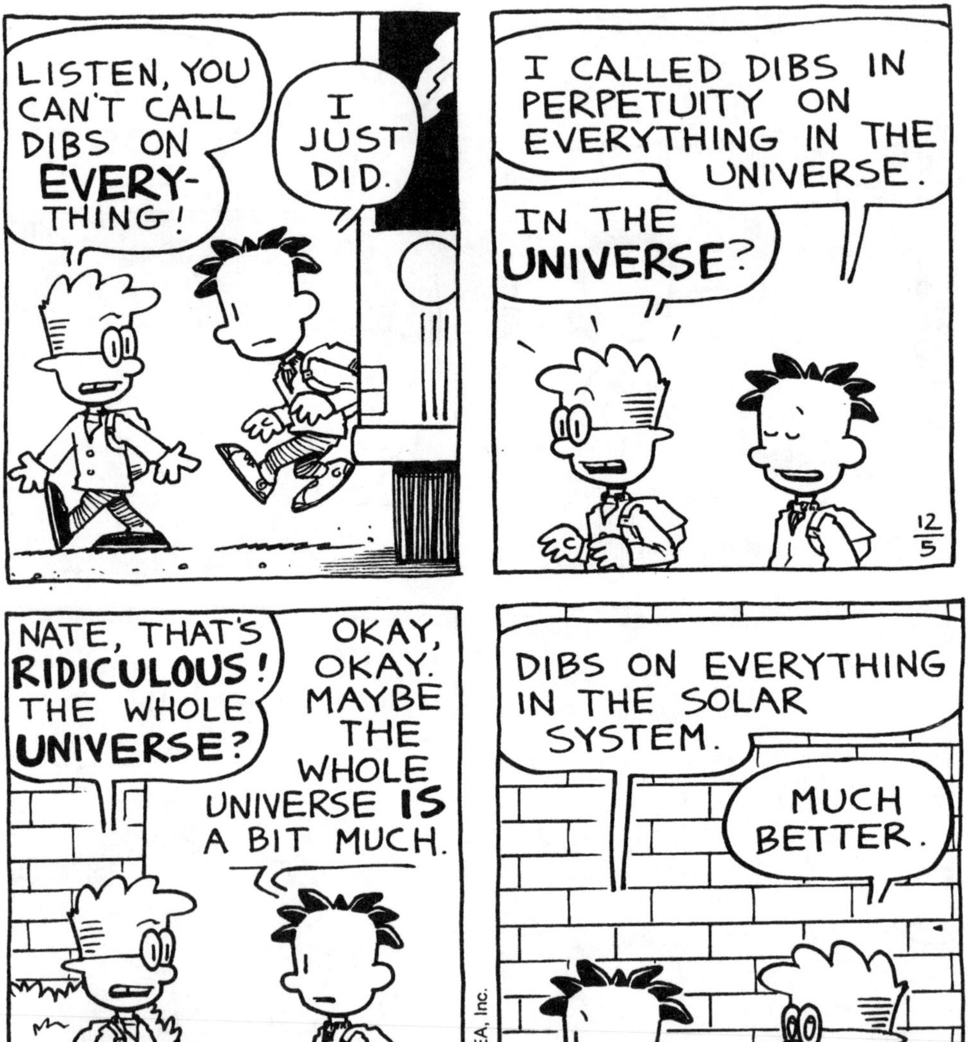
LISTEN, YOU CAN'T CALL DIBS ON **EVERY-THING**!
I JUST DID.
I CALLED DIBS IN PERPETUITY ON EVERYTHING IN THE UNIVERSE.
IN THE **UNIVERSE**?
12/5
NATE, THAT'S **RIDICULOUS**! THE WHOLE **UNIVERSE**?
OKAY, OKAY. MAYBE THE WHOLE UNIVERSE **IS** A BIT MUCH.
© 2006 by NEA, Inc.
DIBS ON EVERYTHING IN THE SOLAR SYSTEM.
MUCH BETTER.
Peirce

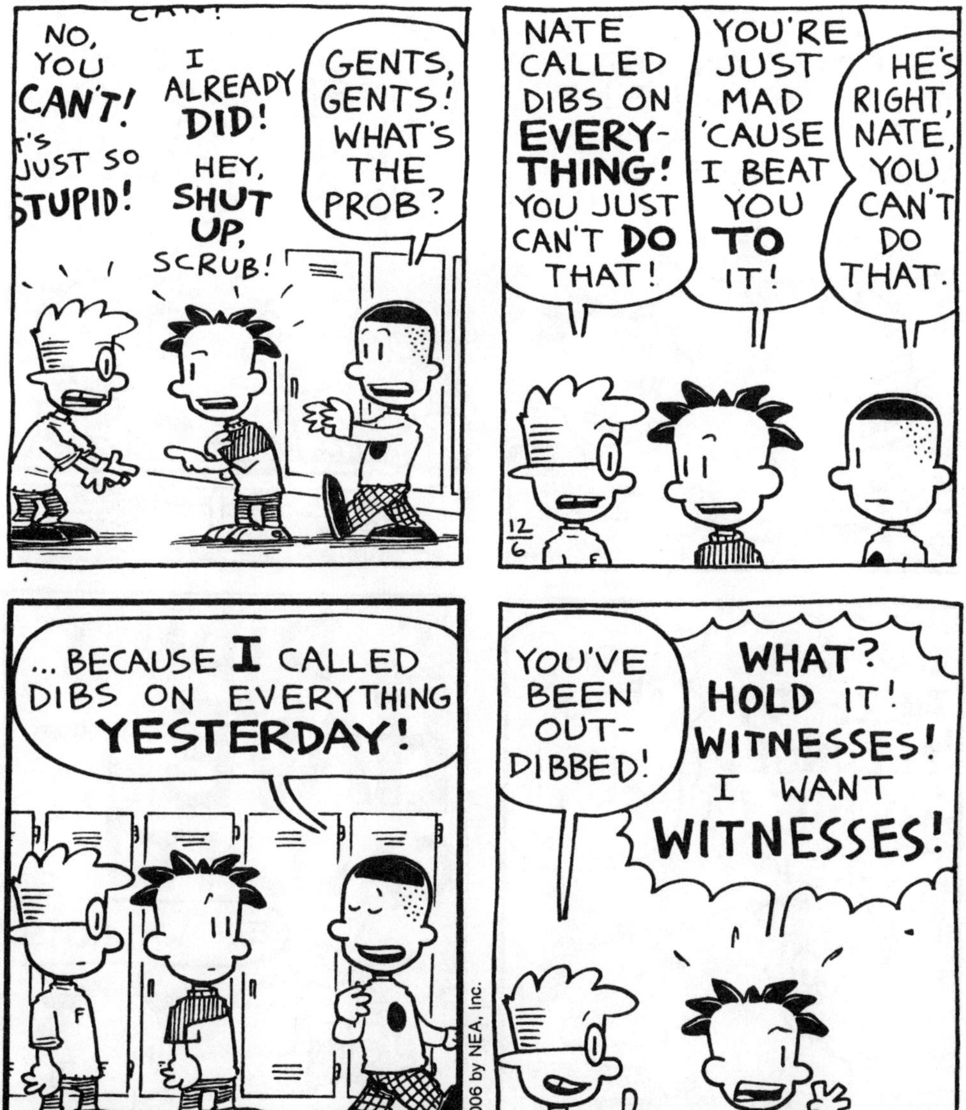
NO, YOU CAN'T! IT'S JUST SO STUPID!
I ALREADY DID! HEY, SHUT UP, SCRUB!
GENTS, GENTS! WHAT'S THE PROB?
NATE CALLED DIBS ON EVERYTHING! YOU JUST CAN'T DO THAT!
YOU'RE JUST MAD 'CAUSE I BEAT YOU TO IT!
HE'S RIGHT, NATE, YOU CAN'T DO THAT.
12/6
...BECAUSE I CALLED DIBS ON EVERYTHING YESTERDAY!
© 2006 by NEA, Inc.
YOU'VE BEEN OUT-DIBBED!
WHAT? HOLD IT! WITNESSES! I WANT WITNESSES!
Peirce

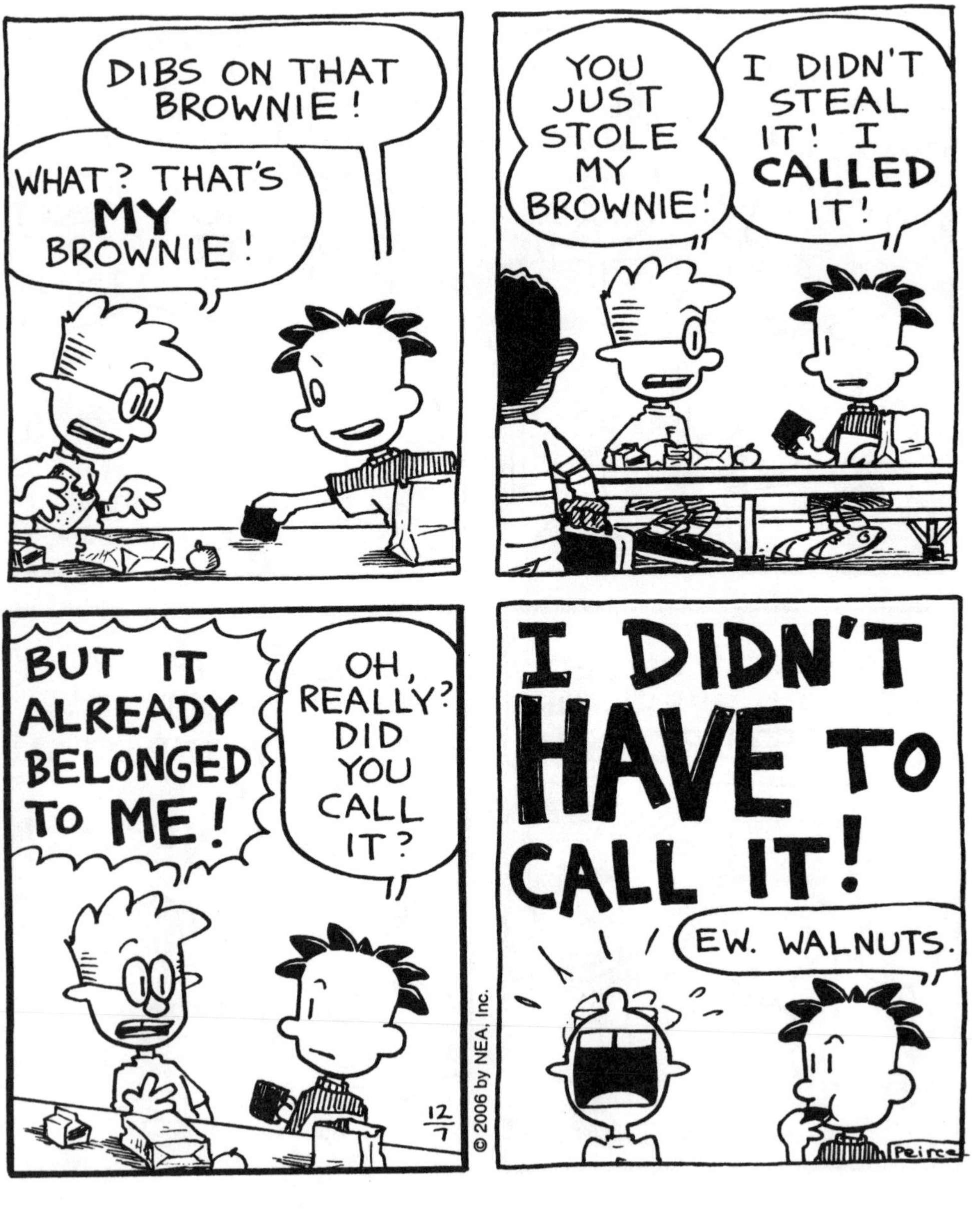
DIBS ON THAT BROWNIE!
WHAT? THAT'S **MY** BROWNIE!
YOU JUST STOLE MY BROWNIE!
I DIDN'T STEAL IT! I **CALLED** IT!
BUT IT ALREADY BELONGED TO **ME**!
OH, REALLY? DID YOU CALL IT?
12/7
© 2006 by NEA, Inc.
I DIDN'T HAVE TO CALL IT!
EW. WALNUTS.
Peirce

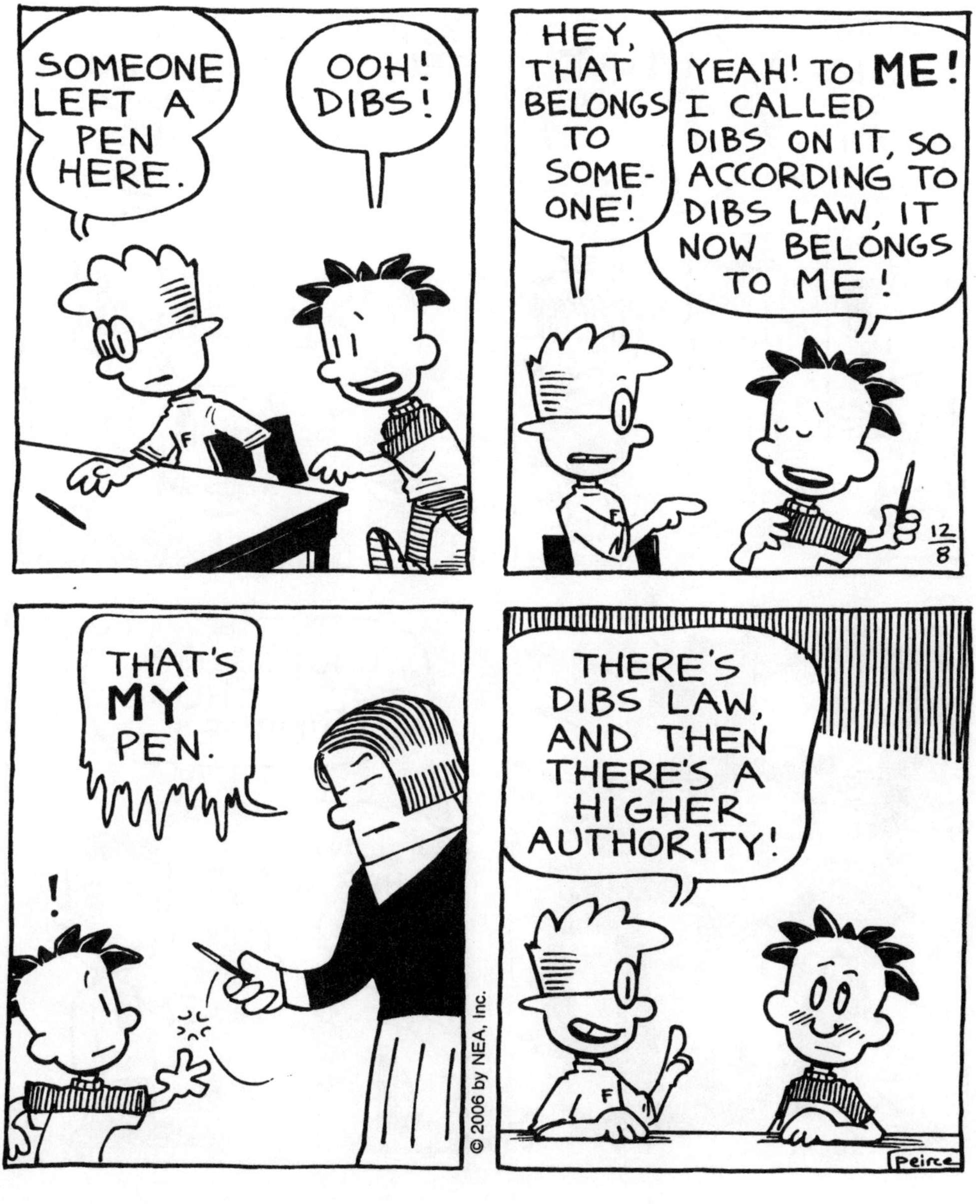
SOMEONE LEFT A PEN HERE.
OOH! DIBS!
HEY, THAT BELONGS TO SOME-ONE!
YEAH! TO ME! I CALLED DIBS ON IT, SO ACCORDING TO DIBS LAW, IT NOW BELONGS TO ME!
12/8
THAT'S MY PEN.
!
© 2006 by NEA, Inc.
THERE'S DIBS LAW, AND THEN THERE'S A HIGHER AUTHORITY!
Peirce

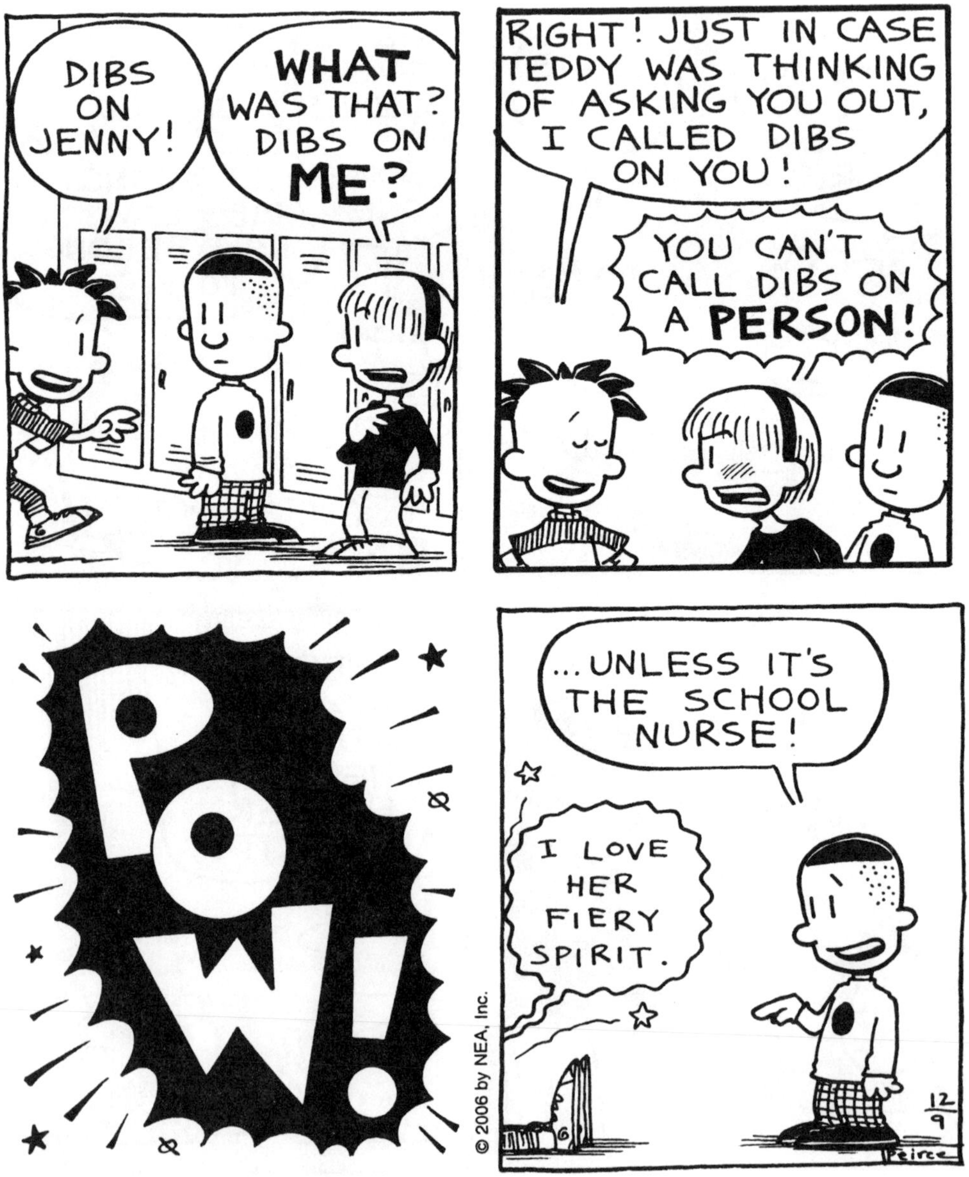
DIBS ON JENNY!
WHAT WAS THAT? DIBS ON ME?
RIGHT! JUST IN CASE TEDDY WAS THINKING OF ASKING YOU OUT, I CALLED DIBS ON YOU!
YOU CAN'T CALL DIBS ON A PERSON!
POW!
© 2006 by NEA, Inc.
...UNLESS IT'S THE SCHOOL NURSE!
I LOVE HER FIERY SPIRIT.
12/9
Peirce

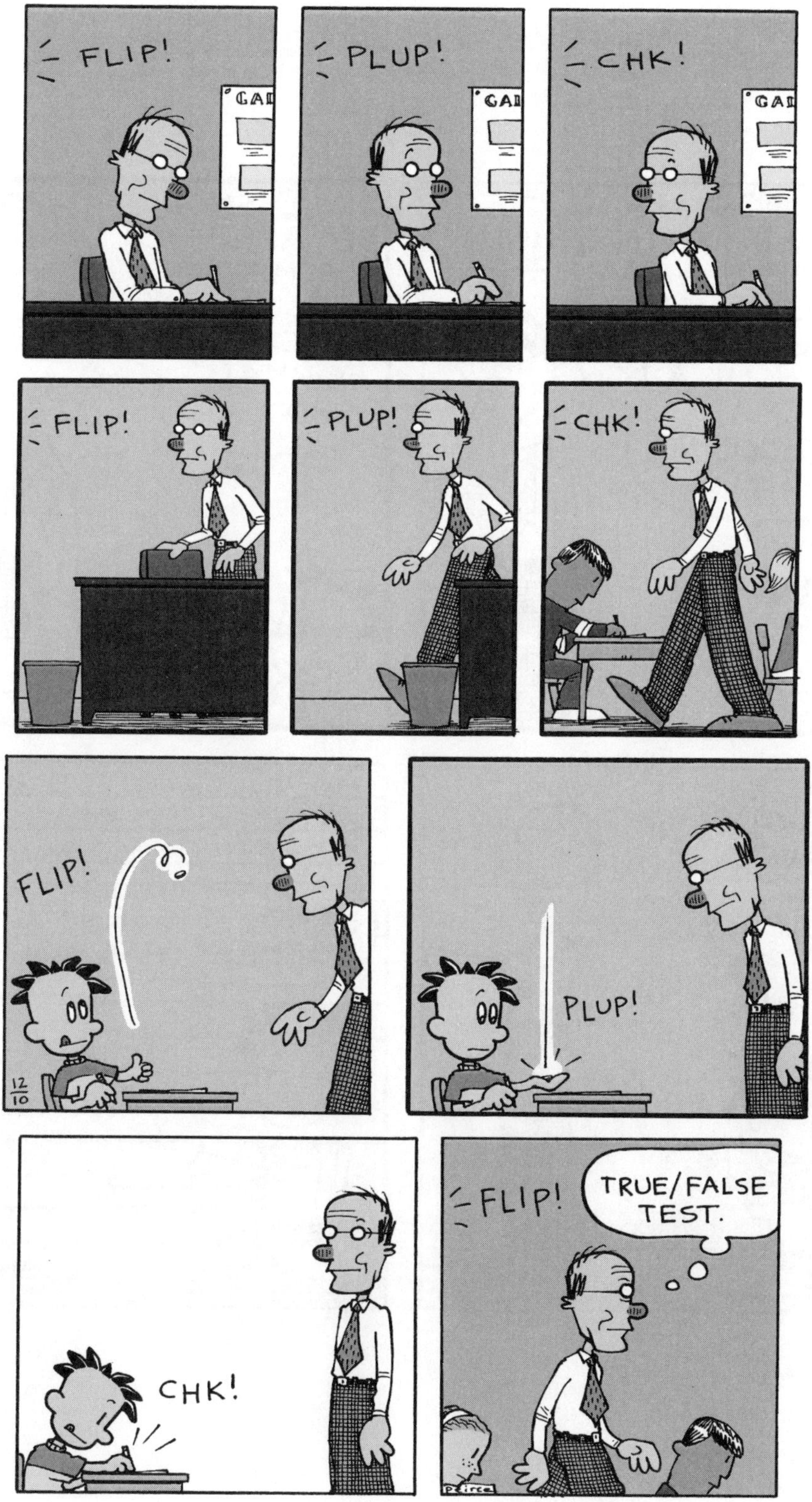
FLIP!
PLUP!
CHK!
FLIP!
PLUP!
CHK!
FLIP!
PLUP!
CHK!
FLIP!
TRUE/FALSE TEST.

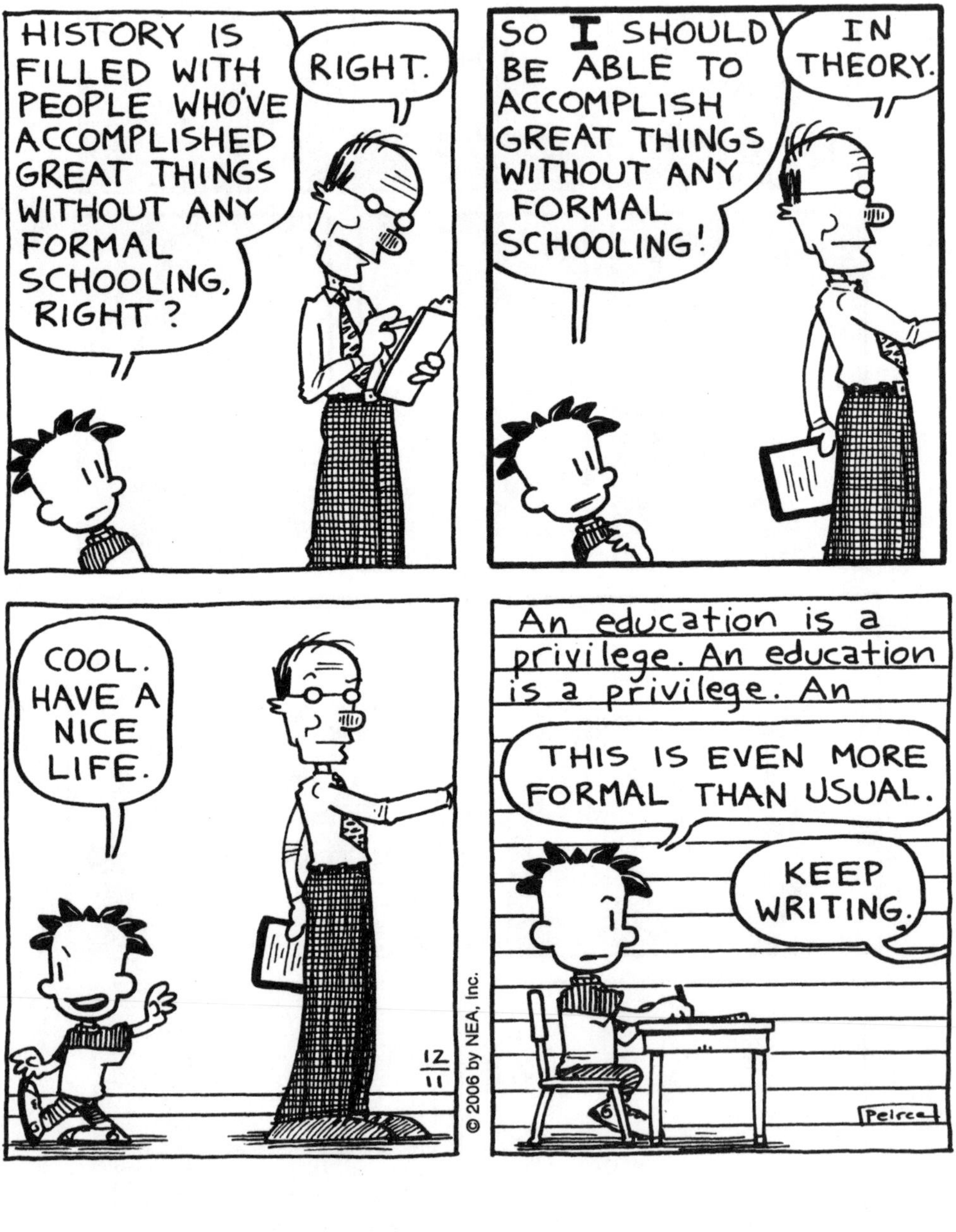
HISTORY IS FILLED WITH PEOPLE WHO'VE ACCOMPLISHED GREAT THINGS WITHOUT ANY FORMAL SCHOOLING, RIGHT?
RIGHT.
SO I SHOULD BE ABLE TO ACCOMPLISH GREAT THINGS WITHOUT ANY FORMAL SCHOOLING!
IN THEORY.
COOL. HAVE A NICE LIFE.
12/11
© 2006 by NEA, Inc.
An education is a privilege. An education is a privilege. An
THIS IS EVEN MORE FORMAL THAN USUAL.
KEEP WRITING.
Peirce

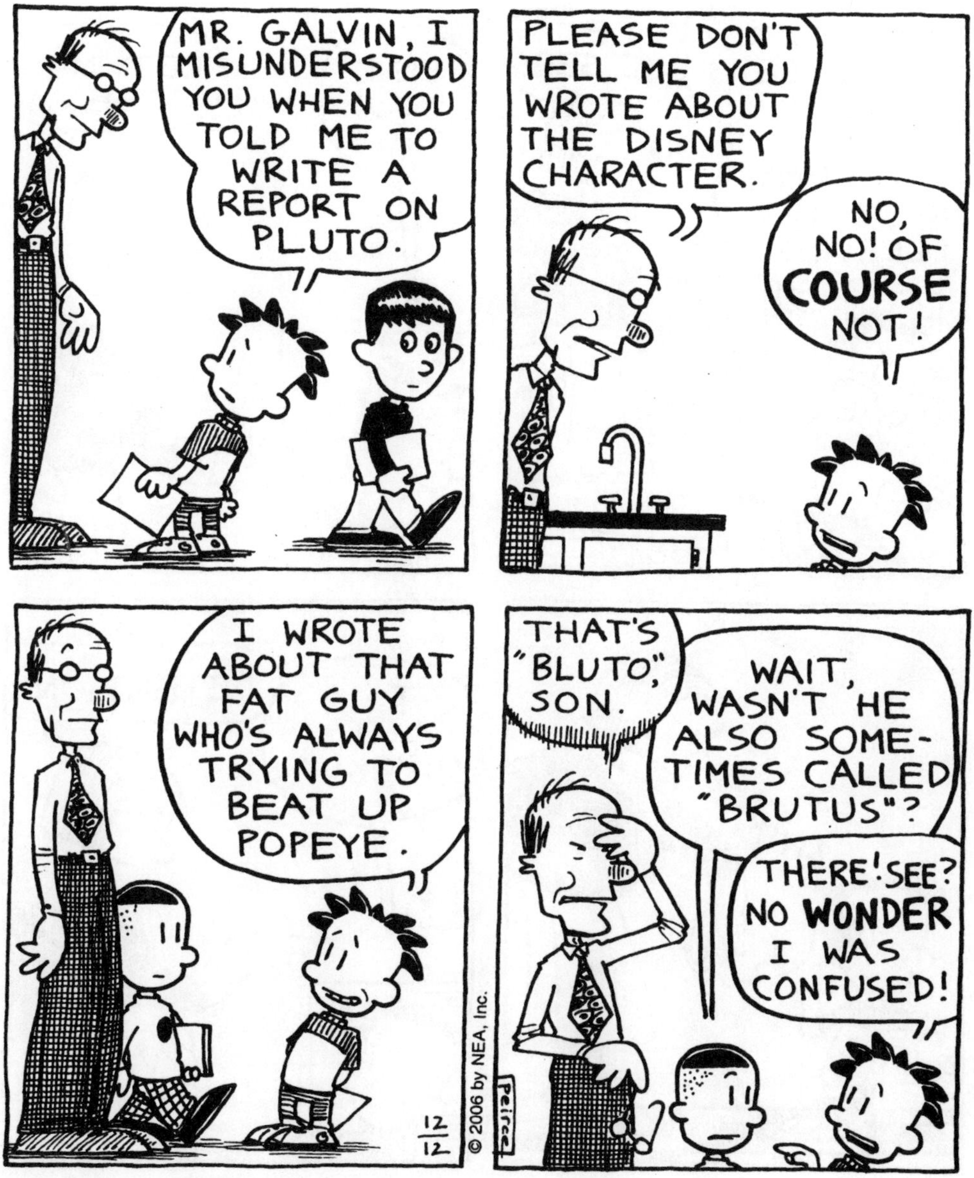
MR. GALVIN, I MISUNDERSTOOD YOU WHEN YOU TOLD ME TO WRITE A REPORT ON PLUTO.
PLEASE DON'T TELL ME YOU WROTE ABOUT THE DISNEY CHARACTER.
NO, NO! OF COURSE NOT!
I WROTE ABOUT THAT FAT GUY WHO'S ALWAYS TRYING TO BEAT UP POPEYE.
12/12
© 2006 by NEA, Inc.
Peirce
THAT'S "BLUTO," SON.
WAIT, WASN'T HE ALSO SOMETIMES CALLED "BRUTUS"?
THERE! SEE? NO WONDER I WAS CONFUSED!

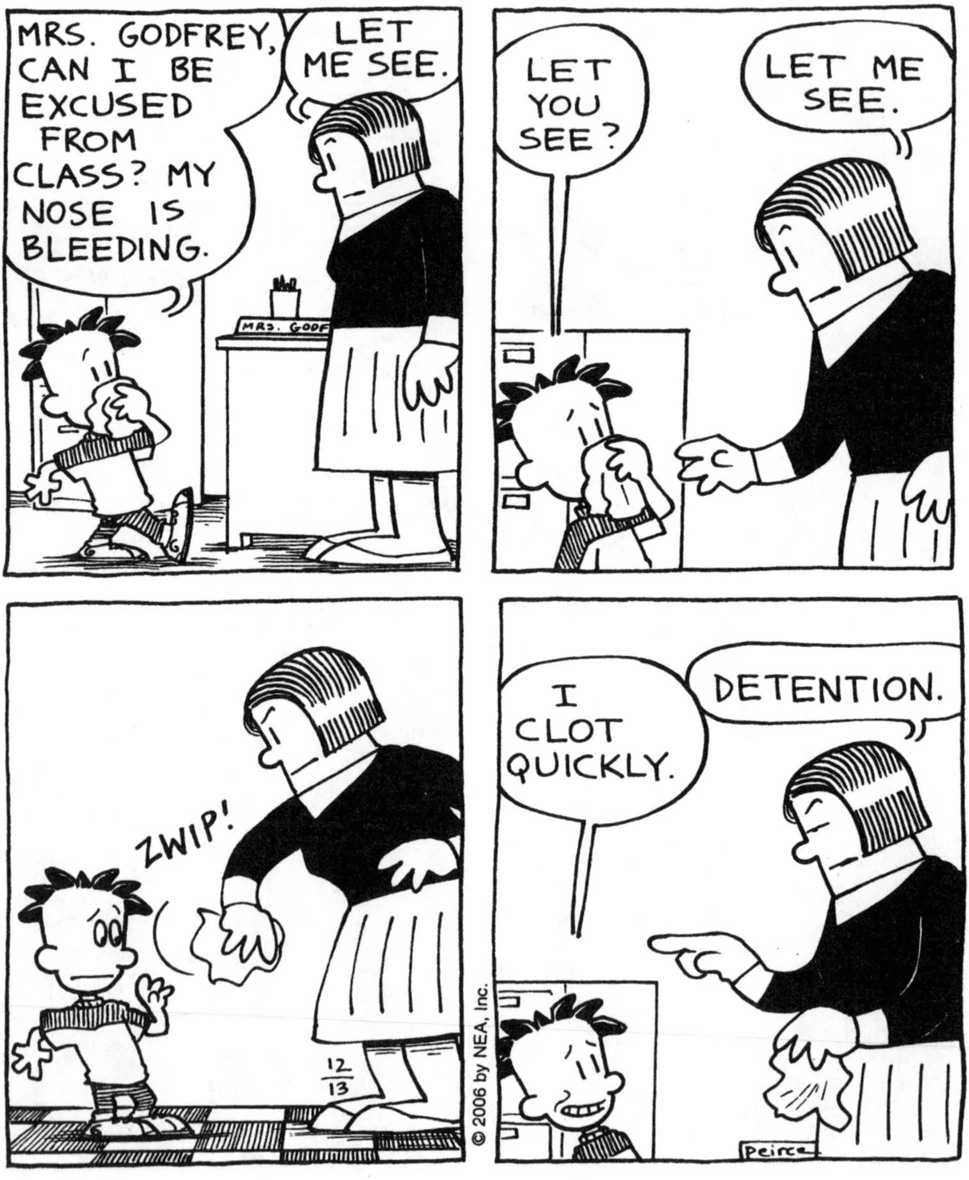
MRS. GODFREY, CAN I BE EXCUSED FROM CLASS? MY NOSE IS BLEEDING.
LET ME SEE.
MRS. GODF
LET YOU SEE?
LET ME SEE.
ZWIP!
12/13
© 2006 by NEA, Inc.
I CLOT QUICKLY.
DETENTION.
Peirce

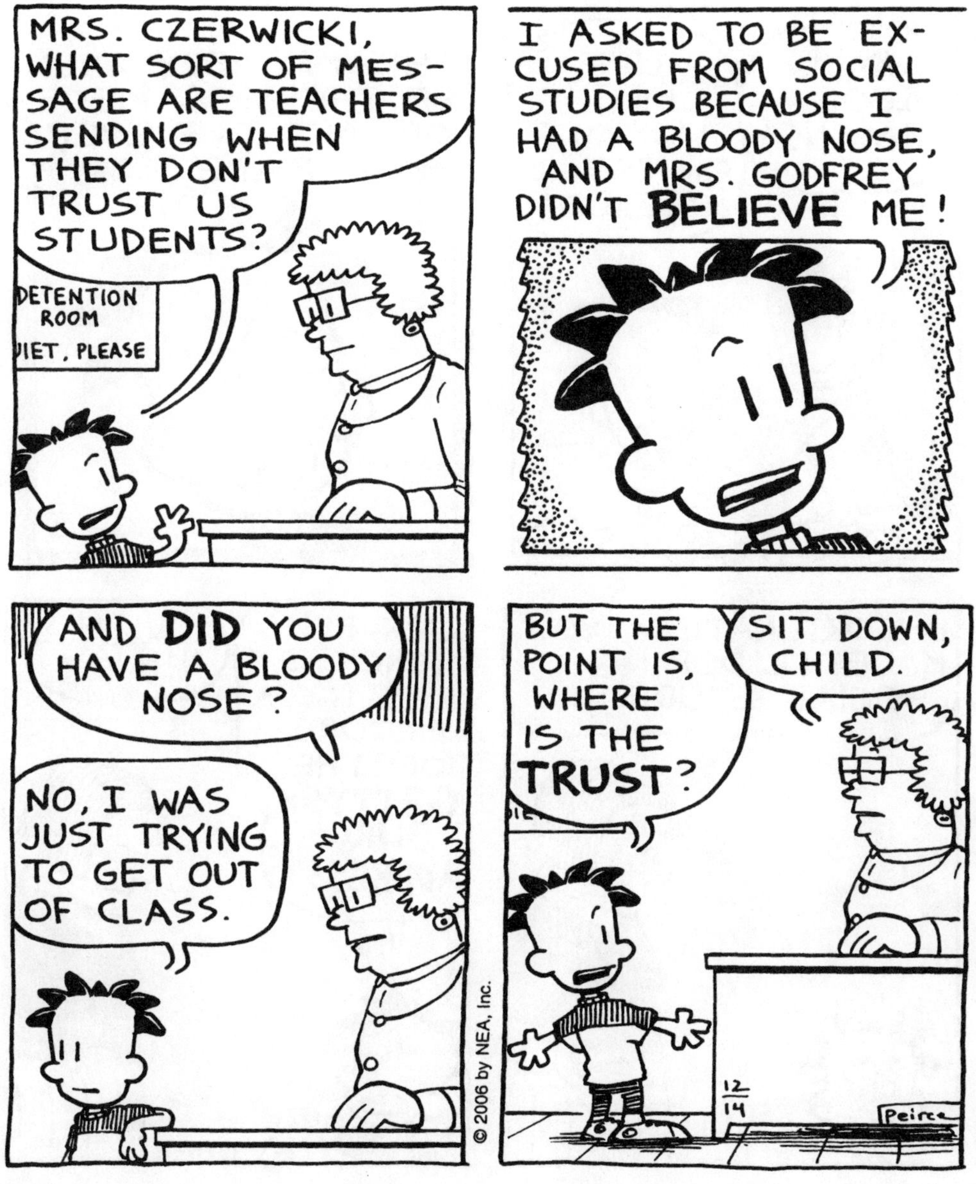
MRS. CZERWICKI, WHAT SORT OF MES-SAGE ARE TEACHERS SENDING WHEN THEY DON'T TRUST US STUDENTS?
DETENTION ROOM
UIET, PLEASE
I ASKED TO BE EX-CUSED FROM SOCIAL STUDIES BECAUSE I HAD A BLOODY NOSE, AND MRS. GODFREY DIDN'T **BELIEVE** ME!
AND **DID** YOU HAVE A BLOODY NOSE?
NO, I WAS JUST TRYING TO GET OUT OF CLASS.
© 2006 by NEA, Inc.
BUT THE POINT IS, WHERE IS THE **TRUST**?
SIT DOWN, CHILD.
12/14
Peirce

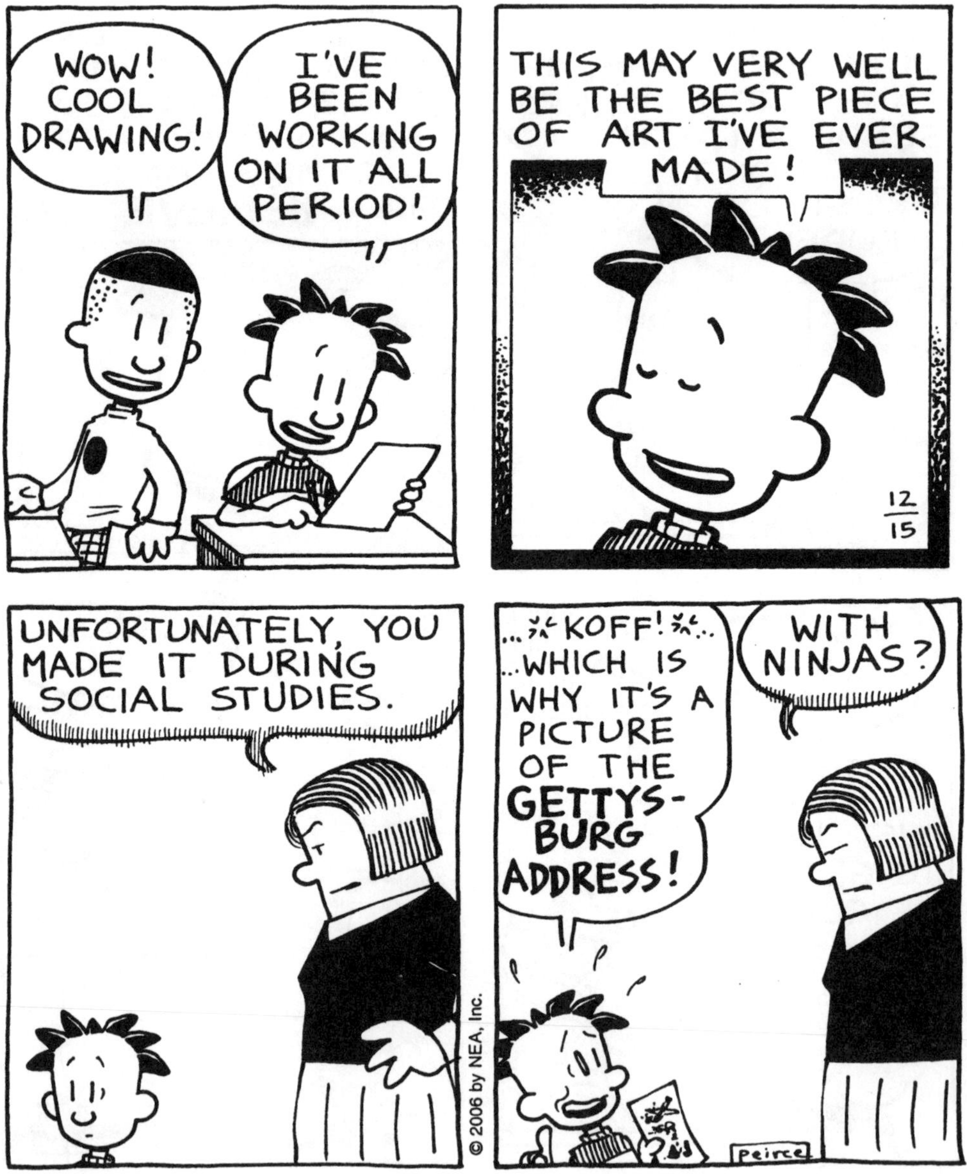
WOW! COOL DRAWING!
I'VE BEEN WORKING ON IT ALL PERIOD!
THIS MAY VERY WELL BE THE BEST PIECE OF ART I'VE EVER MADE!
12/15
UNFORTUNATELY, YOU MADE IT DURING SOCIAL STUDIES.
...KOFF!...
...WHICH IS WHY IT'S A PICTURE OF THE GETTYSBURG ADDRESS!
WITH NINJAS?
Peirce

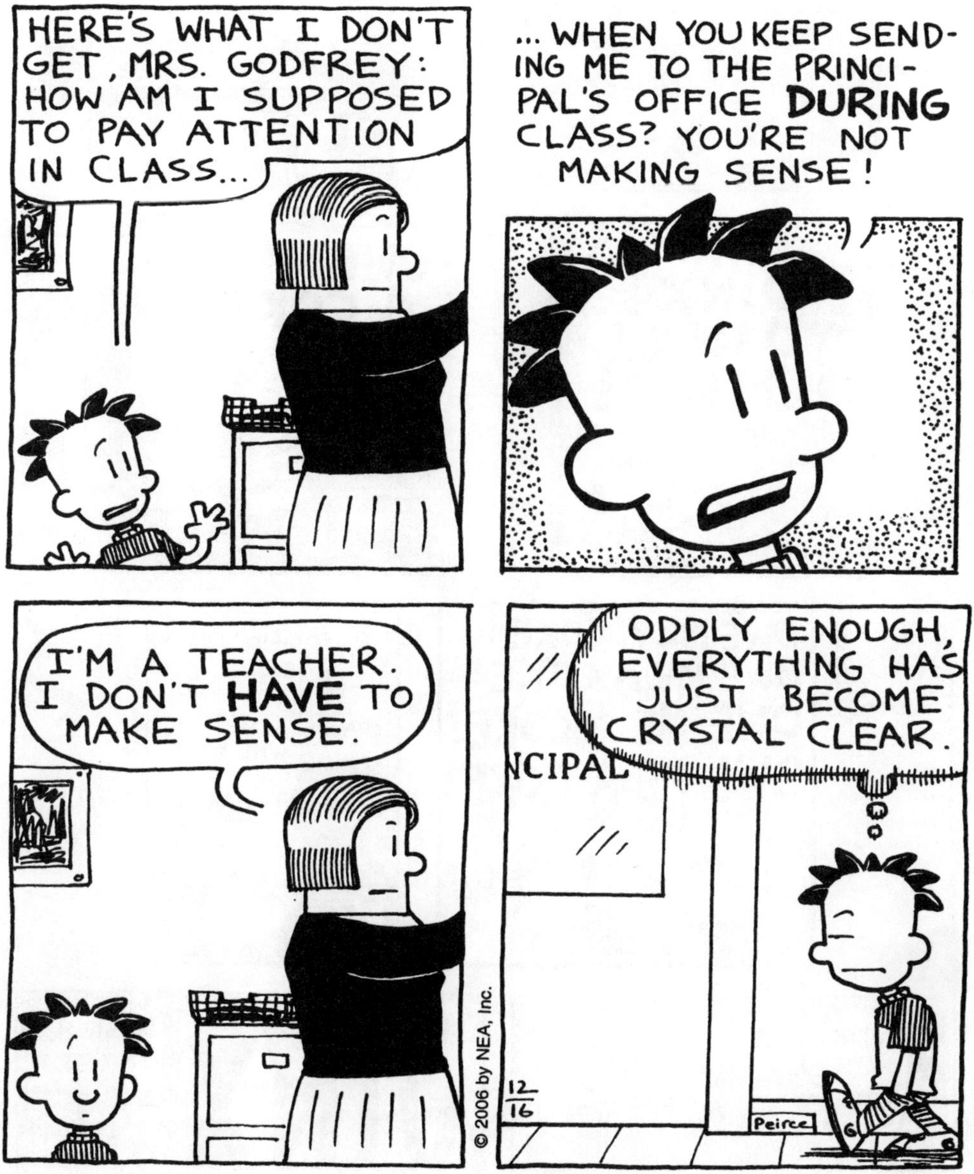
HERE'S WHAT I DON'T GET, MRS. GODFREY: HOW AM I SUPPOSED TO PAY ATTENTION IN CLASS...
... WHEN YOU KEEP SENDING ME TO THE PRINCIPAL'S OFFICE DURING CLASS? YOU'RE NOT MAKING SENSE!
I'M A TEACHER. I DON'T HAVE TO MAKE SENSE.
NCIPAL
ODDLY ENOUGH, EVERYTHING HAS JUST BECOME CRYSTAL CLEAR.
© 2006 by NEA, Inc.
12/16
Peirce

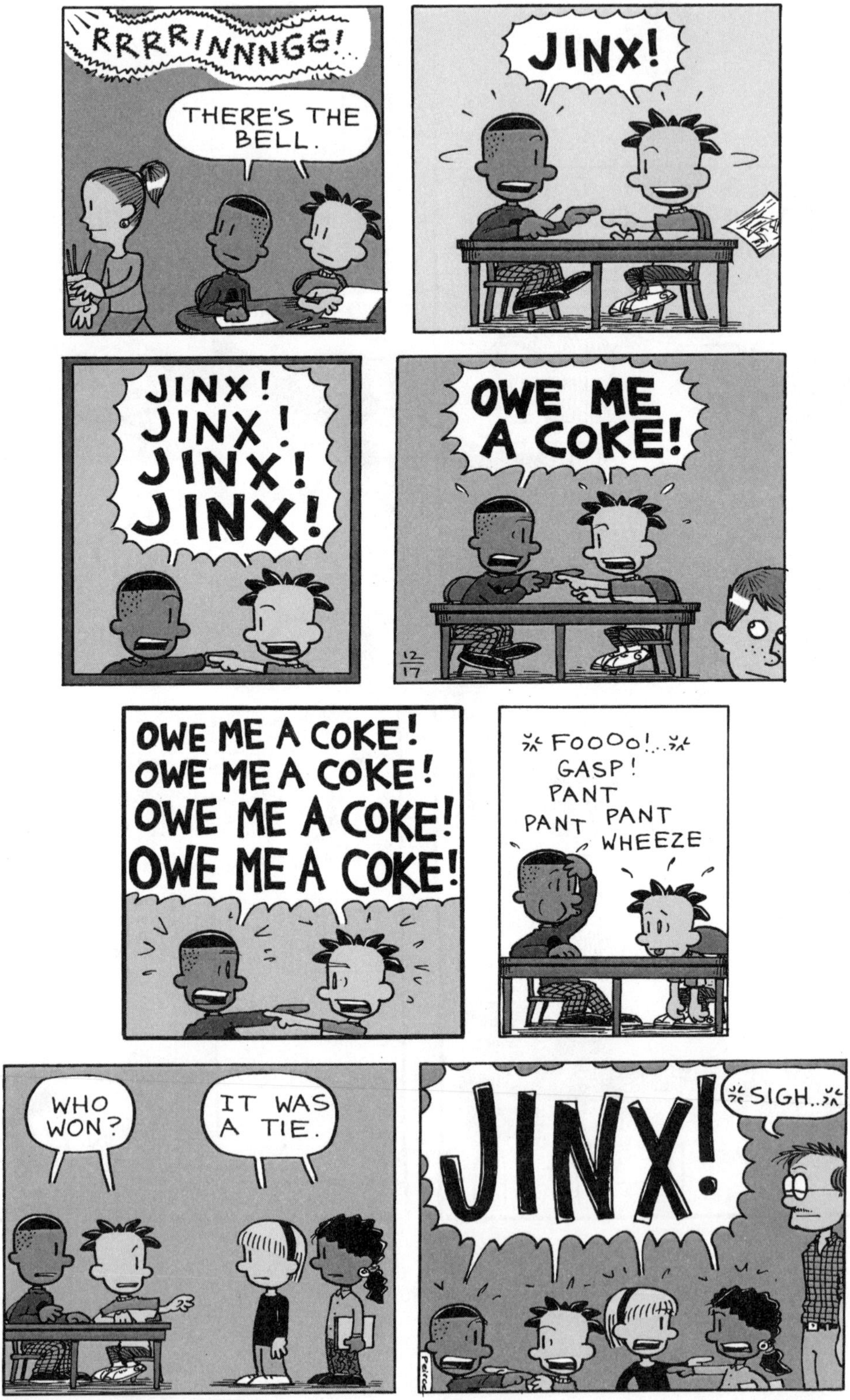
RRRRINNNNGG!
THERE'S THE BELL.
JINX!
JINX! JINX! JINX! JINX!
OWE ME A COKE!
12/17
OWE ME A COKE! OWE ME A COKE! OWE ME A COKE! OWE ME A COKE!
FOOOO!..
GASP!
PANT
PANT PANT
WHEEZE
WHO WON?
IT WAS A TIE.
JINX!
SIGH..
Peirce

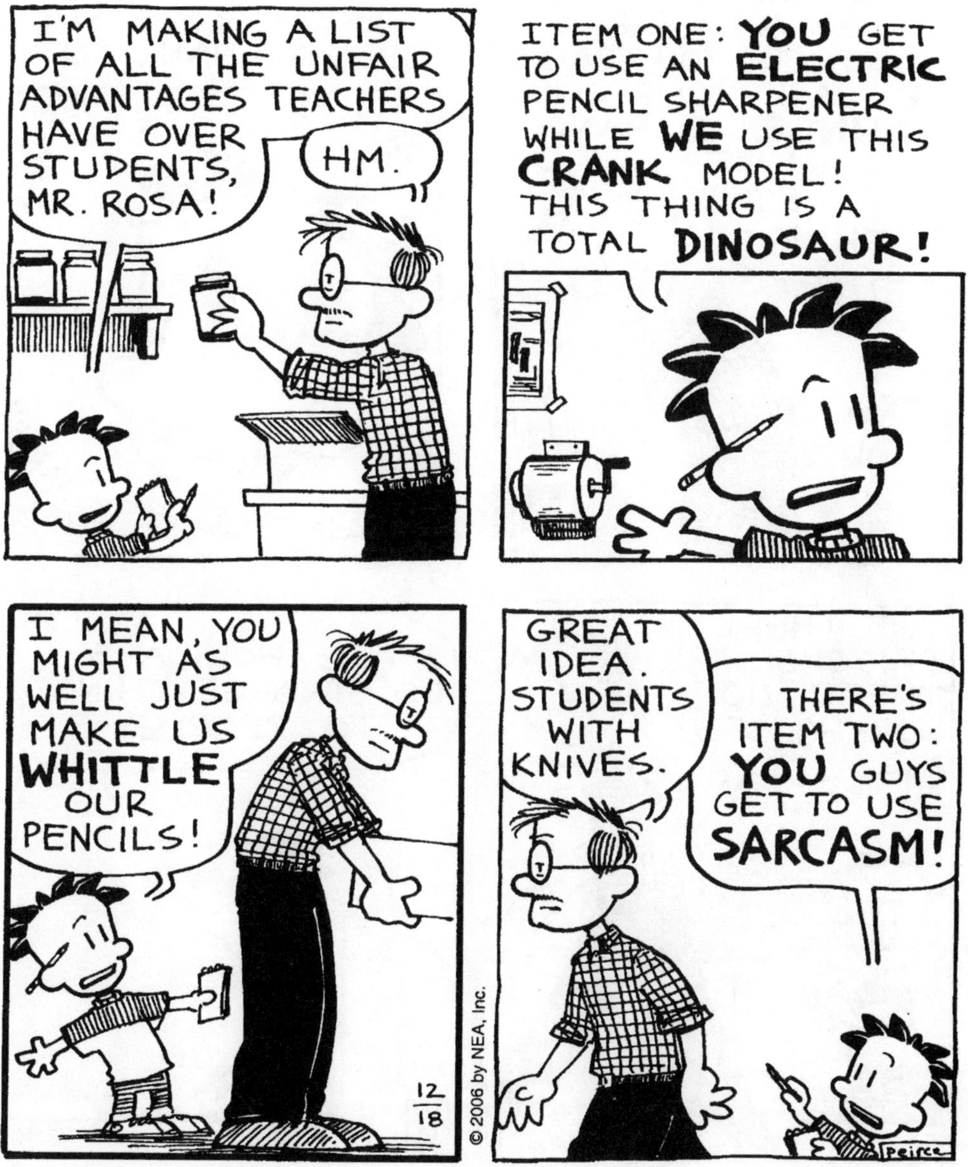
I'M MAKING A LIST OF ALL THE UNFAIR ADVANTAGES TEACHERS HAVE OVER STUDENTS, MR. ROSA!
HM.
ITEM ONE: YOU GET TO USE AN ELECTRIC PENCIL SHARPENER WHILE WE USE THIS CRANK MODEL! THIS THING IS A TOTAL DINOSAUR!
I MEAN, YOU MIGHT AS WELL JUST MAKE US WHITTLE OUR PENCILS!
12/18
© 2006 by NEA, Inc.
GREAT IDEA. STUDENTS WITH KNIVES.
THERE'S ITEM TWO: YOU GUYS GET TO USE SARCASM!
Peirce

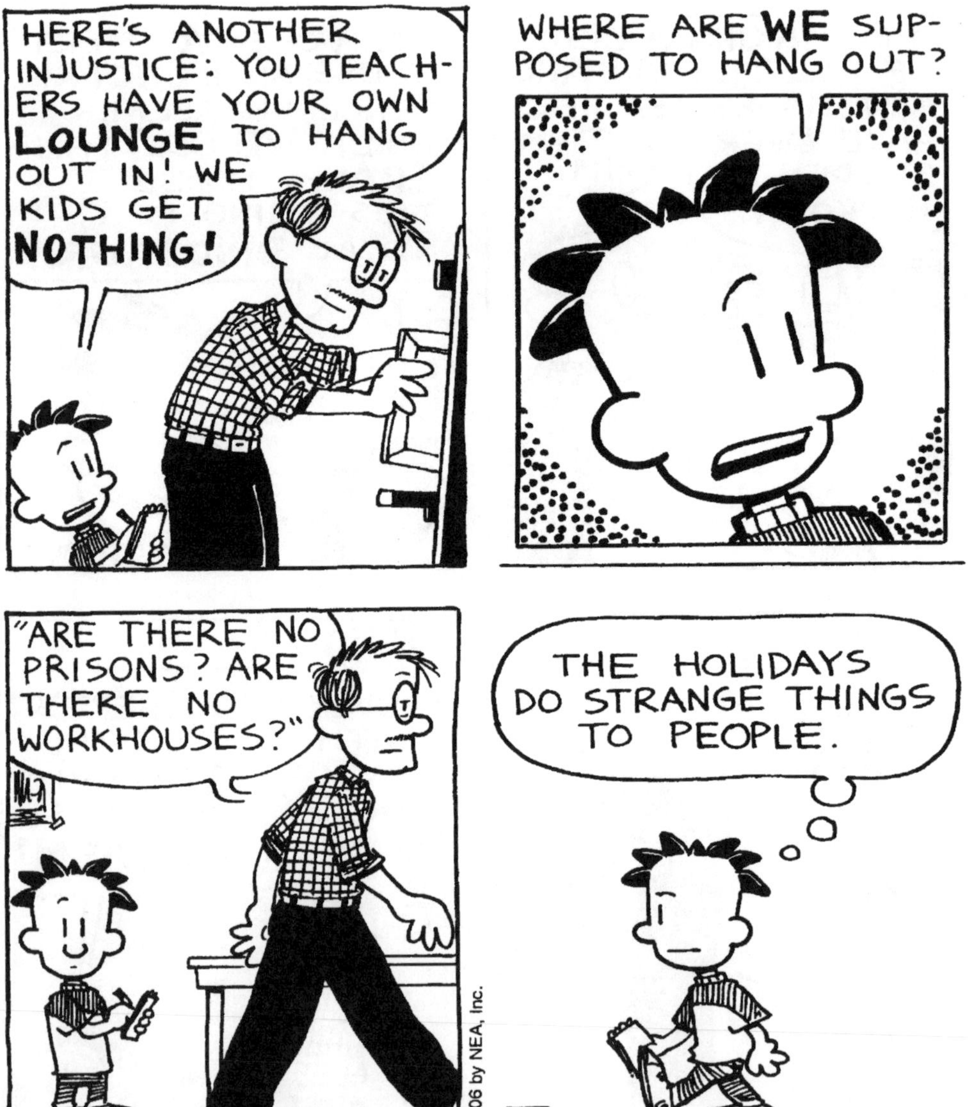
HERE'S ANOTHER INJUSTICE: YOU TEACHERS HAVE YOUR OWN **LOUNGE** TO HANG OUT IN! WE KIDS GET **NOTHING!**
WHERE ARE **WE** SUPPOSED TO HANG OUT?
"ARE THERE NO PRISONS? ARE THERE NO WORKHOUSES?"
THE HOLIDAYS DO STRANGE THINGS TO PEOPLE.
12/19
Peirce

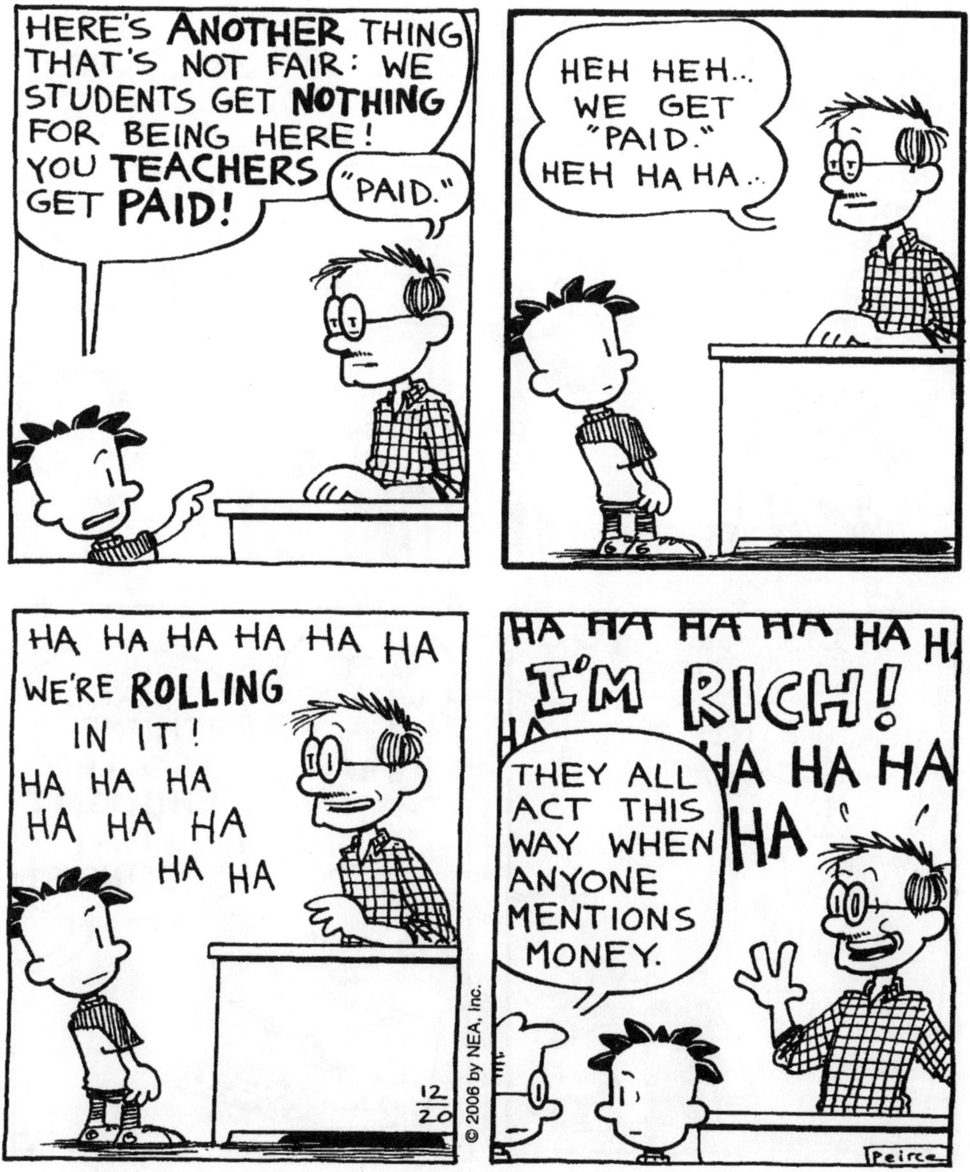
HERE'S **ANOTHER** THING THAT'S NOT FAIR: WE STUDENTS GET **NOTHING** FOR BEING HERE! YOU **TEACHERS** GET **PAID!**
"PAID."
HEH HEH... WE GET "PAID." HEH HA HA...
HA HA HA HA HA HA
WE'RE **ROLLING** IN IT!
HA HA HA
HA HA HA
HA HA
12/20
© 2006 by NEA, Inc.
HA HA HA HA HA H
I'M RICH!
HA HA HA
HA
THEY ALL ACT THIS WAY WHEN ANYONE MENTIONS MONEY.
Peirce

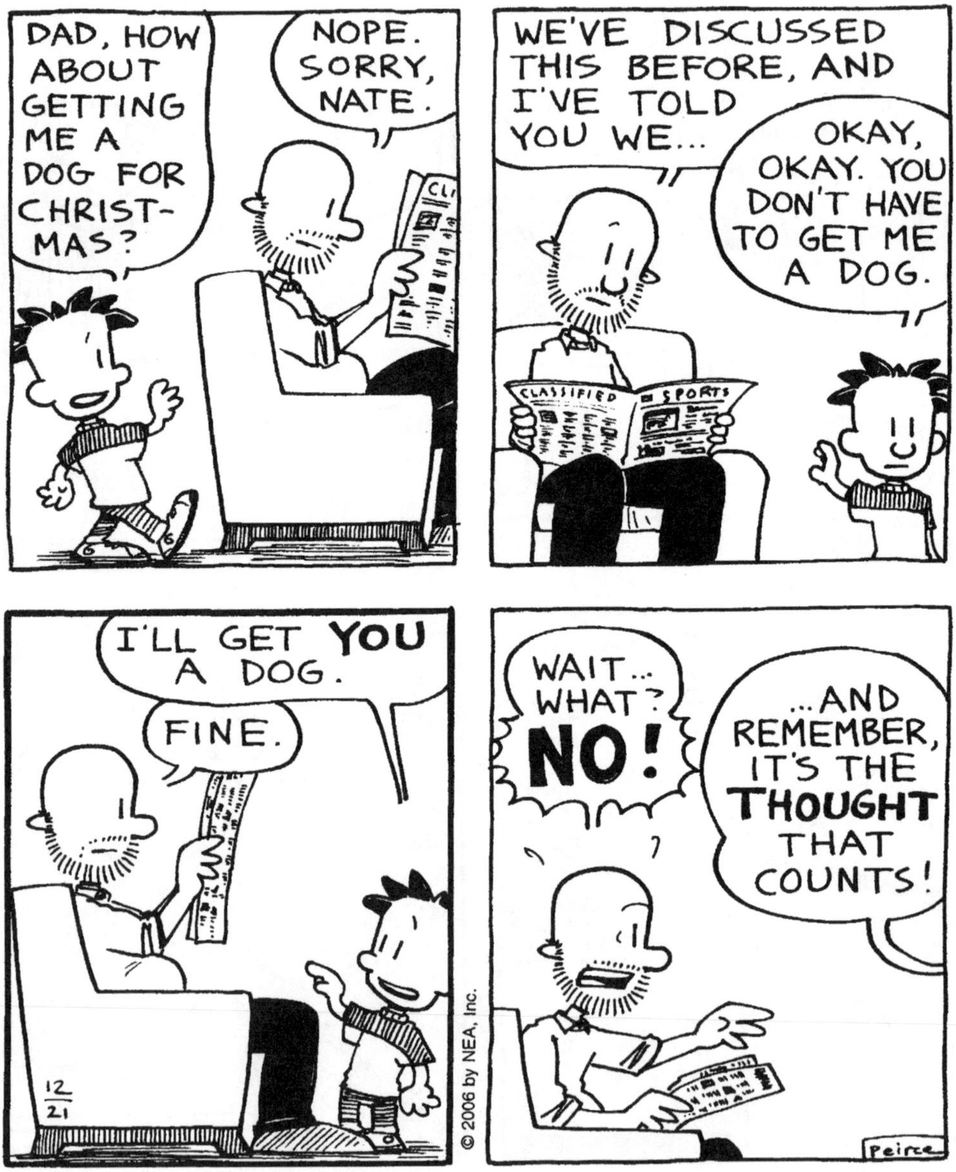
DAD, HOW ABOUT GETTING ME A DOG FOR CHRIST-MAS?
NOPE. SORRY, NATE.
WE'VE DISCUSSED THIS BEFORE, AND I'VE TOLD YOU WE...
OKAY, OKAY. YOU DON'T HAVE TO GET ME A DOG.
I'LL GET **YOU** A DOG.
FINE.
12/21
WAIT... WHAT?
NO!
...AND REMEMBER, IT'S THE **THOUGHT** THAT COUNTS!
Peirce

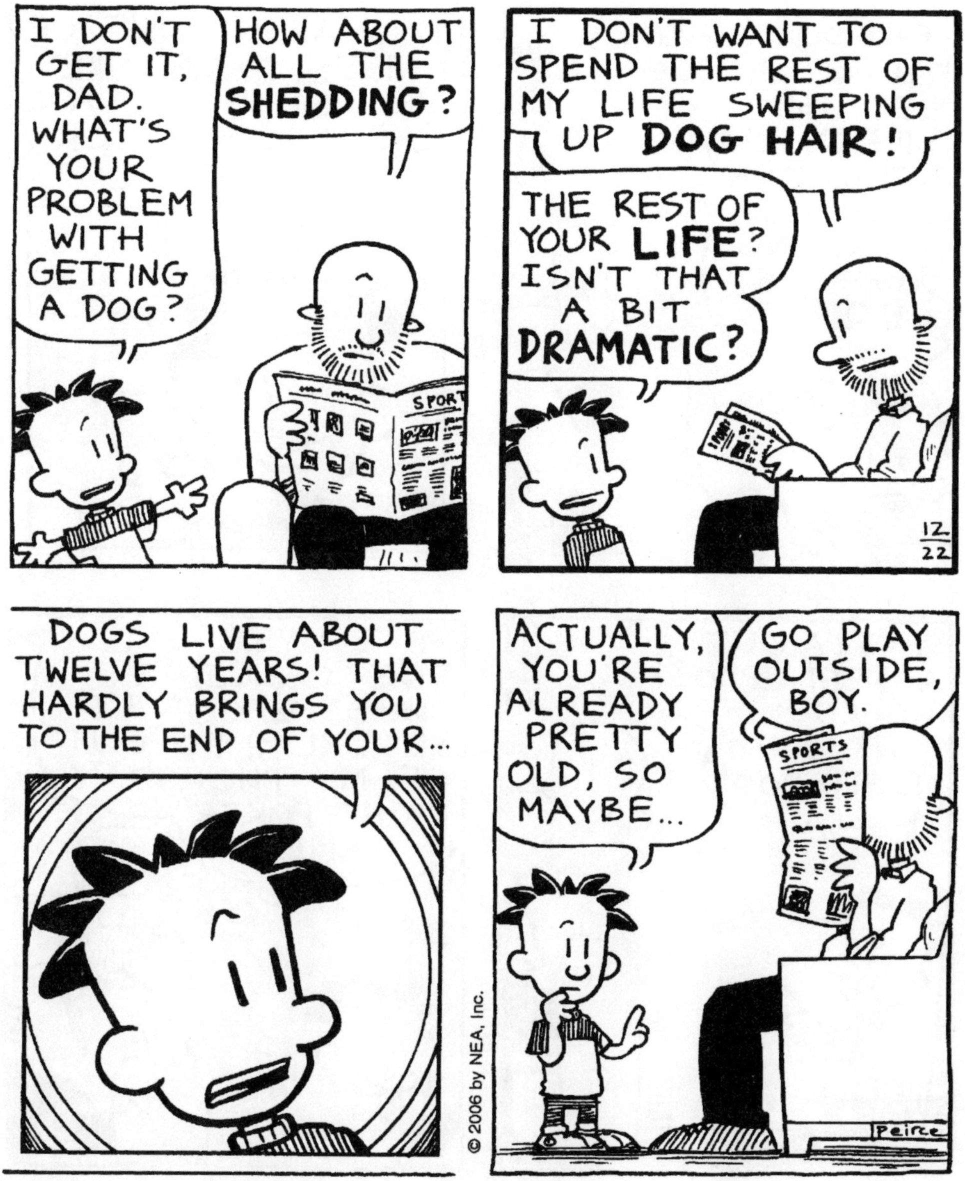
I DON'T GET IT, DAD. WHAT'S YOUR PROBLEM WITH GETTING A DOG?
HOW ABOUT ALL THE **SHEDDING**?
SPORT
I DON'T WANT TO SPEND THE REST OF MY LIFE SWEEPING UP **DOG HAIR**!
THE REST OF YOUR **LIFE**? ISN'T THAT A BIT **DRAMATIC**?
12/22
DOGS LIVE ABOUT TWELVE YEARS! THAT HARDLY BRINGS YOU TO THE END OF YOUR...
© 2006 by NEA, Inc.
ACTUALLY, YOU'RE ALREADY PRETTY OLD, SO MAYBE...
GO PLAY OUTSIDE, BOY.
SPORTS
Peirce

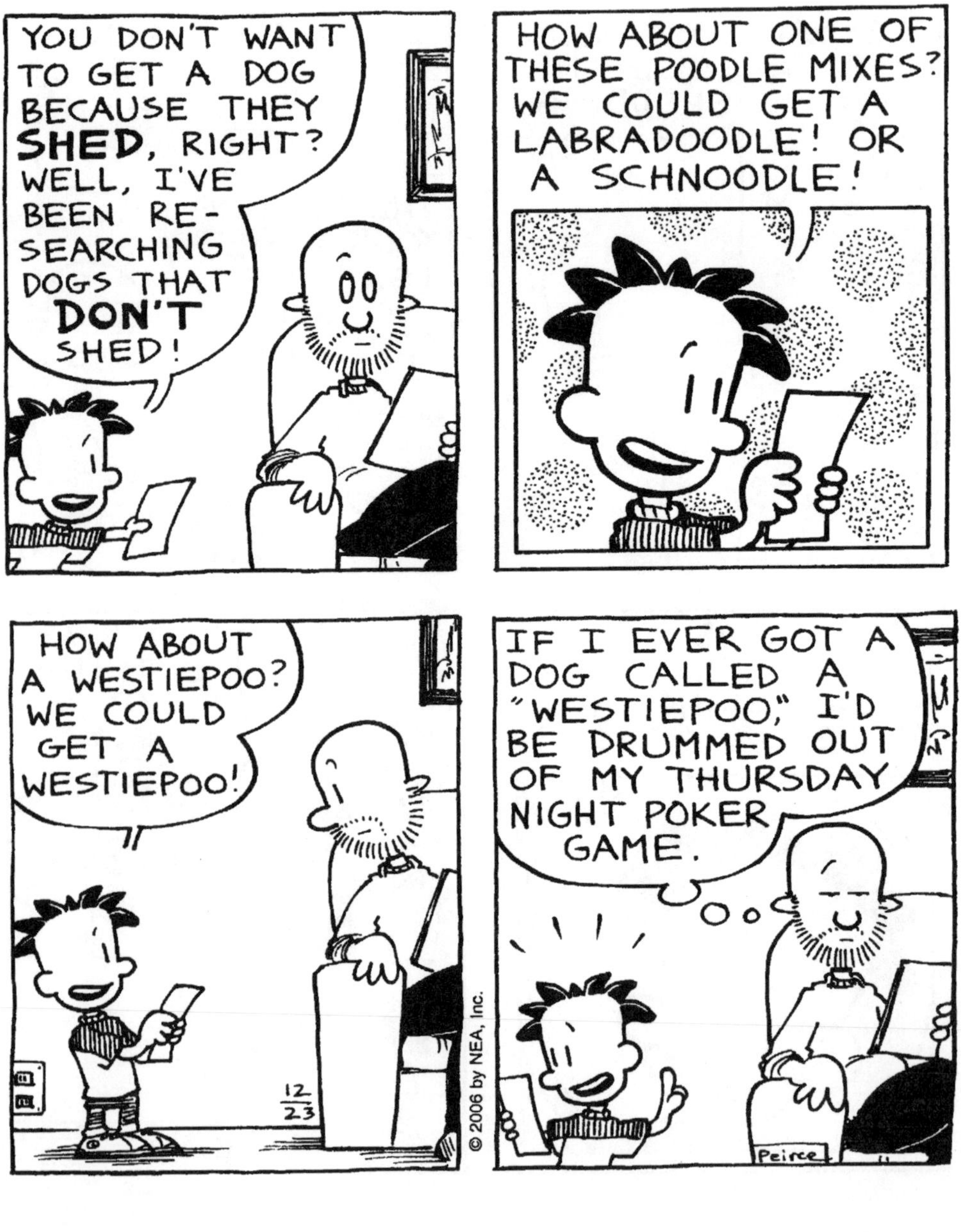
YOU DON'T WANT TO GET A DOG BECAUSE THEY **SHED**, RIGHT? WELL, I'VE BEEN RE-SEARCHING DOGS THAT **DON'T** SHED!
HOW ABOUT ONE OF THESE POODLE MIXES? WE COULD GET A LABRADOODLE! OR A SCHNOODLE!
HOW ABOUT A WESTIEPOO? WE COULD GET A WESTIEPOO!
12 23
© 2006 by NEA, Inc.
IF I EVER GOT A DOG CALLED A "WESTIEPOO," I'D BE DRUMMED OUT OF MY THURSDAY NIGHT POKER GAME.
Peirce

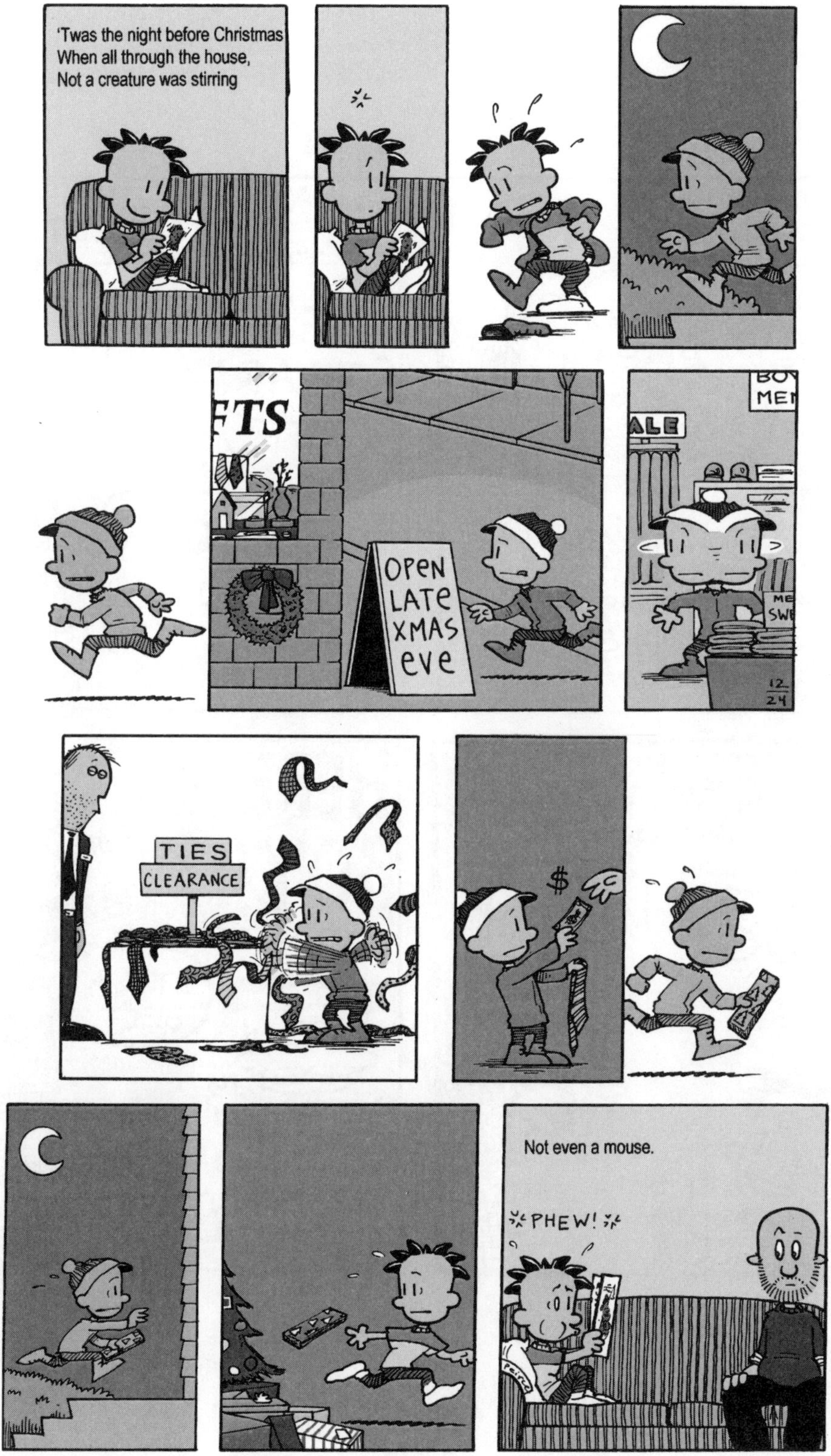
'Twas the night before Christmas
When all through the house,
Not a creature was stirring
OPEN LATE XMAS EVE
12
24
TIES
CLEARANCE
$
Not even a mouse.
PHEW!

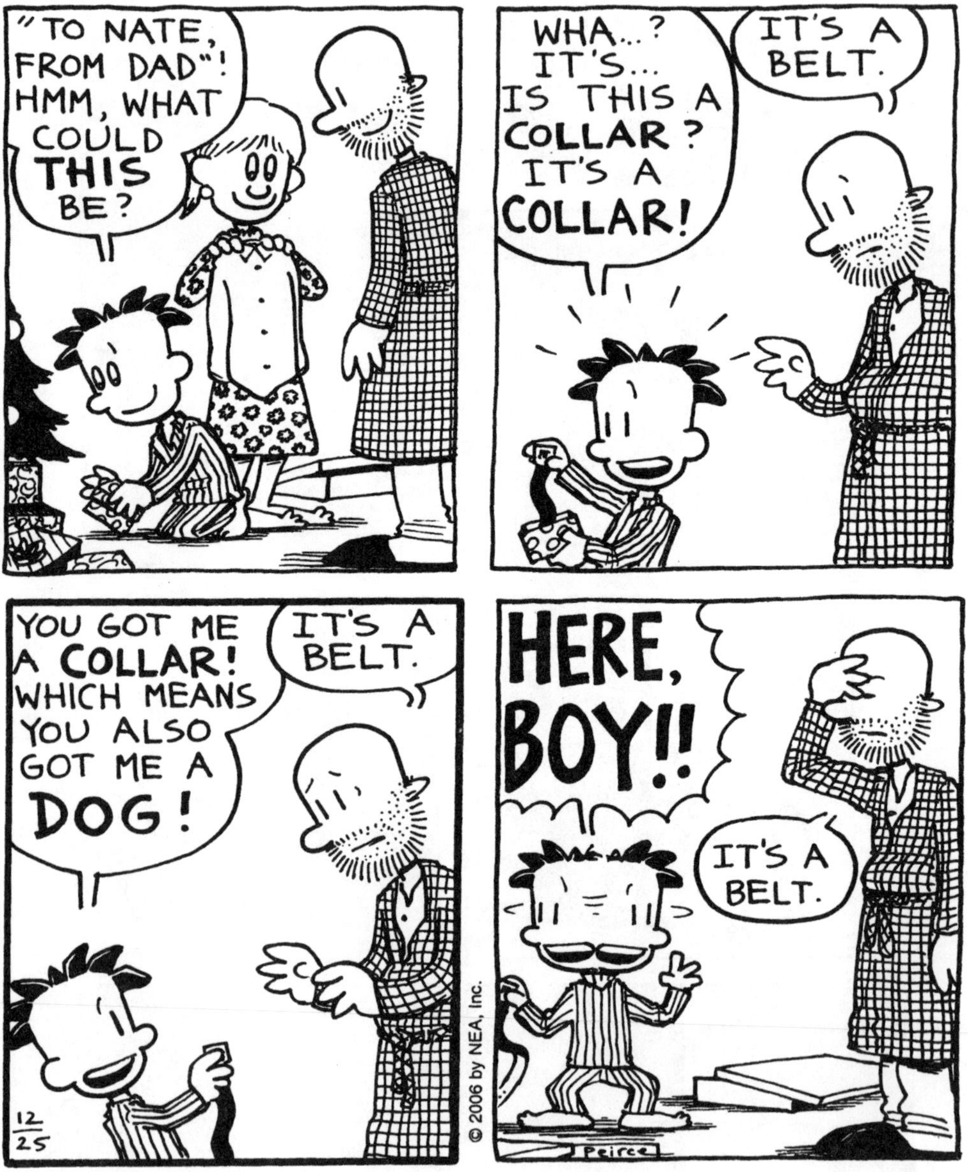
"TO NATE, FROM DAD"! HMM, WHAT COULD THIS BE?
WHA...? IT'S... IS THIS A COLLAR? IT'S A COLLAR!
IT'S A BELT.
YOU GOT ME A COLLAR! WHICH MEANS YOU ALSO GOT ME A DOG!
IT'S A BELT.
12/25
© 2006 by NEA, Inc.
HERE, BOY!!
IT'S A BELT.
Peirce

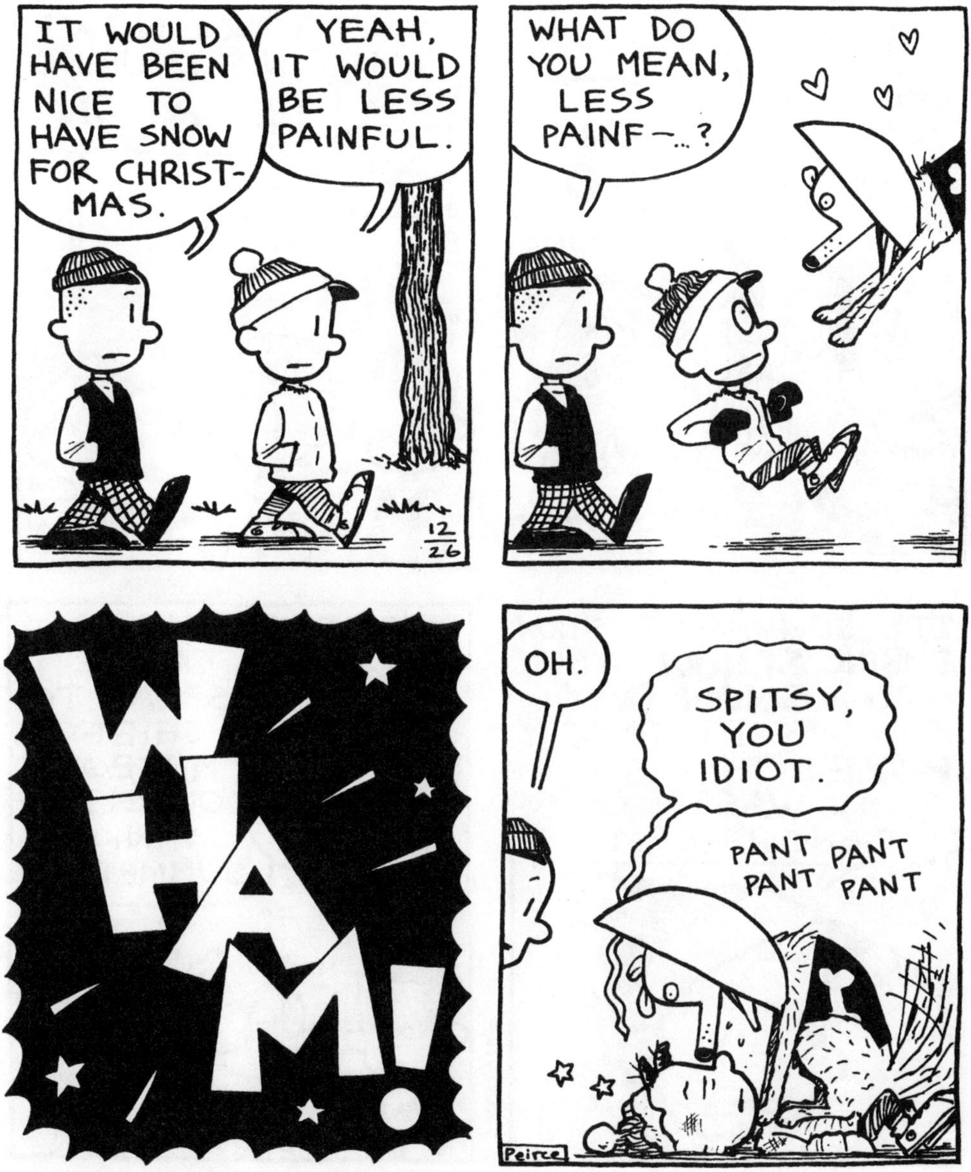
IT WOULD HAVE BEEN NICE TO HAVE SNOW FOR CHRISTMAS.
YEAH, IT WOULD BE LESS PAINFUL.
12/26
WHAT DO YOU MEAN, LESS PAINF—...?
WHAM!
OH.
SPITSY, YOU IDIOT.
PANT PANT PANT PANT
Peirce

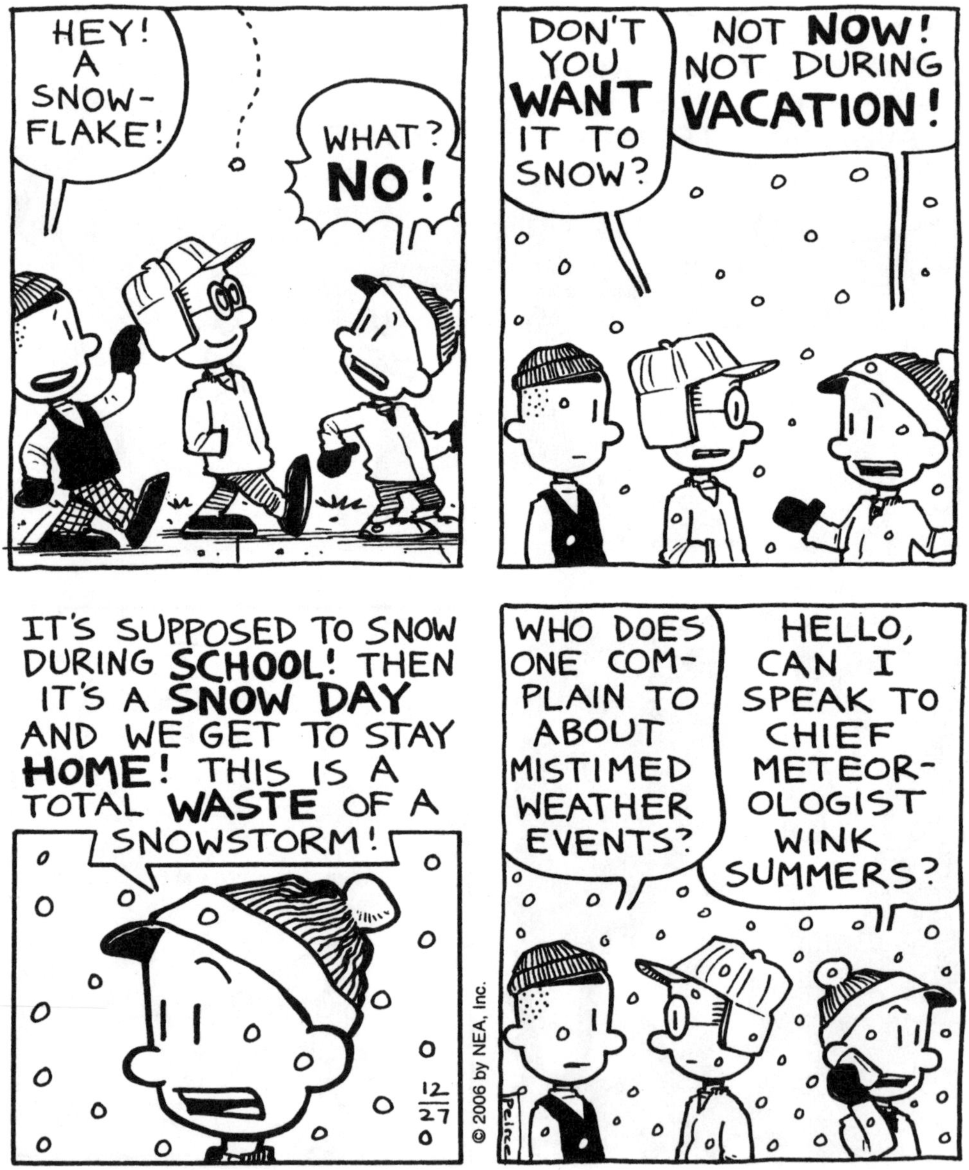
HEY! A SNOW-FLAKE!
WHAT? NO!
DON'T YOU WANT IT TO SNOW?
NOT NOW! NOT DURING VACATION!
IT'S SUPPOSED TO SNOW DURING SCHOOL! THEN IT'S A SNOW DAY AND WE GET TO STAY HOME! THIS IS A TOTAL WASTE OF A SNOWSTORM!
12 27 0
© 2006 by NEA, Inc.
WHO DOES ONE COM-PLAIN TO ABOUT MISTIMED WEATHER EVENTS?
HELLO, CAN I SPEAK TO CHIEF METEOR-OLOGIST WINK SUMMERS?
Peirce

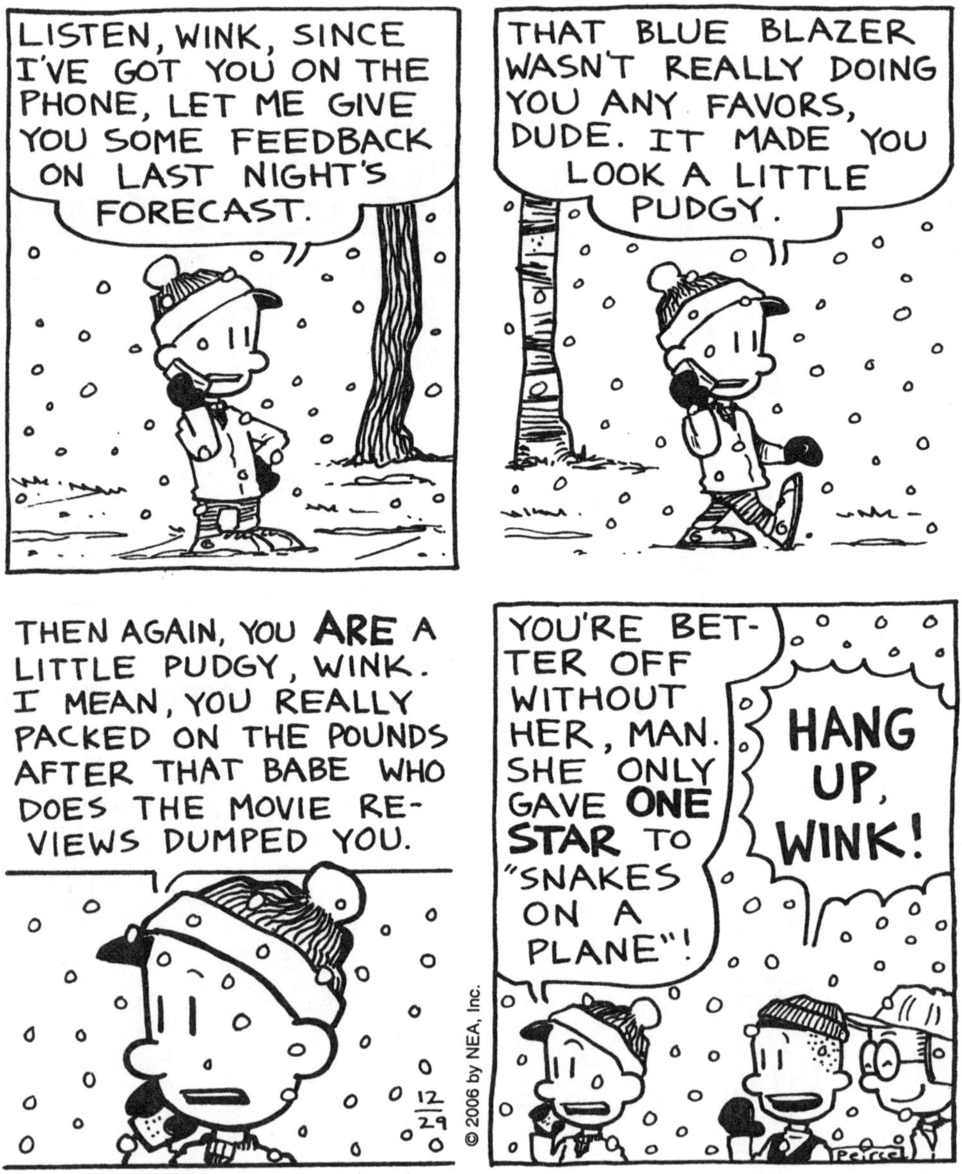
LISTEN, WINK, SINCE I'VE GOT YOU ON THE PHONE, LET ME GIVE YOU SOME FEEDBACK ON LAST NIGHT'S FORECAST.
THAT BLUE BLAZER WASN'T REALLY DOING YOU ANY FAVORS, DUDE. IT MADE YOU LOOK A LITTLE PUDGY.
THEN AGAIN, YOU **ARE** A LITTLE PUDGY, WINK. I MEAN, YOU REALLY PACKED ON THE POUNDS AFTER THAT BABE WHO DOES THE MOVIE REVIEWS DUMPED YOU.
YOU'RE BETTER OFF WITHOUT HER, MAN. SHE ONLY GAVE **ONE STAR** TO "SNAKES ON A PLANE"!
HANG UP, WINK!
12/29
PEIRCE

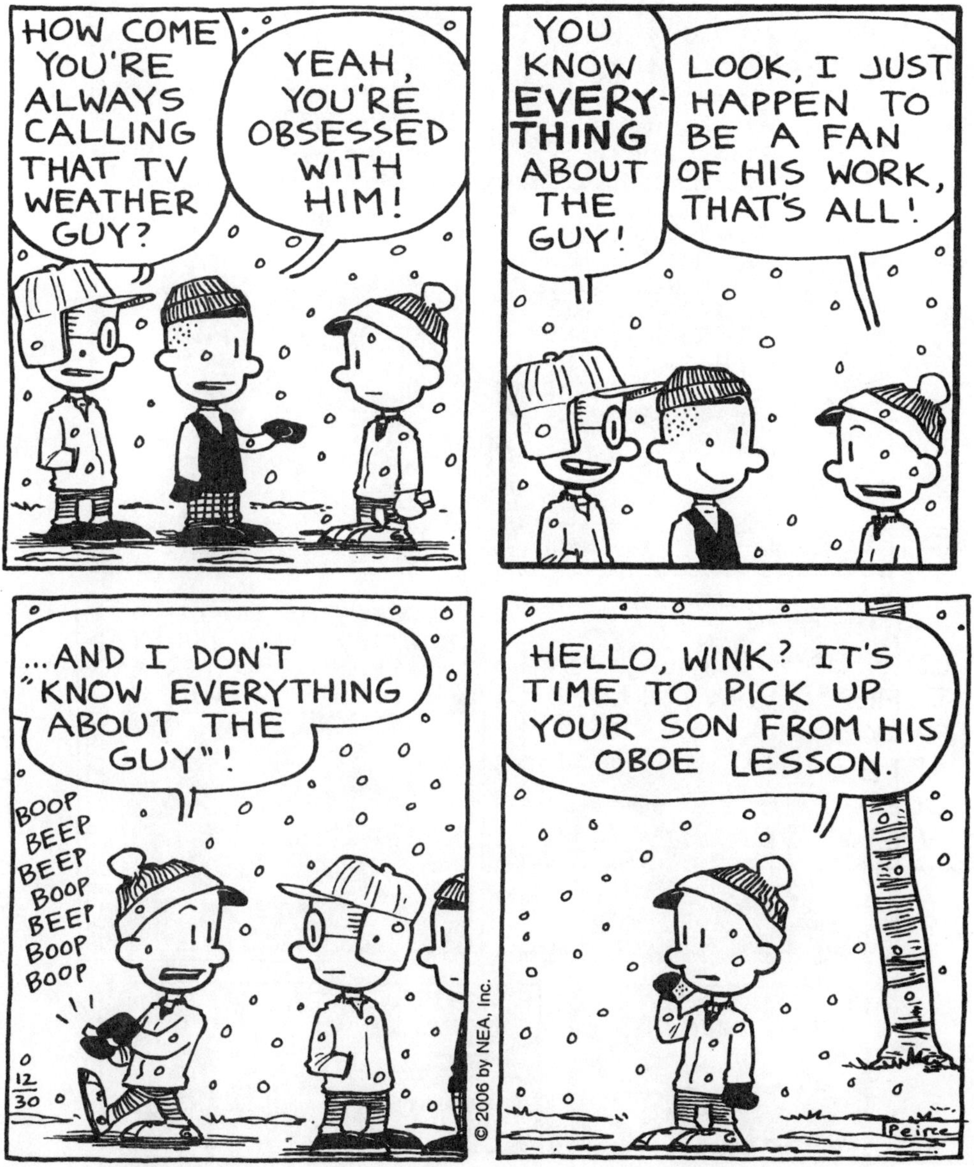
HOW COME YOU'RE ALWAYS CALLING THAT TV WEATHER GUY?
YEAH, YOU'RE OBSESSED WITH HIM!
YOU KNOW **EVERYTHING** ABOUT THE GUY!
LOOK, I JUST HAPPEN TO BE A FAN OF HIS WORK, THAT'S ALL!
...AND I DON'T "KNOW EVERYTHING ABOUT THE GUY"!
BOOP BEEP BEEP BOOP BEEP BOOP BOOP
12/30
© 2006 by NEA, Inc.
HELLO, WINK? IT'S TIME TO PICK UP YOUR SON FROM HIS OBOE LESSON.
Peirce

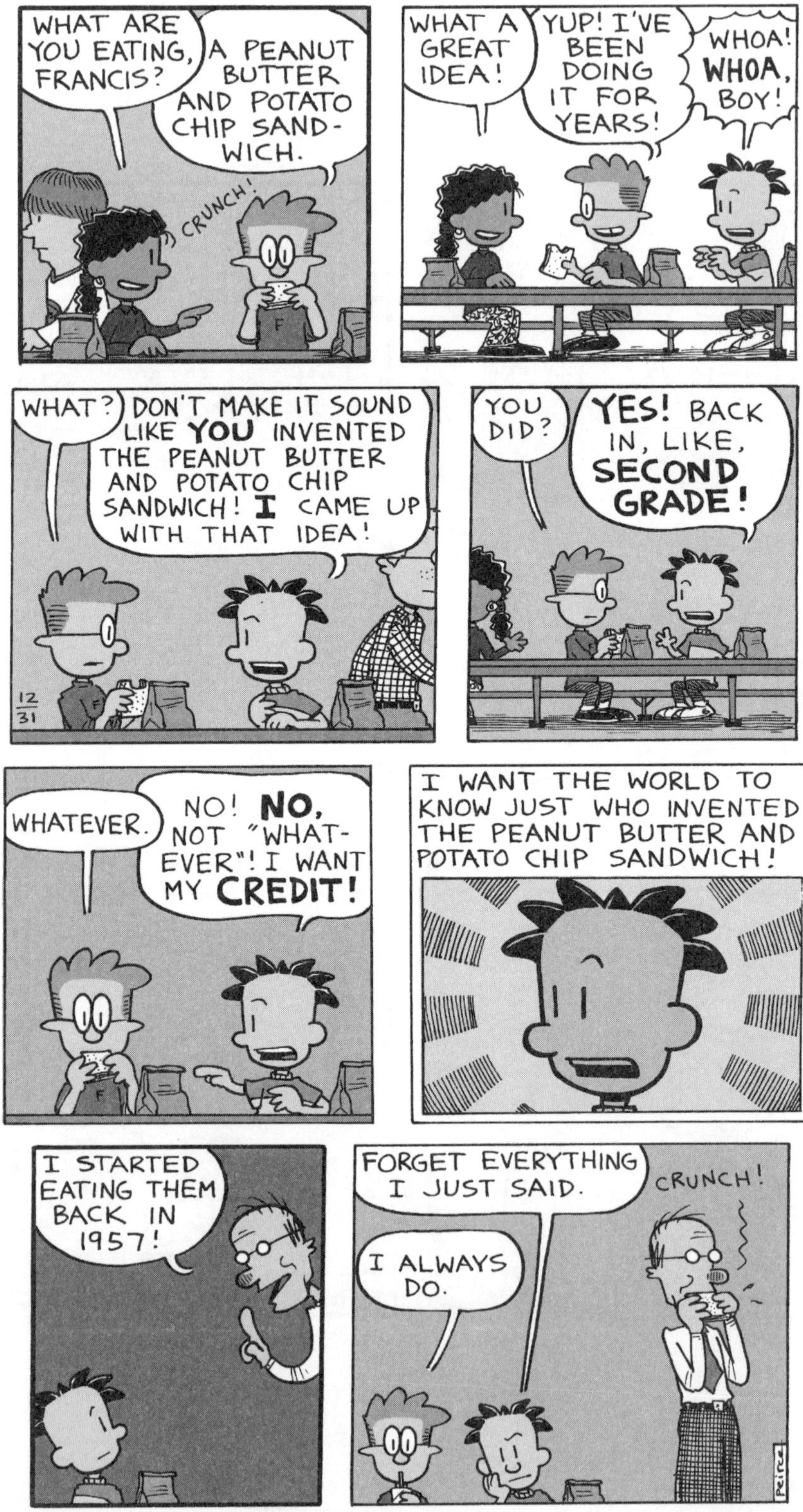

WHAT ARE YOU EATING, FRANCIS?
A PEANUT BUTTER AND POTATO CHIP SANDWICH.
CRUNCH!
WHAT A GREAT IDEA!
YUP! I'VE BEEN DOING IT FOR YEARS!
WHOA! WHOA, BOY!
WHAT?
DON'T MAKE IT SOUND LIKE YOU INVENTED THE PEANUT BUTTER AND POTATO CHIP SANDWICH! I CAME UP WITH THAT IDEA!
12/31
YOU DID?
YES! BACK IN, LIKE, SECOND GRADE!
WHATEVER.
NO! NO, NOT "WHATEVER"! I WANT MY CREDIT!
I WANT THE WORLD TO KNOW JUST WHO INVENTED THE PEANUT BUTTER AND POTATO CHIP SANDWICH!
I STARTED EATING THEM BACK IN 1957!
FORGET EVERYTHING I JUST SAID.
I ALWAYS DO.
CRUNCH!
Peirce

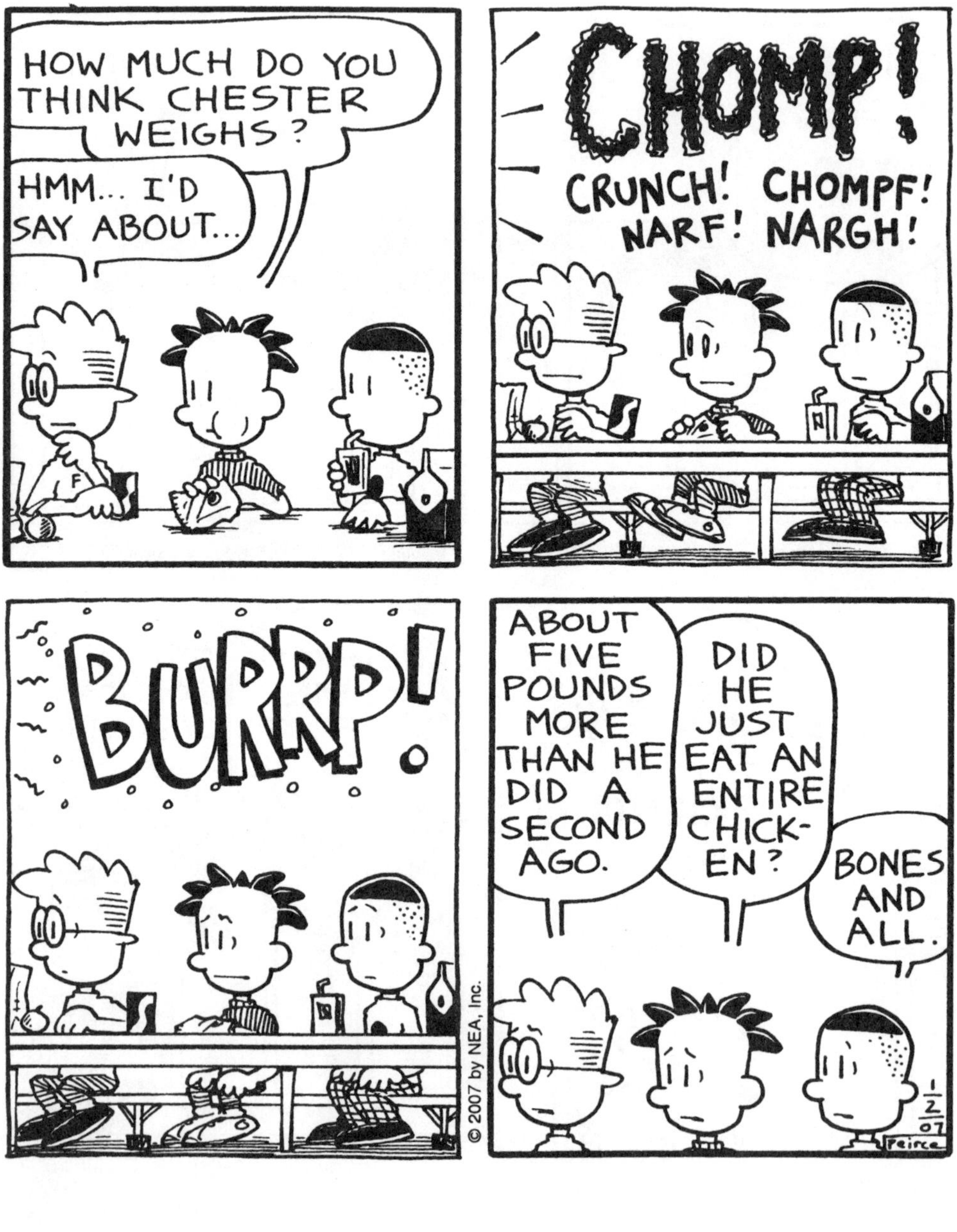
HOW MUCH DO YOU THINK CHESTER WEIGHS?
HMM... I'D SAY ABOUT...
CHOMP!
CRUNCH! CHOMPF! NARF! NARGH!
BURRP!
© 2007 by NEA, Inc.
ABOUT FIVE POUNDS MORE THAN HE DID A SECOND AGO.
DID HE JUST EAT AN ENTIRE CHICKEN?
BONES AND ALL.
1/2/07
Peirce

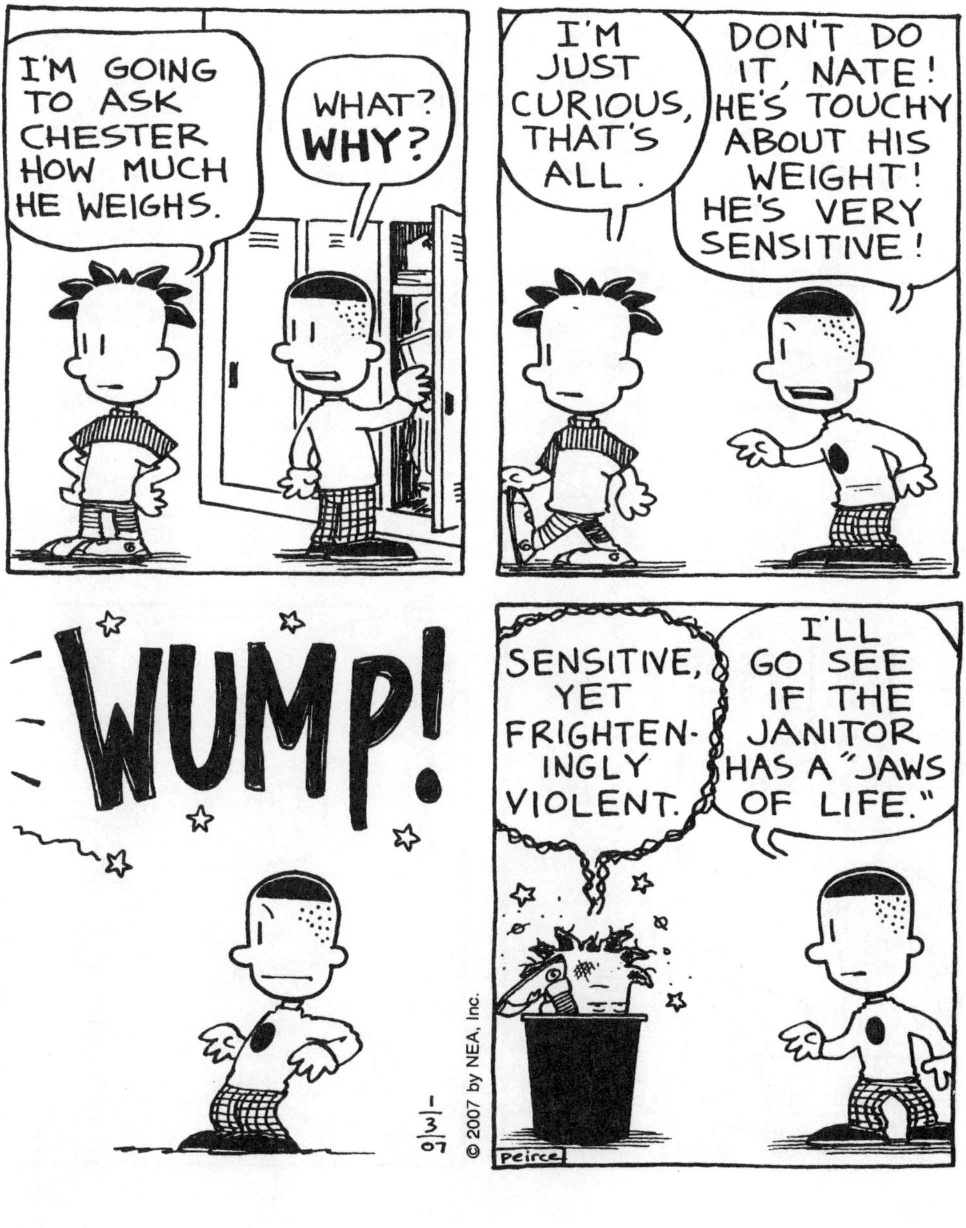
I'M GOING TO ASK CHESTER HOW MUCH HE WEIGHS.
WHAT? **WHY?**
I'M JUST CURIOUS, THAT'S ALL.
DON'T DO IT, NATE! HE'S TOUCHY ABOUT HIS WEIGHT! HE'S VERY SENSITIVE!
WUMP!
SENSITIVE, YET FRIGHTEN-INGLY VIOLENT.
I'LL GO SEE IF THE JANITOR HAS A "JAWS OF LIFE."
1/3/07
© 2007 by NEA, Inc.
Peirce

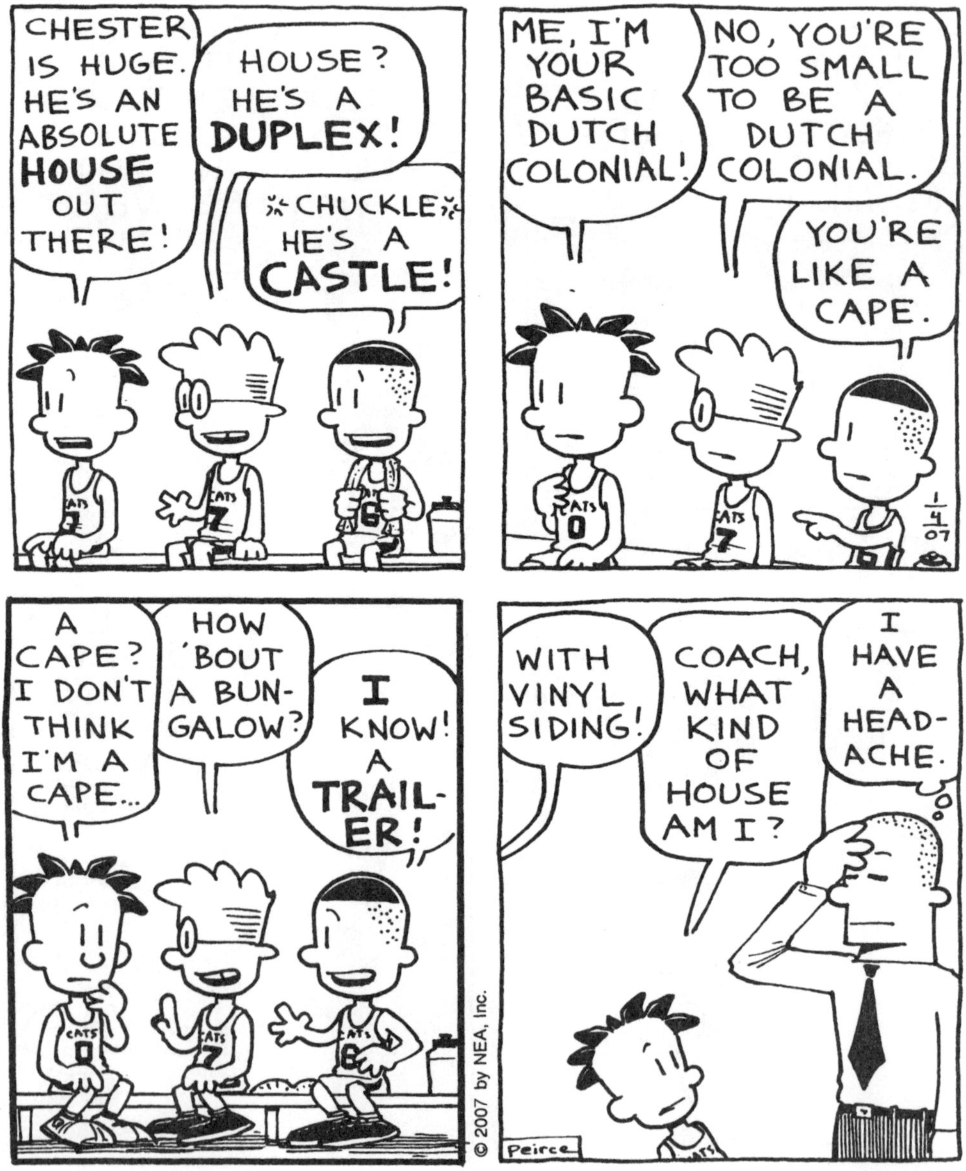
CHESTER IS HUGE. HE'S AN ABSOLUTE **HOUSE** OUT THERE!
HOUSE? HE'S A **DUPLEX**!
CHUCKLE HE'S A **CASTLE**!
ME, I'M YOUR BASIC DUTCH COLONIAL!
NO, YOU'RE TOO SMALL TO BE A DUTCH COLONIAL.
YOU'RE LIKE A CAPE.
1/4/07
A CAPE? I DON'T THINK I'M A CAPE...
HOW 'BOUT A BUNGALOW?
I KNOW! A **TRAILER**!
© 2007 by NEA, Inc.
WITH VINYL SIDING!
COACH, WHAT KIND OF HOUSE AM I?
I HAVE A HEADACHE.
Peirce

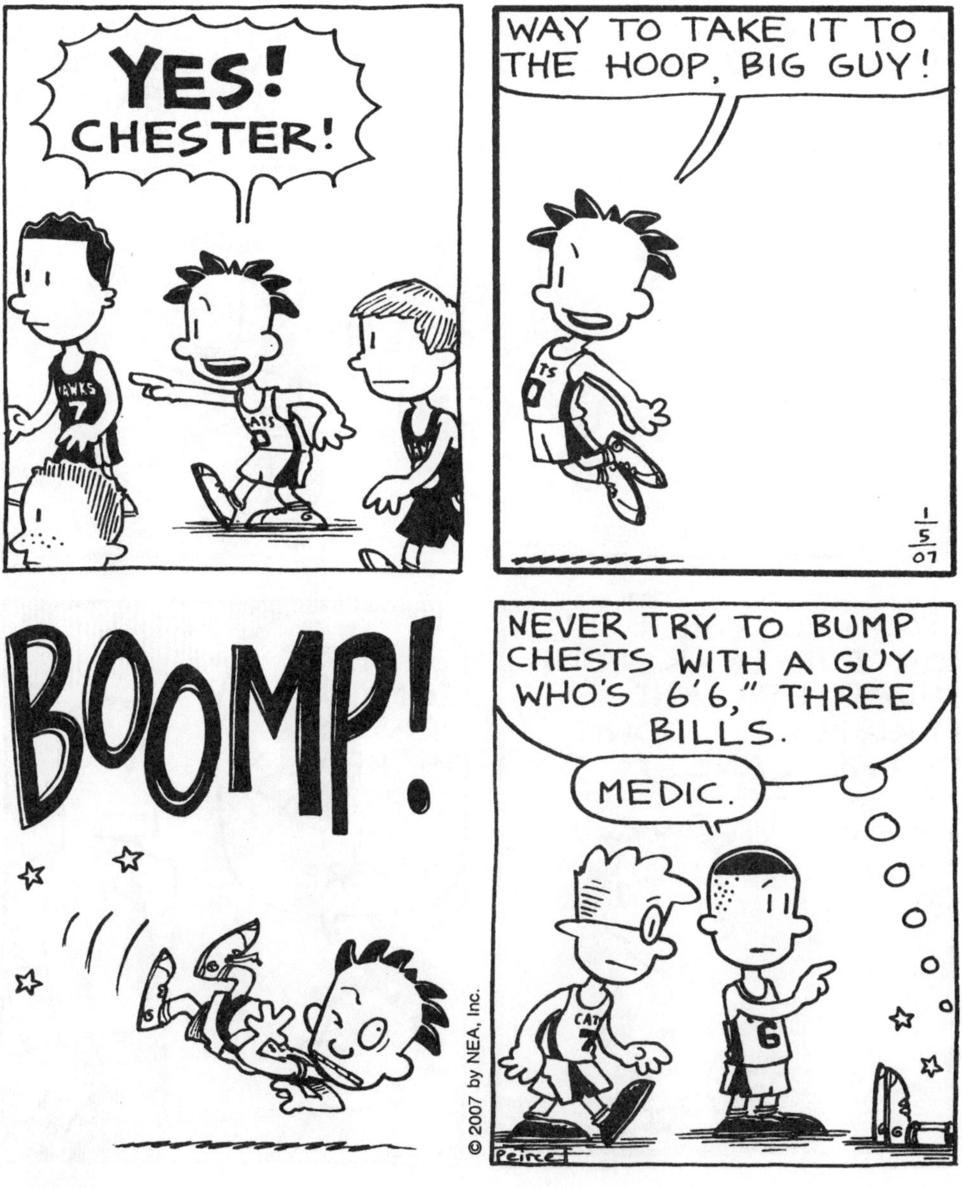
YES! CHESTER!
WAY TO TAKE IT TO THE HOOP, BIG GUY!
1/5/07
BOOMP!
© 2007 by NEA, Inc.
NEVER TRY TO BUMP CHESTS WITH A GUY WHO'S 6'6," THREE BILLS.
MEDIC.
Peirce

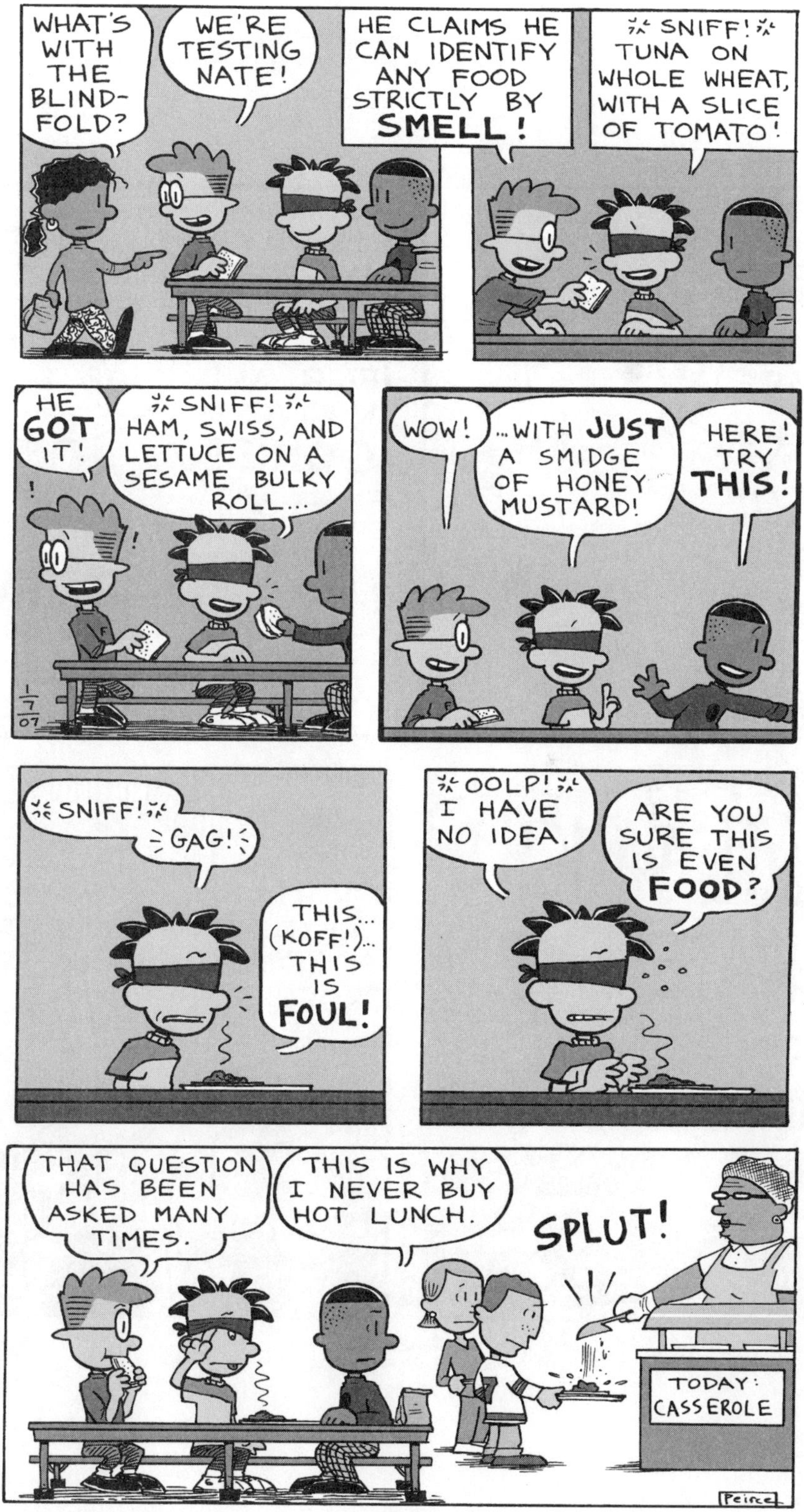
WHAT'S WITH THE BLIND-FOLD?
WE'RE TESTING NATE!
HE CLAIMS HE CAN IDENTIFY ANY FOOD STRICTLY BY SMELL!
SNIFF! TUNA ON WHOLE WHEAT, WITH A SLICE OF TOMATO!
HE GOT IT!
SNIFF! HAM, SWISS, AND LETTUCE ON A SESAME BULKY ROLL...
1/7/07
WOW!
...WITH JUST A SMIDGE OF HONEY MUSTARD!
HERE! TRY THIS!
SNIFF!
GAG!
THIS... (KOFF!)... THIS IS FOUL!
OOLP! I HAVE NO IDEA.
ARE YOU SURE THIS IS EVEN FOOD?
THAT QUESTION HAS BEEN ASKED MANY TIMES.
THIS IS WHY I NEVER BUY HOT LUNCH.
SPLUT!
TODAY: CASSEROLE
Peirce

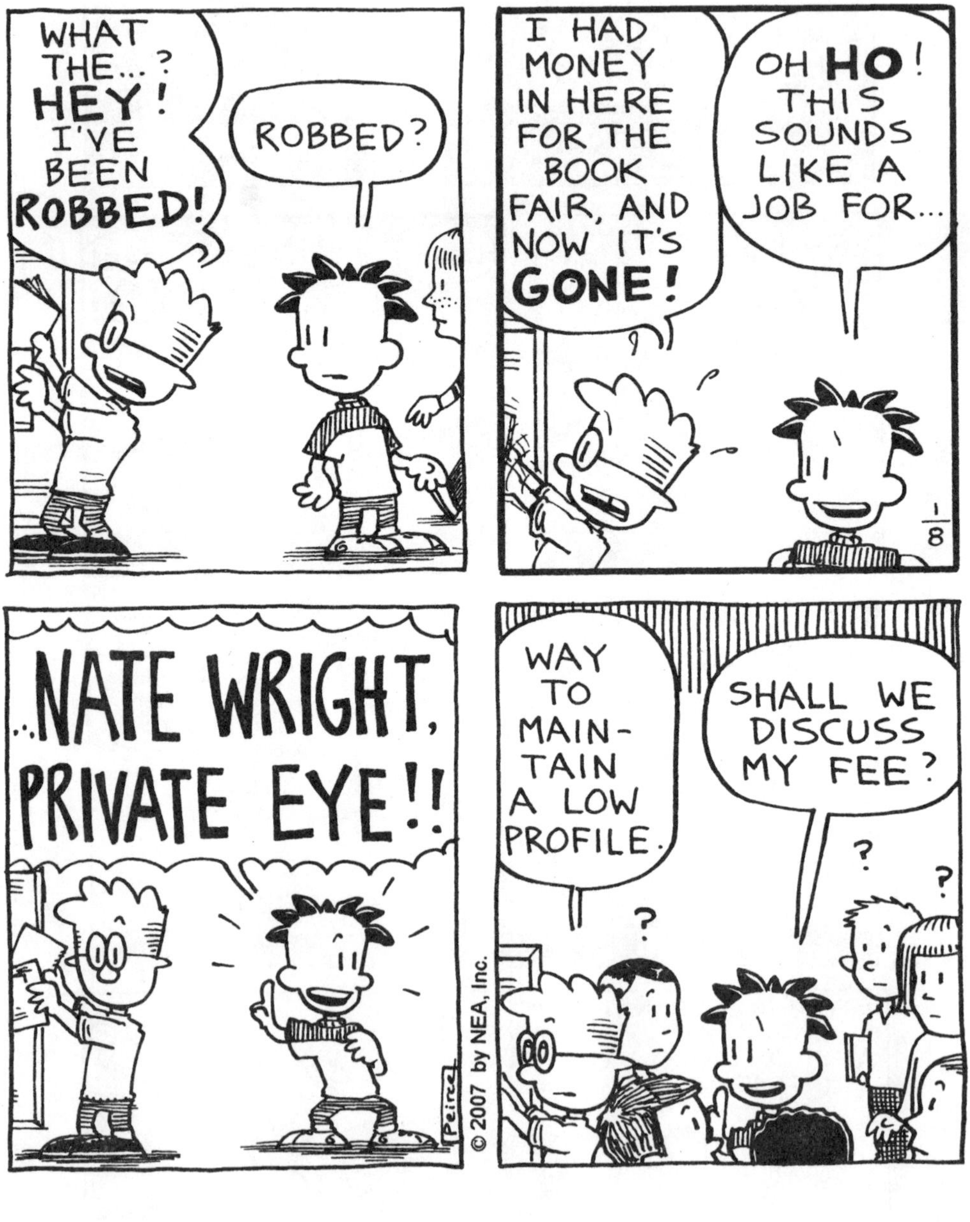

WHAT THE...? HEY! I'VE BEEN ROBBED!
ROBBED?
I HAD MONEY IN HERE FOR THE BOOK FAIR, AND NOW IT'S GONE!
OH HO! THIS SOUNDS LIKE A JOB FOR...
1/8
...NATE WRIGHT, PRIVATE EYE!!
Peirce
© 2007 by NEA, Inc.
WAY TO MAIN-TAIN A LOW PROFILE.
SHALL WE DISCUSS MY FEE?
?
?
?

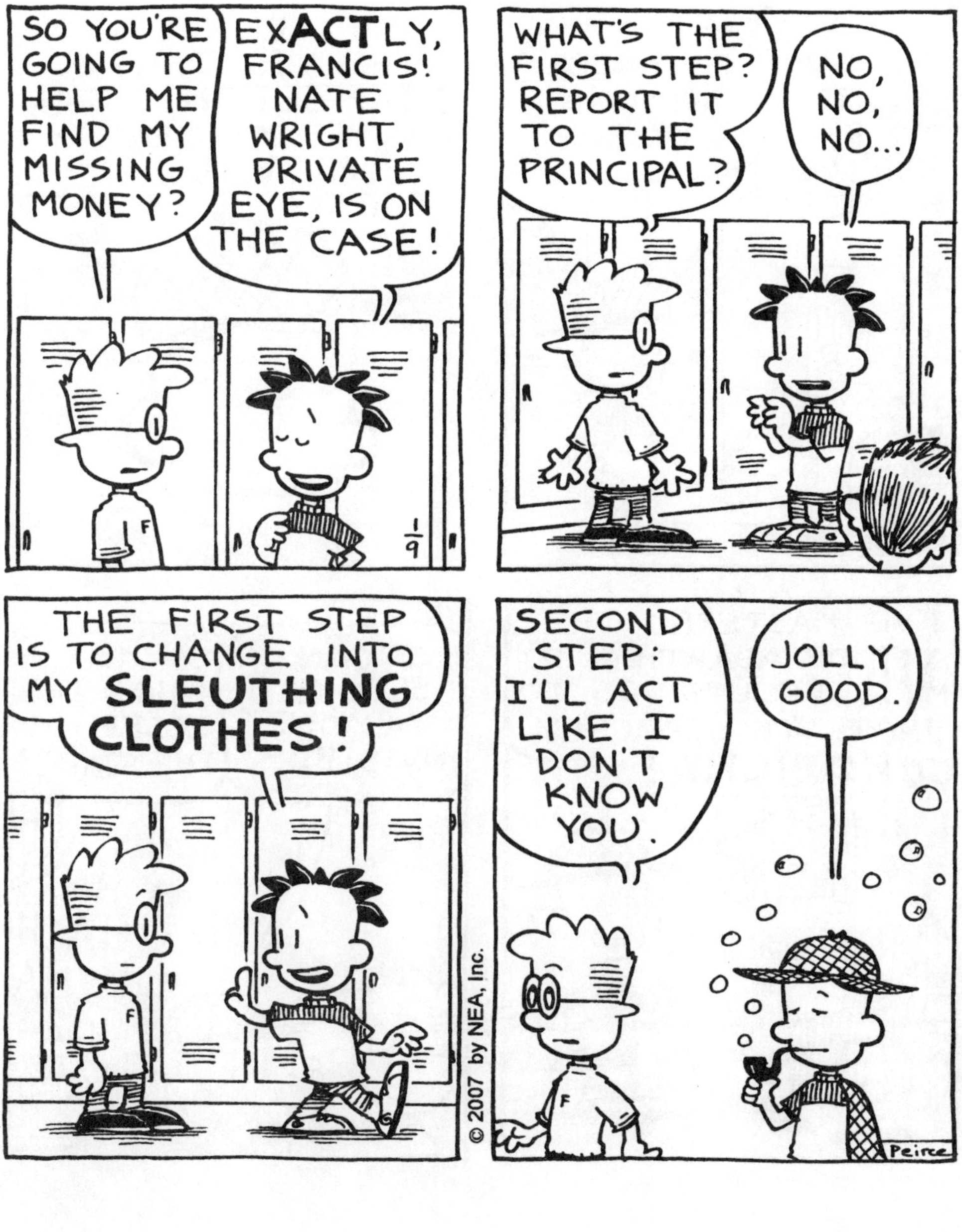
SO YOU'RE GOING TO HELP ME FIND MY MISSING MONEY?
EXACTLY, FRANCIS! NATE WRIGHT, PRIVATE EYE, IS ON THE CASE!
1/9
WHAT'S THE FIRST STEP? REPORT IT TO THE PRINCIPAL?
NO, NO, NO...
THE FIRST STEP IS TO CHANGE INTO MY SLEUTHING CLOTHES!
© 2007 by NEA, Inc.
SECOND STEP: I'LL ACT LIKE I DON'T KNOW YOU.
JOLLY GOOD.
Peirce

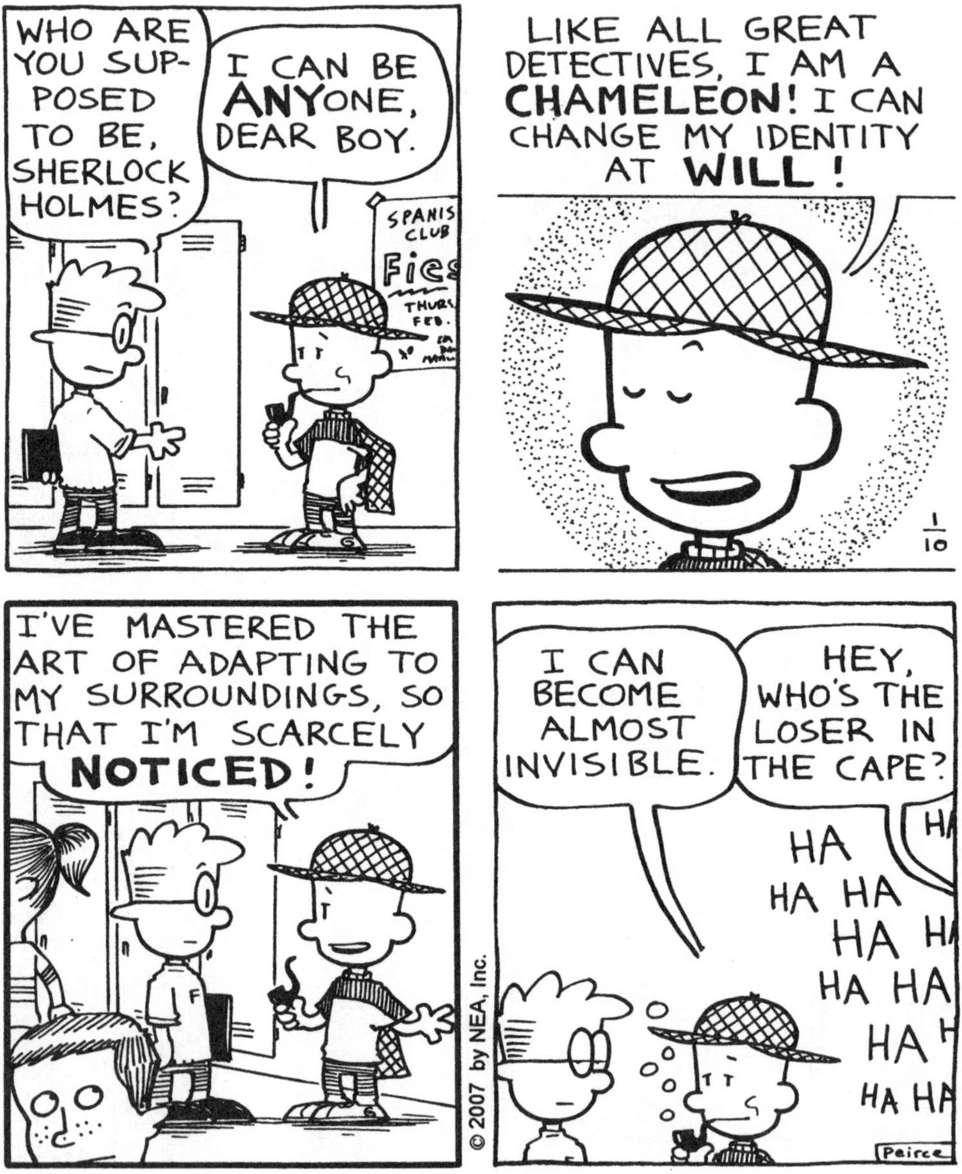
WHO ARE YOU SUP-POSED TO BE, SHERLOCK HOLMES?
I CAN BE ANYONE, DEAR BOY.
SPANIS CLUB Fies THURS FEB.
LIKE ALL GREAT DETECTIVES, I AM A CHAMELEON! I CAN CHANGE MY IDENTITY AT WILL!
1/10
I'VE MASTERED THE ART OF ADAPTING TO MY SURROUNDINGS, SO THAT I'M SCARCELY NOTICED!
© 2007 by NEA, Inc.
I CAN BECOME ALMOST INVISIBLE.
HEY, WHO'S THE LOSER IN THE CAPE?
HA HA HA HA HA HA HA HA
Peirce

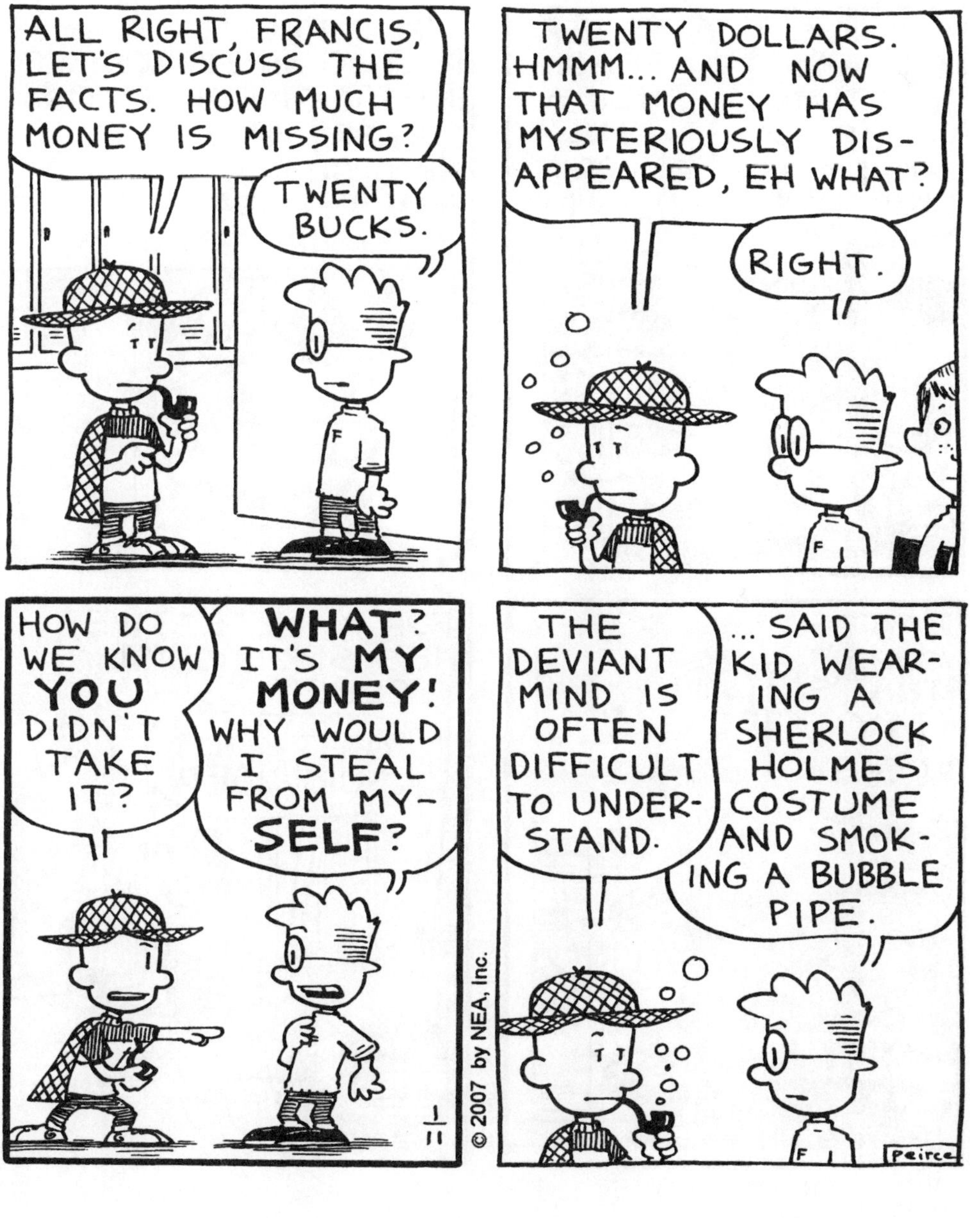
ALL RIGHT, FRANCIS, LET'S DISCUSS THE FACTS. HOW MUCH MONEY IS MISSING?
TWENTY BUCKS.
TWENTY DOLLARS. HMMM... AND NOW THAT MONEY HAS MYSTERIOUSLY DIS-APPEARED, EH WHAT?
RIGHT.
HOW DO WE KNOW YOU DIDN'T TAKE IT?
WHAT? IT'S MY MONEY! WHY WOULD I STEAL FROM MY-SELF?
THE DEVIANT MIND IS OFTEN DIFFICULT TO UNDER-STAND.
... SAID THE KID WEAR-ING A SHERLOCK HOLMES COSTUME AND SMOK-ING A BUBBLE PIPE.
1/11
© 2007 by NEA, Inc.
Peirce

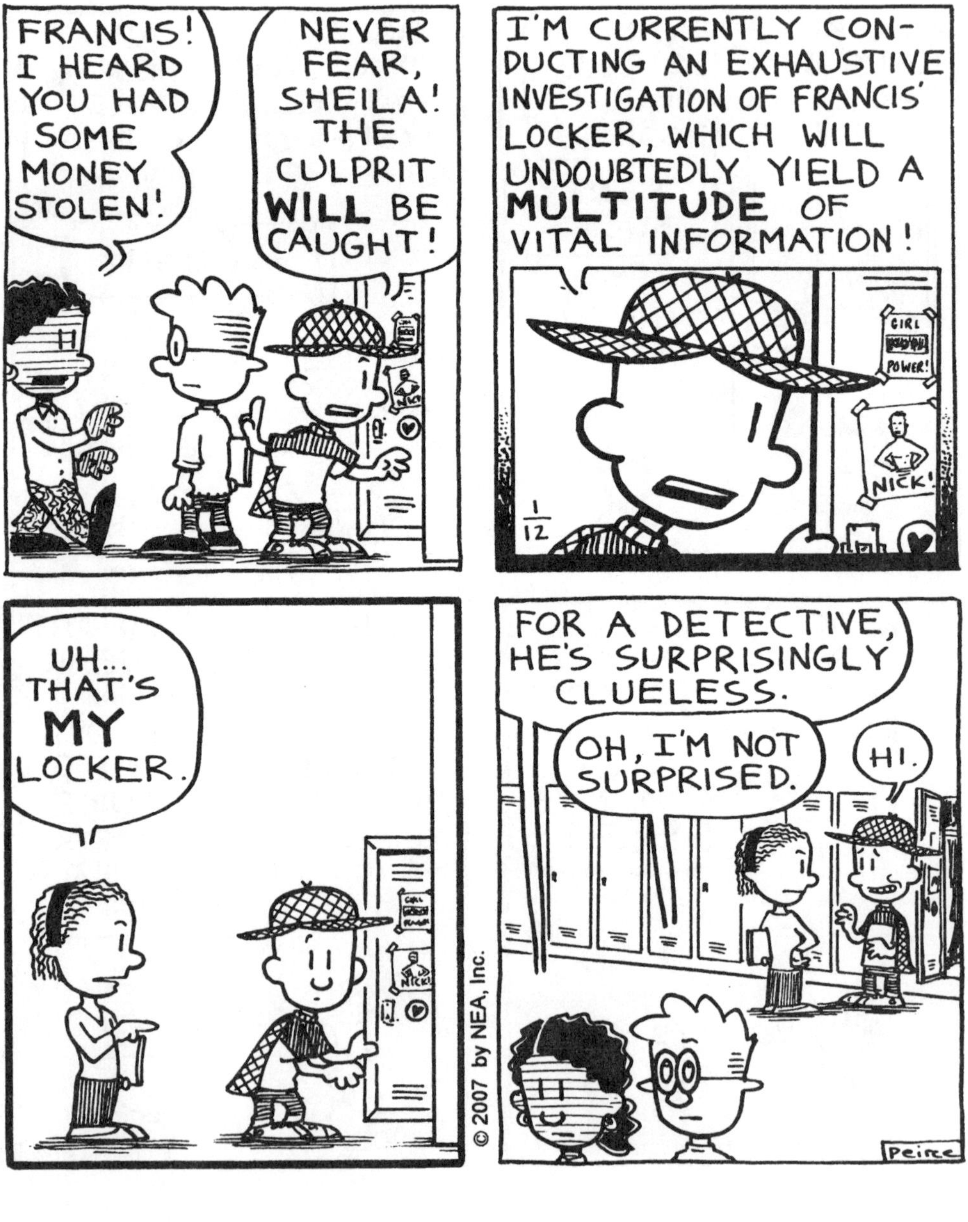
FRANCIS! I HEARD YOU HAD SOME MONEY STOLEN!
NEVER FEAR, SHEILA! THE CULPRIT **WILL** BE CAUGHT!
I'M CURRENTLY CONDUCTING AN EXHAUSTIVE INVESTIGATION OF FRANCIS' LOCKER, WHICH WILL UNDOUBTEDLY YIELD A **MULTITUDE** OF VITAL INFORMATION!
GIRL
POWER!
NICK!
1/12
UH... THAT'S **MY** LOCKER.
FOR A DETECTIVE, HE'S SURPRISINGLY CLUELESS.
OH, I'M NOT SURPRISED.
HI.
Peirce

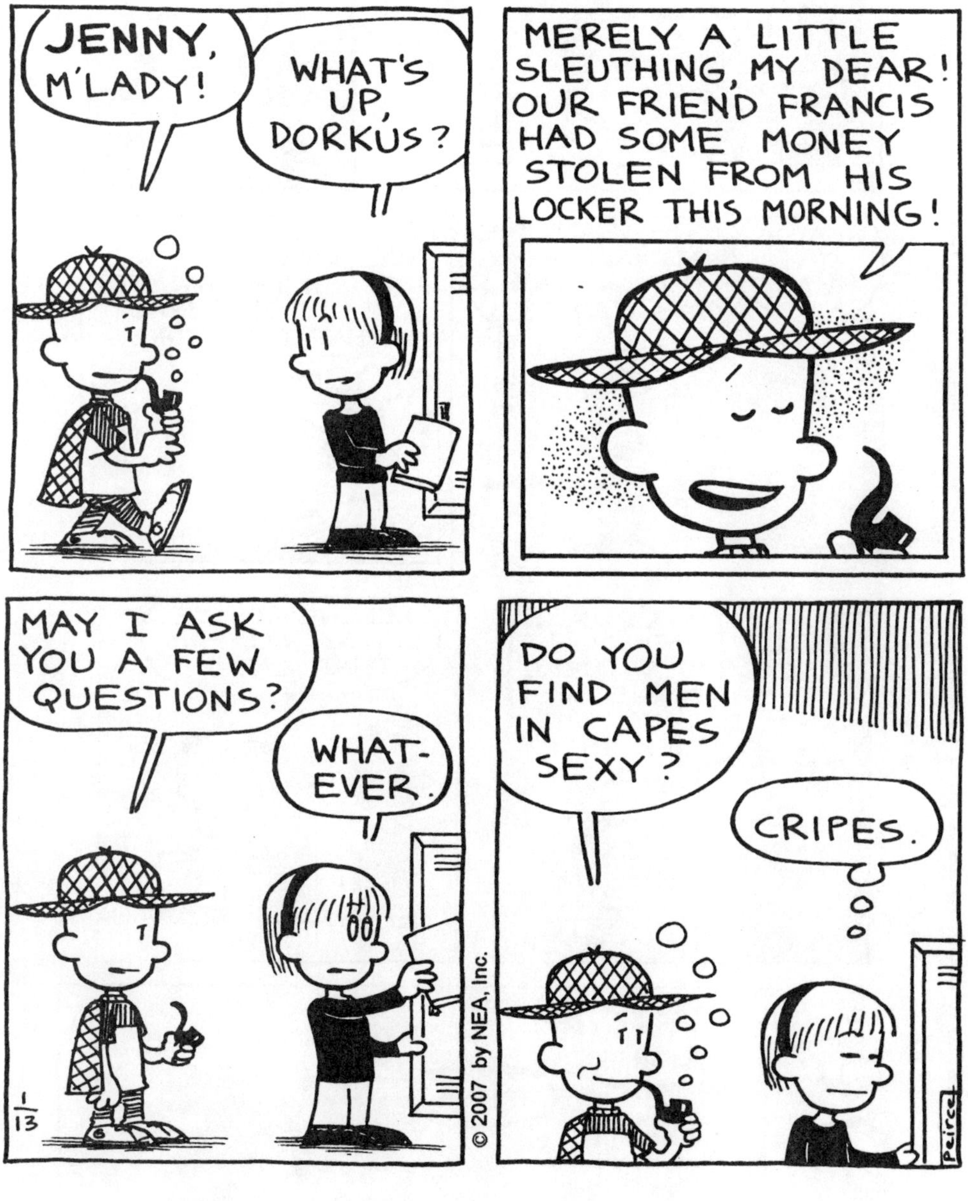
JENNY, M'LADY!
WHAT'S UP, DORKUS?
MERELY A LITTLE SLEUTHING, MY DEAR! OUR FRIEND FRANCIS HAD SOME MONEY STOLEN FROM HIS LOCKER THIS MORNING!
MAY I ASK YOU A FEW QUESTIONS?
WHAT-EVER.
1/13
© 2007 by NEA, Inc.
DO YOU FIND MEN IN CAPES SEXY?
CRIPES.
Peirce

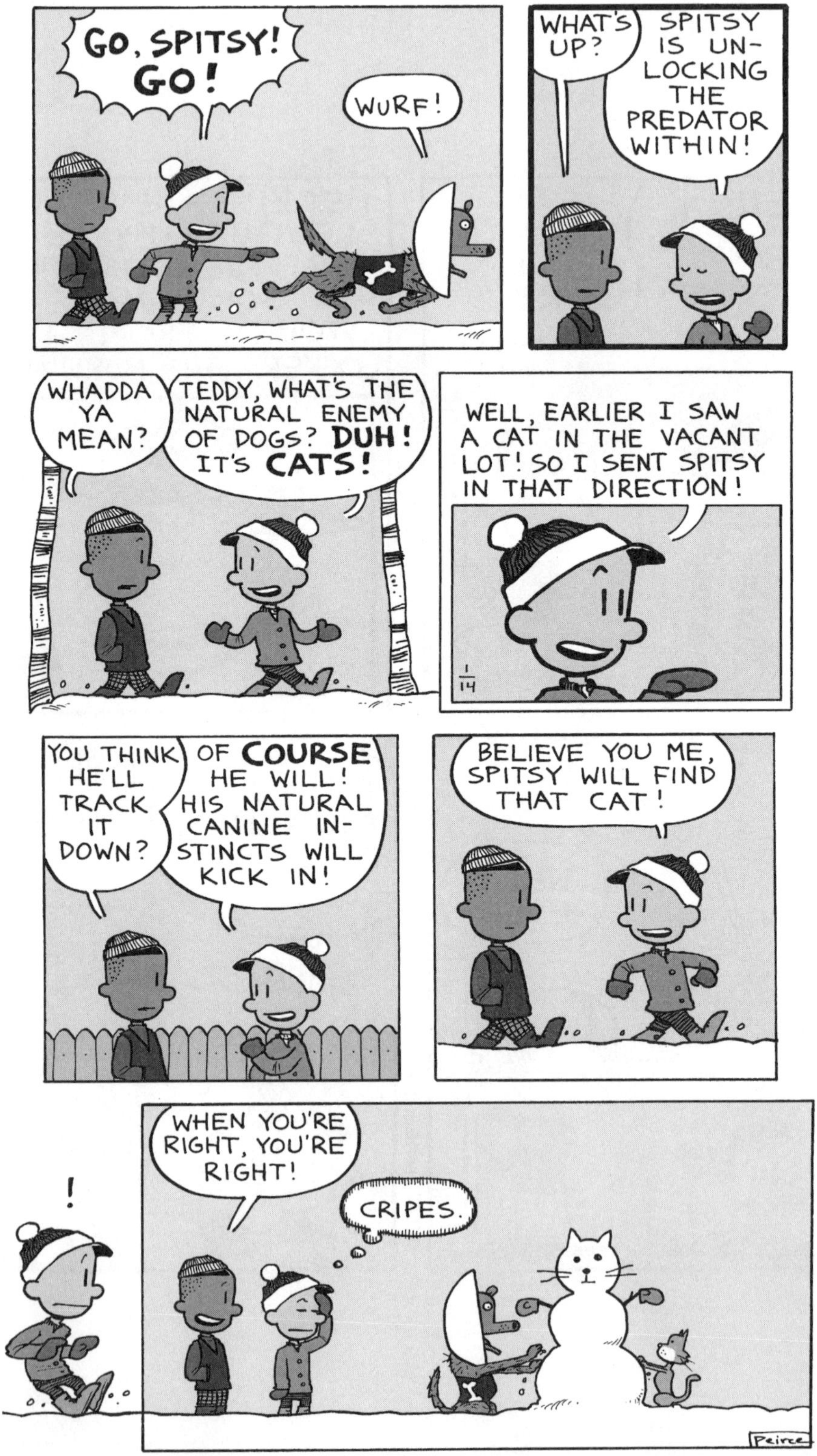
GO, SPITSY! GO!
WURF!
WHAT'S UP?
SPITSY IS UNLOCKING THE PREDATOR WITHIN!
WHADDA YA MEAN?
TEDDY, WHAT'S THE NATURAL ENEMY OF DOGS? DUH! IT'S CATS!
WELL, EARLIER I SAW A CAT IN THE VACANT LOT! SO I SENT SPITSY IN THAT DIRECTION!
1/14
YOU THINK HE'LL TRACK IT DOWN?
OF COURSE HE WILL! HIS NATURAL CANINE INSTINCTS WILL KICK IN!
BELIEVE YOU ME, SPITSY WILL FIND THAT CAT!
!
WHEN YOU'RE RIGHT, YOU'RE RIGHT!
CRIPES.
Peirce

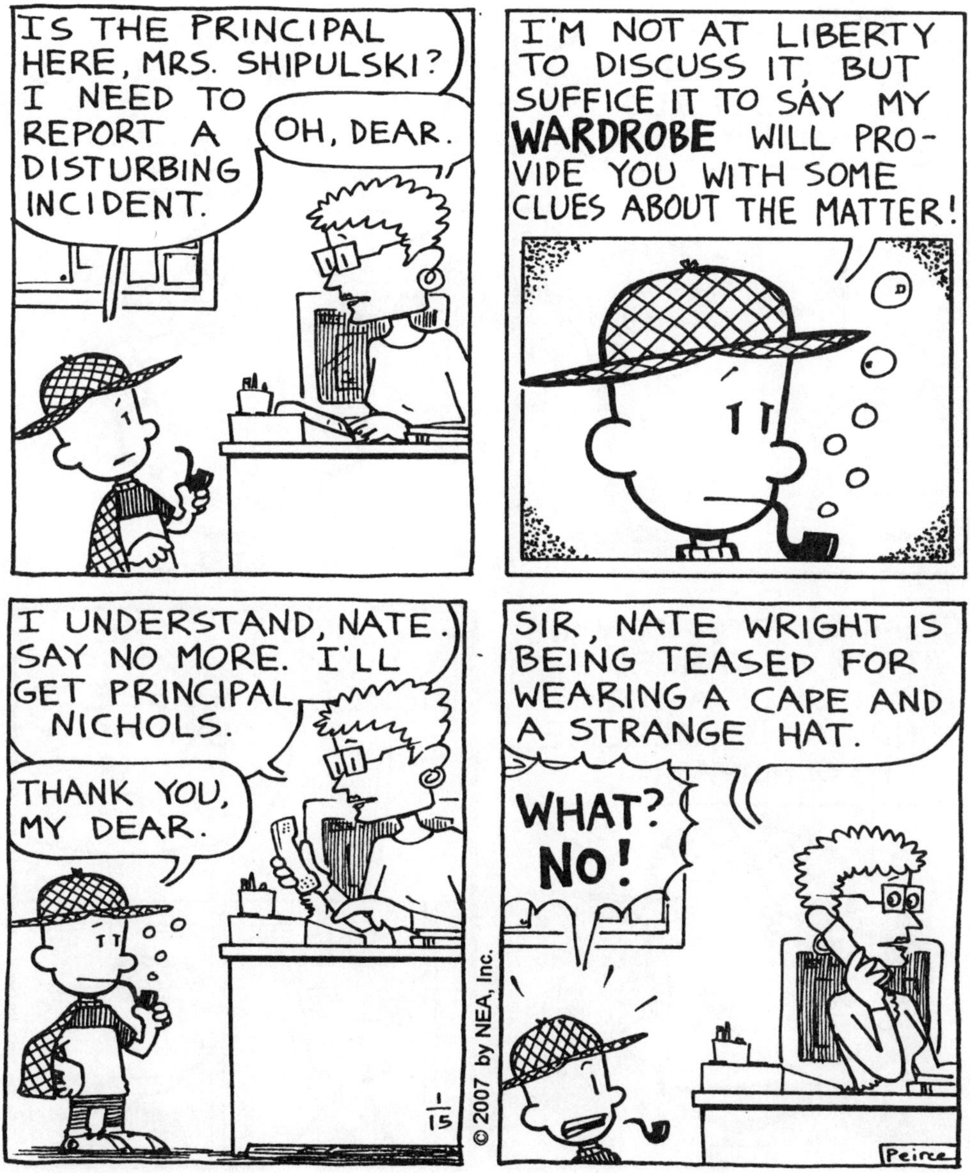
IS THE PRINCIPAL HERE, MRS. SHIPULSKI? I NEED TO REPORT A DISTURBING INCIDENT.
OH, DEAR.
I'M NOT AT LIBERTY TO DISCUSS IT, BUT SUFFICE IT TO SAY MY **WARDROBE** WILL PROVIDE YOU WITH SOME CLUES ABOUT THE MATTER!
I UNDERSTAND, NATE. SAY NO MORE. I'LL GET PRINCIPAL NICHOLS.
THANK YOU, MY DEAR.
1/15
© 2007 by NEA, Inc.
SIR, NATE WRIGHT IS BEING TEASED FOR WEARING A CAPE AND A STRANGE HAT.
WHAT? NO!
Peirce

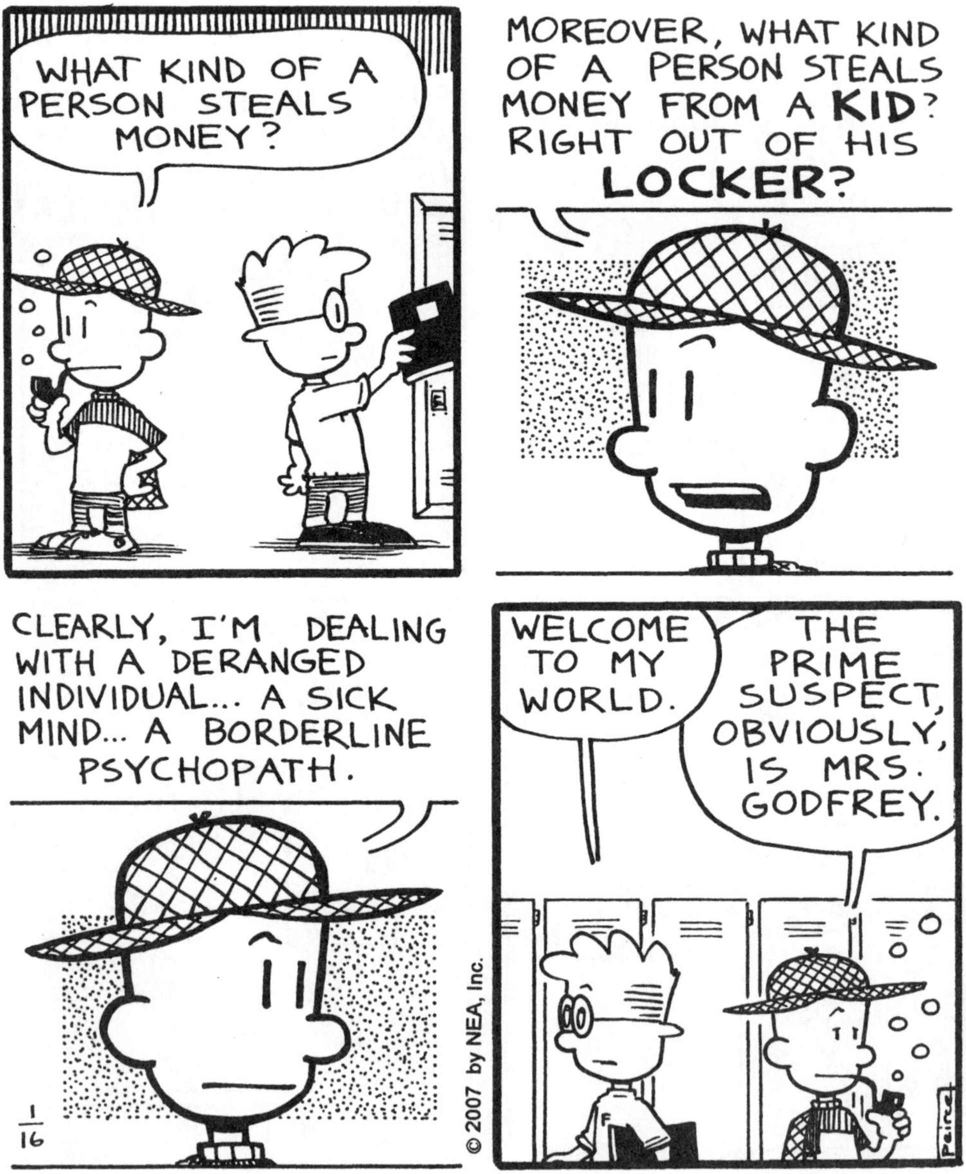
WHAT KIND OF A PERSON STEALS MONEY?
MOREOVER, WHAT KIND OF A PERSON STEALS MONEY FROM A KID? RIGHT OUT OF HIS LOCKER?
CLEARLY, I'M DEALING WITH A DERANGED INDIVIDUAL... A SICK MIND... A BORDERLINE PSYCHOPATH.
1/16
© 2007 by NEA, Inc.
WELCOME TO MY WORLD.
THE PRIME SUSPECT, OBVIOUSLY, IS MRS. GODFREY.
Peirce

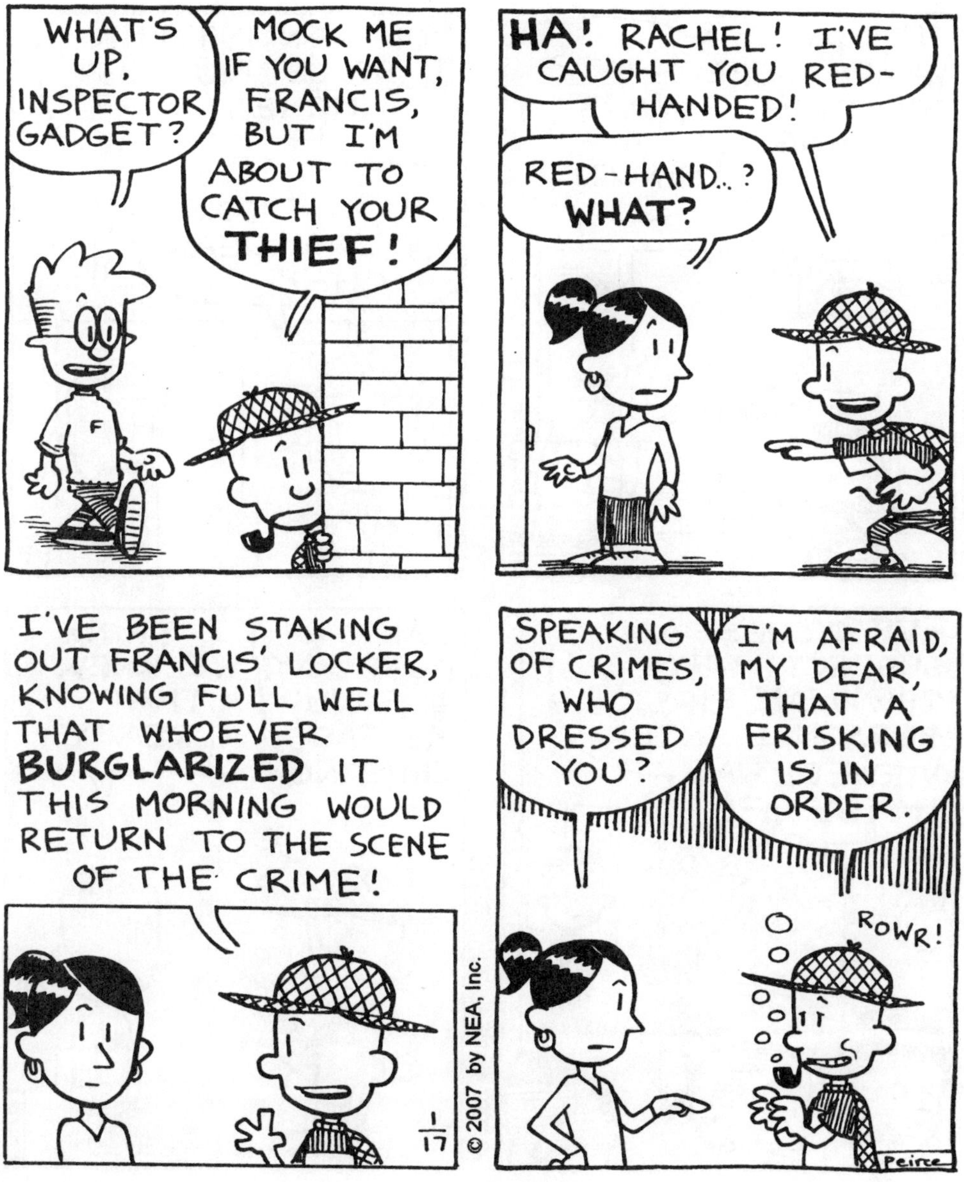
WHAT'S UP, INSPECTOR GADGET?
MOCK ME IF YOU WANT, FRANCIS, BUT I'M ABOUT TO CATCH YOUR THIEF!
HA! RACHEL! I'VE CAUGHT YOU RED-HANDED!
RED-HAND...? WHAT?
I'VE BEEN STAKING OUT FRANCIS' LOCKER, KNOWING FULL WELL THAT WHOEVER BURGLARIZED IT THIS MORNING WOULD RETURN TO THE SCENE OF THE CRIME!
1/17
© 2007 by NEA, Inc.
SPEAKING OF CRIMES, WHO DRESSED YOU?
I'M AFRAID, MY DEAR, THAT A FRISKING IS IN ORDER.
ROWR!
Peirce

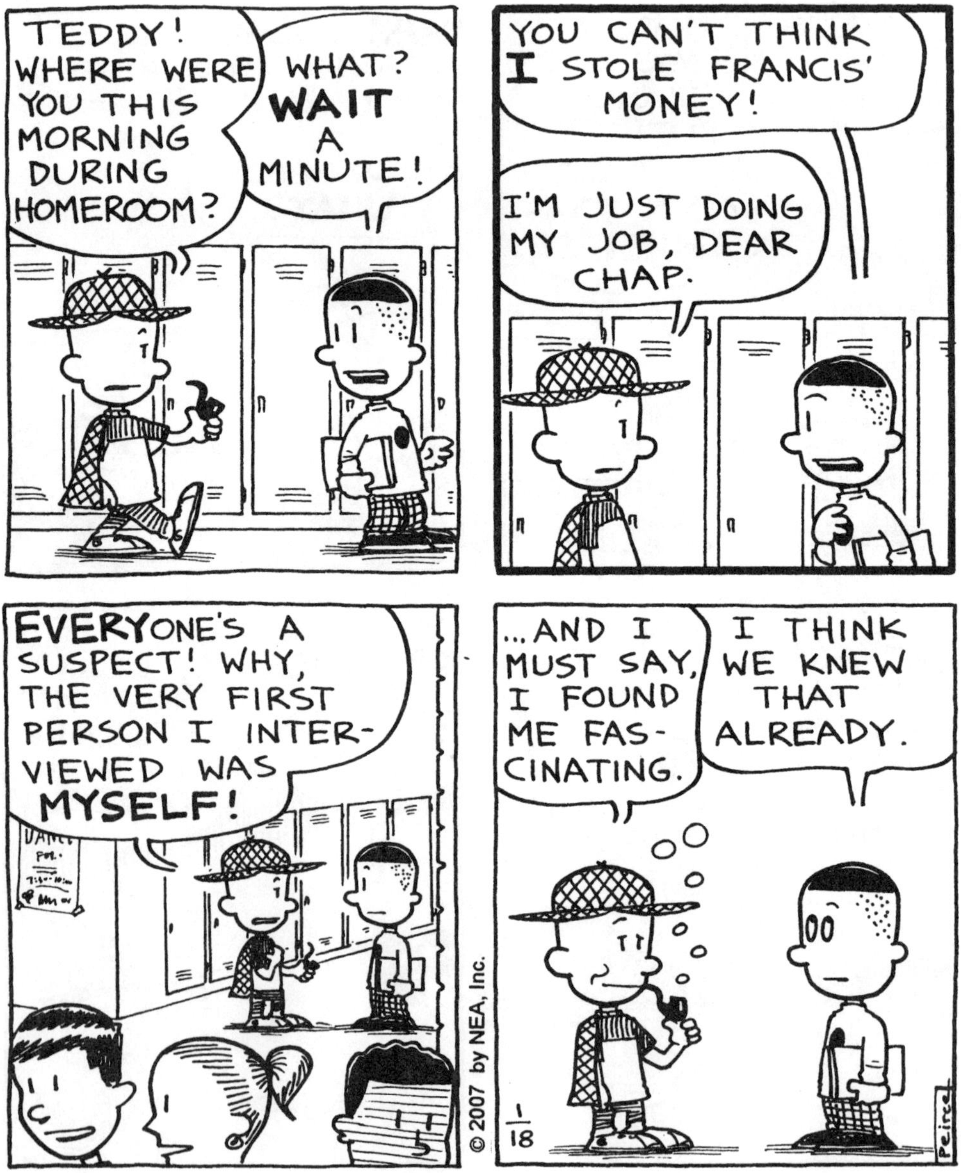
TEDDY! WHERE WERE YOU THIS MORNING DURING HOMEROOM?
WHAT? **WAIT** A MINUTE!
YOU CAN'T THINK **I** STOLE FRANCIS' MONEY!
I'M JUST DOING MY JOB, DEAR CHAP.
EVERYONE'S A SUSPECT! WHY, THE VERY FIRST PERSON I INTER-VIEWED WAS **MYSELF**!
...AND I MUST SAY, I FOUND ME FAS-CINATING.
I THINK WE KNEW THAT ALREADY.
© 2007 by NEA, Inc.
1/18
Peirce

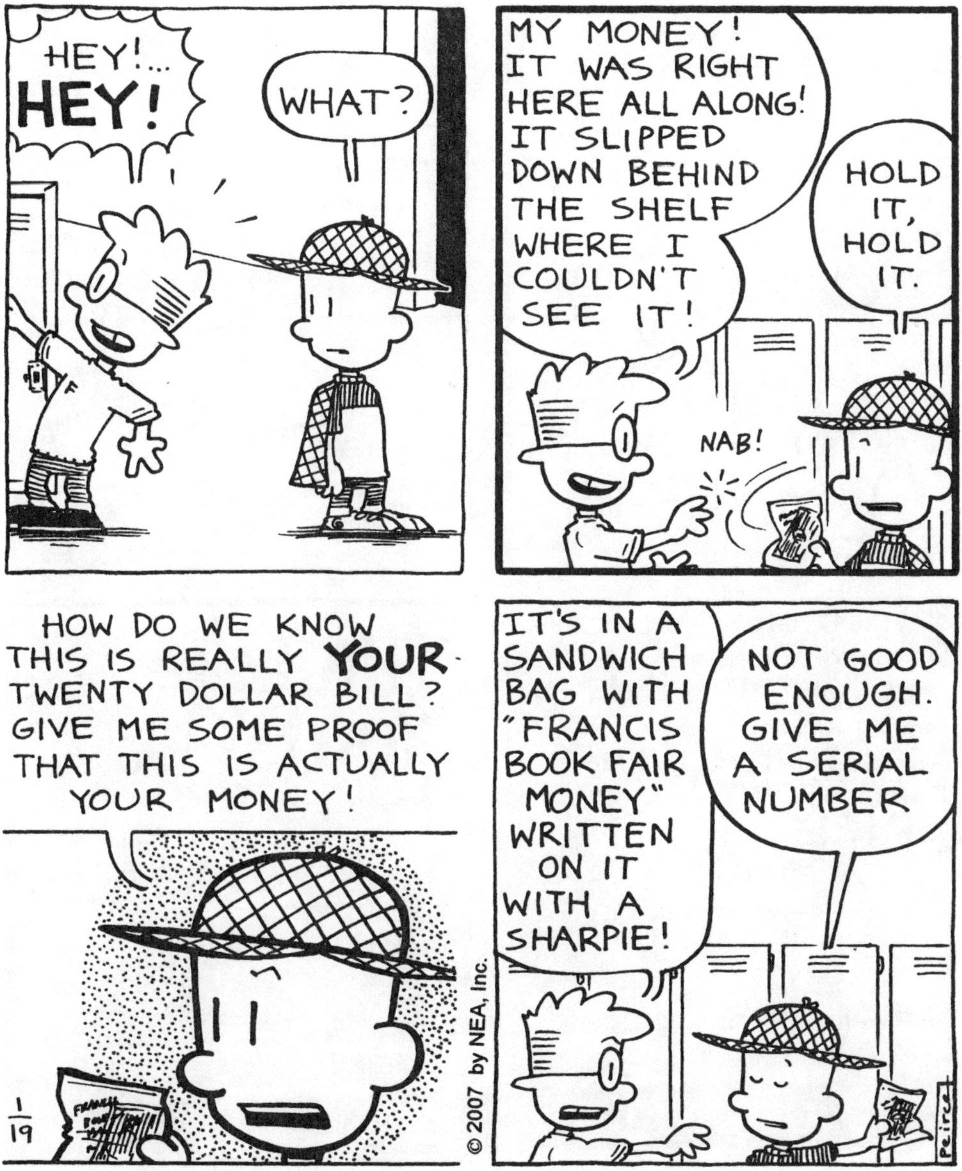
HEY!... HEY!
WHAT?
MY MONEY! IT WAS RIGHT HERE ALL ALONG! IT SLIPPED DOWN BEHIND THE SHELF WHERE I COULDN'T SEE IT!
HOLD IT, HOLD IT.
NAB!
HOW DO WE KNOW THIS IS REALLY YOUR TWENTY DOLLAR BILL? GIVE ME SOME PROOF THAT THIS IS ACTUALLY YOUR MONEY!
1/19
© 2007 by NEA, Inc.
IT'S IN A SANDWICH BAG WITH "FRANCIS BOOK FAIR MONEY" WRITTEN ON IT WITH A SHARPIE!
NOT GOOD ENOUGH. GIVE ME A SERIAL NUMBER
Peirce

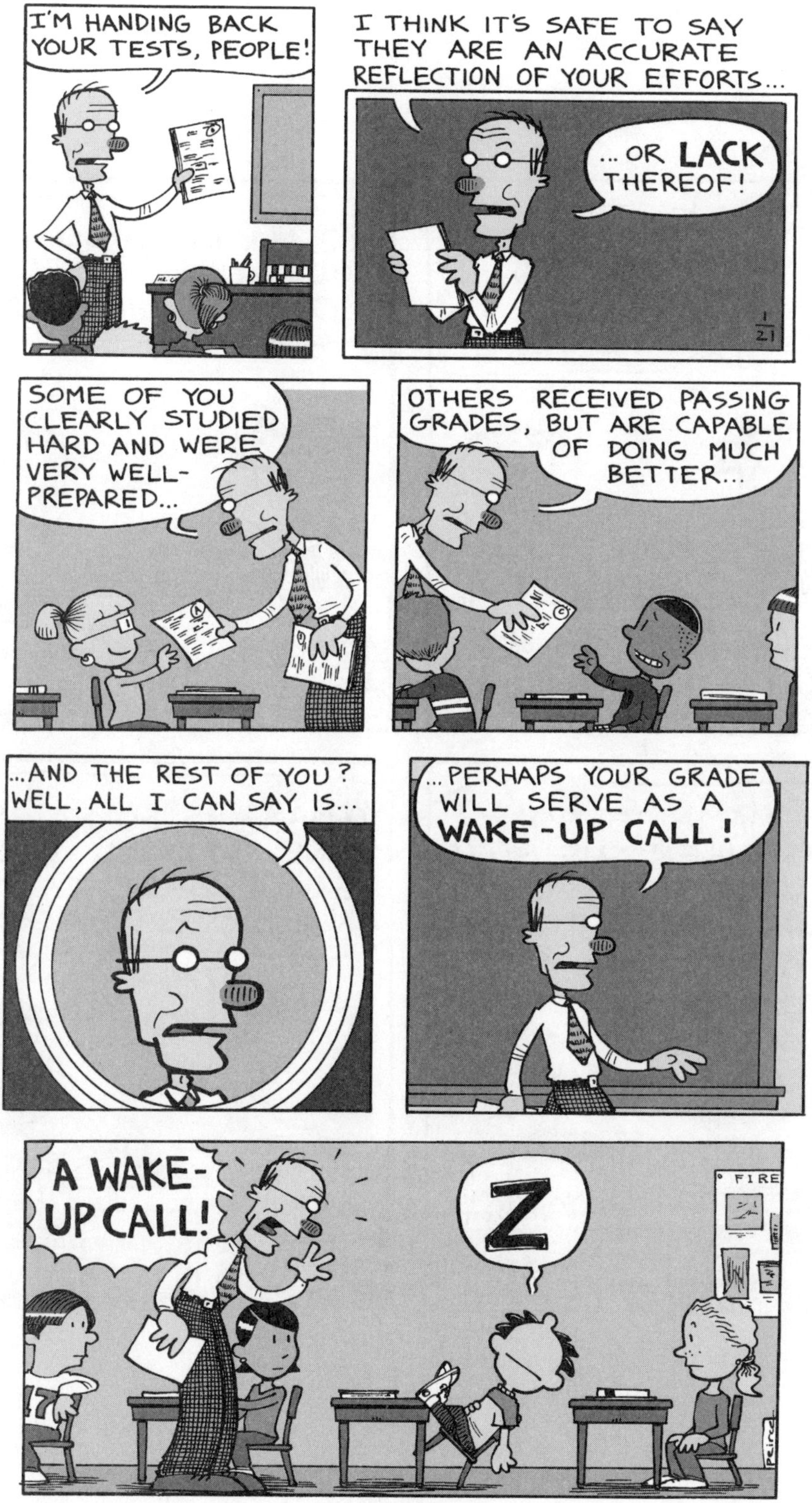
I'M HANDING BACK YOUR TESTS, PEOPLE!
I THINK IT'S SAFE TO SAY THEY ARE AN ACCURATE REFLECTION OF YOUR EFFORTS...
...OR LACK THEREOF!
SOME OF YOU CLEARLY STUDIED HARD AND WERE VERY WELL-PREPARED...
OTHERS RECEIVED PASSING GRADES, BUT ARE CAPABLE OF DOING MUCH BETTER...
...AND THE REST OF YOU? WELL, ALL I CAN SAY IS...
...PERHAPS YOUR GRADE WILL SERVE AS A WAKE-UP CALL!
A WAKE-UP CALL!
Z
FIRE

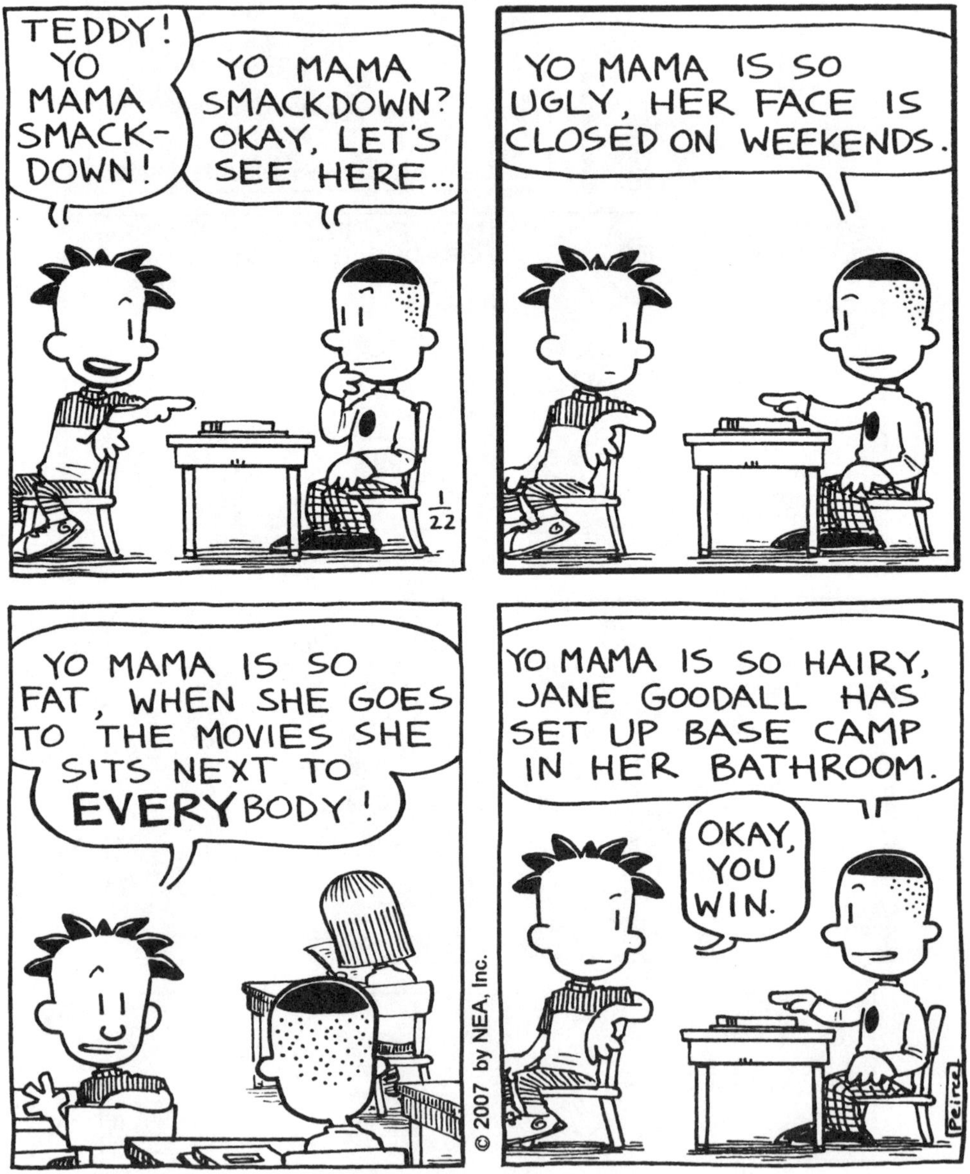
TEDDY! YO MAMA SMACK-DOWN!
YO MAMA SMACKDOWN? OKAY, LET'S SEE HERE...
1/22
YO MAMA IS SO UGLY, HER FACE IS CLOSED ON WEEKENDS.
YO MAMA IS SO FAT, WHEN SHE GOES TO THE MOVIES SHE SITS NEXT TO **EVERY**BODY!
YO MAMA IS SO HAIRY, JANE GOODALL HAS SET UP BASE CAMP IN HER BATHROOM.
OKAY, YOU WIN.
Peirce

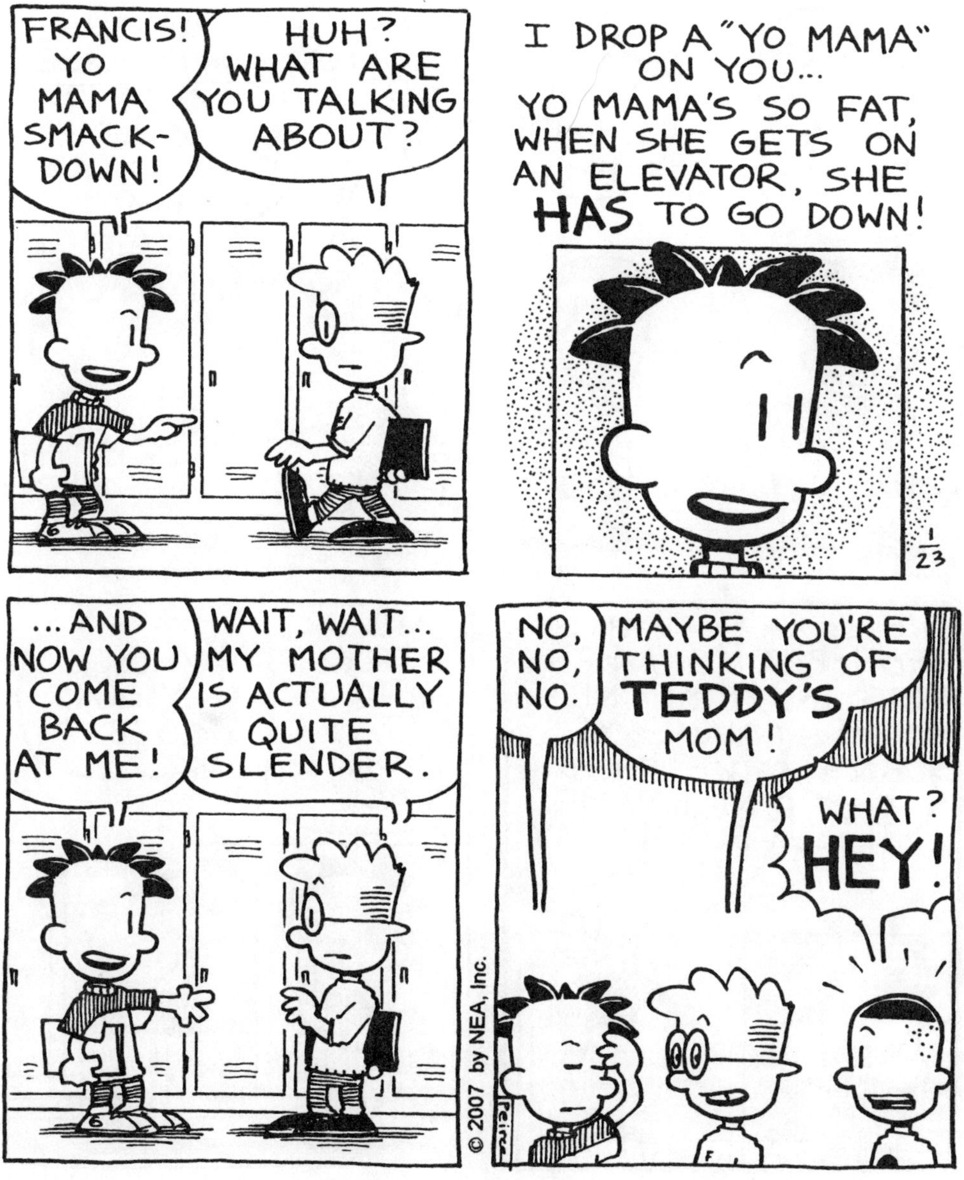
FRANCIS! YO MAMA SMACK-DOWN!
HUH? WHAT ARE YOU TALKING ABOUT?
I DROP A "YO MAMA" ON YOU... YO MAMA'S SO FAT, WHEN SHE GETS ON AN ELEVATOR, SHE HAS TO GO DOWN!
1/23
...AND NOW YOU COME BACK AT ME!
WAIT, WAIT... MY MOTHER IS ACTUALLY QUITE SLENDER.
© 2007 by NEA, Inc.
NO, NO, NO.
MAYBE YOU'RE THINKING OF TEDDY'S MOM!
WHAT? HEY!
Peirce

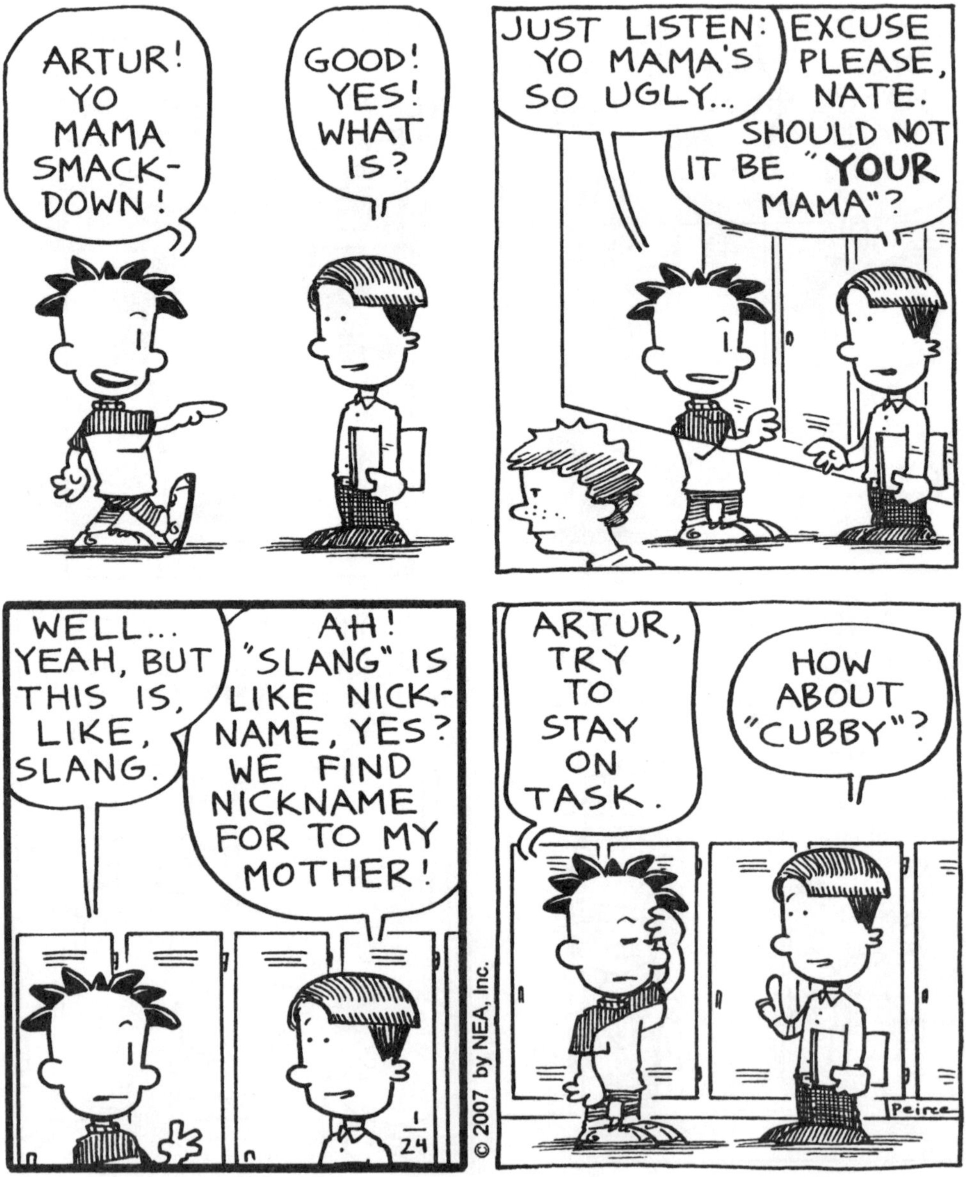
ARTUR! YO MAMA SMACK-DOWN!
GOOD! YES! WHAT IS?
JUST LISTEN: YO MAMA'S SO UGLY...
EXCUSE PLEASE, NATE. SHOULD NOT IT BE "**YOUR** MAMA"?
WELL... YEAH, BUT THIS IS, LIKE, SLANG.
AH! "SLANG" IS LIKE NICK-NAME, YES? WE FIND NICKNAME FOR TO MY MOTHER!
1 24
© 2007 by NEA, Inc.
ARTUR, TRY TO STAY ON TASK.
HOW ABOUT "CUBBY"?
Peirce

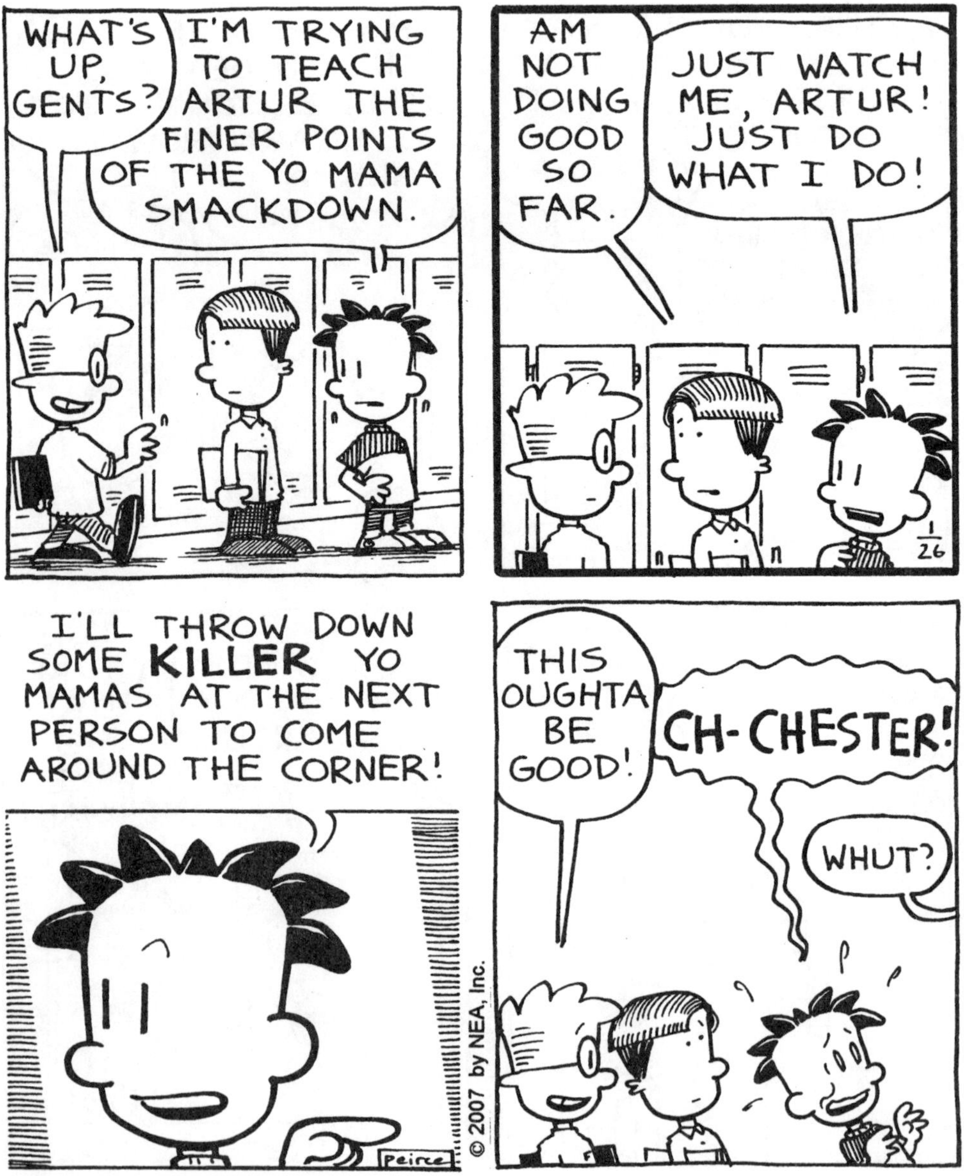
WHAT'S UP, GENTS?
I'M TRYING TO TEACH ARTUR THE FINER POINTS OF THE YO MAMA SMACKDOWN.
AM NOT DOING GOOD SO FAR.
JUST WATCH ME, ARTUR! JUST DO WHAT I DO!
1/26
I'LL THROW DOWN SOME KILLER YO MAMAS AT THE NEXT PERSON TO COME AROUND THE CORNER!
Peirce
© 2007 by NEA, Inc.
THIS OUGHTA BE GOOD!
CH-CHESTER!
WHUT?

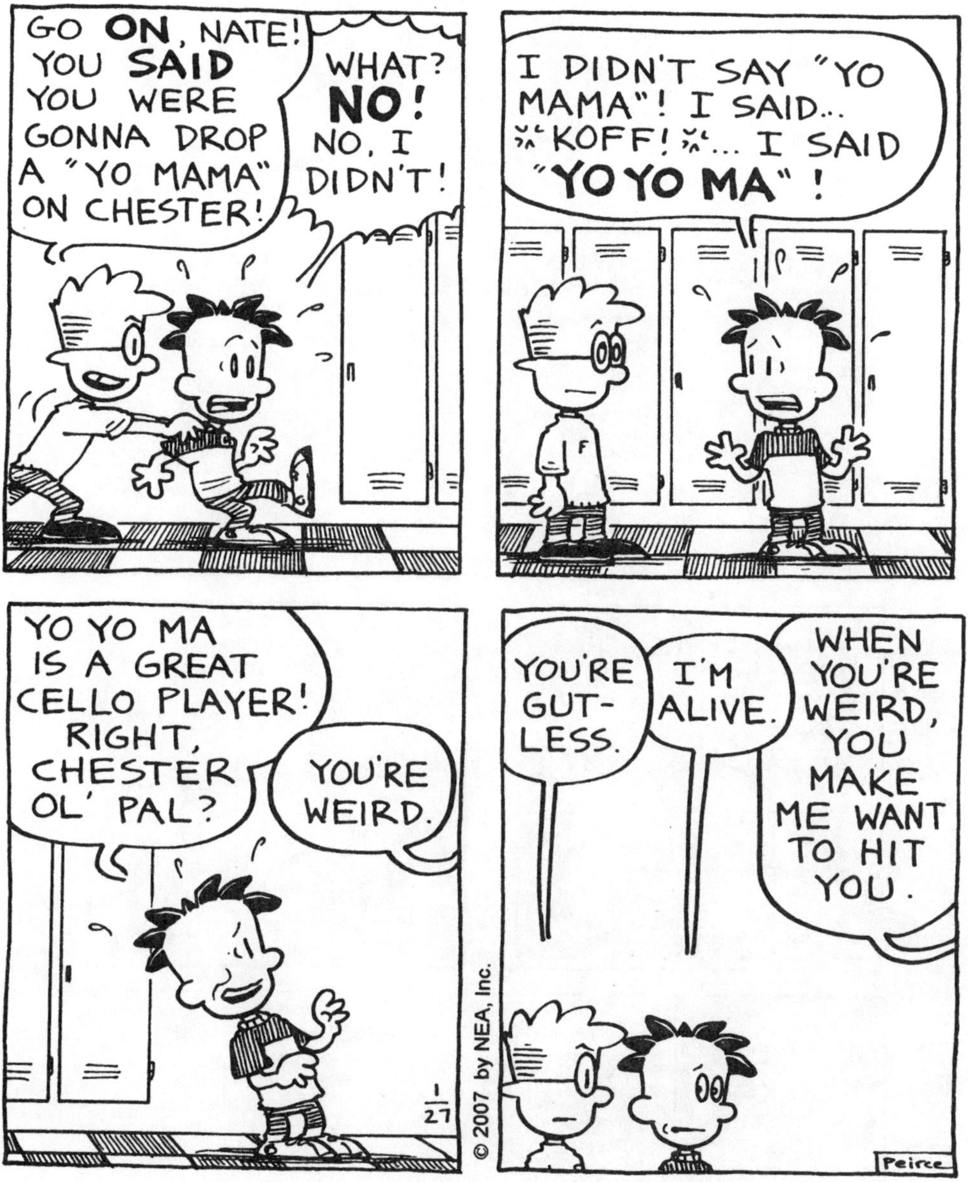
GO **ON**, NATE! YOU **SAID** YOU WERE GONNA DROP A "YO MAMA" ON CHESTER!
WHAT? **NO!** NO, I DIDN'T!
I DIDN'T SAY "YO MAMA"! I SAID... KOFF! ... I SAID "**YO YO MA**"!
YO YO MA IS A GREAT CELLO PLAYER! RIGHT, CHESTER OL' PAL?
YOU'RE WEIRD.
1/27
© 2007 by NEA, Inc.
YOU'RE GUT-LESS.
I'M ALIVE.
WHEN YOU'RE WEIRD, YOU MAKE ME WANT TO HIT YOU.
Peirce

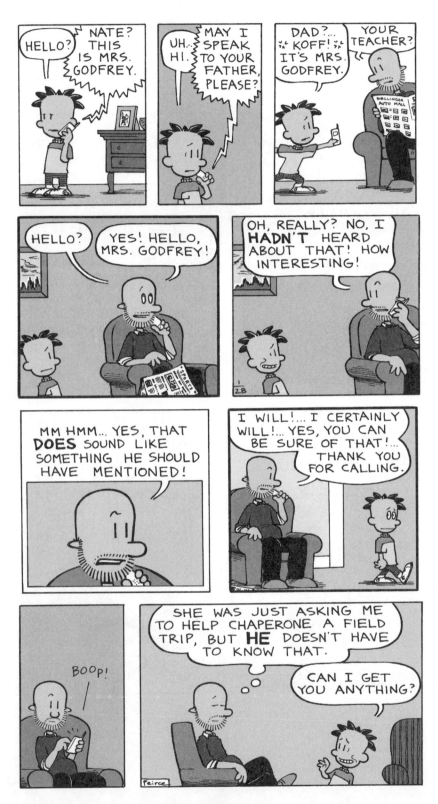

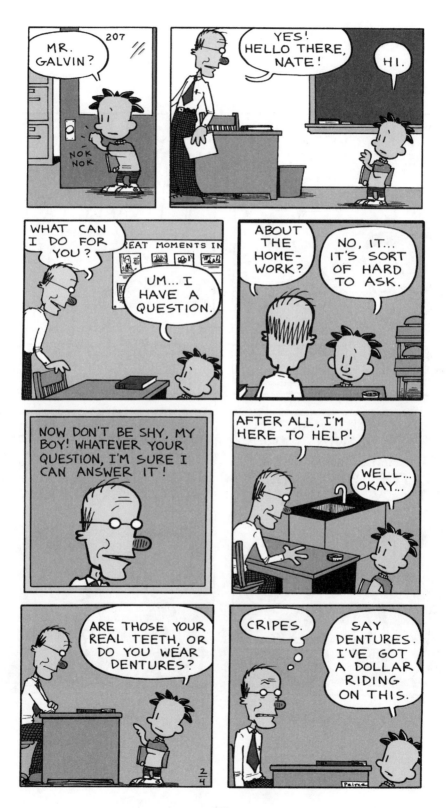

170

You've known me now
For many years,
But never have we dated.

For reasons
I don't understand,
You think our love ill-fated.

But Jenny,
I'm your destiny.
One day we will be mated.

And then you'll know
Just what it's like
To say that you've been "Nated."

WHAT ARE WE DOING IN ART TODAY, MR. ROSA?

MAKING A MESS.

TURNING MY CLASSROOM INTO AN ABSOLUTE PIGSTY THAT'LL TAKE THREE HOURS TO CLEAN UP AFTER SCHOOL, MAKING MY BACK EVEN MORE SORE THAN IT ALREADY IS!

MR. ROSA?

CLAY SCULPTURE.

YES!

I NEED AN ASPIRIN.

© 2007 by NEA, Inc.

Peirce

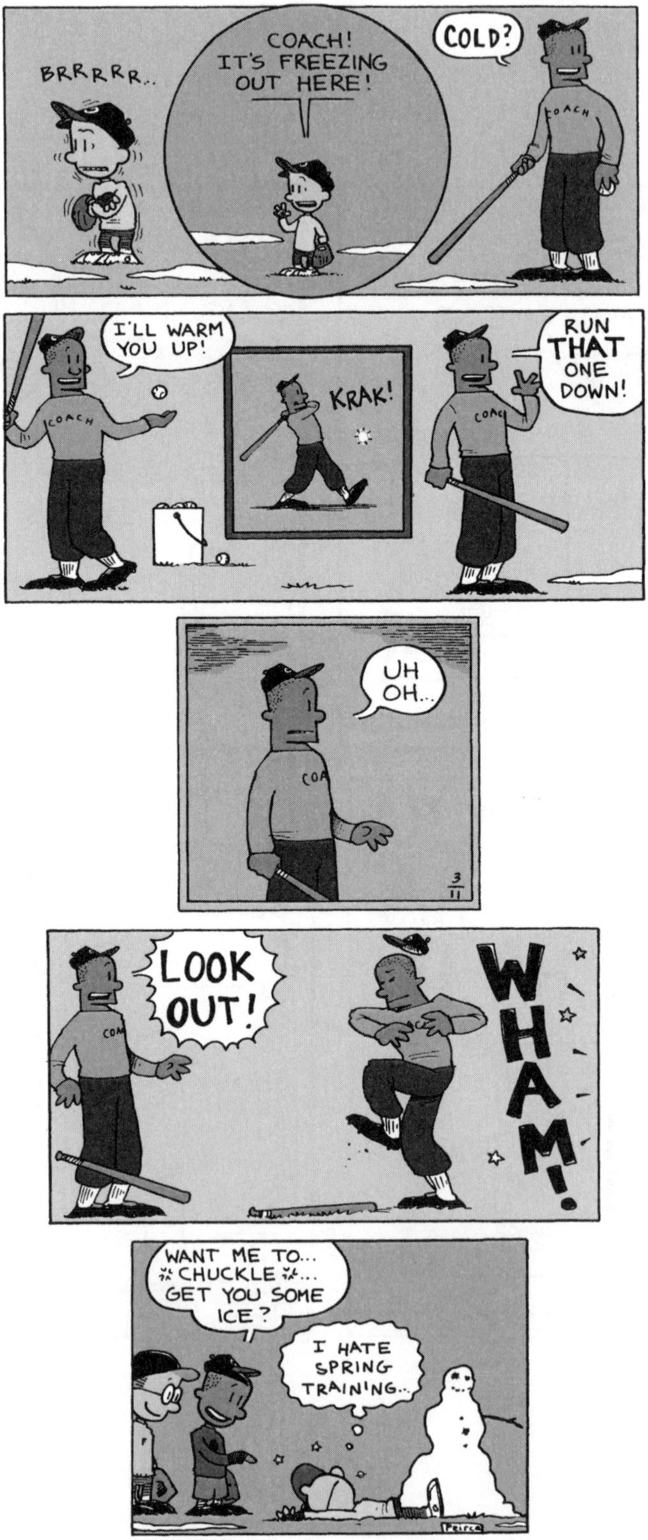
BRRRRRR..
COACH! IT'S FREEZING OUT HERE!
COLD?
I'LL WARM YOU UP!
KRAK!
RUN THAT ONE DOWN!
UH OH...
LOOK OUT!
WHAM!
WANT ME TO... CHUCKLE... GET YOU SOME ICE?
I HATE SPRING TRAINING...